UNDAUNTED

RAMONA FLIGHTNER

Ramona Flightner/Grizzly Damsel Publishing
P.O. Box 187
Boston, MA 02128
www.ramonaflightner.com

Cover design by Derek Murphy

Publisher's Note: This is a work of fiction. Names, characters, places, and incidents are a product of the author's imagination. Locales and public names are sometimes used for atmospheric purposes. Any resemblance to actual people, living or dead, or to businesses, companies, events, institutions, or locales is completely coincidental.

Ordering Information: Quantity sales. Special discounts are available on quantity pur-chases by corporations, associations, and others. For details, contact the "Special Sales Department" at the address above.

Reclaimed Love/ Ramona Flightner. — 1st ed.

Print ISBN: 978-0-9860502-6-8

RAMONA FLIGHTNER

Sheila,
When I was four, you fed my imagination with Charlotte,
Wilbur, Templeton, and the promise of one new chapter a day,
helping foster a lifelong love of reading and creating stories.
Bantiox.

"There is a sacredness in tears.
They are not a mark of weakness, but of power.
They speak more eloquently than ten thousand tongues.
They are the messengers of overwhelming grief,
of deep contrition and of unspeakable love."
Washington Irving (attributed)

CAST OF CHARACTERS

BOSTON

Savannah Montgomery nee Russell: Clarissa's cousin and confidante, recently married to Jonas Montgomery, lives in the Back Bay

Jonas Montgomery: wealthy New Yorker, Savannah's husband

Lucas Russell: Savannah's brother, works at his father's linen store, "Russells," is a talented piano player

Martin Russell: father to Lucas and Savannah, uncle to Clarissa, owns and runs the linen store, "Russells," store and home in the South End, near the Sullivan home

Matilda Russell nee Thompson: Savannah's mother and Clarissa's aunt, sister to Agnes and Betsy

Betsy Parker nee Thompson: childless, lives in Quincy, married to a wealthy man, free-thinking, cryptic comments, Matilda and Agnes' sister, Clarissa and Savannah's aunt.

Richard McLeod: Gabriel's middle brother, a blacksmith, friend to Colin

Florence McLeod nee Butler: married to Richard, orphan, used to teach with Clarissa,

Jeremy McLeod: the youngest McLeod brother, was in the Army, recently returned from fighting in the Philippines

Aidan McLeod: uncle to the three McLeod boys, smart businessman

Sophronia Chickering: feisty suffragette, lives on Beacon Hill, distantly related by marriage to the piano Chickerings

Sean Sullivan: Clarissa's father, a blacksmith, from Ireland

Mrs. Rebecca Sullivan nee Smythe: Clarissa's stepmother, has social aspirations

Delia Maidstone: headmistress at the orphanage in the North End

Zylphia Maidstone: Delia's daughter

Mrs. Wright: Cameron's mother

MONTANA

Gabriel McLeod: the eldest McLeod brother, a cabinetmaker, married to Clarissa

Clarissa McLeod nee Sullivan: suffragist and former teacher, married to Gabriel, sister to Colin, works with Mr. Pickens

Colin Sullivan: Clarissa's brother, a blacksmith

Ronan O'Bara: Matthew's friend who works in the mine with Liam

Amelia Egan: widow to Liam, was a schoolteacher, mother to Nicholas and Anne

Nicholas Egan: Amelia's son

Anne Egan: Amelia's daughter

Mr. A.J. Pickens: works at the Book Depository

Mrs. Bouchard: works on the Library Committee with her sister; considers herself a great arbiter of fashion

Mrs. Vaughan: works with her sister, Mrs. Bouchard, on the Library Committee

Sebastian Carling: mill foreman, befriends Gabriel

Cameron Wright: was a suitor for Clarissa's hand, remained in Montana

CHAPTER 1

SAVANNAH MONTGOMERY SAT ROCKING to and fro on the ornate rococo camelback settee with faded gold fabric. Eyes vacant and expressionless, as though turned inward, she failed to notice the other women in the room. Her hair, fashioned in a stylish manner when she left her house a few hours earlier, had begun to slip out of the confining pins so that wisps fell along her cheeks and down her back. The fashionable silk dress—in cornflower blue to match her eyes—hung on her frame, highlighting her recent weight loss.

"Don't you worry about Savannah, Mattie?" Betsy asked as she watched her niece sitting across from her in a near stupor. She spoke in a low voice, barely heard by her sister, Matilda, seated next to her in the parlor. Although, as she gazed at Savannah, Betsy doubted Savannah would understand any of their discussion.

Even though only midafternoon, lamps were lit, as much of the former light from the windows was now blocked by the recently constructed elevated train tracks. Savannah sat alone on the settee, picking at the lace at her wrists, rocking in place, as conversation flowed around her. A low table in front of her held the detritus of afternoon tea, one of the doilies stained after Savannah had spilled her cup. The wallpaper appeared almost purple in the dull light, rather than its former light pink.

"It takes time to recover from these experiences," Matilda whispered to her sister with a pointed stare. Her eyes flashed as she continued to work on her needlepoint, a lamp lit to aid her.

"It's been six months, and she has yet to improve," Betsy argued. She gripped the handle of her cane in momentary agitation, grimacing with the action as her fingers, gnarled from rheumatism, protested the movement. She relaxed her hands, rubbing them down the front of her sea-blue brocade skirt.

"I find it hard to believe my own daughter carries on so at the loss of her child," Matilda said. "I would think she'd have the strength of character to mourn in private, not persist in showing the world her sorrow."

Betsy raised an eyebrow at her sister's comments. "And thus speaks the concerned mother."

At Betsy's words, Matilda sat even straighter, and her body vibrated with self-righteous indignation. She stabbed the needlework with such force she rent a large hole in the middle of her pattern.

"Do you even listen to yourself and the harmful words you speak?" Betsy asked. "Where is the sister I knew? The sister who flouted all conventions in an attempt to live the life she wanted? How can you desire for your daughter to suffer as she is?"

"You swore you would never speak of my past," Matilda hissed.

"I'm beginning to regret taking such an oath after seeing Savannah pay so dearly for your desire to return to our parents' good graces. You must have realized by now, no matter what you do or don't do, that you will never be forgiven."

"Seeing as I have never forgiven myself, I see no reason for them to have extended such a courtesy." She glared at Betsy. "Every time you are here, you stir up trouble. First before Savannah's wedding, then with Clarissa. When will you learn that we are fine as we are?"

"When I can look at my niece and see the vibrant girl I knew, not a woman in some sort of a stupor."

"If you must know, Jonas informed me that he and his doctors decided it best they give her a tonic to prevent episodes of hysteria."

"You mean to prevent her from actually grieving and recovering from the loss of her daughter? Yes, how shocking it must be for a man of Jonas's refinement to be faced with a normal reaction from a woman. How understandable that the best recourse would be to dull all her emotions and faculties with some horrid concoction."

"Betsy," Matilda said with a warning note in her voice.

"Savannah? Savannah, dearest?" Betsy groaned as she heaved herself to her feet, grimacing with each step as she shuffled the few feet to settle herself next to Savannah on the settee. She clasped her niece's hand, ignoring her sister.

Savannah lifted her head as though it were weighted down and looked toward Betsy with a glazed stare. "Betsy," she whispered. She licked her dry chapped lips, her head bobbing as her unfocused eyes attempted to see her aunt clearly.

Betsy squinted as she studied Savannah for a few moments. She squared her shoulders and firmed her mouth in determination. "That's it, Mattie. I'm taking her with me for a sojourn to Quincy. Jonas can have no complaints as he has shown little interest in her for months. Thankfully his absence is timely, and he cannot object."

"I'd hardly call the death of his mother a timely event," Matilda snapped. "You can't blame the man for traveling to New York City for the services."

"Be that as it may, let us go to Savannah's, pack her trunk and depart," Betsy ordered. "While I'm away, my maid can pack my trunks here and meet us at the station."

"I think we should discuss this with Martin. Her father will surely show more sense than you, Betsy."

"You can discuss all you want. I'm done dithering," Betsy said. She pushed herself up with the aid of her cane and held out her hand toward Savannah sitting next to her. "Come dear, let us prepare for our trip." She took Savannah's hand and led her from the sitting room.

"Not home," Savannah pleaded in a weak voice. She flinched at her mother's grunt of disapproval.

"Only for a few moments and then we shall journey by train to Quincy. Wouldn't you enjoy a nice holiday with Uncle Tobias and me?" Betsy asked in a reassuring tone, as she glared at her sister to forestall any further attempt at preventing Savannah from traveling with her.

"I can't leave my baby," Savannah whimpered.

"We'll visit her at the cemetery, leave her some lovely flowers before we depart," Aunt Betsy soothed, easing Savannah into motion beside her.

Savannah and Betsy made an incongruous pair as they descended the stairs. Savannah leaned heavily on the oak railing, taking each step with two feet, as a child would, before attempting the next one. Betsy leaned onto her cane with her right hand and, with her left hand, held onto Savannah's right arm, causing Savannah to list toward her with each of her unsteady steps. Savannah's father, Martin, emerged from the store at the commotion they made on the stairs, blanching at their chaotic yet harmonious movements as they approached him.

Martin glared momentarily at his wife, who watched her sister and daughter with disdain, before focusing on his daughter as she stood in front of him. His chocolate-brown eyes tracked his daughter's every movement, agony and regret reflected in their depths as she failed to focus on him.

Betsy met Martin's concerned gaze. "I have had enough, Martin. I am taking her home with me."

Martin's broad shoulders drooped, and he sighed heavily. "Good. It's time one of us showed some sense." He approached Savannah, placing his hands on her shoulders and kissing her forehead softly. "I shall miss you, my Savannah. Come back to us, from wherever you are," he murmured in a tortured voice.

He turned away and met his son, Lucas's, fierce frown. "Lucas, help your aunt and sister." At Lucas's nod of acquiescence, Martin moved toward his sister-in-law. "Take care of my girl, Betsy. Bring her back to us."

***

SAVANNAH WOKE WITH A START, stifling her scream. Open pale-green curtains allowed faint moonlight entrance, limning the area near the window and Savannah's bed. Shadows formed by a nearby tree branch created a fluctuating pattern on the gold rug. She rolled over, searching for the sleeping tonic Jonas had purchased and had kept her well stocked with for the past months. Her hands grasped a glass of water, but nothing else lay on the nightstand. She rose to search for the cinnamon water that aided in banishing her nightmares.

As she walked toward the washstand, she stumbled and fell, knocking over the porcelain bowl which shattered. Savannah lay on the floor, too weak to rise. She curled into herself, weeping, while impressions from her delivery flickered through her mind. The never-ending pain. The pleas from the doctor to push. The fear she would die. The …

"Savannah!" Betsy cried as she hobbled into the room. She sat in a chair next to Savannah, stroking her forehead and wiping away her tears.

"No!" Savannah gasped, as the final fleeting memory from the delivery flitted away. The memory she was desperate to remember. "No." Tears leaked from her eyes as she shivered on the floor.

"Tobias!" Betsy yelled. "Don't worry, dear. Soon your uncle will be here to help you to bed. If you were looking for that horrid sleeping tonic, I've thrown it away."

"I need it," Savannah mumbled, raising up to lean against her aunt's chair.

"No, you do not," Betsy said sternly. "I refuse to see my precious niece become a slave to a sleeping drug."

"It's just cinnamon water. That's what Jonas told me."

"Well, he was misinformed," Betsy said as she rubbed Savannah's back gently and stroked her hair.

Savannah nestled into her aunt's embrace as she awaited her uncle. "Thank you, Aunt Betsy. Thank you for helping me."

***

WHEN SAVANNAH WOKE to bright sunlight a few days later, she felt as though she were emerging from a long, dark tunnel. She squinted at the light, her head throbbing. A mild nausea and lassitude prevailed, and she wanted to remain in bed all day. However, for the first time in months, she felt the stirrings of hunger, despite the nausea.

After slowly rising from bed and donning her robe, she tiptoed downstairs to the peaceful glass-enclosed conservatory that her aunt Betsy used as the breakfast room and private retreat in late spring and summer. Savannah paused at the door, momentarily soothed by the calm interior adorned with white wicker furniture, lace curtains and potted ferns. Sunlight streamed in through the windows, and Savannah had the impression she was to enter a haven. She froze as she overheard a conversation.

"Mary, you are certain of this?" Betsy asked Savannah's maid.

"Yes, ma'am," Mary replied in a wavering voice.

"You are in no trouble here," Betsy said. "If you are dismissed by Mr. Montgomery, I'll hire you. Do not fear for your post."

"Thank you, ma'am."

"You are certain the child lived?"

Savannah leaned forward, holding her breath.

"Yes, ma'am," Mary said in a firmer tone.

Savannah's anguished cry rent the air as she collapsed to the floor. She heard Aunt Betsy exclaim in concern, but Savannah was suddenly thrust back into the memories of the birthing room.

"Doctor, you know what you are to do to help her with her pain," Jonas intoned as he left the room. He spared not even a glance for the sweating, groaning Savannah.

"Yes, sir."

"Jonas, Jonas!" Savannah cried out, a hand flailing toward his retreating back. "Don't leave me with a doctor I don't know!" she screamed as the pain became excruciating. He brushed by her without acknowledging her words or her outstretched hand.

Soon Savannah did not care who was attending her birth; she simply wished it to end. Her loyal maid, Mary, remained by her side as the ordeal continued for hours. Just as she thought she wouldn't be able to continue further, the doctor ordered her to push. The pain became nearly unbearable as she pushed and screamed in agony.

"Put this over her mouth," the doctor instructed Mary. "When she is relaxed, you should lift it away."

"But, Doctor ..."

"Do it," he barked, as Savannah screamed once more, and a faint wail was heard. Mary placed the cloth over Savannah's mouth, and she was insensate to pain in a matter of moments.

"Savannah. Savannah, dearest," Betsy murmured as she bent over next to Savannah on the floor, stroking her back.

"That is the memory I couldn't remember. That I wouldn't remember. The baby's cry."

"Shh, dearest, don't weep so," Betsy said as she stayed close.

"They told me that she was stillborn when I woke. How did my baby die?" Savannah demanded as she looked toward Mary. "Tell me, how did she die?"

Mary paled as she watched Savannah. She shared a glance with Betsy, uncertain what to say. At Betsy's subtle nod, Mary squared her shoulders. "She didn't."

CHAPTER 2

MATILDA AND SAVANNAH sat on lady's chairs in the Sullivan family parlor to call on Mrs. Sullivan for tea. Sunlight streamed in the front window, highlighting alterations to the room. Reupholstered settees and chairs in rich gold and ruby formed new seating patterns in the room. A love seat—with two chairs on either side—was placed where the piano had formerly stood near the front window. The fireplace had been refitted with imported Italian marble. The wallpaper, sparkling with its gold highlights, shimmered in the sunlight.

"It is so gracious of you to call. I am delighted to welcome you to see the completed refurbishments of the parlor." Rebecca Sullivan waved around the room. "Now if I can only convince Sean to loosen the purse strings for the rest of the house.

"I'm sure neither of you contend with such an obstinate husband when it comes to financial matters. Sean believes in economy and moderation above all things. He believes I should act as his first wife, Agnes, did and be satisfied with her furbishment of the house. Can you imagine? When this house remains firmly rooted in the nineteenth century? It must be modernized!" Rebecca Sullivan spoke in a sweet alto voice, leaning forward as though imparting great secrets. She wore a teal dress, cut to highlight her voluptuous figure. Her light-blond hair was pulled back into a stylish chignon, enhancing her long, thin face.

"I know how you suffer, Rebecca," Savannah's mother, Matilda, said. "My sister Agnes was a wonderful woman but believed in thrift and economy as the ruling principles behind her decoration. For my part, Martin is much the same. Never understands why the drapery needs to be changed or why new furniture is a necessity. He seems to enjoy living in the past."

"Of course, Savannah must have no such difficulties with a generous husband such as Mr. Montgomery."

"Yes, Jonas is generous in all regards," Savannah said.

"Such a genteel man. One can only imagine how he must be to live with," Rebecca said with an envious smile to Matilda.

"You can only imagine," Savannah murmured.

"You are looking much recovered, Savannah," Rebecca said with a nod of agreement from Matilda. "Your extended mourning was not at all becoming."

"I have felt more like my old self these past few days," Savannah said. "I recovered well during my visit to Aunt Betsy's. I no longer need the tisane recommended by Jonas's physician." She picked up her teacup with her right hand but dropped the cup with a gasp. The cup fell to the table, cracking its delicate china base.

"Savannah," her mother hissed. Matilda stilled her movement to wipe the spilled tea with her white linen napkin when she heard Mrs. Sullivan gasp.

"I beg your pardon, Mrs. Sullivan. I fell and hurt my wrist, and forgot I shouldn't use my right hand," Savannah said. She massaged her wrist as she held it against her lower abdomen. "I will speak with Jonas about a replacement teacup."

"Of course," Mrs. Sullivan said as she edged her new china teapot and plates away from Savannah. She cleaned the spilled tea with her handkerchief. "You are fortunate indeed to have such a man's interest that he would concern himself with something so minor as a teacup."

Savannah forced a smile as Mrs. Sullivan continued to speak. "We have very little word from Clarissa. Do you hear from her? I had thought that ungrateful young woman would write us more, as is our due, as we are her stepmother and father, and yet she seems intent to break her father's heart with her silence."

"She writes us once a week. Their one year anniversary approaches, and I believe she is disappointed she is not yet expecting a blessed event." Matilda took a sip of tea.

"Oh, if she only knew what a bother it is to have a child, she'd rejoice at her childless state. Just last week I was awakened by Melinda, not once, but twice. It seems she is teething again. Why she can't soothe herself is beyond me." Mrs. Sullivan pursed her lips in disgust.

"Did you go to her? Comfort her?" Savannah asked.

"Of course not. She needs to learn to calm herself."

"She's eighteen months old," Savannah said with a hint of steel in her voice. "I'm uncertain how you expect such a young child to know such things."

"If I don't instill such attributes as self-reliance in her now, she'll never learn them." Mrs. Sullivan watched Savannah with a censorious look. "What parenting advice can a childless woman give me, Savannah? I'd count myself fortunate your daughter died rather than have to listen to her mewling cries and constant interruptions in your life."

Savannah paled and wrapped her arms around her middle. "I will never give thanks that my daughter was taken from me. Unlike you, I would have rejoiced at her presence in my life." She rose and nodded to her mother and Mrs. Sullivan. "If you will excuse me, I have other calls to make." She strode from the room, and, after a moment, the table shook from the force of the front door slamming shut.

Rebecca turned to Matilda. "Well, I never, Matilda. I thought you had raised her to be more respectful of her hostess."

"The loss of her daughter continues to haunt her."

"I would think she'd have recovered after six months."

"It's approaching seven months, and I see no end to her grief," Matilda said with a sigh. "I had hoped that today she was beginning to show signs of recovery. She seems to believe she is the only woman who has lost a child. I understand her sorrow, but I cannot countenance such behavior."

"I would think Mr. Montgomery would aid her in seeing the error in her ways."

"I believe he tries, in his way. However, she is reluctant to be persuaded to his manner of thinking." Matilda shook her head. "She has become fanciful in her grief, believing that her daughter lived and was taken from her."

Mrs. Sullivan smirked. "As if that husband of hers would act in such a way. Her behavior's been indulged too long, Matilda. You need to take care with her."

"I fear she has been influenced by Clarissa's radical beliefs about women."

Mrs. Sullivan gasped. "Never say such a thing. Although I know it pains Sean to have her so far away, I'm glad not to have to listen to her spouting her suffragist nonsense nor live with the turmoil she brought to our daily lives. I can't imagine what that man in Montana sees in her."

"And yet you wanted her to marry Mr. Wright."

"You know he would have been like Mr. Montgomery. A steady, strong hand to steer her in the proper direction. I fear that Mr. McLeod will only continue to encourage her radical ideas and she will become wilder." Mrs. Sullivan shuddered.

"Any word about Mr. Wright?"

"I had tea with his mother recently. He has remained in Montana and is enamored of a Mrs. Bouchard's daughter. He has chosen to remain to be near her."

"Do you believe the proximity to Clarissa has anything to do with his desire to remain in Montana?" Matilda took a sip of tea and watched Mrs. Sullivan over her teacup.

"I should think not. She is a married woman now, and her dowry, or what she would have received had she married an acceptable man, has been donated to charity."

"To charity? Any idea to which one?"

"I can't remember the name, but to the women opposing the vote. Isn't it such a wonderful irony? Her defiance has led to the group she despised receiving a generous donation in the amount of her dowry." Mrs. Sullivan cackled with malicious glee. "Mrs. Wright, Cameron's mother, is a member of that group and took great joy in telling me the tale."

"I do feel badly for Sean. I know how he doted on his only daughter by Agnes." Matilda exhaled a long breath. "It's a bit how Martin dotes on Savannah. For some reason, he believes that Jonas is overprotective of her."

"Martin's just being a concerned father. Sean was the same with Clarissa. In the end fathers must learn their daughters will do what they like without their permission."

"Hmm … you may be right," Matilda said. "Although why Martin would ever suspect Jonas of anything remotely nefarious is ludicrous." Matilda shook her head in consternation.

"For some fathers, no man will ever be good enough for their daughters. Even with such an estimable man as Mr. Montgomery, your husband finds fault. I'm sure, with time, Mr. Montgomery's true character will be seen, and Martin will have no cause for concern."

***

SAVANNAH STUMBLED ON the cobblestone as she looked for the New England Home for Little Wanderers. She stood on a street corner with her back to an alley dimly lit in the afternoon sun. Across the street, three- and four-story brick buildings gleamed in the bright sunlight. Businesses from bakeries to locksmiths to cobblers to grocers lined the first floors of the street. The sounds of a baby crying, a heated argument in Italian and the faint strains of a violin solo drifted down from nearby upper-story windows. The smell of freshly baked bread competed with the scent of horse manure and other rubbish in the street.

"Excuse me," she said to a stout woman dressed in black. "Could you …"

"No *Inglesi*," the woman said in a thick accent as she bustled past Savannah.

Savannah glanced up and down Salem Street in the predominantly Italian North End of Boston, a street she had already traversed three times to no avail.

"What am I to do?" Savannah whispered to herself. She blinked away tears as she realized she would be unable to communicate with most of those walking past her.

"Ma'am?" a deep voice said. "Ma'am?"

Now a gentle hand to her arm.

"Are you lost?"

Savannah turned to find a tall, familiar-looking black-haired gentleman watching her with concern. "I know you, don't I?" Savannah whispered.

"You are Mrs. McLeod's cousin," he said. "Clarissa's cousin." At her continued silence, he said, "I'm Jeremy McLeod. We met at your parents' house last year."

"Of course," Savannah said. "Forgive me for not remembering right away."

"Are you lost?" At her quick shake of her head in denial, Jeremy watched her with curiosity. "Are you searching for something?"

Savannah's eyes filled with tears, and she began to shake. "Yes, something very dear to me."

"Come. Let's find a place where you can rest for a moment." He gripped her arm and led her through a maze of narrow streets until he reached a small alley. At one of the entryways, he extracted a key, opened the door and ushered her inside.

"Oh, but this isn't proper," Savannah protested.

"I highly doubt fainting in the middle of a street would be proper either, ma'am," Jeremy said. "Flo! We have company." He continued to propel her down a darkened hallway.

Savannah blinked when she saw the sparse yet clean living area. Jeremy pulled out a scarred chair from the table and gently helped Savannah into it. "Sit before you fall down," he muttered. "Flo, can you make tea?" He paced away toward the back window area, watching Savannah closely.

"Hello, Mrs. Montgomery," Florence said. "I never thought to see you in my home."

"I'm sorry, but have we met?" Savannah asked, as her eyes quickly roamed the room and its contents. Her eyes lit on the shelves filled with books, and she seemed to come out of a dazed stupor. "*Florence.* You were Clarissa's friend. You were at my parents' house last spring." She then turned haunted sky-blue eyes to Jeremy. "And you are Gabriel's brother."

Jeremy nodded as he watched her from across the table.

"You have another brother," Savannah said.

"Yes, Richard. My husband. He will be home soon from the forge," Florence said, unable to hide the connubial contentment from her voice. She set a mug of tea in front of Savannah. "Richard, Jeremy and I live here in the home they used to share with Gabriel."

"Do you think Clarissa is as happy as you?" Savannah whispered after she took a sip of sweetened tea. Florence blushed and nodded.

"I should hope so. If not, Gabe's a damn fool," Jeremy said as he joined them at the table.

"Don't you know how Clarissa is?" Florence asked.

"I can't remember if I've heard from her lately," Savannah said. She saw Jeremy and Florence exchange a concerned glance.

"What do you mean? Either you received a letter or not," Jeremy said.

"But that's just it. I might have received a letter. And I might have responded. But I can't remember," Savannah said in a soft, anguished voice. "Until recently there's so much I can't remember."

"Ma'am, what is it that brought you to the North End? I would think you'd have little cause to leave the Back Bay and its exalted environs," Jeremy said.

"I hate the Back Bay," Savannah muttered, then blushed.

Florence raised her eyebrows in surprise.

"I'm sorry. Please forgive me for speaking out of turn."

"There's no one here to care how you speak, ma'am," Jeremy said, still watching her intently.

"I have no right to burden you with my problems," Savannah said as she set down her mug. She massaged her wrist absently. "Please forgive my thoughtlessness."

"There's none to forgive," Florence said. "And if there is some way we could help you, I like to think you'd turn to us."

"I couldn't," Savannah protested.

"You're Clarissa's cousin. Thus, you are our cousin." Jeremy paused. "You'd be the first cousin I'd care to claim in a while."

Savannah burst into tears, burying her face in her palms as her shoulders heaved. "I'm so sorry. This is unseemly," Savannah gasped out.

"Quit your nonsense and have a good cry," Florence ordered as she moved to sit next to Savannah and embrace her. Florence continued to pat her back and hum soothing noises as Savannah sobbed. "That's it. Get it all out. You'll feel better for it."

"Flo, I'm home!" Richard yelled as the front door slammed shut. When he entered the room, he noted his brother's worried expression and the crying woman in Florence's arms. "What's the matter?"

"Mrs. Montgomery is under duress," Jeremy said.

"Clarissa's uppity cousin has called here for help? Not likely," Richard said with a half laugh. Savannah turned a tear-streaked face toward him as she hiccupped out a sob, and he immediately sobered.

"You're Savannah," Richard said. He studied her, from her tousled hair, her gaunt appearance, all the way to her disheveled, outdated clothes. "What happened?" He pulled up a chair to sit next to her, with Florence on Savannah's other side.

At Savannah's silence, Richard looked from Florence to Jeremy. "Why is she here in our kitchen, crying, rather than in her fancy house in the Back Bay or her father's shop in the South End?"

"Because they don't believe me!" Savannah cried out as fresh tears poured down her cheeks.

Richard grasped her hand gently and looked into her eyes. "Well, why don't you tell us, and we'll see what we think?"

"You'll think I'm crazy too. Threaten to send me away," Savannah rasped. She shuddered as she recalled all that Jonas had warned.

"You may find us more charitable than your husband," Jeremy said.

After a long pause, where Savannah gripped Richard's hand tightly, she whispered, "He stole my baby."

"What?" Florence and Richard asked at the same time.

"Jonas. My husband. He had the doctor give me something during the delivery to put me to sleep. When I woke, he told me the baby had died," Savannah said, as tears streamed down her cheeks again. "I had trouble sleeping. There was always a baby in my dreams, wailing, desperate for me to find her. Jonas had me see another doctor, and I was given a sleeping potion."

She took a trembling breath. "Finally, a few weeks ago, my aunt Betsy visited and brought me to Quincy. She threw away my sleeping potion, and it was as though a fog had lifted. Jonas had kept me drugged all that time."

"How long?" Jeremy demanded in a hard voice as he rose from his chair.

"Six months," Savannah said. "Six months I lost with my baby. I knew I was missing something every time I remembered the birth, and finally, when I heard my maid talking with my aunt, I realized that I had heard the baby cry. She wasn't a stillbirth. She had lived."

"Why do such a thing?" Florence asked.

"Jonas wanted a son. Anything else was a failure," Savannah said. She rubbed at her cheeks and the errant tears that continued to fall.

"You think he brought the baby to the Home?" Richard asked as he looked up to watch Jeremy pacing the small space by the sink.

"I don't know! But I have to find her. She has to know that she is wanted and loved," Savannah said on a sob.

"You aren't mad," Florence said fiercely. "I believe you. Richard and Jeremy believe you."

"You do?"

"Of course. Remember? We know Clarissa. And we know the type of man your husband is," Richard said.

"Any friend of Cameron's is, by association, a bastard," Jeremy growled.

"And we'll help you," Florence said with a glare to Jeremy for his language.

"Thank you. Thank you so much," Savannah said. "Everyone else, every-one except Aunt Betsy, thinks I'm unhinged after the loss of my little girl." She released Richard's hand and scrubbed her face. Finally she raised her eyes to meet Jeremy's gaze. He studied her guardedly.

"Well, I imagine you are," Florence said with a soft smile. "But I don't believe you're mad. You just need to find your baby girl. What day was she born?" Florence asked as she filled Savannah's mug.

"November 14."

"We can start tomorrow at the Home and go from there," Jeremy said.

Savannah nodded, gripping the mug to the point she thought she might crack it. "I will try to meet you."

"Will your husband allow you to leave again so soon?" Jeremy asked, provoking a startled look from Savannah at his perceptiveness.

"I'll find a way," she whispered.

"The Home is not a terrible place, but I would rather your baby be with you," Florence murmured. Richard clasped Florence's hand, smiling tenderly at her.

Savannah rose to leave. "Thank you. Thank you more than I can ever express."

***

AFTER SAVANNAH DEPARTED, Jeremy continued to pace the small liv-ing area.

"Well, Jer?" Richard asked as he sank into the couch. Florence settled next to him. At Jeremy's glare and stubborn silence, Richard sighed. "You're more like Gabriel than you like to admit."

"I am nothing like Gabe."

"But you are. You've taken an interest in a woman who is far above you. And worse, beyond unavailable. She's married, Jer," Richard said with urgency in his voice.

"What makes you think I'm interested in her?"

"You're prowling around like a caged animal. You couldn't keep your eyes off her. And you are protective of her, though you want us to think the opposite."

"I have nothing to offer her. And I'm nothing like Gabriel," Jeremy said, bitterness and fatigue leeching into his voice.

"Jer, at some point, you have to let go of what happened in the Philippines," Richard urged.

Jeremy shook his head as he paced again. "You don't know of what you speak, Rich, or you'd never say such things. You have no idea …" He broke off as he spun to stare outside the darkened window.

"I know you killed men. That you did things you are not proud of," Richard said as Jeremy turned to look at him.

"How?"

"How else were you to survive?" They shared a long look. "And I cannot regret what you had to do to survive, Jer. It brought you back to us." He rose and walked toward him, clasping him gently on the shoulder.

Jeremy met Richard's eyes. "If I can help Sav … Mrs. Montgomery find her baby, I will have done something good. Something I can think about in the middle of the night that doesn't cause me shame."

"You've already done so much. Think of what you did for Clarissa, helping her with Cameron. That may have seemed small to you, but it meant a great deal to her."

Florence joined them. "I think you believe that, no matter what you do now, nothing will ever rectify what you did in the Philippines. Am I correct?" Florence asked.

Jeremy glared at her for a moment before nodding tersely.

"You may not wish to speak to us about what happened, but you need to speak with someone," Florence urged.

"I did once. I spoke with Clarissa," Jeremy whispered.

"You did?" Richard asked. "And how did she respond?"

"How do you think? With compassion and caring," Jeremy said.

"Why do you think we'd react differently?" Richard asked, attempting and failing to hide his frustration that his brother would not speak with him about his war wounds.

"Because you knew me before. You both knew me before." Jeremy paused. "You would never have thought that I would turn into such a man."

"We all have darkness inside us, Jeremy," Florence whispered. "It's whether or not you let the darkness rule you."

"I can't seem to find the light," Jeremy murmured. He patted Richard on the shoulder and left the sitting room.

"Richard," Florence said. He reached for her, holding her close. "Richard, he will recover."

"Will he?" Richard asked, hopelessness and despair evident in his tone. "He's been home for over a year. I don't know what to do for him."

"Maybe it's not what, but who. Savannah may be just what he needs."

***

SAVANNAH SLIPPED into the large four-storied brick corner-lot mansion with its mansard roof on Marlborough Street in the Back Bay. Formal gardens in the front bloomed with peonies and a bleeding heart wept in its patch of shade. She sent a pleading look to the butler as he closed the black walnut door for her, the sound of the closing door echoing through the large foyer and down the long hallway. An incandescent green vase on the entryway table held a large bouquet of white peonies, already starting to close as dusk approached.

Although she had hoped otherwise, she knew the butler would inform Jonas of her absence. After handing the butler her light wrap, she slipped up the carpeted front staircase to her bedroom on the second floor.

After changing into an appropriate evening gown that matched her mood, one of black silk with lace at the neck and cuffs, she sat at her vanity as her maid, Mary, placed the finishing touches on her hair. "Are you all right, Mrs. Montgomery?" Mary whispered.

"Fine," Savannah whispered back. She knew she was in the privacy of her bedroom, but she feared Jonas could have a spy nearby. "They believed me."

"Who, Missus?"

"My friends," Savannah said, nearly breaking down into tears to realize she had friends.

"That is good, Missus," Mary said.

"I've never mentioned what you told me, Mary. I don't want you to lose your position." Savannah met Mary's grave eyes in the mirror. "And I need an ally in this house."

Mary nodded, draping a necklace around Savannah's neck. Savannah smiled her thanks at Mary as she rose to descend the stairs to the formal parlor to await her husband, Jonas Montgomery.

"Where did you go this afternoon, dearest?" Jonas asked from his gentleman's chair, one refined leg crossed lazily over the other.

Savannah sat in her lady's chair next to him, as was expected.

He was exquisitely attired in a black evening suit with crisp white shirt and cravat, his muddy-brown hair tamed by pomade and his beard with no whisker out of place. He inhaled from a cigarette, blowing the smoke in Savannah's direction. His intentional air of relaxation belied the barely restrained fury emanating from him.

Savannah attempted to prevent a start of surprise but still grimaced unintentionally. "I visited my mother and then a few friends."

"I was unaware you had friends. After your prolonged illness, you fell out of favor with your set," Jonas said with a mocking laugh as he tamped out his cigarette.

Savannah shrugged, unwilling to expound on her whereabouts.

"I'm certain I need not remind you that you are to have no further excursions with dubious acquaintances without my permission."

"May I visit my parents tomorrow? My mother wanted me to call for tea again."

Jonas watched her with patent dislike. "No, I think you need a few days to contemplate your error in leaving our home when you are still unwell."

"Jonas …"

"Do you really think I don't know what you attempted today, Mrs. Montgomery?"

"Pardon?" She tried to hide from Jonas the hitch in her breathing indicating her fear of him.

"If you are thinking of replacing me, I will have you know, no man will ever want you. Not now that you have shown yourself to be the pathetic female that you are."

"Jonas," Savannah whispered as she choked down a sob.

"Why would any man want you now?" His gaze skimmed over her silk-clad body with contempt. "You had one purpose in our marriage, Mrs. Montgomery. One! And that was to give me a son," he roared.

She leaned away from him as he rose and paced, his movements jerky with his anger.

"Instead, you cry and wail in that birthing bed as though you were no more than a low-class barmaid. It made me ashamed to have married you.

And then, instead of giving me a son, you produced a mewling girl."

"Jonas," Savannah said at the thought that he would admit their daughter had lived.

"I'm only thankful she died," he said viciously. "She saved me the shame of having to look upon your weakness daily."

"Jonas, she was our daughter," Savannah pleaded.

"No, Mrs. Montgomery. She was never my daughter. I never wanted a daughter. Daughters are meaningless when it comes to business and legacies. They are only an unwanted, unneeded expense."

"Jonas, please." Savannah began to sob.

He moved toward her abruptly, gripped her shoulders and hauled her to her feet. "If there is any justice in this world, it is that we are both childless," he hissed, his eyes taking on a maniacal gleam. "You, who only wanted children, now will never have one."

He pushed her down to her chair again, and she landed with a heavy thud. "What do you mean?" she gasped.

"The doctor informed me that the birth had gone so poorly, that you had done your one job so badly, that you will never be able to have another child. You are useless to me."

"What will you do?" Savannah whispered, anguish from his words pervading her.

"I have yet to decide," he said, as he paced about again. He spun to face her. "But you will heed me on this and remain in this house until I give you permission to leave."

"Jonas, if I want to call on my parents, I will," Savannah said with a defiant lift of her chin.

"Do not cross me on this, Mrs. Montgomery. I assure you, you will not like the consequences." He turned and left the room.

CHAPTER 3

"BREAK, DAMN YOU, BREAK!"

The harsh voice matched the fierce green eyes, fingers like talons gripping his mouth open as the tube passed his lips into his throat. He arched his back as a fiery agony invaded his belly, swelling it past bearing, in an attempt to garner information he did not have.

A kick to his side enhanced the agony in his belly, and he writhed in an attempt to escape this torment.

"Hold on to him, dammit."

Strong hands clasped his legs and arms, impeding any further movement. He looked into the merciless green eyes promising only pain—

Jeremy woke screaming, gasping, his arms flailing in front of him to ward off his imaginary tormentors. One arm connected with someone's hand and was grasped. "No!" he yelled, writhing to break the contact and restraint.

"Jeremy," a familiar voice said. "Jeremy, you're safe." Richard released Jeremy, and he fell to the bed to curl onto one side. The dregs of the nightmare faded, and Jeremy could recognize his surroundings.

"Boston," he gasped, shaking as he lay on his side.

"Yes. Home." Richard reached out to pat Jeremy on the shoulder, but Jeremy cringed from the contact. "Can't you tell me what torments you?"

"No, never," Jeremy said. "I …"

"Jeremy, I'm your brother. I will stand by you through whatever you've done and whatever you imagine you've done."

"I don't need to imagine anything. There is no absolution for all I've done."

Florence's soothing hands swept the sweaty hair off his brow and cupped his cheek. "We are your family, Jeremy. Never doubt our love for you."

31

Jeremy opened stricken eyes to see Florence crouched over him, mothering him. "Flo." He inhaled a stuttering breath in an attempt to forestall a torrent of grief.

She traced his jaw, then moved her hand to his shoulders and massaged them with a gentle pressure. She would not be forestalled and continued her ministrations. After a few moments, she eased onto the bed next to Jeremy and pillowed his head on her lap. She continued her soothing caresses.

Suddenly Jeremy pushed away. He rose, and Richard gripped his arms. "Jer?"

Jeremy shook as though suffering a malarial ague and fell into Richard's arms as he sobbed. Richard clasped Jeremy to him, as Florence rose and left the room.

After a few moments Jeremy began to calm and backed away from Richard. "Forgive me."

"No, Jer." He gripped Jeremy's head, cradling it with his large hands. "Let me be your brother. Talk with me. Let me help you."

"I don't want you to despise me," Jeremy whispered. "I think I could handle anything but that."

"I will only ever give thanks you came home to us, Jer. Talk to me and Flo. It can do you no more harm than keeping it all inside."

"Florence can't even stand the sight of me. She left."

"No, I know Florence. She's in the kitchen making us tea." Richard released Jeremy's head and gripped his shoulder. He propelled him into movement, having him walk in front of him toward the kitchen.

Florence stood at the dining room table arranging mugs, a pitcher of milk and sugar, as a pot of tea stood steeping on it. Jeremy glanced at the battered clock on the bookshelf and blanched. "You two should be in bed. Richard, it's 3:00 a.m. You have work tomorrow."

"Nothing is more important than family, Jer." Richard's intense blue eyes dared him to argue.

Jeremy groaned as he collapsed into one of the large chairs Gabriel had built. He covered his face with his hands for a moment before meeting their worried gazes. "I'd enjoy a cup of tea, Flo."

She smiled and prepared him a cup with milk only.

He wrapped his fingers around the mug, staring into its depths.

"From your recent nightmares, we have a good idea of what happened in the Philippines. Let us help you," Florence said.

Jeremy raised his eyes. "I don't wake you every night, do I?"

"You thrash and moan and scream most nights, Jer," Richard said. "Whatever torments you is in deep."

"You should have told me. I would have moved out. Given you some peace."

"The only peace we want is the peace that comes from knowing you are free of this at last," Florence said. She reached forward to grip his hand.

"There are things I need to say, but, Florence, you shouldn't listen to them."

"Because I'm a woman? Too sensitive to understand what you could have suffered?"

"Because I want to protect you from the darker aspects of this horrible world."

"Jeremy, my own mother didn't want me. I know how dark this world can be. Let me support you too," Florence said.

Jeremy nodded, gripping her hand once before releasing it. He took a deep breath and drummed his fingers on the table in a nervous pattern. As he spoke, he lowered his head, tracing granules of sugar on the table.

"In the beginning, I enjoyed the army. I loved it. I was used to a regimented life after living with Aunt Masterson, so it was no hardship. But in the army, if I followed the rules, I was left alone. I wasn't punished for something I didn't do.

"I made friends, enjoyed the camaraderie. I believed it was a just and noble fight. I believed the … propaganda, I guess you'd call it. We were the liberators of an oppressed people who wouldn't know how to rule themselves. I thought I'd have an adventure, travel to an exotic tropical island and that there'd be no true fighting because we'd be welcomed by the natives."

He rose and paced. "They didn't want us there. At least not when it meant more war and death and suffering for their loved ones." He pinched the bridge of his nose.

"Do you know I actually offered to obtain intelligence? That's how it all started. I was friends with one of the men who was specially trained in it, but he got sick with malaria. Rather than wait for someone to be sent out from Manila, I offered to give it a try. I thought, if we could obtain the information, the fighting would end sooner."

He snorted. "God, how naive I sound. I believed them when they said that force was needed to extract information. Never mind that half of what we learned was useless. Just desperate men fabricating anything they could think of to make us stop.

"I took pride in what I did because men broke the fastest under me. I caused them the most pain in the shortest amount of time, and I was hailed as the ideal soldier." He sat in a chair across from Richard and Florence, and held his head in his hands.

"What do you dream about, Jeremy?" Florence asked in a near whisper.

"I'm in this dream I can't get out of. But instead of being the torturer, I'm the one being tortured. I can't move and ... and ..." He broke off, rubbing a hand over his face. "How could I have done that? It wasn't me! That's not who Mum and Da raised me to be."

"Jeremy, look at me."

Jeremy's head jerked up as though complying with an order from a commanding officer. Richard gave a small smile, tinged with bitter satisfaction. "That's how you did it. You were ordered to."

"I should have known better."

"What would have happened to you if you'd declined?" Florence asked. "I can't imagine your troop mates would be happy to have a pacifist in the army."

"That's just it. I was far from a pacifist. I liked the fighting. I liked outsmarting the enemy. Figuring out where they'd hide and how to best attack. How to break them the fastest."

Richard waited, watching him. He gripped Florence's hand to signal her to keep quiet.

"I even enjoyed battle, as long as it wasn't hand-to-hand." He ran a shaky palm over his face. "But the screams and carnage after battle." He shuddered. "I realized all I was good at was bringing pain to others."

"That's not true, and you know it," Richard snapped. He met Jeremy's eyes, and his voice softened as he saw Jeremy's torment. "You were forced to do and live through terrible things. But you survived, Jer. And I will only ever be thankful you returned to us."

CHAPTER 4

"I TOLD YOU THAT she wouldn't come," Jeremy said, as he paced the living area he shared with Florence and Richard. He approached the bookshelf, tracing the spines of the novels, staring blindly at the titles.

"She sent a note, apologizing for the delay and asking for us to go to the Home today. I'm sure she'll be here soon," Florence said.

"Delay? Two weeks' worth of silence and then she expects us to be free to help her?" Jeremy spun away from the bookshelf and approached the sink overlooking the empty lot to the rear.

"Jeremy. You know what type of man her husband is. Maybe he wouldn't let her leave the house."

"Why would any woman marry a man like that?"

"Some don't show their true colors until after the wedding," Florence said wisely. "Especially if there is money involved."

"Makes you thankful to be poor. Things are simpler," Jeremy said, causing Florence to laugh.

"Simpler maybe, but not easier."

"No need to worry, Flo. Rich has a good job, and he can support the two of you well. And I'm starting to sell my work. A little extra income helps."

"I know, Jer. I know. I just wish there were something I could do. It's so unfair that married women are not permitted to teach."

"Well, with the likes of you agitating to change things, I'm sure that will not always be the case," Jeremy said with fond affection in his voice. "Flo, are you certain you want to return to the Home?"

"There's no reason for me to dread returning. They were always very good to me there." Florence sighed and closed her eyes. "And yet I hate the thought of walking through those doors again. All I'll think about is the day my mother brought me there, wearing her tattered Sunday best, and her promise to return for me. I didn't know what was happening, so I didn't even cry when she left. It was only hours later, when I understood I'd been relegated to the unwanted, that I cried."

"You've never been unwanted, Flo," Jeremy said. He was interrupted from saying any more by a tentative knock at the door. He strode down the hallway, reached the door and flung it open. "Hello, ma'am. I was beginning to think you'd never come."

"I'm sorry I was unable to return until today," Savannah whispered.

"Please come in," Jeremy said as she slipped past him into the dark hallway. She preceded him into the living area where she smiled at Florence.

"Are you all right, ma'am?" Jeremy asked.

She flinched but nodded. "Yes, thank you. Thank you both for believing me and being willing to help me. Do you know where the Home is?"

Jeremy exchanged an amused glance with Florence. "Yes, we do," Jeremy said when Florence remained silent. He led them from the living room area, down the hallway and into the dim alley.

Jeremy continued to walk in front of them, and Savannah linked arms with Florence. She stumbled a few times on the uneven cobblestones of the sidewalk before noting the small businesses they passed. She inhaled appreciatively as they walked past a bakery.

"I'd love to go in there some day," Savannah said.

"They make delicious cakes for tea," Florence said with a smile. "Especially if you are entertaining."

Florence sobered as they turned a corner and approached a large oak door with a brass knocker in the shape of a lion's head. Narrow windows on either side of the door and an arched window over the door's lintel caused the entrance to appear imposing. Except for the large door, the faded brick building blended in with its neighbors, and Savannah realized why she'd had such trouble finding the orphanage.

Jeremy turned to study both Florence and Savannah for a moment, before nodding and tapping on the knocker a few times. They were met by a young woman in severe plain black clothes and led to a bench halfway down a narrow hallway.

Florence turned in a slow circle, appearing to look in all directions at once. She stared at the walls, the ceiling and the doorways, before finishing her small circuit. She approached a picture on a wall, studying a photo of recent residents.

"Florence Butler! It is Florence Butler, isn't it?" a low-pitched voice called out as they waited in the foyer of the New England Home for Little Wanderers. Florence spun to face the woman rushing toward them. Her black skirts whipped around her legs, and her salt-and-pepper hair was restrained in a tightly coiled bun.

"Delia," Florence breathed. "You're still here? It's been fifteen years." Her question went unanswered as Delia flung her arms around Florence, grasping her in a tight embrace.

"Oh, it is wonderful to see you again. I have worried so for you, my little Florence, ever since I learned of Mrs. Kruger's death." She paused for a moment, her almond-shaped eyes taking in Florence's appearance. "But look at you now, all grown and with a husband." She looked toward Jeremy with a nod of approval, before she frowned as she studied him longer.

"This is my brother-in-law, Jeremy McLeod," Florence said hastily. "Though you are correct in that I am married. To Richard McLeod." She flushed with pride, failing to note Delia paling at the name. "Jeremy, this is Delia Maidstone. She has worked at the home for years." Jeremy nodded. Delia pursed trembling lips and firmed her jaw before attempting a weak smile of welcome that failed to reach her hazel eyes.

"Then you have been blessed. I hope you did not suffer, alone in that big home with only Mrs. Kruger for company?" Delia said as she looped her arm through Florence's and led her toward the rear offices of the orphanage. Savannah and Jeremy followed as they walked through the dim hallway.

"No, she treated me well. Saved me in many ways," Florence said.

"Wonderful. And now you are here to take a child?" Her curious gaze flit from Florence to Jeremy, her mouth firming as she studied Jeremy.

"No, no, not at all," Florence stammered. She glanced toward Jeremy with a lost expression, as though looking for help. Her eyes lit on Savannah standing behind Jeremy, belatedly recalling she had yet to introduce her. "I'm here with …"

"Are you here looking for your family?" Delia asked, interrupting Florence. She patted Florence's arm. "I just wish we'd been able to place your brother and sister with you. But, by the time we had realized they were your siblings, Mrs. Kruger had no need of more help. She knew she didn't have long for this world and couldn't take on any more responsibilities."

"My siblings were here?" Florence whispered.

"Yes, for a few years. No one wanted them, poor dears. Terribly scrawny things. I thought the influenza would get them at one point, but they survived." She paused to study Florence's ashen expression. "I assumed you knew they'd come here. Been brought here by your mother."

Florence collapsed onto a chair in the hallway, bone white. "No, I've had no contact with my family since the day I was left here." She raised devastated eyes to Delia. "Where are they now? I haven't been able to find any of them."

"That would prove difficult," Delia said. "They were sent west on one of the trains. We were overrun, and it was decided the most prudent action." She shrugged, either with chagrin or embarrassment before turning to smile broadly at Savannah, noting her fashionable dress and coat.

Savannah stiffened, melding an instinctive grimace into a practiced, impersonal smile.

"Oh God," Florence said as she leaned forward.

"Breathe, Flo. Take deep breaths. Nothing is ever accomplished by fainting," Jeremy said urgently as he crouched by Florence's side. He rubbed her back and glared at the woman to remain quiet.

Mrs. Maidstone paused as she moved toward Savannah. Mrs. Maidstone's brow furrowed as she noted Florence's distress while she watched Jeremy intently. "Be thankful they weren't still with your parents, for they fared better than the rest of your family. Died in one of those pestilent outbreaks in one of the tenements."

Florence gasped, raising her head. "Is that why I can't find them? They're all dead?"

"Yes, all but Victor and Minerva, who went west on the train," Delia said.

"Mrs. Maidstone," Jeremy hissed, "I think you need to desist your chatter."

"Mrs. Maidstone," Savannah said at nearly the same moment, when she noted the woman taking a deep breath as though to continue her prattle. "Might I have a word about a child?" She glanced toward Jeremy, and he flashed her a grateful smile.

"Oh, wonderful. I knew my Florence would not forget us." She bustled into a back office, and Savannah followed her.

"Please have a seat, Mrs. ..."

"Mrs. Montgomery," Savannah said as she sat on the edge of the seat with her hands on her knees, her small purse resting on her lap.

"Yes, Mrs. Montgomery." Her smile faltered for a moment before beaming brightly again at Savannah. "What sort of child are you looking for, dear? Is there a specific age?"

"I would like to discern if you have, at any time, had a child in your home who was born last year in mid-November. A girl," Savannah said in a soft voice.

"A baby?" Mrs. Maidstone asked. She sat at a large desk, opening a side drawer for a ledger. "Mid-November, you say?"

"Yes," Savannah murmured.

"No babies were brought to us from early September until January," she said as she looked up from the ledger. "I have many fine young children here for you to consider, Mrs. Montgomery."

Savannah paled before nodding. "I'm sure you do. I thank you for your time." She departed the office to find Jeremy still crouched in front of Florence.

Jeremy glanced up and watched her as she reentered the hallway. "Any luck?" he murmured.

"No."

"I'm sorry," he said with a sad smile. He turned back to Florence. "Flo, we should leave. Let's get you home to Richard."

"How can it hurt this much, Jeremy?" Florence whispered, her low voice resonant with pain. "I haven't seen them in years."

Savannah moved to her other side and bent over to rub her back. "I imagine it's the loss of the dream that hurts. It's that which must be mourned," she murmured.

Florence gripped her hand. "Thank you, Savannah. Thank you for understanding," Florence said on a sob.

"We have much in common," Savannah said with a rueful smile.

As they helped Florence to rise and then depart the orphanage, Savannah began to fidget. "I must return to my house in the Back Bay. My husband will be angry enough with me upon learning that I left today to visit my parents. I don't wish him to suspect anything."

"Stay safe, Savannah," Florence said. "Come visit us again soon."

Savannah nodded, turning away from Jeremy's intense stare. She walked down Salem Street toward the nearby trolley stand and home.

***

"HOW DARE YOU DISOBEY my instructions?" Jonas said in a soft voice as he entered the front sitting room that night, Savannah already in her lady's chair. Lamps cast a warm glow on the walls, and no fire was lit in the marble fireplace. The curtains in the bow-fronted window were closed, engendering a sense of warm intimacy in the room. His tailored black suit highlighted his thin frame, while the amber waistcoat enhanced the brown in his eyes. The thick Turkish carpets dulled his stalking footsteps.

Savannah attempted to quell a shudder at the tone she had come to dread.

"I thought you knew better by now than to disappoint me, Mrs. Montgomery."

"I advised you last night I wished to visit my parents." She bit her lip in frustration at her inability to hide the quiver in her voice.

He strolled toward her until he stood behind her. Jonas placed his hands on her shoulders as though to massage them and leaned down to whisper into her ear. "Do you desire my wrath? Have you missed my attentions?"

"No, no, Jonas," Savannah said quickly. She tried to rise, but his firm grip pushed her back onto the chair.

His fingers worked to knead her neck as Savannah panted with agitation. "Then I would think you would obey my dictates," he hissed as he gripped her neck, thrusting it back so that her head faced upward, and she saw him. Her startled whimper of pain appeared to please him as she stared, upside down, into his irate eyes, and he tightened his hold around her neck.

"Jonas, please!" Savannah said on a weak gasp, as she struggled in an attempt to breathe.

"Never disobey me again," he said as Savannah turned white. "Or you will be disappointed by the consequences." He released her abruptly and strolled out of the sitting room.

Savannah fell forward, collapsing onto the floor as she gasped for air. Futile tears fled from her eyes as she stared dazedly at the refined splendor of the formal sitting room. The perpetually joyful, flute-playing cherubs in the ceiling mural mocked her misery.

When she had recovered to the point she could stand, she walked upstairs to her bedroom, latching the door. She collapsed against it, knowing no way out of this prison she had fashioned for herself.

A connecting door opened, and she squinted, expecting to see Jonas cataloging her every fault. Instead her maid, Mary, was there, a look of horror and concern in her expression.

"Missus!" she gasped as she shut and latched the door. She hurried to Savannah and gripped her hands. "What has happened?"

"I … I …" Savannah shook her head, unable to express her agony.

"Can you write?"

"Writing Clarissa will do me no good," Savannah whispered.

"Write those friends of yours who you mentioned a few weeks ago, Missus. If you tell me where they live, I'll deliver the letter myself," Mary said earnestly. "Tomorrow I have a few hours to go to the post office and run my weekly errands. I can deliver it then."

Galvanized by Mary's idea, Savannah pushed away from the door and rushed toward her escritoire. She scribbled a hastily written note and, after ten minutes, sealed the letter. She turned to Mary. "I am trusting this to you. Please, do not let anyone find this or I …" She shook her head, unable to finish the sentence.

"I will not fail you, Missus. And don't fear. I'll bring you some dinner later." She turned to leave. "Lock the door after me." Savannah rose, locked the door and crawled fully dressed into her bed. She wondered when she would stop shaking.

CHAPTER 5

THE FOLLOWING AFTERNOON, Savannah sank into her chair in her upstairs sitting room. She placed the book she had attempted to read on a nearby table and stared at her embroidery. Faint light shone behind the curtained windows. The gray satin wallpaper, the ice-blue parlor suite and dark brown mahogany furniture gave no relief to Savannah's dark mood. She glowered at the pitcher of purple hydrangeas. She closed her eyes, imagining throwing them out and filling the room with the sweet scent and vibrancy of pink peonies.

"Do not even think of barring me entrance," a loud, imperious voice declared.

Savannah heard rustling skirts and footsteps approaching on the thick rugs. She rose from her chair to see a woman near her grandmother's age barging into her second-floor sitting room. The woman's vivaciousness was more startling for her age.

"I beg your pardon," Savannah said, although she wondered why she was asking this woman's pardon. She marveled at the gall of the woman dressed in jade-green silk, the color highlighting her silver hair.

"As you should. If you had any sense, you would have come to see me and not forced me to call on you." She sighed as she glanced around the room. "This is a rather depressing room, isn't it? I should think you'd want lighter colors in a more soothing tone to highlight the afternoon sun."

"Who are you, and what do you want?"

"I was sent to you by Clarissa." With this the woman turned the full force of her stare on Savannah, looking her up and down, her aquamarine eyes squinting in displeasure at what she saw. "I understand why she was concerned."

"You will leave this house at once," Jonas hissed from the doorway, having been summoned upstairs to Savannah's sitting room by the butler. "Mrs. Montgomery is not accepting callers at this time. She is recovering from her illness."

"Any illness that requires seven months to recover from would be better treated at the hospital, Mr. Montgomery. Or by a competent physician rather than by useless tonics peddled by charlatans. Or is it that you prefer to keep her here, sequestered away from her friends and family, for some other reason?"

"Mrs. Chickering, I would thank you to leave things well enough alone. This is not your place."

"Oh, but it is. Your mother would have wanted you to behave in a more gentlemanly manner. If she could see you now, she would be ashamed of her only son." A flush highlighted her cheeks, and a fiery gleam of displeasure lit her eyes. Sophronia straightened her shoulders as she faced Jonas.

"How dare you speak of my mother in such a way?"

"Didn't you know I summered with her in Newport? We attended the loveliest parties together. She had such elegance and grace. Knew the importance of decorum, tradition and family. She understood that all members of the family, both male and female, were to be cherished."

Jonas glared at Sophronia, and his face reddened. "I think I knew my mother better than you to know that she would never have willingly associated with …"

"With a firebrand suffragette?" Sophronia smirked. "Didn't you know she was one of our greatest supporters? Had a lovely luncheonette each summer to support our cause." She raised an eyebrow at him. "I imagine she didn't inform you. Always did think you were too stodgy, even for someone so young." She turned toward Savannah with a dismissive gesture toward Jonas. "Now, Mrs. Montgomery, I was hoping to have a cup of tea and discuss your future."

"Mrs. Chickering," Jonas hissed.

"And you, Mr. Montgomery, may retire to your library or to wherever it is you spend your afternoons. We will be fine without you." Her aquamarine eyes appeared more steel-like in their distaste, daring Jonas to contradict her. He inhaled deeply but then turned on his heel, and the sound of a slamming door reverberated up the stairs.

"How, how ..." Savannah stammered, as she stared after Jonas.

"A bully rarely knows what to do when one stands up to him," Sophronia said with a small, satisfied smile.

"Please, I will ring for tea," Savannah said but was forestalled by Sophronia moving toward the sitting room door and shutting it.

"I have no need for tea. And my dressmaker will despair if I eat many more tea cakes," Sophronia said with a long sigh. She sat on a stiff-backed chair and grimaced with distaste. "This is as uncomfortable as it is ugly."

"Yes, well, Jonas wanted a distinctive-looking room," Savannah murmured.

"Pompous and overbearing in an attempt to proclaim his importance, even in your private sitting room," Sophronia said censoriously. She studied Savannah, and her expression softened. "Savannah, you look terrible."

"I know I've never met you. Why should you take an interest in me? How do you know how I normally look?" Savannah shook her head in confusion.

Sophronia examined her from head to foot, looking increasingly worried. "You are becoming emaciated. Your skin has no luster, and your eyes have no sparkle. If you are anything like my girl Clarissa, you used to sparkle."

"Clarissa," Savannah whispered.

"Yes, Clarissa. She has been very worried about you, especially when she has received no word from you for months. And then your aunt Betsy wrote me of your recent visit to her lovely home in Quincy. Made me postpone my usual sojourn to Newport. I had to come and see for myself how you were faring."

"You know Aunt Betsy?"

"Of course. We traveled to Minneapolis together last spring with Clarissa to the NAWSA convention for the suffragists. Wonderful time we had together. Although I'm afraid our enthusiasm for the cause was momentarily overshadowed by Clarissa's hasty departure for Montana.

"Thus, when I received letters from two of my favorite people, and I don't have many of them," Sophronia said with a raised eyebrow and a mocking half smile, "I knew I needed to determine for myself how you were. I will be disappointed to write them you are not well. Not well at all."

"Please, Mrs. Chickering, you mustn't exert yourself on my account. I chose—"

"I highly doubt anyone would believe this is the life you imagined for yourself. Locked away in a stifling second-floor sitting room, dreaming of what life might have been. Your life has barely begun!"

"I can't ..." Savannah whispered.

"Can't bear to see reality? Can't bear to realize that you were a fool when you let your miserly, narrow-minded grandparents manipulate you into a marriage with one such as your husband?"

"You know them?"

"Of course. And, no, we do not get along." Sophronia *harrumphed*. "I have the misfortune of meeting them at social outings. I take great comfort in always grating on their nerves with my impolitic comments."

"They must have disapproved of your friendship with Clarissa."

Sophronia laughed. "Ah, they did. But then they never truly cared what Clarissa did. They looked upon her and saw a failure. Someone not worth their notice."

Savannah flushed and lowered her eyes. "I wish they had gifted me the same consideration."

"Well then, what are you to do?" Sophronia asked. "I can't imagine this is how you want to continue." She watched Savannah closely as she remained mute. "As I see it, you have two options. Continue to live a miserable existence and die an early death, or decide you want more from life."

"You make it sound very simple," Savannah snapped, a flush lighting her cheeks.

"If you don't sound like Clarissa," Sophronia said with a chuckle as she thought about Savannah's cousin. "She said much the same when circumstances forced her to make difficult choices. Life's hardest decisions are rarely simple, and sometimes they are made for us by a cruel fate. However, sometimes we must make our fate."

Savannah looked away, uncertain what to say. "I don't have that strength. Or the courage," she whispered.

Sophronia *harrumphed* again but then leaned over and clasped Savannah's hands. "Of course you do. But first you must decide what you want. And what you are willing to forego to obtain it." Sophronia watched Savannah with passion-filled aquamarine eyes, as though daring her to dream for more from her life.

"I must leave. And I hope someday soon you will follow me. This is the address of my residence in Boston. I will soon journey to Newport, but I always leave a full staff at my residence here. I will be sure to inform them of your"—she raised an eyebrow—"impending arrival." Sophronia handed Savannah her card.

Savannah sputtered. "Mrs. Chickering, you presume too much! I … I …"

"You what, dear? You could never leave your husband? And why is that? Because he treats you with such respect and consideration?" She patted Savannah on the hand and rose. "Good-bye, my dear. I will see you soon."

***

"JEREMY!" FLORENCE GASPED as she flung open the door and entered the workshop. "Jeremy!"

"Flo, what is it?" he asked, turning to face her. She paused, trying to catch her breath, waving a piece of paper. "This just arrived. Delivered by a maid."

"A maid? Who do we know with a maid?" he asked in confusion before whispering, "Savannah," and grabbing the letter out of Florence's hand.

> *Dear Florence,*
> *Please forgive my presumption in writing you. I have no one else whom I can trust.*
> *Oh, what to say! I fear for my safety. I fear that Jonas will finally make good on his threats and harm me irreparably. He was very angry with me tonight for being away from the house, although he thought I'd only visited my parents.*
> *Please forgive me for writing. I know there is nothing anyone can do for me. I married him and must accept this fate. If I am absent for a while, I wanted you to know it is due to my husband's dictates.*
> *Savannah*

Jeremy lowered the letter, staring at Florence in horror. "What in God's name does she mean by saying she fears for her safety? She fears he will harm her irreparably?"

"I don't know, Jeremy. I didn't know what to do when I read that letter. I couldn't sit at home, waiting for you and Richard to return tonight, and I know Richard's new foreman has little patience for wives when they visit."

"We must go to her," Jeremy said.

"Like this?" Florence asked, waving at her ratty dress and Jeremy's dusty, worn clothes. "We have no business in the Back Bay."

Jeremy paced, picking up pieces of wood and setting them down again. "She can't be forced to live in a place where all she knows is fear." The anguish in his voice tore at Florence.

"Jeremy, it isn't up to us to save her."

"Isn't that what she is asking us to do?" he asked as he twirled away from the workbench to face Florence. "Isn't she begging, in her aristocratic, so-sorry-to-bother-you way, for help?"

Florence nodded reluctantly. "But what are we to do?"

"Have you ever met him?" At Florence's blank stare, Jeremy said, "The bastard husband. Have you ever met him?"

"No, I don't believe I have."

"I've only met Cameron. Not this Jonas. He wouldn't know who we are."

"Although we couldn't use the McLeod name. He'd recognize that after Clarissa's scandal."

Jeremy began to pace. "We'll use my mother's maiden name, Sanders. He won't have heard that in relation to Clarissa. Let's go home, clean up and go to her house."

"We don't know where she lives, Jeremy."

"There can only be so many Jonas Montgomerys who live in the Back Bay. Someone will tell us."

CHAPTER 6

SAVANNAH SAT IN A DAZE in her upstairs sitting room after Sophronia left. She had never imagined such a woman would come to her aid. Could she really leave Jonas? Savannah glanced around the room, taking in the large mirror, the pale-gray silk-covered walls with filigree highlights and the sumptuous furniture. She closed her eyes as she imagined walking away from this luxury. It was everything she had been taught to value. And yet, as she opened her eyes to take in the room again, she could not remember one moment's worth of happiness in this room. Not until Sophronia presented her card, offering her freedom.

There was a moment's warning before her sitting room door was flung open. "Jonas!" Savannah sputtered as she took in his enraged countenance. "Have your meetings for the afternoon concluded?"

"I canceled the rest. I found that I needed to deal with a pesky domestic issue."

"Has one of the maids spilled claret on the rug again?" Savannah asked. She kept her voice calm and refrained from gripping her hands together, although she was unable to prevent tensing involuntarily as he stalked toward her.

"No, my sweet, it has to do with an errant wife and her unfortunate liaisons. How dare you have a friend such as Mrs. Chickering? She is an abomination to womanhood, and I am ashamed to learn my mother associated with her. It makes her no better than your cousin, Clarissa."

"Jonas, I did not know her before today. I had no idea she would call," Savannah protested in an attempt to soothe him.

"Why did she come?"

"She is friends with Aunt Betsy and wanted to make my acquaintance."

He leaned down and gripped her arms, half lifting her from the chair. "Why now, Savannah?"

"Aunt Betsy was worried about me after I visited with her in Quincy last month. I haven't written her since my return, and she wanted her friend to call on me and see how I fared."

Jonas roared as he threw her back into her chair. He then slapped her so hard across the face, she fell onto the rug. Savannah recoiled, bringing up her hands to her cheek to guard against further attack. She turned onto her belly, attempting to crawl behind an overstuffed chair.

"How dare your family gossip about the goings-on of your marriage?" he hissed as he leaned over her, reaching down to hold her shoulder and keep her in place. "I know I should expect no better from a shopkeeper's daughter, but I had hoped you had learned some refinement from your grandparents."

"No. No, please!" Savannah begged as she curled into a ball. His booted foot connected with her shin but missed her belly.

"I will teach you about the proper public persona you must always don." He clasped her arms and dragged her to a standing position. Savannah struggled, trying to break free from his merciless grasp. She gasped as his fingers dug into her arms.

Suddenly Savannah was dropped to the floor with a thud as Jonas flew backward and crashed into an ornate bookcase. She backed into the side of the settee, her knees pulled up to her chest as tears poured down her cheeks.

"Don't you ever touch her again," a menacing voice hissed as another loud *thwack* sounded of a fist meeting bone.

Savannah heard Jonas groan weakly while she sat huddled on the floor, shaking. She whimpered when strong arms picked her up, and soon she was moving from the sitting room, down the stairs and out the front door.

"Sir! Sir!" her maid, Mary, yelled as she ran after them down the sidewalk. "Take this," and she handed him a bag so jammed full of clothes it could not be closed.

"Mary," Savannah whispered as she flung out an arm to grasp her hand. "You're her maid."

Savannah recognized Florence's voice.

"You will come with us. If you return to the house, he will harm you. Come!"

The man holding Savannah maneuvered them into a carriage. "Ma'am, are you all right?" Savannah relaxed fully when she recognized Jeremy's voice.

"Mr. McLeod," she said. "How did you know to come?"

"I received your letter today. Mary delivered it. We became frantic with worry and wanted to ensure you were well," Florence said, as she leaned over to stroke Savannah's forehead.

"Where are we going?" Savannah whispered.

"To my dragon lady friend. She's a fellow suffragist, a friend of Clarissa's and mine, and not one to be trifled with. She'll not allow anything to happen to you," Florence said.

Savannah shook at the realization that she was safe.

"Shh, ma'am, you'll be all right," Jeremy crooned into her ear as he caressed her back, soothing her. He continued to hold her protectively on his lap.

Upon their arrival at a row house on Beacon Street across from the Boston Common, Florence walked toward the door and banged on the knocker a few times.

"Flo, I hardly doubt anyone who lives here expects the likes of us to call," Jeremy said as he stared at the imposing bow-fronted brick home with green shutters beside all its windows. The white trim around the door gleamed in the bright sunlight, as did the brass knocker on the door.

"Nonsense. I'm good friends with her," Florence said, and Savannah, carried in the sure arms of Jeremy McLeod, saw Florence greet the butler with familiarity.

"Ah, Mrs. McLeod, a pleasure to see you again. Please allow me to inquire if Mrs. Chickering is receiving this afternoon."

"Please inform her that Mrs. Montgomery is with us and is injured. She may require a doctor." The butler nodded imperiously and made his slow ascent upstairs, refraining from touching the gleaming mahogany banister. Florence entered the front hall, nodding for Jeremy to follow her inside.

Jeremy turned sideways, shielding Savannah from jostling against the doorway and moved into the entranceway. He sat with Savannah on his lap on a chair beside the black walnut hallstand and continued to look around. "I had forgotten how impressive these homes are," Jeremy said in a near whisper to Florence. "Aunt always made us stay in the servants' quarters, unless she dragged us out to be seen by friends in an attempt to exemplify her

Christian charity." His glance took in the white wainscoting, the mauve satin wallpaper that covered the upper half of the walls and the fine furniture relegated to the entranceway. He bit his lip from saying anything more as he noted the butler returning.

He motioned for them to follow him. "Mrs. Chickering just returned home and was desirous of a quiet afternoon. However, she will make an exception for you. Please follow me."

They followed him up the stairs to a sun-filled yellow sitting room, with flourishing ferns sitting in a bow-fronted window overlooking Beacon Street and the Common.

"Florence, what do you mean, Mrs. Montgomery might need a doctor?" Sophronia demanded as she stood near the fireplace waiting for them. She had been staring into the painting of a quiet mountain glen with light sparkling through the tree branches as at dawn but turned toward them at their arrival. "Please, lay her on the settee."

Jeremy did as he was bid, stroking Savannah's hair once before he backed away a step.

"I don't need a doctor," Savannah said. "It's not that bad this time."

"This time?" Jeremy bellowed. "How many times has that man hurt you?"

Sophronia moved toward the settee, pushing Jeremy out of the way. "Mr. McLeod, it's nice to see you are one male with good sense. I suspected as much when I met you last year at Clarissa's when you called with your brother, Richard. However, I must insist you let Savannah breathe. Give her some space." Jeremy backed up a few paces, his gaze never leaving Savannah's prostrate form on the settee.

"Now, Savannah, you will tell me what he did and allow me to determine what needs to be done," Sophronia said.

"He gripped my arms, struck my cheek and kicked me in the shin. Nothing that requires a doctor."

"What has he done in the past?"

Savannah curled into a ball, squeezing her eyes shut. "Nothing that needs to be discussed now. It has no bearing on today's events."

"Oh, but I disagree. It has everything to do with today's events, and our ability to show a court that you left him due to cruelty."

"Court?" Savannah whispered as she opened her eyes to meet Sophronia's. She flinched as Sophronia traced the red welt rising on her cheek below her left eye.

"Of course, my dearest Savannah. You wouldn't think your aunt Betsy or I would have you simply leave and be a scorned woman in society? We want you to be a divorced woman."

Jeremy hissed and Florence gasped. Savannah watched as Sophronia turned her icy aquamarine eyes on them to silence them. "If you are going to be scandalous, dearest, you might as well be a true sensation. Why allow Clarissa to have all the notoriety?" She smiled tenderly at Savannah as she tucked a strand of hair behind one ear. "And you must be free of that man."

"What must I do?"

"Never fear. I've asked my butler, Poole, to send for my lawyer, and I'm sure he is en route by now. He will know what needs to be done."

"Mrs. Chickering, thank you," Savannah said, as tears streamed from her eyes.

"None needed. I had hoped you would come to me, but I had never expected it would be so soon nor in quite so dramatic a fashion."

CHAPTER 7

THE DRY, HOT BREEZE blew down the canyon and into town, and small funnels of dust formed in the front walkways of the homes we passed. The mountainsides in the distance were a baked gold, incandescent in the early evening light. I maintained a loose hold on Gabriel's arm as we walked toward his uncle's house.

Gabriel reached out and clasped my arm as I stumbled in a rut on the side of the road. I steadied myself and moved away from him, brushing down my skirts. "I'm sorry, Gabriel."

"No need to apologize, Rissa." He offered his arm again, and I reached for it with shaking fingers. Gabriel reached down to cover my hand with his, holding it firmly in place. I moved a step closer to him, and we walked at a sedate pace to Aidan's home on Pine Street. Although Aidan was currently in San Francisco, Amelia lived there as his housekeeper and cook. We spent many evenings there with our friends, at what had become our informal gathering place.

"Clarissa," Gabriel said with a note of hesitancy in his voice. "Won't you tell me what troubles you?"

"It's nothing. Nothing that won't be resolved with time."

"Have I done something?"

"Of course not," I whispered. I blinked rapidly to prevent any tears from falling.

"You've been distant lately, darling. Tell me what I can do to help."

"There's nothing you can do. It's all my own doing." My voice cracked, and I cleared my throat.

He paused for a moment on the walkway toward his uncle's house. "You say there's nothing troubling you. Then in the next breath that there's nothing I can do to help. Don't you want what we had? Why did everything change in April?"

"Gabriel, now is not the time," I whispered, as I forced a smile at a passing couple.

"When is the time? You're never home. You don't want me near you. I thought we'd moved past what happened in Boston."

"Gabriel—"

"Dammit, Rissa," he said, as he stepped in front of me and gripped both of my arms and glared at me with azure eyes lit with pain. "Be honest with me. Tell me what I can do to make you happy."

I shook my head. "There's nothing you can do. I—"

He backed away, releasing my arms before I finished. "I see. Well, can you at least act as though I make you happy for our friends? They've gone to some trouble for our anniversary dinner." He motioned for me to precede him up the walkway.

"For my sake, can you please try?" Gabriel asked again, as he knocked on the front door of his uncle's house.

I nodded, moving a step toward him and gripping his arm as Colin eased open the front door.

"Welcome!" he said in a booming voice. He enveloped me in a warm hug before releasing me to slap Gabriel on the back. "Amelia's in the kitchen, putting the finishing touches on dinner. Seb and Ronan are in the living room, playing with little Nicholas, and Anne's had her supper and is already asleep."

We entered the small foyer to Aidan's house with its staircase leading upstairs. The main doorway was in the middle of the house. To the right was a large room he used as an office. To the left was a formal sitting room connected to a dining room. The previous owners had added a kitchen in the back, transforming the once-square, two-story building into an irregularly shaped residence. A pantry and another small storage room were next to the kitchen. Behind Aidan's formal office was a bedroom, currently used by Amelia and her children. Upstairs, three nice-size bedrooms remained largely unused.

"*Gavriel!*" Nicholas yelled as he rose from the floor and clamped onto one of Gabriel's legs. "We get to eat cake!"

Gabriel chuckled as he ruffled Nicholas's russet-colored hair. "That we do, little man. Today is a day to celebrate."

Nicholas scrambled back to Sebastian to continue their marbles match. Sebastian, our friend and overseer of one of the local lumber mills, glanced toward us and nodded, his long, lean frame still sprawled on the floor. "Gabriel, Mrs. McLeod." He smiled, before returning his attention to Nicholas.

I managed a wan smile as I met Ronan's gaze. "Hello, Ronan. How did you travel here?"

"Seb took one of the wagons from the mill and picked me up." Ronan sat on his wheelchair in the living room, watching Nicholas's and Sebastian's antics, his sherry-brown eyes lit with pleasure.

"Doesn't weigh more than a few two-by-fours," Sebastian said, before he began to tickle Nicholas.

Over Nicholas's delighted shrieks, Colin said, "That's not what you were muttering as I helped you. You were carrying on worse than an old woman."

Amelia swatted him on his arm as she hugged first me and then Gabriel. "Men will do no end of bellyaching if they think there's a receptive audience." She smiled at Ronan, Sebastian, her son Nicholas, and Colin before retreating to the kitchen.

I moved to follow Amelia. However, Colin directed me to a dining room chair. "Don't even think about it, Rissa. This is one meal that I'm looking forward to eating!"

"I'd have to agree with Colin," Ronan said with a wink. He wheeled his well-used wheelchair—made of sturdy maple, designed by Gabriel; and steel to form the wheels, forged by Colin—into the dining room. The steel wheels were a simple design with little ornamentation. However, with enough determination and arm strength, Ronan was able to move himself short distances. "Not that I don't appreciate your attempts to feed me, Clarissa. But a man does look forward to a good home-cooked meal."

"I'm not that bad in the kitchen." At their smirks, I remained seated.

"Disastrous is the word most often used with you and the kitchen," Colin said with a grin.

I knew their remarks weren't intended to harm, but, in my present state, they only added to my melancholy.

Soon Sebastian rose from the floor, carrying Nicholas with him toward the kitchen to wash their hands. Gabriel settled next to me at the dining room table with Colin sitting at my left, Ronan on his other side. Amelia scurried to and from the kitchen, carrying platters of food, and before long the large oval table was covered with a delicious feast. Green beans, beets, mashed potatoes, homemade rolls and slabs of a carved roast filled bowls and platters.

Sebastian emerged from the kitchen, sat next to Ronan and propped Nicholas by him. Whenever Amelia settled, she would sit next to Gabriel and Nicholas.

"Amelia, sit down so we can begin. I can't imagine you have any more food out there for us," Colin said. He reached for a roll but stilled his movements as Amelia entered the room from the kitchen. He flashed her a quick grin as she glared at him.

"I want this meal to be perfect for our celebration." She beamed at everyone present and took her seat, setting down the bowl of mashed potatoes.

"Clarissa and I thank you, Amelia, for this fine meal," Gabriel said. He reached out to grip my hand.

I smiled and nodded.

"We couldn't have you celebrate your anniversary with Clarissa's cooking, Gabe," Sebastian said as he served himself a slice of the roast and passed the tray.

"Although you might have appreciated being alone," Ronan teased with a twitch of his eyebrows.

"Ronan," Amelia scolded, but he only laughed as I blushed. "I know Clarissa continues to improve in her cooking, but a day like today calls for a feast."

"Any word from the eastern McLeods?" Colin asked.

"Yes, I just received word today from Richard," Gabriel said. "I haven't even been able to share it yet with Clarissa. Florence and Richard are intent on making us aunt and uncle."

"Oh, that's wonderful news!" Amelia gushed.

"I agree," Colin said with a wry smile. "Hard to imagine Richard a father, though he or she will be one lucky child."

"He sounds scared out of his britches." Gabriel laughed and a wistful smile remained on his face as he thought of his brother in Boston. "I can see him now, fussing over little Florence."

"Why so pensive, Colin?" Ronan asked.

"Oh, just wishing I'd be around to help teach him or her the black-smithing songs I'm learning. They're different from the ones in Boston."

"As though you can sing," Ronan said with a laugh.

I paled and gripped my fork tighter as they continued to tease each other, Sebastian joining in to comment on Colin's attempts at yodeling.

"Ah, it will be wonderful to have a little one in the family again," Amelia said. "It seems baby Anne is growing up too quickly already."

"Yes, wonderful," I whispered. "I'm very happy for them." My knuckles had turned white, and I had to force my hand to relax.

"Well, I for one, hope to hear similar news from other McLeod relatives," Colin said.

I knew he meant well but still flinched at his words.

I heard Gabriel chuckle as he caressed my neck. "All in good time, Colin. And I will remain hopeful the baby will have Lucas's musical abilities."

"Ah, Lucas. I do miss hearing him play the piano. That's the one thing missing from our gatherings," Colin said. He leaned away from the table, taking a momentary break from the dinner.

"When's the baby coming, Mama?" Nicholas asked as he looked at me and then poked his head under the table as though he was trying to see my belly.

I flinched at Nicholas's question while everyone else laughed. As the laughter subsided, I noticed that Amelia was watching me with an assessing look in her blue eyes.

"Never mind that there is no baby," I said as I blinked away tears. "If you will excuse me a moment?" I rose from my chair and stumbled into the living room and then out the front door onto the front porch, hearing a confused, "Mama?" from Nicholas as the front door closed behind me. I collapsed onto the bench next to the door. A soft breeze blew, cooling the town after a warm July day.

"Clarissa?" Gabriel asked, as he poked his head out the front door. "What's the matter? I would have thought you'd be delighted at the news for Richard and Florence. And there's no reason to be upset with Nicholas."

"Of course I am delighted." I swiped at my cheeks, rubbing away an errant tear. "Happy for them. And I'm not mad at Nicholas."

"It's not like you to be jealous of others' good fortune. We'll have similar news soon."

He crouched down in front of me and caressed my cheek. I closed my eyes. I neither leaned into nor away from his touch. After a moment he dropped his hand.

"I'm sorry I haven't been able to give you what you desire, darling."

"I'm happy. Of course I am," I said around a sniffle.

"This is a fine way to show it." He grasped my hands as he met my gaze. "What's wrong? I can't seem to do anything right recently."

"It's nothing you've done, Gabriel." I hitched in a stuttering breath as I battled tears.

"No? Maybe it's something I've failed to do." He rose, walking a pace away before turning to look down at me, sitting crumpled on the bench. "Can't you at least act like you're happy to have married me on our anniversary?"

I paled, placing one of my hands to my chest at the pleading in his voice. When I stared at him wordlessly, he strode into the house, the screen door slamming shut behind him.

After another moment outside, I rose to follow him. As I opened the door, I heard the conversation continuing without me. "She'll come around soon, Gabriel. Don't worry."

Amelia's soothing voice.

"It's an adjustment from Boston. Never fear she'd rather be there than here."

Colin's deep voice, unable to hide his concern.

"You know what I think, so no need going over it again," Sebastian said.

"Whatever you've done, figure it out, man. You don't want your woman angry with you for much longer," Ronan said.

I waited for Gabriel to speak. After a long silence, he said, "I wonder if I should have listened to Richard's advice in the beginning."

I stifled a gasp as my mind raced to the moment Richard had confronted Gabriel about his interest in me at his workshop in Boston. *It will only lead to pain. For pity's sake ... find another one, more suitable, more of our class.*

"Colin, will you see Clarissa home?" Gabriel ran a hand through his ebony hair. "I need ..."

"Gabriel, you haven't eaten any of your anniversary cake," Amelia said.

"Cake won't make this better, Amelia," Gabriel said before he marched toward the kitchen and exited the rear door.

I looked out the side window to see his long, loping gait striding down the boardwalk toward the center of town.

"That was poorly done, Rissa," Colin said. He had risen and seen me standing in the living room.

"I know, Col," I said. I fell into an overstuffed armchair, curling my legs up under me, holding onto my knees as I rocked to and fro. My mind raced at the disastrous evening. "I'll apologize to Nicholas."

Colin glanced over his shoulder and saw that Amelia, carrying Nicholas, moved with Sebastian and Ronan into the kitchen. "It's not just Nicholas, Rissa. Can't you tell me what's wrong? Why are you acting like this?"

"It's nothing, Col."

"Don't treat me like a fool. It's obviously something. Do you regret marrying Gabe?"

"That's not the question, Colin. It never will be." I let out another stuttering sigh as I leaned my head against my knees, a terrible weariness filling me.

"Then what it is? Are you ill? Is that why Amelia saw you visiting the doctor recently?"

"Is that all you do? Gossip about me?"

"It's what people do who care about each other. Especially when one of them refuses to share anything and acts like a wounded badger."

Colin glared at me, daring me to contradict him.

"I'm of sound health, Colin. Nothing to fear." I closed my eyes in resignation.

"Then why are you acting like this?" Colin asked again as he gripped my hand. "I've never seen you with such little spirit. Not even last spring in Boston. Now you act as though all the fight has left you. That's not who you are, Rissa."

"You'd never understand, Col. And I fear Gabriel never will either."

"Whatever it is, you must tell him."

"No, Colin. The last thing I should do is tell Gabriel. Because once I do, he will despise me."

***

AMELIA MOVED FROM THE KITCHEN to the dining room. She held a teal-blue cast-iron coffeepot in her left hand while four mugs swung from the fingers of her right hand.

"Here, let me help you, Mrs. Egan." Sebastian reached for the coffeepot.

"No, take the mugs. I have the towel to protect my hand." She nodded to the table, smiling her thanks as he set down the mugs with loud clunks. She filled them before returning to the kitchen for sugar and milk, leaving the coffeepot warming on the stove.

She joined Colin, Ronan and Sebastian as she stared at the carved anniversary cake. "Is there anything we can do?" She blew on her mug of steaming coffee a few times before taking a tentative sip.

"I doubt it. Clarissa won't admit to what's wrong, and that's unlike her," Colin said, as he added milk to his coffee.

"Could be she's unsatisfied with her life with Gabe," Sebastian said. He drummed his fingers on the tabletop, a distant look in his eyes.

"Or she's still running from her past. Can't be easy to have that man here, taunting her every time she sees him," Ronan said. "She's strong, but that kind of thing can wear a person down."

"How could she be unhappy with her life with Gabriel? They have a good home. She works with Mr. Pickens. She could want for no better man," Amelia said.

Sebastian met her earnest gaze with marked intensity, causing her to lower her eyes.

"This ain't Boston. I imagine she misses her life there," Sebastian said.

"I don't know why she would," Colin said. "The last few months weren't pleasant for her. She wasn't allowed to teach, even though she wasn't married. She couldn't visit her friends or participate in her suffragist activities. All that was attractive about Boston was taken away from her."

"Would she want that good-for-nothing?" Sebastian asked, as Ronan scoffed at the idea.

Colin started as though Sebastian had struck him. "I can guarantee, never."

"Maybe now that she sees what life is like with Gabe, she realizes she should have opted for the easier life." Sebastian met Colin's steely glare.

"If Cameron were her only option, she would never choose him." Colin sighed. "She suffered too much at his hands."

"And appears to continue to suffer from it. Only now she's making everyone, especially Gabe, miserable," Ronan said, as he took a sip of coffee.

Sebastian squinted at his friend's words, before letting out a long sigh. "Well, whatever it is, she needs to tell Gabe. There's nothing worse than not knowing how to make your woman happy and waiting for the day she leaves for good."

"Mr. Carlin?" Amelia asked Sebastian, sensing he spoke from experience.

"I'm afraid I've overstayed my welcome, and I need to return the wagon to the mill. I thank you, Mrs. Egan, for a delicious dinner and fine company. Colin."

Ronan nodded his thanks, as he must leave now with Sebastian, maneuvering his wheelchair to the kitchen and out the side door. Colin had also risen, and he and Sebastian carried Ronan in the wheelchair down the porch steps. They hoisted Ronan into the front seat of the wagon, where he had a special rope he tied around his waist to prevent sliding out of the seat. Sebastian moved toward the wagon to tie the wheelchair securely, before climbing in beside Ronan.

Colin reentered Aidan's house and sat again next to Amelia. He took a small sip of coffee, the quiet of the night descending as they sat in silent contemplation.

After a few moments, Amelia turned to Colin. "Would you like some cake?"

"I thought you'd never ask," Colin said with a broad smile. "Sweets are one of my weaknesses."

"They were one of Liam's too," she said with a wistful smile.

"You miss him still."

"Of course. I'll always miss him." She rose, moving toward the cake to carve two generous portions. "I still turn to speak with him or to meet his amused smile when Nicholas says or does something humorous. And then I remember he's not here. He'll never be here again."

"I'm sorry, Mrs. Egan. I didn't mean to ..."

"I'd rather speak of him. It's as though a code of silence was erected around his name after his death, and everyone is afraid to breach it. I know I helped erect it, but now I need to speak of him again. He'd want his children to hear me talk about him. *I* want his children to know who he was. A good, kind man who would have loved them. Who did love them."

"And their mother," Colin murmured.

"Yes. Thank you, Mr. Sullivan."

"We're family, of sorts. You should call me Colin."

She smiled and nodded. "And you must call me Amelia."

Colin sighed in contentment as he took a bite of her chocolate cake. "I hope Rissa and Gabe have the good sense to eat this."

"I'm afraid that's the one thing they've been lacking for a few months, Colin."

Colin grunted his agreement as he devoured his cake in earnest.

CHAPTER 8

HAVING REFUSED COLIN'S OFFER to escort me home, I returned to the workshop and apartment Gabriel and I shared on Main Street in Missoula. I paused to marvel at the sunset. To the west, the mountains shone crimson, while the wisps of clouds in the sky changed from fuchsia to a carnation pink, before night finally descended and the beautiful display ended. I sighed, turning to face the workshop, knowing that I'd see another beautiful sunset again, if not tomorrow, soon.

I unlocked the workshop, re-locked the door and trudged up the stairs to the loft-like living area. I carried the slab of anniversary cake Amelia had sent home with me for us to share, any of Amelia's optimism that our disagreement could be resolved by consuming her confection fading with each step.

As I neared the top of the steps along one sidewall, long shadows entered our apartment through the three large windows overlooking the street. The small kitchen area was near the stairs along the back wall. A small dining room table sat next to one of the windows, covered in a colorful, poppy-covered cloth. The living area consisted of two gentleman's chairs, a rocking chair and two small side tables covered in lace doilies tatted by Amelia. I enjoyed the small touch of home.

My desk sat at the edge of the living area, toward our bedroom area and in front of the second window. In truth, Gabriel and I shared the desk, as he often worked there, going over his books and orders during the evenings. Our bed was in plain view across the room.

I entered the kitchen area near the top of the stairs and set the plate on the dining room table. Gabriel stood with his back to the far window, in our bedroom area. He had pushed the privacy screen aside, allowing him to see the entire room.

"So, you came home."

I shuddered at his chill tone. "Of course. Amelia sent cake." I unpinned my hat, setting it on a small table near the top of the stairs. I avoided looking in the mirror and turned toward him. Gabriel remained across the room, his arms crossed as he leaned against the ledge of the window.

"Who is he?" Gabriel asked.

"I beg your pardon?"

"You'll have a lot more to beg than that, Rissa. Who is he?" Gabriel growled, as he pushed away from the window and prowled toward me.

"I don't know what you're talking about."

"You don't come home anymore after you leave the depository. You wander in, hours later, breathless and disheveled. Acquaintances tell me that they've seen you walking in parts of Missoula they'd never seen you in before." Gabriel's eyes flashed, and he gripped his hands at his sides, although he refrained from touching me.

I gave a surprised laugh at his conclusion. "Gabriel, there is no one else."

"Don't laugh at me," Gabriel hissed, as he reached up and gripped my arms almost to the point of pain.

I jerked at his sudden movement, and he released my arms but not before I saw the hurt flash in his eyes.

"Gabriel, there is no other man. I ... I have a lot to think about. I go on walks." I blushed. "You know I'm clumsy." I smiled, hoping the shared memory of how we'd met—me knocking him off a ladder and landing on top of him at my uncle's store in Boston two years ago—would lighten his mood. I frowned as he continued to glower at me. "When I sit next to the streams, I like to take off my hat, cool down. I nearly fell into the stream a few times."

"You mean you'd prefer to spend your time alone, rather than talking with me?"

"It's not like that." I hated the pleading in my voice, but I couldn't hide it.

"How is it then, Rissa? You won't talk with me. You don't want me to touch you." He backed up a step. "You prefer to spend all your time away from home." His eyes flashed pain and disappointment.

"Gabriel, I wish you could understand—"

"How? How am I to understand when you won't tell me anything?" he roared. "I'm not one of those clairvoyants. I don't know what you want without you telling me."

"I … I …" I tried to speak, but no words emerged, as though I were choking.

He turned away from me and took a deep breath. "Happy anniversary, Clarissa." He spun around to face me, and he watched me with tormented eyes for a moment before he moved past me and down the stairs. I heard the resounding slam of the workshop door.

I stood in the middle of the room, a welling desire to tell Gabriel everything filling me. I swayed, almost to the point of following him before I collapsed into my rocking chair. *No one will want you but me.* I shuddered at the whisper of memory, at the possibility of truth in those words.

***

GABRIEL THRUST OPEN the swinging shutters of the Turf Bar, his boot heels forming a resounding clunk with each step on the battered wooden floors. He stalked toward the wooden bar with its scarred top, edging his way around customers leaning against it. He nodded his agreement when the bartender held up a glass and turned to look around. The darkened, seedy interior matched his mood. A man sat in a far corner, playing discordant music on a button accordion. Many of the low tables were occupied, most of the men sipping their drinks rather than telling tall tales.

Gabriel slapped down his coin, picked up his beer and moved to a table in the shadows toward the rear of the bar. He sat with a thud and sighed. His glower and unfocused gaze prevented those who knew him from approaching. He continued to replay his argument with Clarissa, each time finding a way to breach her resistance to speak with him about what truly concerned her.

"What's the matter, McLeod?"

Gabriel jerked toward the voice to his left, his body stiffening and readying for battle. "Cameron. I'd hoped you had enough sense to leave."

"Why would I? The town's got other wealthy women." His honey-brown eyes blurred with drink, he gripped his tankard of beer and glared at Gabriel.

"I'd think you'd go to Butte. That's where the real heiresses are." Gabriel fisted his hands as he confronted the man who'd tormented his wife.

"You just want me out of town. Away from Clarissa. So she isn't re-minded of what she gave up by marryin' you." His voice slurred, he waved one hand toward Gabriel.

"Think what you like."

"What's it like, bein' with your wife, knowin' that another had her first?" Cameron's voice was low and taunting. "That no matter what you do, I'll al-ways be a part of her life? That every time you touch her, she'll have the memory of my touch to compare it with?"

In an instant, Gabriel had him by his shirt collar, dragging him from his chair and slamming him against the rear wall of the saloon. "Don't you dare speak about her with me. You have no right. Not after what you did."

"I have every right." Cameron gasped as Gabriel tightened his hold. "She should have been mine. *Mine.* She should have borne my children, rather than run off to you, you worthless immigrant."

"All you wanted was her money. And when you knew she didn't want you, you tried to ruin her spirit, destroy her in the worst way. For that alone I should kill you." Gabriel leaned his face into Cameron's, his fiery gaze met by Cameron's taunting brown eyes.

"You should, and yet you haven't. You've let me live. Seems that all your purported love for Clarissa doesn't extend to defending her honor."

"You have no idea what honor is. I honor her by loving her. By cherishing her. By building a life with her. I can't do that if I'm in jail for killing your worthless carcass." He shook Cameron once more and then flung him away. Cameron fell to the floor and glared up at Gabriel.

Cameron rose, brushing his hair into place and running his hands down the sleeves of his tattered jacket. "Seems to me, if you believe what you said, you wouldn't be in a saloon looking miserable. You'd be home with your wife."

Gabriel glared at him and then turned to the other patrons in the room, noticing their hasty attempts to avert their curious stares. He grabbed his hat and strode from the room.

CHAPTER 9

"HOW WAS THAT ANNIVERSARY, Missy?" Mr. Pickens sat in his chair in the rear of the Book Depository, next to a table of recently returned books.

"Fine. Amelia cooked us a lovely meal." I moved around the stacks of books, putting them away.

"Seems a mighty strange way to spend an anniversary. No sirree. When my Bessie 'n' me had our anniversaries, we were all by our lonesome." He smiled his near toothless grin. "An' what a time we had." He thumped his cane down once in emphasis. "Though with your cooking *incapacitations*, makes sense to have someone else prepare the meal, else you'd both die of starvation." He guffawed at his own joke.

His eyes narrowed when I failed to laugh, and he focused on me. "What's got you in a bad mood, Missy?"

"Nothing, Mr. A.J."

"You look like a woman headin' to her funeral, rather than a blushin' bride," he said, clamping his mouth around his imaginary pipe, as he frequently did.

"Mr. A.J., it will all be sorted soon."

He motioned me toward him with his cane, and I stumbled as I went to sit on my small stool next to him.

I began to sort the books he had failed to look at.

"If you want to know somethin' about menfolk, Missy, it's *don't make 'em feel vulnerable*. Word has it, yer unhappy at home, an', if that's the case, your man knows it. Find a way to show him that's a bunch o' malarkey."

I stared at him, unable to hide the shock from my eyes.

"It's a small town, Missy. And people like to have somethin' to talk about. Yer the most interesting thing to come around in some time. 'Specially since that good-fer-nothin's still here and courtin' Mrs. Bouchard's daughter."

"Cameron." I shuddered as I said his name.

"Afore you know it, they'll start sayin' you wished you'd married him, if you keep carryin' on the way you are." He watched me with solemn eyes.

"Never!" I said.

"Well, show that husband of yours, an' the townfolk'll know well enough the truth. 'Cause you keep actin' like this, no one'll ever believe yer happy, married to the man you chose."

"Mr. A.J., why can't people just leave us alone to solve our problems?" I stood and picked up a few books, slamming them onto the table as I vented my frustration.

"Where's the fun in that, Missy? Asides, you enjoy a little gossip just like the rest of us. It's just no fun when it's pointed at you, now is it?"

My shoulders stooped, and I collapsed onto the stool again. I pinched the bridge of my nose in an attempt to ward off a headache.

"Whatever you think's so terrible to tell that young man of yours ain't no worse than what yer already doin', Missy. Just tell him."

"How do you know what I'm going through?"

"I know women. Well, as much as a man can. Yer all a bit mysticalerious. But I knew my Bessie. An' when she got all ornery like you, was 'cause she had some bad news to tell me. The imaginin' was always worse for me than the reality."

I half smiled as I puzzled through his word. *Mysterious? Mystical?* At his broad smile, I nodded. "What's the worst news Bessie ever told you?"

"Other than she was dyin'?" He shook his head from side to side a few times and rubbed his face. "There's nothin' worse than death, Missy. An' we do all kinds o' things to protect those we love from the pain of it. Sometimes it's a pain that should be shared. An' there ain't no protectin' those we love from it."

He sighed as he settled onto his chair. "My Bessie did no end of tryin' to protect me." A wistful smile spread across his face. "In the end she learned that we were together to protect each other." He pierced me with a fierce stare. "You remember that, Missy. You and that man o' yours are together for each other."

I blinked rapidly, nodding as I turned away toward the books. Mr. Pickens ignored my sniffling as I returned to work.

***

GABRIEL SAT IN THE BACK of the shop, staring at a sketch. He tapped at it before erasing half of it. Ronan worked at his low workbench at the base of the stairs, sunlight spilling in from the window. He sang ribald songs from the saloon, pausing in his singing when he needed to focus on a task. Ronan looked up at the heavy footsteps entering the workshop.

"What's gotten into you, McLeod?" Sebastian asked. He took off his hat, slapping at his pants, brushing off dust from his fawn-colored pants.

Gabriel glanced toward the door, setting aside the pencil he held, and straightened. After a quick glance at Ronan, who shook his head in a near imperceptible movement, Gabriel frowned. "I don't know what you mean, Seb."

"Getting into bar brawls. Doesn't seem your style."

"I was in no brawl," Gabriel snapped, as he picked up a piece of wood and slammed it down onto his workbench.

"Nearly stranglin' a man to death seems close enough to me," Sebastian said. "What's got you so riled? You haven't been acting like yourself for weeks."

"Months," Ronan murmured. Gabriel shot a steely look at him, but Ronan shrugged. "It's the truth, Gabe. Something's bothering you, and you've been hell to be around."

At Gabriel's persistent silence, Sebastian wandered over to Ronan and sat on a stool near him. "Seems it's that lovely wife of his who's got him so tied in knots." Ronan nodded his agreement.

Gabriel growled at them before marching toward the door. "Gabe!" Ronan said, but, instead of leaving, Gabriel shut the door and locked it.

"You never know who's listening in," Gabriel said. Less light entered the room with the door shut, although enough light entered through the two windows on either side of the door to illuminate the room.

Gabriel pulled over a dusty chair and sat in it with a loud thud. "I wanted to kill him last night. I would have too, if I hadn't remembered that I'd be separated from Clarissa."

"What's going on, Gabe?"

"I don't know. I think she regrets marrying me." The words came out in a tortured whisper, and he refused to meet his friends' gazes. "She's been so different the past few months."

After a few moments, Ronan asked in a quiet voice, "How is she different, Gabe?"

"Prickly. Like she doesn't want me near her. Doesn't want me to touch her." He rose and paced. "And that's not like her. Well, not like her since she overcame her fears."

"Maybe she has other fears you don't know about," Sebastian said.

"I've tried to think of what they could be, and I can't. She's survived the worst. What more could she fear?"

"Well, it's a large fear, because who you're describing isn't the Clarissa I know," Ronan said as he leaned back in his chair.

"Do you think she's upset you haven't taken care of that varmint?" Sebastian asked.

Gabriel shook his head. "She insists I do nothing to harm him so that I won't go to jail and be separated from her."

"Well, almost starting bar brawls isn't the way to go about honoring that request," Sebastian said with a sardonic lift of his eyebrows.

"Gabe, the only one who can end your misery is Clarissa. Talk to her. Insist she tell you what is occurring. You have that right. You've earned it," Ronan said.

"What if she truly regrets being my wife?"

"The only way you'll know is if you ask her. Otherwise, you'll just continue to torture yourself." Ronan tapped his fingers on the arms of his chair. "The woman I met last summer didn't seem anxious to escape you. She wanted to be with you, even with everything that had happened."

"It's better to know than to spend your life wondering. Take it from me," Sebastian said.

"What do you mean?" Gabriel asked.

"I was married before," Sebastian murmured, a mocking half smile gracing his lips as Ronan and Gabriel gaped at him. He rose and paced the workshop. He picked up tools, traced patterns in the dust and remained in perpetual motion as he wandered.

"What happened to her?" Ronan asked after sharing a long glance with Gabriel.

"She left me for a drifter, traveling to New Mexico. Thought it sounded like a more interesting life than living in a small house near a sawmill. I can still see her, brown hair shot with red, flying loose in the wind. Pointing around at all I had earned for her, for us, and her snickerin'. Didn't want any of it. Never had envisioned the sort of life I craved. Wanted a man with bigger dreams."

He spun to face Gabe. "I should never have married her—knew she was fickle. But the heart's not always rational. I paid for my folly."

"Are you still married?" Gabriel asked.

"No, she died in a carriage accident a few years ago. She and our daughter. The child I never knew I had, not till I received the letter from the lawyer telling me about their deaths."

"Seb—"

"There's nothin' to say, Gabe. I made the greatest mistake a man can make, and it cost a child, my child, her life. I hope you chose better than me."

"For God's sake, Seb, you know he did," Ronan snapped. "It's Clarissa you're talking about. She'd never treat Gabriel false."

"Well, whatever she's doing, she's not treating him true, now is she?" Sebastian asked with a glare as he moved toward Ronan and Gabriel to sit on his stool again.

Ronan hissed in a breath. "She wouldn't do that to Gabe."

"We like to think we know those we love, but love can give us blinders. I'd hate it if she was playing you false," Sebastian said as he turned to watch Gabriel. "What're you going to do about her, Gabe?"

"Continue to try to talk with her. Listen when she does speak." He closed his eyes. "Hope I have the ability to let her go, like you did, Seb."

"I near drank the town dry, Gabe. You don't want to be anything like me." He clapped Gabriel on the shoulder. "Whatever happens, you've friends to support you. Remember that."

CHAPTER 10

AMELIA WIPED HER HANDS on the kitchen cloth as she turned toward the soft tapping on the kitchen's screen door. "Mr. Carlin, I hadn't thought to see you tonight." She pushed open the screened door and backed up a step to allow him to enter the kitchen.

Sebastian doffed his hat and scuffed his boots before entering. He looked at the small kitchen table already set for dinner and then at Amelia. "I thought we were meeting here for dinner tonight." His brow furrowed in confusion. "This is the normal night for our weekly dinners, isn't it?"

"Yes, it is, even though it's only six days since the anniversary dinner for Clarissa and Gabriel. However, Gabriel sent word that he and Clarissa weren't coming. Thus, Ronan and Colin decided to cancel. I assumed that meant you weren't coming."

"I never heard from them. It was busy at the mill today, and I could have missed a message. I had a stack of them on my desk that I left for tomorrow."

"It's no bother to set another place, and Nicholas will be delighted to have you here." She turned away toward the cupboard and extracted another plate and cup.

"Mr. Seb! Mr. Seb!" Nicholas called as he ran into the kitchen. He jumped up and down in front of Sebastian in his excitement, until Sebastian pulled him high into the air before settling him on his hip.

Sebastian closed his eyes for a moment, tilting his head back as he inhaled appreciatively. "Whatever you're cooking smells wonderful."

"It's a chicken! We gotta pick it out today at the butcher's," Nicholas said. "It still had its neck on, but Mama didn't want it, so he pulled out a big knife an'—"

"Nicholas," Amelia interrupted. "We know what he did."

"An' he chopped it off!" Nicholas wriggled around so much that Sebastian lowered him to the floor. He happily made chopping motions with his hand. He banged into the side of the table, oversetting a glass and knocking a few pieces of silverware onto the floor. Amelia grimaced at the clattering sound of forks and spoons landing on the wood floor. She reached forward and set to rights the tablecloth.

"Nicholas," Amelia began but was interrupted by Sebastian.

"I think you and I need to pick up that silverware, little man," Sebastian said, as he moved to peer under the table. Soon he and Nicholas were crawling on the floor looking for a missing fork.

"I found it!" Nicholas said, thrusting up his hand from under the table.

"Good work. Now let's wash and dry these for your mother," Sebastian said. He grasped Nicholas's hand and pulled a chair over to the sink for him to stand on. In a few moments Nicholas's arms were covered in sudsy water, and he looked as though he had just taken a bath. He held out each piece of silverware for Sebastian to dry and babbled about his day, playing cowboys and Indians with the local children, before the eventful trip to the butcher's.

"An' I was an Indian, but I didn't want to lose. Got in a fight with snotty Bobby Hunter 'cause I tried to scalp 'im."

Sebastian choked back a laugh. "I hope you didn't really try to do that."

"No, just grabbed his hair and yanked on it." Nicholas pulled his hands from the water, where he was now playing rather than washing anything, and demonstrated on his head what he did, soaking his hair.

Sebastian grabbed a towel from Amelia and wiped the boy's head with it, causing Nicholas to giggle. Sebastian shared an amused glance with Amelia as Nicholas described the trip to the butcher's in enthusiastic detail. "Do you want to be a butcher when you grow up?" Sebastian asked.

"I don't know," Nicholas said. "I think I want to work in a blacksmith shop like Uncle Colin."

"A very good profession," Sebastian said, as he wiped at Nicholas's arms and lifted him off the chair. He placed the chair at the table again and helped settle Nicholas.

Amelia grabbed the cleaned silverware and placed it at the missing settings around the table. She moved to the living room, picking up Anne from an enclosed play area Gabriel had constructed for her. She sat Anne in her high chair. Anne clapped her hands and smiled at seeing Sebastian. He stroked a finger down her cheek and then sat at his indicated spot, between Nicholas and Anne's high chair and across from where Amelia usually sat at the square table covered in a red-checkered cloth.

Amelia moved to the stove, pulling out the roasted chicken. She scooped up mashed potatoes from a pot on the stove and boiled carrots from another, placing each in bowls. She placed the bowls on the table and then sat.

"How are things at work?" Amelia asked as she mashed carrots and fed small amounts to Anne.

"Busy, but with no recent accidents." Sebastian placed a small amount of mashed potatoes on Nicholas's plate and then grabbed the butter dish to prevent Nicholas from slathering on half the bowl. He placed a small dab on top of Nicholas's potatoes and set it aside.

"I'm glad to hear that."

"Accidents and fire are always a concern in a mill. We've been lucky, and I try to instill in my men that they need to be careful to prevent tragedy. So far, it's worked."

"I hope it continues to," Amelia said before Nicholas entertained them with more stories from his day.

After supper Amelia rose to bring Anne to the back room the three of them shared. Amelia readied her for bed and rocked her a few minutes while singing a gentle lullaby before laying her in her crib for the night. When she reentered the kitchen, she paused in the doorway to see Sebastian doing the dishes. His shirtsleeves were rolled up; his arms were immersed in soapy water nearly to his elbows, and he whistled a soft, lilting tune as he worked. She glanced into the living room to see Nicholas asleep on the sofa.

"Seb … Mr. Carlin, you shouldn't be doing that," Amelia whispered. She moved toward the sink, intending to push him away. He turned toward her, his light-brown eyes flashing with amusement.

"Of course I should. You've enough to do with those two young ones, 'specially after making such a delicious meal." He nudged her shoulder as she tried to force herself in front of the sink. "Why don't we compromise, and you dry, seeing as you're already holding the towel?" he asked with a smile.

After a few moments where he handed her objects to dry, he murmured, "I'd hope you'd see me more as a friend than a guest."

She turned confused hazel eyes to him, nodding. "Of course. You're very fond of the children."

Sebastian turned toward the soapy water, muttering to himself. Amelia couldn't make out the words but had a sense by his tense shoulders and disgruntled tone that she had said the wrong thing. He spun toward her, thrusting a platter at her.

"Did you never stop to think that it's not just your children …" and then he broke off as a flush started rising up his neck. "I'm saying I hope we are friends too, Mrs. Egan."

"Oh. Of course," Amelia said as she focused on drying the platter until it shone. She heard Sebastian remove his hands from the water and saw out of the corner of her eye as he wiped them on his pants legs to dry, as she was using the only visible towel. His gentle grip of her chin startled her, and she gasped. Her gaze flew to his as he traced her jaw with a few of his fingers.

"Amelia," he murmured. He leaned forward and kissed her gently on the lips. A soft caress, a fleeting touch, and then he released her.

"Mr. Carlin," Amelia said, trying to control her breathing and not hyperventilate. "I … I am flattered. I—"

"*Flattered.*" His deep voice lost all traces of tenderness and humor, and he turned away, running his hands through his short red hair, making it stand on end. "Of course. I beg your pardon, ma'am."

"No, please, Mr. Carlin. I value your friendship. Nicholas—"

"Don't worry, ma'am. I'll continue to befriend your son. He's a fine lad." He turned flat, defeated eyes to her as he studied her for a moment. "It's good for me to know where I finally stand with you."

"No, Mr. Carlin—"

"Evening, ma'am." He turned, picked up his hat and coat, and exited the back door.

Amelia watched him leave, confused and hurt by his actions. She collapsed into a kitchen chair, tracing her lips gently as she closed her eyes and remembered the brief kiss. Her heart leaped at the memory but then began to pound as she became uncertain about what had just happened.

CHAPTER 11

"MR. A.J., DO YOU THINK the depository will close early today?" I wiped away at dust on the tabletops, moving with restless energy from table to table. The puce curtains were pulled back, and the windows were open, letting in a gentle breeze. A week and a half had passed since the disastrous anniversary dinner, and I yearned for a distraction from my distressing thoughts about my marriage.

"Why should it, Missy?" He thunked his cane on the floor as he watched me walk around the room. "These books ain't goin' to get sorted with no one workin' on 'em."

"You know darned well why I'm asking, Mr. A.J."

He hooted his glee. "Course I do, just happy to get my Missy so riled. You want to go see those big elephants. You probably hope to see a leper too."

"Of course I don't!"

"You tellin' me you ain't got no interest in seein' those creatures bein' brought in by the circus?"

"Oh, a *leopard*."

"Course. That's what I said. A leper. Now you ever seen one of those big elephants? Men ride 'em, you know? Get right up on their backs and steer 'em one way, then another. Tugging on their big ears. I hear they have to use a ladder to get up there."

I laughed as I watched him act out his words. "Mr. A.J., yes, that is why I would like to leave early. I think they'll parade them down Higgins. I'd like to go with Amelia and her children."

"Ah, the lovely widow."

"Don't start, Mr. A.J."

"Still don't seem right to me that one such as she slaves away makin' another man comfortable in his home, and she don't have a real home of her own. That woman should be married. Have a proper place of her own."

"She needs to grieve, Mr. A.J."

"Grieve my foot. It's been over a year. An' no matter how good a man her husband was, she's a young woman who needs a little consideration. Her children need a father." He thunked his cane down again as he glared at me.

"It's been over a year for you, Mr. A.J. I don't see you moving on."

"Don't you start, Missy. If I were a young buck rather than this old wore-out bag o' bones, I'd a found me a good woman. My Bessie would've wanted that for me."

"I'm sure she would have. I think the question is whether or not you would have wanted the same for her?" I raised one eyebrow as I watched him.

He flushed red, then scratched his head. "Now yer bein' mean, Missy. Askin' me to imagine my Bessie off with some other man."

"I'm just showing you that it isn't always as easy as you seem to believe." I groaned as I lifted a heavy pile of books and shuffled toward another table. "It can be difficult to find a good man."

"Any fool could see she's already found him. She's just got to see it for herself."

"If you listen to the gossips."

"No, Missy. I listen to you jabberin' on as you work. I learn plenty that-aways and never have to give no mind to the likes of the Prattlin' Prisses." He watched me with a studied look. "You give away more 'n you think. Why'd no other young men go sniffin' around, tryin' to make her acquiescence?"

I gasped and looked up at him from the table where I worked. "*Acquaintance?*" At his nod, I shook my head. "You're a menace with your big words."

"But I sound learned." He tilted his head with pride, beaming at me.

I took a deep breath, uncertain if I should dispel him of this notion. I was prevented from having to decide by the arrival of Amelia, Nicholas and Anne. Nicholas launched himself at me, and I tumbled backward with him in my arms.

"Hello, little man," I said as I kissed his head.

"Can we play hide-and-seek?"

"Not today. We have to watch the parade come through town." I smiled toward Amelia. She held a squirming Anne.

"Let that little girl down, missus." A.J. reached out a gnarled hand toward Anne when she teetered, and she grasped his fingers. She stood in front of him, bouncing and giggling. "What a precious jewel." A.J. swiped at her silky red curls, mussing her hair.

Amelia smiled at A.J. "She is that, Mr. Pickens. Thank you for not minding our visits. I know that Mrs. Bouchard and Mrs. Vaughan don't like us to call."

"Well, they don't keep this place runnin', do they? It's my Missy who does," A.J. said. "And I enjoy seein' my favorite kids." He reached down to steady Anne as she almost fell over.

I heard faint music in the distance and knew I wanted to be on the boardwalk as they marched the animals through the streets. "Mr. A.J., I'll be back soon," I said with a breathless smile as Nicholas jumped up and down with excitement.

"Take your time, Missy. I plan on watchin' the entertainment from up here." He tottered over toward the windowsill to stare down at the streets becoming more crowded by the minute. I brought his chair to him, and he sat with a groan.

"There, you won't miss a thing," I said as I patted him on his shoulder.

"Have fun!" he said with a broad smile as I grabbed Nicholas and Amelia hauled Anne to her hip. We emerged onto the boardwalk to find it filling with townspeople vying for a place to watch the circus come through.

"I wish we weren't so short," I muttered, as we tried to push our way forward.

"Here, Clarissa, let me help you."

I jolted and then turned with a faint smile at Gabriel's presence.

"I was just coming to see if you were planning to watch the spectacle when I saw you emerge." He plucked Nicholas from my aching arms and put him on his shoulders.

"Ouch, Nicholas," Gabriel said as he untangled the child's fingers from his hair. "Hold on to my shoulders." Gabriel gripped Nicholas's legs as he turned toward the street. The sound of lyrical music became louder with each passing minute.

"Do you hear that, Nicholas?" I asked.

"It's a calliope," Sebastian said as he joined us. "Gabe, missus," he said to both Amelia and me. "Can I take her?" he asked as he reached for Anne. Anne was already holding her arms out for him, and he smiled as he held her high for a moment before snuggling her to his chest. He smiled as Anne patted him on his cheeks.

With Gabriel's and Sebastian's help, we maneuvered until we were at the front of the crowd. Amelia and I stood in front of them, able to see the passing animals. "Look!" I said, pointing down the street to see the slow, ponderous walk of the elephants. "They're enormous."

"I never thought to see such a creature," Gabriel said as he caressed my arm.

For a moment, I leaned into him. The animals passed, the elephants leading, followed by the wagons pulling cages filled with prowling felines. Spotted leopards and lions. One large male lion sat with his paws crossed, watching us as though bored, his gold mane framing tawny eyes. I jumped as he opened his jaw, roaring at us. Nicholas shrieked with glee, gripping Gabriel's hair again.

The last horse-drawn wagon approached, a small stream of black smoke curling toward the sky from its rear. The music, a mixture of church organ music and a high-pitched lyrical squeal, approached. Soon it was so loud we would not have been able to speak had we tried. Two prancing gray horses pulled the brightly painted red-and-gold-colored wagon containing the calliope. Panels on the side of the wagon were folded up so that we were able to see the interior and the gleaming brass organ-like calliope, with the woman playing the keyboard at the front of the carriage. A small engine at the rear provided the steam for it to play.

As it moved away from us, Gabriel turned toward Sebastian, Amelia and me with a broad grin. "I hear they'll raise the circus tent in the empty field across the river. If we rush there, we can watch them as they raise it."

I bit my lip. "I don't know that I should be away from work that long."

Gabriel looked up toward the depository. "Old man!"

Mr. A.J. poked out his head. "Yes, young'un?"

"I'm stealing my wife away for the afternoon."

"'Bout time, Sonny. Bye, Missy."

I heard Mr. A.J.'s faint cackle as I turned to face Gabriel. "I have a job, Gabriel. This is unseemly."

"To spend an afternoon with your husband?" He reached forward and traced the edge of my jawline. "Please, Clarissa."

"Please, Auntie!" Nicholas said as he bounced on Gabriel's shoulders.

I smiled as I watched Nicholas. "All right." I reached for Gabriel's arm. "Let's hurry. I want to see those elephants in action." I reached up, and Gabriel closed his eyes, but I stroked Nicholas's head instead. I heard Gabriel sigh and met his gaze after he opened his eyes, filled with longing and sadness.

"Let's go," Sebastian said as he held out his elbow for Amelia.

We made our way across the wooden bridge spanning the Missoula River. The walk was farther than I had thought it would be, and I was tired by the time we arrived thirty minutes later. We had passed a new neighborhood on the other side of the river and finally approached a large meadow. The tall field grass had been trampled with the arrival of the circus, and swallows flew overhead, diving and swerving to catch the insects stirred up by all the commotion.

A small army of circus employees worked to erect a multitude of tents in a wide oval shape. A few of the employees ushered those of us who had ventured across the river to a small area deemed safe.

One man, who appeared to be a foreman, let out a series of whistles, and a stream of men appeared with sledgehammers. They worked in unison, battering enormous stakes into the ground. Finally they raised the main pole, and I gripped Gabriel's arm as the pole swayed for a moment or two until it stood perpendicular to the ground. At another whistle, a sea of canvas was laid out on the ground and hitched by pulleys to the main staff. Soon the canvas covered the main tent area, and men were rushing to the point of each stake to place a smaller pole for support.

I glanced at Gabriel, seeing him attempt to understand everything that was occurring and smiled. I leaned into this arm and felt him sigh with contentment as he reached up to grip my hand.

"Have you ever seen anything like it?" Gabriel asked with wonder.

"Never. Let's see the circus come to town every year," I said.

Gabriel watched me, searching my eyes. "Yes, every year."

CHAPTER 12

"AMELIA," I SAID, as I knocked on her back door. I poked my head in to find her staring into space. "Are you all right?"

She started at my voice and presence in the kitchen. "Rissa! Forgive me, I hadn't realized the time." She moved to rise, but I placed a hand on her shoulder, keeping her in her seat. I glanced into the living room to see Nicholas playing on the floor with a set of tin soldiers.

"Is Anne asleep?" I asked. At her nod, I said, "Then let's chat for a bit. We haven't had a chance to catch up in a while. Our errands can wait." I studied her, noting her distracted air. "What's upset you, Amelia?"

She glanced into the living room, noting Nicholas's deep attention to his toys. "Mr. Carlin came for dinner the other evening."

"Sebastian came for dinner alone?" I hid my smile when I saw how distressed Amelia was.

"Yes, a week ago. He hadn't realized our plans to meet here had been canceled. He's a favorite of the children and stayed for dinner."

My eyes clouded as Amelia became more upset. "Did something happen?"

"He kissed me!" Amelia whispered. At my delighted smile, which I tried to bite back, she glowered at me. "Stop that right now, Rissa. You know nothing could come of it."

"I know no such thing." I spoke in an equally soft voice to prevent Nicholas from overhearing. "Your Liam's been dead for over a year. You've a good man interested in you, one who genuinely cares for your children. Why should nothing come of it?"

"He's only interested in me for the children."

"That's nonsense, and you know it. No man courts a woman for her children." I watched as she traced patterns on the tabletop. "What scares you, Amelia?"

"I'm terrified to care again. To love again. I couldn't handle losing another man." She raised tormented eyes and met mine.

"I would think it would be equally hard imagining a life lived alone, with no one to share the joys and burdens of life." I clasped her hand. "I can only imagine what you've suffered, but I know you to be a brave woman, and I hope you can trust in finding happiness again."

I studied her for a moment, as she seemed to become more upset as our conversation continued. "If you don't want a relationship with him, tell him. It's not fair to lead a good man on. Are you interested?"

"More than I should be. I think I ruined it though. I told him that I was flattered by his kiss, and he became upset."

I giggled. "I've seen Colin in a snit enough times over a woman to know that no man likes to think a woman's flattered. Flummoxed maybe, but never flattered."

"I was caught off guard. I've never kissed any man but Liam, and Seb was so gentle. Not at all like Liam, who was like a wildfire."

"You'll always miss Liam, as you should. But live the life you have ahead of you rather than attempting to remain in your memories."

Amelia nodded. "The same applies to you, Rissa. Don't let the past dictate your future." I nodded, and we sat in quiet companionship for a few minutes until Anne's cry rent our peace.

***

"YOU CONFOUND ME, CARPENTER," Mr. Pickens said as he glared at Gabriel, his mouth clamping down on his imaginary pipe.

"Listen, old man, I came to see Mrs. McLeod. I appreciate your concern, but it's misplaced. And I've had about all I can take with advice right now."

"Missy's runnin' an errand with the loverly widow." A.J. waved his cane around as though to indicate somewhere in the town's vicinity, causing Gabriel to dodge backward a step to avoid a blow to his chest. "I figured you'd finally found sense. Gave up on that tomfoolery notion 'bout courtin' and married my Missy last year. Thought you'd spend your time canoodlin', not arguin'." He stomped his foot and cane at the same time, causing the books to rattle.

"Mr. Pickens, it's none of your concern."

"It ain't my concern when my Missy's actin' like she's got the hay fever to hide her broken heart? Ain't my problem when anyone with sense"—A.J.'s cane hit Gabriel's chest with a thump—"could see the woman just needs a babe to love? Now what're you doin' about it?"

Gabriel flushed red and inhaled until his chest was full, as though he were the bellows at Colin's forge. After a moment he breathed out and sank onto an overturned crate, holding his head in his hands. "It's difficult for a man to admit that some things are beyond his control."

"You blamin' Missy?"

"No, not at all. We've just been unlucky. And, as the months pass, she becomes more ..."

"Haunted, McLeod. Haunted. I may not know my fancy words, but I know when a woman's still runnin' from her past. Seems Missy's havin' trouble stayin' ahead of hers."

"You're a perceptive old goat, aren't you?" Gabriel asked.

"When a man has been married as long as I was, he knows to look for the signs. An' Missy ain't done tryin' to defeat her past."

"I can't kill him."

"Who said anything about killin'? Find some other way. And gettin' into bar brawls ain't the way." He thunked his cane again when Gabriel flushed. "Show that woman of yours that you'll protect her, even from sly insinnuendos. Townsfolk ain't always as nice as we'd like."

Gabriel shook his head as he watched Mr. Pickens. He held up his hand to stop A.J.'s onslaught of advice. "Insinu—*insinuation*? *Innuendo*? Which did you mean?"

"Both, I guess. Seemed a good sort of word. Now, pay attention, young'un. You gotta let Missy know yer still happy to be married to her. Only a damn fool storms away from a pretty woman on his anniversary." He thumped his cane down. "Thought this generation had more sense."

Gabriel bit back a startled laugh and shook his head. "I need to reconsider if you really are a good influence on my wife."

"Nothin' to consider. I'm the only one out of the three of us showin' any sense."

"Old man, this is advice that would be better shared with Clarissa."

"Never forget fear makes us irascible, young'un."

"*Irascible* or *irrational?*" Gabriel asked.

"Both," Mr. Pickens said. "Yer near as good as my missy at figurin' out my words." His almost toothless smile faded as he watched Gabriel. "I already gave Missy my advice on men. Now listen up, Sonny. Here's mine for you." He glared at Gabriel, although a hint of male kinship lit his eyes. "Don't let Missy think yer disappointed in her."

"How could she imagine that? She knows I don't care that her cooking is edible at best. Or that she is not great at sewing." Gabriel leaned forward to hear any wisdom Mr. Pickens could impart.

"There's nothing worse than wanting a child and then not having one. The want eats away at the soul," Mr. Pickens said, a haunted look crossing his face. "My Bessie did no end of trying to shield me from her grief when she failed to …" He waved his cane around. "And I was almost too much a fool." He clamped his jaw shut as he shook his head, as though pushing away the memories. "Don't be like me, Sonny."

***

I WALKED DOWN MAIN STREET past Gabriel's shop, and continued on past saloons and other businesses toward the small first-floor rooms Ronan rented. It was within the same block as the workshop so he could travel easily from his home to work daily. A warm breeze ruffled my skirts on this early August day, nearly two weeks after my anniversary.

"Mr. O'Bara?" I knocked again on his door. I leaned toward the door, straining to hear the sounds of his chair rolling toward it. I heard a scraping noise inside, and, after a few moments, the door opened.

"Mrs. McLeod," Ronan said with a half smile.

"I was told Colin was here," I said. I peered over his head into the interior of his room.

"He's going to come by, but he hasn't yet. Why don't you come in and wait for him with me? We're to have a grand cribbage match tonight."

"Cribbage. Yes, I'll wait."

He rolled his chair out of the way, and I stepped around him. The door clicked shut behind me. Faint light entered through a window to the side of the door. A single bed, set at the height of his wheelchair, was along the back wall. A small table with a lamp, a bookshelf and a few chairs made up the rest of the furniture, the wooden walls bare of any decoration.

"Do you play, Clarissa?"

I smiled at his use of my given name. He always remained proper, using my last name in public. However, in private, he used my first name.

"No, but it reminds me of the matches Col used to have with my da."

"You miss him still," Ronan said. He rolled to the low table and shuffled cards.

"Yes. I'll always miss my da. And my family in Boston. It's hard to realize I'll never see them again."

"You've been here a year now. Do you regret coming to Montana?"

"Of course not. Why would you ask?"

"Well, forgive me for speaking so plainly with you, but it's obvious things aren't going well between you and Gabe. I thought part of the reason was your desire to be elsewhere." He shuffled the deck of cards, while at the same time watching me with worried brown eyes.

"First it's another man, now my desire to be elsewhere," I muttered.

"What other man?" Ronan asked with a raised eyebrow and amusement glinting in his eyes. "Any fool could tell you don't have another man."

"Tell that to Gabriel."

"Well, any fool but a confused, wounded husband." He gave me a pointed stare.

"I can't talk with you about it, Ronan. I'm hoping it will resolve on its own."

"Seems to me, you've been hoping that for months. And the longer you hope and the longer it continues, the more miserable the two of you become."

"Gabriel deserves a wife who—"

"Stop that rubbish right now. I thought we'd discussed this last summer. Gabriel deserves *you*. He's chosen *you*. Whatever you can and cannot do in the domestic front doesn't matter. Whatever indiscretion you imagine you've done, tell him. If he finds out some other way, he may not forgive you. Because whatever you think you cannot tell him, if he learns it from you, you'll both be able to move past it.

"Have you ever stopped to consider what you deserve, Clarissa?"

At his gentle question, my eyes filled with tears, and I blinked them furiously.

"Have you ever once thought about what you need from Gabriel? Or have you been so consumed with fear about how he'll react that you haven't allowed yourself to reveal what you need and want?"

"Ronan ..."

"I've never been married. But after watching Liam and Amelia, and watching you and Gabe the first months, I thought I had an idea of what I wanted if I were to marry. I would desire a marriage where you could depend on the other person. And, from where I'm sitting, the way you're acting says you don't have faith in Gabriel. Imagine how that makes him feel."

"That's not fair."

"Maybe not, but then none of us have any idea what demon you're fighting. Not this time." He paused. "If it's more to do with that lecher from Boston, you know there are many who'd help with him."

"Oh, Ronan, if only it were that simple," I whispered.

"Whether it's simple or not, talk to Gabe, Clarissa."

I nodded at his gentle urging and turned to leave. "Will you tell Colin that I was here and that I'll try to speak with him tomorrow?" Ronan nodded, and I left for home, determined to overcome my fears and speak with Gabriel.

CHAPTER 13

"GABRIEL, WE NEED TO TALK." I paced the small area between the dining room table and the chairs in the living room. Gabriel was hunched over the small desk in front of the middle window, working on the books for his business. He stilled, and I saw him close his eyes before forcing himself to relax and set down his pencil.

I moved toward him, pulling his comfortable chair around to face him. I reached forward, grabbed his arm and had him turn toward me. "Gabriel, I have to talk with you. I can't ..."

His eyes remained closed, and a deep sigh escaped him. "I know we need to talk, Clarissa. I've told myself that we must resolve this. Are you ready to tell me what's been bothering you?"

I blinked away tears. "Yes."

"There's no good way to tell a man you don't love him anymore."

The agony in his voice tore at me, but I firmed my jaw to prevent any tears from falling.

I gripped his face, turning it toward mine. I stroked his ebony hair, brushing a strand off his forehead to the side. "Good. Because that's not what I have to tell you. And I hope you remember the same goes for women."

He gifted me with a lopsided grin and turned to face me fully, a subtle nod my only indication to continue speaking.

"Gabriel, I'm so afraid of you hating me," I whispered.

"The only way I'll come to hate you is if you continue to act like you are."

I cringed. "I, ah ..."

After many moments of silence, he whispered, "Why are you afraid to talk with me? Why don't you want me to touch you?" The anguish in his voice ripped at my heart. "I know this isn't the life you envisioned. I'm trying to become as successful as I can, to provide for you as you deserve. Can't you see that?"

"Gabriel," I choked out as I fought tears. "Forgive me." I leaned forward and placed my forehead against his for a moment before leaning away again.

"Is it because you're not yet with child? Don't you know that doesn't matter to me? All I want is you." Gabriel traced the track made by one of my tears.

"It's all my fault, Gabriel. It's all my fault, and I can't stand for you to feel trapped here with me." I tried to rise, but he now had a firm grip on my arms and wouldn't allow me to move. "I thought if I could give you a perfect home, you'd forgive my failings, but I was never meant to be a housewife! I can't do anything a husband expects." My voice broke.

"What are you talking about? No one's to blame if we don't have a child. And I've never cared about a perfect home. I've only ever wanted a home with you."

"Oh, Gabriel. You don't understand. It is! It's all my fault."

"What?" Gabriel released my arms, and I rose to pace away. He stood, leaning against the desk, his eyes trailing my jerky movements. "What are you talking about, Clarissa?"

"I don't deserve you!" I sobbed as I raised a hand to my face, attempting to hide from him. "If you knew what I'd done, you'd hate me."

I dared to meet his face. He watched me with shuttered eyes, all emotion carefully hidden. "Tell me, Clarissa."

"After Cameron's ... after Cameron's attack," I paused as I fought the memories from the spring a year and a half ago when I had lived in Boston, and Gabriel had already moved to Montana. I shivered as I recalled my helplessness and pain. Images of a sun-drenched sitting room, Cameron's victorious smile as he loomed over me and blood-stained fabric cascaded through my mind. I opened my eyes to meet Gabriel's gaze, forcing myself to face his condemnation. "I feared I would become pregnant with his child." He jerked as though I had slapped him. "I didn't know what to do. I had no one to guide me. I was so ashamed. And the thought of having Cameron's ... of being forced to marry him because of that, I couldn't, Gabriel. I just couldn't."

Gabriel gripped the edge of the desk until his knuckles turned white and nodded once.

Tears flowed unchecked down my cheeks. I moved toward him, my arms wrapped around my waist. "About a week after … after, I visited Sophronia. She somehow understood what had happened to me. Gave me the option of what to do to prevent being bound to Cameron. She gave me a tea to brew." I took a shuddering breath, pausing for a moment.

"I've always liked my tea strong," I whispered. "I fear I made this too strong."

"What are you saying, Clarissa?"

"I've spoken to the doctor here. The capable one who helped save baby Anne. He's concerned that the heavy bleeding I had after I took the tea might have affected my ability to have a child." I choked out the words, paling as I saw Gabriel's jaw tighten. "I wanted to be sure, so I've visited colleagues of his, who have confirmed his concern. It's why I've been seen visiting so many doctors."

"Christ," Gabriel said, as he pushed away from the desk and stepped around me. He faced away, toward the kitchen for a few moments before spinning toward me. "That's why you've been seen in areas you don't generally visit? Because you've been consulting with this doctor and his cronies?" At my nod, he asked, "Are you telling me you were pregnant with Cameron's child?"

"No! I don't know if I was. I was terrified of becoming pregnant," I whispered. "I didn't know what else to do. I only had Sophie to help me, and she'd had to badger an old doctor friend of her husband's into helping at all. I just wanted to come to you."

"So you acted in such a way to ensure you would remain free of Cameron?"

"Yes," I whispered.

He met my gaze with one filled with anger. "Why didn't you think this was something to share with me before our wedding?"

"I could barely believe you really wanted me after … after Cameron's attack. I knew you would despise me if you learned what I'd done willingly."

He shook his head as he studied me. "How can I despise you for showing more courage than anyone else I know? Do you know you could have died?"

"I do now." I took a deep, shuddering breath. "Are you saying you aren't angry with me, Gabriel?"

"No, I am furious with you," he roared as he turned away, pacing the kitchen's length. If he were in the workshop, I knew he would have thrown a piece of wood against the wall to release his anger. He reached up and massaged the nape of his neck. After a moment he turned fiery eyes to me. "How could you, Clarissa? How?"

"I had to, Gabriel. I had to have my freedom and come to you."

"No, dammit. I'm not talking about your excess of courage, allowing you to do what most women would never have had the ability to do. How could you doubt my love for you?"

The soul-deep pain I saw in his expression shattered me.

"Gabriel, I—"

"I love you, Clarissa. All of you. I hate that you suffered more than I could ever have imagined to come here to me. I hate even more that you continue to doubt yourself worthy of my love. I hope someday you'll believe that I am not a fool to love you."

"Gabriel, I …" My voice broke, and I shook my head. Tears fell unheeded as I watched him studying me. After a few moments, he sighed, and his anger seemed to evaporate.

He gazed at me with a yearning tenderness, a look I hadn't seen in far too long. He approached me carefully, like he had last year when I had first arrived from Boston. When I didn't flinch as he raised his hands to cup my face with his strong, callused palms, a relieved smile flickered over his lips before he sobered.

"Forgive me, Clarissa," he said in a voice thickened with emotion. "I should have exalted in your ability to fight and demand the life you wanted. Instead, I acted like a wounded idiot, thinking only of myself."

"That's not true," I whispered. "I love you, Gabriel. I don't believe you're a fool for loving me. I've always feared that, one day, you'd feel a fool for having loved me."

"Never, my love. Never," he vowed, as he leaned forward to kiss me.

Against my will, I sobbed, with no ability to stop. Gabriel clasped me to him, rubbing his strong hands soothingly over my scalp and back.

"I want a child desperately," I sobbed into his chest.

He pushed me away with a gentle insistence until I met his gaze. I continued to stutter in gulping breaths while his fingers chased away my tears.

"You must forgive yourself, my love. Imagine your life if you hadn't taken the tea. If you had married Cameron."

I blanched and shook my head in denial.

"I hope you find pride in your strength, as I have. I will always dream of us having a child. But seeing as, being here, now, with you in my arms, has been my greatest desire for months …" He smiled, flashing his dimple.

I collapsed against his chest, my tears abating. "I feared you wouldn't want me anymore when you found out what I had done," I whispered against his neck.

"You thought I wouldn't desire you?"

His chest rumbled as he grunted out a laugh, and I heard the incredulousness in his voice.

"A day hasn't passed since you got that foolish notion in your head that I haven't wanted you," Gabriel whispered in my ear.

He turned his head and began to nibble along my neck. I giggled as his whiskers tickled, and he stopped abruptly, his brow furrowed, but deep contentment shone from his blue eyes.

"I've missed your laugh," he said huskily before he leaned forward to kiss me.

Soon our hands were grasping at buttons, hems and ties in our agitation to free ourselves from our clothing. I heard Gabriel swear softly as he tripped when stepping out of his pants and giggled again. My breath caught as he winked at me, his face lit with an all-consuming happiness.

I backed toward our bed, and he followed. For some reason, I was suddenly shy and dove under the covers, lying on my side.

"Rissa?" Gabriel asked. His fingertips traced down my back, barely touching. I arched backward, hoping for more of his caress. I felt his weight settle on the bed behind me and then a soft kiss to my nape. "Darling, talk to me."

I rolled over so that I lay on my back, and he leaned over me, his weight resting on an elbow. He caressed the hair at my brow line, as though to soothe me.

"I'm sorry," I said. "I'm sorry for all the time we lost because I didn't speak with you sooner. Because I wasn't brave enough to share my fears." I raised my hand, tracing his eyebrows, cheek and lips. "Watching you, just now, devastated me. I had always blamed circumstances or those such as my stepmother for separating us. But this was my doing. Please forgive me."

"There is nothing to forgive, my beloved darling." He shifted his position slightly, leaning over me so that the weight of his hips and legs bore me into the soft mattress. I lay on my back, looking up at his serious face.

"I will never regret our life together. I will give thanks, every day, that you are my wife." He leaned forward, and kissed first one eyelid and then the next. His thumbs swiped away my tears. "I have nothing to forgive, only a plentitude to be thankful for."

"I hate that the specter of Cameron remains between us." I was unable to mask my bitterness.

"He is not between us, darling. He has not separated us, nor will he ever be able to. He hurt you terribly, more than I ever realized. You have always been so strong, Clarissa." He leaned forward and kissed my nose. "Let me be strong for you. Share your fears as well as your dreams with me. I would carry any burden you give me, so long as we are together."

I leaned up, kissing him tenderly. "I love you, Gabriel, so much. I've been terrified of losing you."

"Let me love you," he whispered, as he nuzzled my neck and moved lower. "I've missed you so much, my Clarissa."

I reached up and grasped his face between my palms. "I've missed you with an equal fervor."

He took a deep breath, watching me closely. His eyes shone with a fierce love and nodded. His hands skimmed up my sides, over my breasts.

I gasped as he suckled my breast. I arched into his caress, rubbing my hands through his hair.

He moved to my other breast, while his hands stroked over my belly. "Gabriel," I gasped.

"I want you to know how much I've missed you," he whispered.

"I missed you too."

He nibbled on my shoulder before kissing me deeply again. "What a pair of fools, living in the same house, but never speaking. Barely touching." He sighed as he eased into me.

I arched up again to meet him. "Love me, Gabriel. Love me." I gripped his back, fingers digging into his strong muscles.

"Always, my Clarissa, always," he vowed, and we were beyond words.

***

I LAY ON MY SIDE with Gabriel's arm across my belly, holding me close. He breathed deeply in my ear, but it didn't sound like he was asleep. "Gabriel?" I whispered.

"Yes, darling?" he murmured, his voice thick with sleep.

"What if we never have a child?" I tensed involuntarily at the question.

His hand tightened around my belly, and his face nuzzled the back of my neck. "You must know, Clarissa, my love for you is boundless. Nothing could make me love you more. If we have a child, I will cherish her. For I would love to have a daughter with your mixture of strength and beauty. If we are destined to be without children, we will be the best aunt and uncle around."

"Every time I sense someone looking at my belly to see if I'm increasing or when I hear about others' good news, I feel ..."

"What, my darling?"

"Inadequate," I whispered.

He rolled me to my back so he could see my expression, his hands cradling my face, preventing me from looking away. "You are not, and never have been, inadequate." A wondrous smile spread as he traced my cheeks with his thumbs. "You've believed for too long you could never be loved for who you are. All I want is you, Clarissa. You. Anything else is—"

I didn't let him finish as I leaned up to kiss him, an overwhelming happiness spreading though me.

CHAPTER 14

FLORENCE ENTERED THE Arlington Street gate to the Public Gardens, glancing around for Sophronia. The sounds of passing trolleys and carriages faded as Florence moved farther into the verdant sanctuary in the heart of the city. She strolled at a leisurely pace along tree-shaded paths, past the small lake at the center of the gardens. The swan boats, only half full on this bright, humid afternoon, slowly floated around the lake. As she approached the side of the gardens toward Beacon Street, she saw Sophronia.

"High time you arrived," Sophronia said from a park bench in the shade of a tree. "I'd not thought you would be so tardy." She sat with her back ramrod straight, her hands holding a walking stick. Her cream-colored hat, tilted to one side, failed to hide her inquisitive aquamarine eyes, and her matching suit remained starched and wrinkle free, even in the oppressive heat and humidity.

"I'm sorry, Sophie," Florence said as she settled next to her. "I wasn't feeling my best this morning, and it delayed me."

"I hope it is not some sort of illness?" Sophronia frowned as she looked Florence up and down.

"No illness. Just the nine-months' sort," Florence whispered with a blush.

Sophronia cackled her delight. "Wonderful, girl. Wonderful! And what does your young man have to say for himself?"

"He's overjoyed but terrified something will happen to me. We've known for some time, but I haven't wanted to tell anyone. I wanted to wait until I felt the baby move."

"Well, your husband's is a natural reaction. When he holds the baby in his arms and sees you are well, he'll be fine." Sophronia patted her hand a few times. "Have you written Clarissa?"

"No."

"Why ever not? I should think she'd be elated." Sophronia nodded to a passing acquaintance but did not welcome her to join in their conversation.

"I know. And I will write her."

"Well, I'll keep your secret, although I know it will make my girl Clarissa happy. I know she frets that she hasn't yet found herself in a family way. But, all in good time," Sophronia said. "And you might not be able to stop your husband from writing his brother."

"I know. I fear he wrote him when we first suspected," Florence said with a blush. After a moment's hesitation she asked, "How is Savannah? I was worried when I received your note."

"Mourning," Sophronia said bluntly. "If I ever see that man again, I fear what I will do." She turned fiery blue eyes on Florence. "He attempted to shatter her spirit, and, for that, I will never forgive him." Sophie sighed. "I didn't want to meet at the house because Savannah insists she's not ready for visitors, and yet, had you called, she would have made an attempt. After so many months where her wishes and desires were ignored, I'm trying to demonstrate that what she wants will be respected."

Florence squinted her eyes as she looked at Sophronia. "But you don't agree."

"No. She's spent enough time crying in her room, staring out the back window. She's been in my home, refusing to leave, for over a month. We're nearing mid-August. She needs to reenter the world."

"She needs to find a new purpose, Sophie."

"Well, a few weeks of crying are not going to heal the wounds she has suffered. You and I know that. And she is quite reticent at becoming part of the movement. But I'm sure we can find something for her."

"Maybe it is for her to discover," Florence murmured. "I believe she will have no interest in any movement until she has found her child."

"I believe you are correct. I presume you will aid her?" Sophie raised an eyebrow and smiled faintly at Florence's nod of agreement. "Excellent. I have begun to make discreet inquiries for her but have yet to meet with success."

"I'm sure we will discover something, Sophie."

"For her sake, I hope so. As for the divorce, it is not proceeding as I had hoped, but I am convinced it is the correct way forward for her. I find comfort that she is safe in my home away from her horrid husband."

"Has he called again?"

"Not since I threatened summoning the police," Sophronia said. "Savannah remained in her room for four days after hearing his voice."

"We'll provide the support we can, and the McLeods are family, of a sort," Florence said. "However, Savannah needs to determine what she desires, Sophie. She may not be ready to face the infamy of divorce."

"Maybe so," Sophie said with a sigh. "There are tough days ahead for Savannah, Florence. She will need her friends. I was hoping you'd write her. Encourage her to call on you. Try to convince her to come to one of the meetings. Show her that you're her friend, as well as Clarissa's." Sophronia paused, gripping her walking stick for a moment before releasing it along with her agitation.

"I'll write her tonight," Florence said with a sad smile. "I shudder to think what more she suffered at his hands. The little I witnessed was horrible enough."

***

"SAVANNAH, ARE YOU AMENABLE to visitors for tea? I'm afraid a few of my friends insist on calling," Sophronia asked as she sat at her desk in her private sitting room. The lower half of the walls were covered in white wainscoting, with dusty-rose-colored wallpaper covering the top half of the walls. Like her more formal sitting room, there were few pieces of art on the wall. In this room, the focal piece was a scene of a mountain glen after a heavy snow. Sophronia's desk sat in front of the rear window, and comfortable chairs were scattered throughout the room. Savannah sat in the rocking chair.

"Yes, of course. I would hate for you to curtail your social calls due to my presence." The tightening of her grip on the rocking chair arm betrayed her agitation.

"Most of my set are away for the summer. Doing mostly useless activities in Newport and the like. However, a few are in town, and I look forward to a lively discussion about the cause and hearing about their efforts to save birds."

"Birds?"

"There are many good causes to dedicate your energies to. You're too young to simply lay about with no purpose to your life."

Savannah nodded and intrepidly avoided committing to any of Sophronia's causes. "Would you prefer if I were absent? I would hate to cause you any more scandal."

"Ah, Savannah, when are you going to learn that a little scandal is good for the soul? If you live your life too much by society's dictates, you will have nothing interesting to relive when you age." Sophronia raised one eyebrow as she spoke. "Besides, I think a few of them are quite interested in making your acquaintance."

"I have no desire to be seen as a circus act," Savannah said.

Sophronia cackled and returned her attention to her correspondence.

Savannah rose and wandered to the small room she had chosen on the third floor. Sophronia had protested heartily, insisting she occupy a grander room, but Savannah enjoyed its soothing mint-green silk wallpaper, the understated elegance in the mahogany four-poster bed, and the simply carved walnut armoire. Her favorite aspect of the room was the chaise longue set next to the window. It overlooked the green area of Sophronia's neighbors. Savannah enjoyed passing the afternoon, watching the light move across the walls, listening to the birds and trying to heal.

A few hours later, Mary knocked gently on her door, and Savannah rose from the chaise. "I'm coming, Mary." Savannah wore a simple light-blue cotton muslin dress, perfect for the hot, humid day. "I can't imagine why anyone would want to drink tea on such a warm day."

She exchanged an amused glance with Mary as she left her room. Savannah walked slowly toward the front parlor, uncertain if she should enter after hearing the raised voices.

"When I think of the damage you have already wrought on this family due to your interference with Clarissa …" A long pause followed. "And now you seem determined to destroy Savannah's future. Do you have no decency, Mrs. Chickering?"

"Apparently not, at least where you're concerned," Sophronia replied, and Savannah could hear a hint of amusement in the outspoken woman's voice. "As for your estimation of what is decent, I know we will always have differing definitions."

"How dare you sit there like the Cheshire cat, smug and all knowing, when you have ruined Savannah's marriage!"

Savannah leaned forward to see Mrs. Sullivan, Clarissa's stepmother, snapping at Sophronia. Savannah blanched to see her mother sitting next to Mrs. Sullivan, glaring at Sophronia. Savannah backed away, remaining hidden in the hallway, not wishing to be seen but wanting to overhear the conversation.

"I'm surprised you would know of such a creature, Mrs. Sullivan. I had thought your intellectual leanings were more in the domestic vein."

"My mother read me that story. And I have always abhorred those who mock others," Mrs. Sullivan hissed.

"Ah, yes, such a terrible thing to mock someone. Much better to undermine and destroy their lives by stealth. I'm sure Mr. McLeod much prefers your method," Sophronia said with a chill in her voice.

"We are not here to discuss Clarissa and her unfortunate alliance with that worthless laborer. She has only brought scandal and ridicule onto this family. We refuse to allow you to do the same to Savannah," Clarissa's stepmother snapped.

"We demand that you allow Savannah to leave with us. We have spoken with Jonas, and he is very understanding of her nerves after the loss of her child. He is quite happy to accept her home after this small hiccup," Savannah's mother, Matilda Russell, said.

"Is this your definition of maternal love then, Mrs. Russell? Send her back to the lion's den? Or do you prefer the medieval entertainment of bear-baiting? For I can assure you, either description is applicable to what it would be like if Savannah were to return to that house."

"How dare you—"

"How dare I actually open my eyes and see that that young woman has been tormented and beaten down to the point where she has trouble seeing her own worth? How dare I desire her to have a life filled with happiness rather than fear and trepidation? How dare I dream that her family loved her more than any aspirations for improved social standing? Yes, what a cruel woman I must be."

"You have no right—" Mrs. Sullivan sputtered.

"I have every right. I am a woman of means, with quite a bit more respectability and clout than either of you could ever imagine. I have accepted into my home a young woman who has been treated cruelly by her husband. She will be welcomed here for as long as she wishes to stay."

"What if she desires to leave?" Matilda asked.

"We can ask her," Sophronia said. "Savannah, please join us."

Savannah gasped but then squared her shoulders and entered the parlor. "Hello, Mother. Mrs. Sullivan."

"It seems the circus came to us," Sophronia murmured with a wry gleam in her eyes. "Please join us, dear. I'm sure you've found the conversation enlightening."

"Savannah, quit your petulant outburst and return home where you belong with your husband," her mother ordered. She was flushed and glaring at both Savannah and Sophronia.

"Do you—" Savannah began but was interrupted.

"It's not as though you could possibly want to remain here. With this woman. She is so uncouth," Mrs. Sullivan snapped.

"I wish you would—" Savannah said.

"And why you would come here rather than turn to us, Savannah? It shall not be borne! What will the grandparents say when they hear of it?" her mother wailed.

"Silence, the pair of you. You're worse than a pair of jackals," Sophronia demanded. She turned toward Savannah and raised an eyebrow. "Would you care to explain to your loving family how you fared at that home on Marlborough Street?"

Savannah watched them, a dull pain in her eyes. "You knew what he was and yet you still encouraged me to marry him." She glared at her mother. "How could you?"

"The social standing—"

"Yes, of course. Always the social standing. The money. The prestige you would win in the grandparents' eyes if I were to marry one such as him. A shopkeeper's daughter marrying such a man!" Savannah choked back a sob. "I can't believe I allowed myself to be blinded into agreeing with you. Into believing any of that mattered."

"Your dowry—"

"Yes, my dowry. The only reason why a man such as him would ever deign to marry a woman such as me, and yet I wasn't even allowed to know that I was being auctioned off like a prized horse. How dare you criticize

Clarissa for wanting more from life than meeting societal expectations. Why didn't you want more for me?" Savannah sobbed. "Why weren't kindness, respect and love as important to you in that invisible tally of yours, Mother, as Jonas's perceived respectability?"

"I'm sure Jonas has more kindness than you give him credit for," Matilda said stonily.

"Do you? Did you believe that when he wrote solicitous letters telling you that I was ill again? Did you never wonder that all my illnesses were caused by his cruelty?"

"I will not sit and listen to any more of this," Matilda said as she picked up her purse.

"Does it not bother you that he beat me? That he took away my baby and gave her to the care of strangers, simply because she was a girl?" At her mother's stony silence, Savannah whispered, "How can you be my mother?"

"You will come to understand that some sacrifices are required in this life, Savannah. I hope you will soon come to your senses and return home to your husband."

"I will never return to him. I am seeking a divorce."

"What?" Mrs. Sullivan and Matilda gasped at the same time, Matilda collapsing into her chair as she had half risen to leave.

"Oh, Savannah, don't do this to the family. Don't do this to your father's business. Have you no decency?" her mother asked.

"Why can you never worry for me, Mother?" Savannah whispered in a tear-choked voice.

"Because this isn't just about you, you selfish girl!" Matilda snapped. "What did we ever do to deserve two women in our family such as you and Clarissa?" She shared a long-suffering glance with Mrs. Sullivan.

"I believe it is time for you to leave," Sophronia said. "I would ask you to refrain from visiting my home again. I pride myself on the quality of my company, and you do not meet my standards."

"You would stand by her as she embarks on this folly?" Mrs. Sullivan asked.

"Of course. It is what women do for each other. Or so they should," Sophronia said with a note of reproach in her voice. Matilda and Mrs. Sullivan stalked out of the room, and Sophronia sat, watching the trembling Savannah. "You did well."

"She never really cared about me, did she?" Savannah asked in a daze. "I never mattered."

"I imagine something happened to your mother to alter how she sees the world. Something caused her to esteem social respectability more than anything else."

"What am I to do?"

"Continue as you are. You know you can't return to Jonas and that life, Savannah." Sophronia gripped her hand until Savannah met her eyes. "You know that." Savannah finally nodded. "Good."

"Yes, he would kill me if I returned. I know that deep inside. And, if he didn't, I would want to die." Savannah let out a stuttering sigh. "I want more from life than that, Sophie."

"Good. Now you must determine what it is you do want."

"I want to find my baby," she said in a whisper, barely giving voice to her words.

"What was that, dear?" Sophie asked with a raised eyebrow.

Savannah cleared her voice and spoke in a firm voice. "I want to find my baby."

Sophie smiled triumphantly. "Very good. You must continue to voice your desires, Savannah. As for finding your daughter, I have begun to make inquiries on your behalf. However, you should do whatever you deem necessary to find her."

"Thank you for your help, Sophie."

Sophie nodded. "I want to see you flourish, my dear."

***

"HELLO, FLORENCE," Savannah said after Florence inched open the door. "I'm sorry to interrupt your day."

"Nonsense. I'm baking bread, and it's a tedious process. You can keep me company." She smiled as she led Savannah toward the back room. The smell of yeast and flour permeated the air, and the dining room table, turned into a workspace, was covered in flour. The far end of the table had mounds covered by a cloth.

"Could I help you?" Savannah asked, as she took off her hat and gloves. "I used to love to bake."

"Really? I would have thought you'd always have a cook."

"We did. She was a lovely woman from Scotland, Mrs. McDuffie. She made the best breads. I loved spending time with her. Thought my mother would be delighted that I was learning to cook."

"I gather she wasn't." Florence handed Savannah the bowl with the other half of the dough to be kneaded. Savannah covered her hands in flour and leaned into the dough.

"No, she wasn't. When I told her at dinner one evening that I had made the bread we were eating, I thought my mother would faint. I was sent from the table with no dinner and told I was never to enter the kitchen again, unless requesting food."

"What did your father say?"

"He was proud of me. But, as in most things, he allowed my mother to determine what was proper for my upbringing."

"Did you never want to cook again?"

"I missed the stories Mrs. McDuffie told. Wild stories about growing up in Scotland among a large family. She only moved to Boston because she was number three of sixteen, and she had hoped she'd be able to earn some money to send home.

"And I missed the cooking. Even when I was young, my mother had a strict idea of what I was to do and not do. She believed there were certain activities that were beneath me, and cooking was one of them."

"Does Mrs. McDuffie still cook your favorite meals when you visit your parents?"

"Oh, no. She … left my parents' employ a few weeks after I was barred from the kitchen."

"That's horrible," Florence whispered.

"Thankfully she began to cook for a prominent businessman, a bachelor. And now she has a cook while she entertains in his drawing room."

Florence watched her with serious eyes. "You learned your lesson well, though, didn't you? Do what your mother wants or the consequences will affect more than just you."

"Yes, well, you can see where that got me." She swiped at her cheek, smearing it with flour.

"Married to a maniac with a penchant for brutality," Florence said with a shake of her head.

"She still wants me to return to him. To uphold the family's honor by sacrificing myself." She punched the bread dough and leaned in to knead it with all her pent-up fury.

Florence stopped kneading for a moment to stare at Savannah. "But you won't. Tell me you will never return to that man."

"No, I won't. I can't. No matter how much my mother says it is hurting the family and the business, I can't."

"They're adults. They can manage without having you harmed in the process," Florence said as she slapped the dough with renewed vigor. She blew a huff of air, blowing a strand of curly black hair out of her eyes. "If I knead this anymore, we won't be able to chew it." She turned, found two clean cloths, handed one to Savannah, and they covered their loaves to rise.

"How is Mr. McLeod?" Savannah asked after she had settled on the couch with a glass of water.

"If you mean Jeremy, he's better each day. His business continues to grow, although I know he wishes Gabriel were here to help him. Wouldn't it be wonderful to have Gabriel and Clarissa home?" Florence smiled wistfully.

"I doubt Rissa would want to come back. From what I understand, she likes her life out there. Not nearly as restrictive as life here."

"Yes, and it seems Gabriel has fallen in love with the outdoors. It does seem hard to imagine him enjoying horseback riding."

Savannah giggled at the thought. "Hmm … although I bet he's a handsome sight."

She and Florence shared a laugh before Savannah sobered. "Do you think you and Mr. McLeod would be able to help me find my little girl? I can't imagine traveling to the orphanages alone."

"I'll help you in any way I can, Savannah. I'm sure Jeremy feels the same, although he might not have as much freedom with the new commissions he's receiving."

"Thank you, Florence. You don't know what it means to have your friendship."

"Is it really true that no one in your family believes that Jonas took your baby?"

"My aunt Betsy does. I've never spoken with my father or brother about it. I used to worry they'd believe as my mother, but I've begun to wonder if that's fair to them. I plan on visiting my father tomorrow at the store, and I will hopefully see Lucas too." She sighed. "I dread going there. My mother is irate and would bar me from setting foot in the store if possible. I must hope she's absent during my visit."

***

THE FOLLOWING DAY, Savannah opened the door to her parents' fine linen store, Russell's, and maneuvered her way around milling patrons. She smiled at Lucas who stood behind the counter and walked toward the back area to enter her father's office, a small rectangular room behind the main storefront. Her father sat at his desk in a comfortable swivel chair, head bowed over piles of papers. He appeared busy, adding up the books and reviewing receipts. He glanced up, frowning for a moment as he saw someone in the doorway, but his expression lightened as he beheld Savannah.

Upon seeing her, he stood, moved from behind the desk and enfolded her in his strong arms. "Ah, my Savannah," he murmured as he held her. After a few minutes, he released her, cupping her face for a moment as he studied her closely. She settled in a chair in front of his desk while he shut the door and then returned to his seat.

"I'm happy to see you looking healthy," he said as he watched her, frowning as she wiped away tears. "It's been two nearly months since you left Jonas's home in mid-June. Are you sure you are well?"

"Yes, Father. I'm finally well again." She sniffled into a handkerchief and smiled weakly.

"You are safe now?"

"Yes."

"Your mother told me that you were concocting wild tales of abuse in an attempt to instill sympathy."

"I spoke only the truth," Savannah said.

"That's what terrifies me," he whispered.

A knock sounded an instant before Lucas opened the door. "Hi, Sav. Great to have you back! But you need to know, Mother's home, and she's heard you're here."

Martin closed his eyes for a moment before firming his shoulders for the battle to come. "My daughter has every right to visit me," he snapped at Lucas.

"Father," Savannah said as she rose. Martin stood and rounded his desk to stand in front of her. "I'll leave because I can only imagine how difficult life already is with Mother. What matters is that you would have fought for me. Thank you." She leaned forward for a short embrace before moving toward Lucas and the doorway to the store.

"May I visit you at Mrs. Chickering's?" her father asked as he followed them into the store.

"Of course."

"Lucas, I'll man the store. Please see your sister home."

Savannah waited as Lucas removed his apron. She smiled at her father and walked outside as she heard her mother approaching. Lucas gripped her elbow and propelled her forward, slamming the store's door shut behind them.

"Let's go, Sav. I wish there were more customers in the shop to prevent Father from receiving another verbal lashing from Mother."

"Why can't she understand my desire to be away from Jonas?" Savannah said, sighing with relief when they slowed to a more sedate walk as they turned down Waltham Street. The trees provided a canopy of shade, and birds trilled overhead.

"Why didn't you ever tell me how terrible it was?" Lucas asked, unable to hide the hurt from his voice. "I hate that he kept you locked in the house as though you were in a prison." He paused, gripping her shoulders as he searched her eyes. "And the baby? He placed her in an orphanage?"

Savannah closed her eyes for a moment, blinking away tears. "I thought no one would believe me. Mother would never let me speak a word against him, and I began to believe everyone would think it was my fault. And then, when I learned the baby lived, I worried you'd believe I was unhinged, like Jonas said, and that I should be placed in a mental institution."

"Why would you doubt Father and me? Why would you believe such things?" Lucas asked.

"I chose to marry him. I could have left after … I realized how he was. But I stayed. I believed what he told me." At Lucas's inquisitive stare, she continued. "That whatever happened to me, I had provoked him to do it. That it was all my fault."

"You had to have known he was feeding you a pack of lies, Sav."

"Some part of me, deep down, did. But I was so afraid, all the time. You don't know what it is to live your life like that."

"Are you safe now?" Lucas asked as he offered his elbow, and they began their slow walk toward the Public Garden and then to Sophronia's house.

"Yes. Sophie is powerful and fierce. She'll not let anything happen to me."

"It seems strange you'd go to another woman rather than to your father and brother."

"Mother would never allow me to stay. And I think Jonas is afraid of Sophie. She's one woman he can't charm or intimidate. He doesn't know what to do with her."

"Please tell me that you'll call if you ever need me or Father."

"Of course." After a moment Savannah asked, "Lucas, why is Mother so upset with me?"

"Mother wants you to continue with your marriage so that she maintains her esteem with the grandparents. She hopes to receive a generous amount on their death if she does."

"That's so … That's so …" Savannah stammered, unable to think of an appropriate word.

"Mercenary. Cruel. Selfish," Lucas said. "Yes, all those things. And all could be applied to Mother. But their health has begun to fade, and she thinks that she will soon reap her just deserts, as she calls them."

"But for that to happen, I must continue to play the part for her."

"Exactly. And you couldn't have chosen a worse time for your rebellion."

She turned to glare at Lucas but then smiled when she saw that he had a satisfied gleam in his eyes.

"She tried to convince Father that the store was having financial difficulties due to your scandal. However, he is savvy enough to know it has nothing to do with it."

"What is causing trouble for the business, Lucas?"

"Mother doesn't like to admit that the store is suffering due to the new aboveground trolley line. It's uglier than we thought it would be and creates a near-constant rumbling that patrons say precludes them from thinking clearly about their purchases." He smiled at Savannah's unladylike snort. "At any rate, due to it, there are now fewer people walking along the streets. Everything is darker. Fewer pay attention to our shop's front window displays, and it's harder to entice customers in."

"Besides the fact that fashion is changing, Lucas," Savannah murmured. "People are purchasing more ready-to-wear clothes."

"I know," Lucas said. "At any rate, none of this has to do with you and your decision to live the life you want." He gripped her hands. "The life you deserve, Sav."

"Thank you, Lucas," she whispered, before gripping his arm with such force he grimaced. "Will you do something for me?" At his nod, she said, "Will you go to City Hall where they keep the birth and death records, and look for my baby's death certificate?"

"Why? You know Adelaide didn't die, Sav." He brushed away her stray tear.

"But I don't know where she is! I've visited orphanages, and none have any record of her. I keep thinking, maybe she did die, and I'm deluding myself. If there's a death certificate, that would mean she was gone, wouldn't it?"

Lucas's jaw clenched, and Savannah flinched. "I'll never forgive him. Not for what he did to you. Not for what he's done to Adelaide, stealing months from you, her mother," Lucas whispered, moving forward to grasp both of Savannah's arms and meeting her eyes with a fiery intensity. "He lied to all of us. I've never seen Father as upset as these past months, watching you mourn Adelaide."

Savannah nodded, blinking rapidly, unable to forestall the shedding of tears. "I knew I couldn't remember something from the birth, but, when I finally emerged from the drug-induced fog, I realized I remembered hearing her cry. That she wasn't a stillbirth. I have to find her. Find out what happened to her."

"You feel strong enough to leave Mrs. Chickering's? To venture forth each day in your pursuit?"

"Brave enough, you mean?" Savannah asked with a self-deprecating laugh. "I'll always be afraid Jonas will find me. Attempt to force me back with him. But I've realized I can't allow my life to be dictated by fear, Lucas. I want more than that."

"There's the brave Savannah I know," Lucas said with a hint of a smile, his glower fading. "As for your request, why don't you look for the record yourself, Sav?"

"The man working at the desk said a lady shouldn't concern herself with such matters and should look to her husband for guidance in such a case. He refused to help me."

"If there is anything to be found, I'll find it," Lucas vowed before he pulled Savannah close for a tight embrace. "I hate that you suffered more than I'll ever know."

Savannah stifled a sob and clung to him. "Thank you for believing me."

"Of course I believe you. You never lied before, Sav. Well, except to yourself." He leaned away to meet her eyes, and his regret-filled smile made her cry harder. "Hush, don't cry so, or that Chickering woman will think you've had a run-in with Jonas."

Savannah shuddered. "Not even in jest, Lucas. Will you visit me at Sophie's? Come play for me?"

"You'd like to hear my music?" Lucas asked, unable to hide the pleasure from his voice.

"Yes, I've always loved it. I didn't have enough sense to appreciate it until I'd moved out."

"I'd love to. I have missed you, sister," he said, before he kissed her gently on her forehead. "Even when you visited, you seemed distant. Not at all like the Savannah of old."

"Well, I may never again be the pre-Jonas Savannah ..."

"No, you're even better. Stronger and wiser." He hugged her at Sophie's door. "Never forget that, Sav. You might have changed due to your association with Jonas, but it hasn't altered you irreparably."

CHAPTER 15

"PLEASE, SIT WHILE I prepare us a cup of tea," Florence said. She bustled around the kitchen, putting the kettle on the stove, stirring the dregs of the ashes while adding a piece of new coal to rekindle the fire. She pulled out a teapot and two mugs, placing them on the table. "I'm afraid we don't have any milk today," Florence said as she placed the sugar bowl on the table.

"Florence, please sit," Savannah coaxed. "I can't thank you enough for all your help."

"You're welcome, Savannah. I know that Jeremy would have been with us if he hadn't received such a good commission."

"I'm happy for him that he did. He should have more to do in his day than escort women to orphanages on a wild chase."

Florence rose, filling the teapot with boiling water before placing it on the table to steep. She sat on a chair facing Savannah. "I just wish we'd been able to find your child, Savannah."

"I'm beginning to think she really did die. That everything Jonas told me about her was a mixture of half-truths, and I will never decipher truth from lie." She bit her lip as she fought tears. "Even if she is alive, I have to accept I may never find her."

Her gaze became distant as she envisioned each trip to the different orphanages in Boston and the surrounding cities. She cringed as she recalled her inability to ward off a fleeting hope as she ascended the stairs outside each new orphanage, that this day's orphanage would bring her resolution. Perhaps even a reunion with her daughter. The inescapable grief had continued to grow as, every time, her hopes were dashed, and her possibilities became more limited.

Savannah shook her head and smiled sorrowfully at Florence. "As I feared, Lucas discovered there was no death certificate. Nothing corresponding to an Adelaide Montgomery. At the same time, Sophie's contacts have yet to yield any information." She played with the spoon in the sugar bowl. "I wonder what Jonas did to her." She raised tormented eyes to Florence.

Florence gripped her hand in an attempt to impart solace. "You must take heart that you have done all you can."

"But I lost so many months," Savannah whispered as she brushed at tears on her cheeks. "It's already the end of August. She'd turn one in November. I've lost so much time, Florence."

"Thanks to your husband. Do not blame yourself for mourning." Florence studied her with wonder for a moment. "You don't know what it means to have watched you these past weeks search for your daughter." Florence glanced away, reaching toward the teapot to pour the tea.

Savannah stilled Florence's movement with a gentle touch to her hand. "Why has it meant so much to you, Florence? I would have thought, after the way I'd treated you, that you would gloat at my misfortune." She made a face as Florence frowned.

"Well, if not gloat, at least not be eager to help me. I was not kind to you. I scorned you for being a poor, orphan teacher, thinking myself above you because I was marrying a man such as Jonas. I couldn't have been more wrong, and you married the better man," Savannah whispered.

"Do you know much about me?" Florence asked. Savannah shook her head and released Florence's arm as Florence poured the tea. "Did it never seem odd to you that the head mistress of an orphanage would know who I am?"

"Aren't you an orphan like the McLeod brothers?"

"No, Savannah." Florence gripped the handle of her mug and continued to speak. "My mother gave me to the orphanage. She didn't want me."

"That can't be true," Savannah argued.

"On some level you are right. I'm sure she thought she was giving me a better future by bringing me when I was seven to the orphanage to be raised. My father was a drunk, and there was never enough food in the house. She was pregnant with another child."

"You can't think she chose your siblings over you."

"For the longest time I did," Florence whispered. "Until we returned to the Home, and I realized two of my siblings had been brought in."

"You must know that your mother acted as she did to ensure you had the best future possible, Florence," Savannah urged. "No mother gives up her child without feeling as though her heart is breaking."

"Well, whatever the case, I'll never know what my mother felt as she and the rest of them died in some sort of outbreak in the tenements a few years ago. My other siblings were sent on those orphan trains. I'm the only one left in Boston." Florence blinked away tears.

"I know what it is to have family, Savannah. To have siblings and a mother to tuck me in at night. To have a father that tells wondrous stories when he's not sick with drink. You have no idea what it does to you to be torn away from all that is familiar."

Savannah gripped Florence's hand, her brow furrowed with concern. "I'm sorry, Florence. I wish there was more I could say. I'm sorry you had to suffer as you did."

"It's why I no longer focus on how you thought of me in the past. You were blinded by Jonas's and your grandparents' values. The true woman, the Savannah I've come to know, fights to find her baby daughter. Fights to escape her husband and to not die an early death. Learns that all those trappings of wealth won't bring happiness. That's the woman I call friend."

"Thank you, Florence." Savannah sniffled.

"Because, like you, I know what it is to lose everything, I'm protective of the family I have now. Gabriel and Jeremy are the only brothers I will ever have. I don't want to see them hurt." She wiped at her eyes. "I hate to admit it, but I can understand Gabriel's protectiveness of Richard and why Gabriel tried to separate Richard and me when Gabriel thought I would harm his brother."

"You're being too understanding," Savannah said with a wry smile.

"When you're alone in this world, I understand doing everything possible to protect those you love from harm. You have family, Savannah. It's something you'll never understand."

"You seem to be under the misapprehension that family always has the best intentions for its members. Often it's quite selfish and manipulative. Or at least, that's what I've found to be the case."

"But you still have your father, brother, aunt and Clarissa for support. Not to mention Colin," Florence argued. "You might have to battle your mother and grandparents, but they haven't turned everyone against you. You're not alone, Savannah. Be thankful for that."

***

"DO YOU MIND IF I interrupt?" Savannah asked as she entered the work-space. Bright sunlight streamed in through the windows on this late summer day, the first of September. She noted the pieces of wood piled haphazardly about, the workbench along one wall of the room, the table off to one side and the rocking chair. "I tried to visit Florence, but she wasn't at home. I hope you don't mind."

"Not at all," Jeremy said as he motioned for her to enter. "Today she's visiting an elderly widow. She won't return home until Richard does."

Savannah blushed and glanced away from the frank approval she saw in his gaze. She fidgeted, fingering the sleeve of her new plain yellow cotton dress. "I see you kept Clarissa's rocking chair." At Jeremy's nod, Savannah wandered to it and sank into it. "He made her a comfortable chair."

"Yes, Gabriel always was talented," Jeremy said.

"What are you making, Mr. McLeod?"

"A dining room set for an apothecary. He wanted cherry, but I convinced him maple was more practical."

"I would think cherry would be a more beautiful wood."

"Yes, though not on his budget," Jeremy said with a smile. He watched her for a moment as he leaned against his workbench, absentmindedly wiping his dusty hands on his workpants. "What brings you by, ma'am?"

"I … I just wanted to see a friendly face," Savannah said and then blushed, looking away.

"How are things with your family?"

She grimaced before attempting to smile. "Lucas and my father are willing to visit me."

"Your brother, the musician?" Jeremy asked.

"Yes, he's supporting me through all this. I hadn't realized until I saw him a few weeks ago how much I'd missed him."

"I'm glad then, ma'am," Jeremy said with a smile.

"As for my parents, my father's supportive, but my mother would prefer if I were barred until I had the good sense to return to Jonas," Savannah whispered.

"Who would ever wish for you to continue to suffer at his hands?" Jeremy asked as he moved toward her.

"My mother worries about what her parents will think of her. And about her hoped-for inheritance. How can money ever be worth more than me?"

"I imagine your mother fears poverty. At least her version of poverty."

"I doubt she's known a moment of hunger in her life," Savannah said.

"Well, then the fear of it can make you irrational. Have you any idea what it is to be poor?" he asked. "Do you know what it is like to wonder where your next meal will come from?"

"No, but I know what it is to have every material possession I could imagine and still wish I were dead, because anything would be better than the reality I was living," Savannah murmured. "And I will not return to that. Never." They shared a long, mournful look before turning to stare around the workshop.

"Oh, ma'am," Jeremy murmured. "I've never known the type of hunger where you think your insides will eat themselves. But I know those who have. And that sort of desperation and fear will make you do drastic things."

"But my mother knows of no such reality!" Savannah cried. "My father will always provide for her. Why would she consign me to such a life?" Savannah scrubbed at her face a moment.

"I imagine there is much about your mother you don't know or understand."

"Sophie said much the same," Savannah said. "At any rate Lucas explained to me it isn't my scandalous desire for a divorce forcing customers away from the linen store but the new, ugly raised tramway. But my mother can only see me as the cause of all her problems. Why must I be the one to blame?" Savannah demanded as she barreled on. "She sends me scathing letters daily about my lack of propriety and decency, saying that the shame I have brought on the family is worse than anything Clarissa had done."

"I'd throw away her letters before opening them in the future," Jeremy muttered.

"Sophie says they're best used for kindling," Savannah said with a grin. "Why is what I've done so terrible?"

"There are some who are afraid that women will become too independent. And others are afraid of the changes that will bring to society."

"Is this what you think, Mr. McLeod?"

He flashed a fleeting smile. "No, ma'am. I prefer that women speak their minds. Even if I don't agree with all they have to say. Sometimes their viewpoint is fascinating." He chuckled. "I might think it's wrong but still fascinating." He watched her closely for a few moments. "Besides, why would any man want a woman who is a parrot to him?"

"You'd be surprised," Savannah murmured. "I'd always been taught that was the ideal woman. That I should think and feel as my husband does. That I had no need for anything more."

"You have no need for anything more than a husband's opinions?" Jeremy asked, raising an eyebrow. "What a bunch of hogwash, if you don't mind me saying. You're an intelligent woman. You just need to find faith in your own ideas."

"Thank you," Savannah whispered as she blinked rapidly.

He cocked his head to one side. "You're welcome, although I don't know for what." He winked at her as he returned to his work.

"Thank you for not ridiculing me." She laughed then. "Oh, if Gabriel could only hear this conversation!"

"Why is it humorous?"

"Because, when I was convincing myself to marry Jonas, Gabriel and I had an argument about domestic animals. He equated domestic horses to domesticated women. Said that they were docile, demure creatures and that he had longed to meet a woman who could think for herself."

Jeremy laughed at the thought. "Sounds like Gabe. What did Clarissa do?"

"She defended him of course. I think she already knew at that point that life without Gabriel wasn't for her. I became irate and stormed out of here. I felt as though he were attacking my way of life. And I couldn't believe Clarissa would want to tie herself to such a man." Savannah paused, sighing. "After a few months with Jonas, I realized the wisdom of Gabriel's words."

"What did he do to you, ma'am?" Jeremy asked softly as he moved toward her. He sat on a bench across from her and clasped her hand in his, tracing patterns on her palm. "You can trust me," he coaxed.

"It's not that I don't trust you," Savannah stammered out, refusing to meet his gaze. "I'm just so ashamed."

"There is no shame in survival," Jeremy whispered as he wiped away one of her tears.

Savannah closed her eyes as tears continued to course down her cheeks. "The first time he hit me was our wedding night. No one had ever hit me before. I had prepared for bed and had my maid pattern my hair in a pretty style, loose, over one shoulder. When he came into my bedroom, he was irate, saying that I had spoiled the night for him by denying him the pleasure of taking down my hair. He slapped me across the face and ..." Savannah paused, choking on a sob.

"You don't know what it's like, always waiting for the next blow. Sometimes there would be weeks, maybe a month between them. And yet it would always come. You begin to live in this state where everything makes you jump—any small noise or creak on the stair—because you think, now is the time for the next punishment.

"He rarely struck me where anyone would see the bruises. But the worst was how he spoke to me. As though I were beneath his contempt. As though I were stupid. As though everything he did I made him do." Savannah bowed her head as she fought back a sob.

"Ma'am," Jeremy murmured. He pulled the bench closer, plucked her out of the rocking chair and sat her next to him, enfolding her in his arms. "You must know none of that was your fault." He rocked her, soothing her, crooning in her ear. He stopped talking, simply held her and let her cry.

After many minutes, Savannah began to calm. She stiffened and tried to rise from his embrace. "Shh, love, let me hold you," he murmured. He continued to caress her hair and to sing gentle words in her ear.

"You have a lovely voice," Savannah murmured.

"Gabe whistles. I sing," he said. "You will be well again. Someday you'll find a man whom you can trust."

Savannah snuggled into his arms, content for the moment. "Thank you, Mr. McLeod. Thank you for listening and understanding."

"Anytime, ma'am. Anytime."

***

SAVANNAH RETURNED to Sophronia's, riding partway in the new underground subway. She stepped out of the trolley, ascending the stairs at Park Street in the Common, breathing a small sigh of relief to be aboveground again. A cool breeze ruffled her skirts, and she walked at a moderate pace in the warm afternoon air. She followed one of the paths toward Sophronia's stately home on Beacon Street, across from the Common.

After entering the front hall and taking off her hat and gloves, she walked upstairs to the front sitting room to look for Sophronia. She entered the soothing pale-yellow front sitting room with the painting of a mountain glen at dawn over the mantel. Savannah wished she could banish the memories of her mother's visit in this room.

"Hello, dear," Sophronia said. She sat in a comfortable lady's chair, sipping a cup of tea. She appeared to have been deep in thought. "Are you well?"

"Of course," Savannah said. "Why wouldn't I be?"

Sophronia studied her closely. "You appear somewhat rumpled and as though you've been crying."

Savannah flushed. "I visited Mr. McLeod at his workshop. I wanted to see a friend."

"Don't you think it would have been more advisable to visit Florence?"

"I tried to visit her, but she wasn't home." Savannah tapped her fingers on the edge of her seat. "My visit with Mr. McLeod was ... enlightening."

"Really? In what way?" Sophronia asked, humored interest sparking in her aquamarine eyes.

"He doesn't seem appalled that I wish to have my own ideas and dreams. He says that there are men who believe that women should be their own person." She shared a wondrous look with Sophronia.

"Ah, yes, there are such men, dearest. Although they are more elusive than you may wish them to be. If there were more of them, we would have our amendment by now."

"Must it always be about suffragism?" Savannah asked, unable to hide her impatience.

"No, although I believe that, if you'd had more freedoms, more rights to your own opinion, including who you wished to vote for, you might not have married the man you did."

"Thus my miserable existence is due to a lack of the vote?"

"Partly. And partly due to an antiquated society that doesn't fully value half its citizens." Sophronia held up one hand. "I'm not here to argue women's rights with you, Savannah dear. Either you will come around to it on your own or you won't." Sophronia gave her a fierce frown. "And I refuse to agree that your existence is miserable." After a moment, she said, "Would you care to tell me why you are looking rumpled?"

Savannah nodded. "I also spoke with him about what life had been like with Jonas. Mr. McLeod was very understanding. When I cried, he held me." Savannah looked up, eyes swamped in memories of misery. "He told me someday I'd find a man I could trust. But I don't know as I ever will. How can I?"

"You have too big a heart to leave it locked away due to the misfortune of having married a brutal man," Sophronia snapped. After a moment, her voice calmed. "And I'd quit searching for that man, if I were you."

"I don't know what you mean."

"Just think about it," Sophronia said with a grin. She sobered, and Savannah watched her with curiosity. "Now, unfortunately, I have disturbing news to impart."

"Yes?"

"I have spoken with my lawyers, and they do not believe they will be successful. In their estimation, they do not have enough proof of Jonas's cruelty to ensure obtaining a divorce decree."

"What more proof do they need?" Savannah wailed. "All the servants heard, and some saw, how he treated me."

"None, besides your maid, are willing to corroborate your claims."

"Even if that means lying in court?" Savannah asked, anger lacing her voice. "And what my maid, Mary, Florence or Mr. McLeod saw? Does none of that matter?"

"There is the fear that their testimony would be construed as biased due to their association with you. They need to have irrefutable testimony as to his cruelty to have a successful case." Sophronia watched Savannah with an intense stare. "As we can find no evidence of your daughter's placement in an orphanage, we cannot use that as evidence of his cruelty toward you. The courts would believe him, especially as he has a doctor to provide testimony to his claim."

"If the court would believe Mary, believe me, they'd know what kind of man he is. Stealing away my child," Savannah rasped. "Why would they believe him over me? Over what I've suffered?"

"Without irrefutable proof of her birth and either time in an orphanage or adoption, the court will not consider it evidence of cruelty against him." Sophronia sighed. "You know that divorces are not frequently granted in Massachusetts, and you must be willing to provide all the evidence necessary for the case."

"I can't return to him. I can't …" Sobs tore from Savannah's chest, and she bowed over, curling herself into a ball in her chair. "I can't detail everything I suffered at his hands. I refuse to be an object of gossip and ridicule for the papers."

"No, you will never return to him. I have summoned your aunt Betsy, and we will help you determine what is to be done."

"Aunt Betsy?"

"Yes, the only member of your family, besides Clarissa—but she is too far away to render any help—who is capable of showing any sense." Sophronia *harrumphed* again. "You'll remain safe and free of him. I promise you."

"Thank you, Sophie."

"Now, as for the other matter at hand, I know you have enlisted the aid of your friends, the McLeods, in your search for your daughter." At Savannah's nod, Sophie continued. "I, too, have turned to those I can trust in an attempt to discover what occurred last November."

Savannah gripped her hands together on her lap. "What have you discovered?"

"I spoke with a physician who was a good friend to my husband. He aided me a little over a year ago when I was in need of guidance for Clarissa. He was generous with his time again and agreed to speak to his colleagues. Unfortunately he hasn't heard any rumors of babies whisked away in the middle of the night."

All hope leeched from Savannah, and she shrunk into her chair. "Thank you, Sophie, for doing what you could."

"If you think the extent of my influence ends with speaking to a physician, you don't know me, Savannah." She looked at her with amusement. "I've numerous friends and acquaintances who are on the boards of orphanages throughout the area, and I've written them with the hopes they'll be able to discover if your daughter was placed in an outlying orphanage."

"Have you heard from any of them?"

"I'm afraid many are away for the summer. However, those who have written have made inquiries on my behalf but with no success," Sophie said.

"I fear I must resign myself to the truth that my daughter is lost to me."

"Never give up hope, Savannah. It is something not even that wretched husband of yours can ever take away from you."

CHAPTER 16

"WHAT'S THE MATTER, Mrs. Montgomery?" Jeremy asked as he set aside a piece of sandpaper and faced her. He turned toward the doorway to see her hovering a few steps inside the room, swaying as though with indecision if she should stay or leave. The stove to the side of the room pumped out anemic warmth on this chilly mid-September day.

"There are no more orphanages to visit. I just received a letter today from the last possible one in Connecticut. I … My baby must have died," Savannah whispered.

"I thought you'd begun to believe that a few weeks ago. Florence mentioned it to me after you had tea with her." He inched toward her as any sudden movement seemed to startle her.

"There's a difference between saying the words and truly understanding there is no hope, Mr. McLeod," Savannah rasped.

"Why do you come to visit me?" he asked as he continued his slow progression toward her.

"Because I like to think we're friends."

"We are," he said in a soft voice. "Why else?"

"Because … because I don't know," she whispered as she turned to leave.

He reached out and grasped her upper arm. "Stay. Speak to me. As your friend. As someone who wants you to stop hiding behind a brittle smile. Tell me what you're really feeling. Please?" He released her arm and squeezed her shoulders with his hands in encouragement.

"Why would you want to hear what I'm thinking? What I'm feeling?"

"Because I know what it is to live in darkness. Just like you, Savannah," he soothed.

"I don't know what happiness is," she blurted out. "I sometimes wonder if I've ever been happy. The memories from before Jonas seem to have happened to another woman. How could that have been me?"

Jeremy watched her, his silent compassion encouraging her to speak.

"I continue this so-called life because it is expected of me. I converse. I eat. I go on walks. But none of it really matters. All I will ever know is darkness." She bit her lip as she swallowed a sob. "I know I am a coward because ..."

After a few moments of silence where Savannah closed her eyes and leaned away from him, Jeremy asked, "Because?"

"Because I wish it would all end. I'd be reunited with my baby, and I'd finally have some peace. But I'm too much of a coward to do anything."

Jeremy gripped her arms, at the last moment remembering not to hold her too tightly. "Look at me, Savannah." He reached up, tracing her cheek and then one eyebrow until finally she opened her eyes. Tears leaked from her sky-blue eyes. "There's no cowardice in not wanting to be enveloped in constant darkness. In wishing you could see light where otherwise all you see is pain infused with hopelessness. You are braver than I can say for continuing your struggle to find a good life. To live a life free of a man such as Jonas. You're not a coward, Savannah."

"Stop it. Stop it," she demanded. She took deep breaths as she attempted to swallow her sobs. However, they poured from her, and she was unable to tamp them down.

"Cry, Savannah. Cry." He pulled her into his arms. "I'll hold you. Shh ... " He rocked her to and fro as she began to keen.

"No, no, no!" she wailed. "I don't want to feel." She punched at his back a few times before gripping him tightly.

"Ah, but you do. Too much. And I hope you never stop." He kissed her head as he cradled her quaking body. "Cry, sweet Savannah. Let it out." For long moments he held her as she sobbed, his silence a shared acceptance of her sorrow.

Even when Savannah settled, Jeremy continued to hold her. "You will always miss your baby, Savannah. But you need to live. Find joy in the everyday."

She pushed away from him, allowing him to see her red-rimmed eyes and runny nose. "How can I find joy, Jeremy? My baby is gone. Even if she didn't die, I'll never find her. I'll forever be separated from her. How can I be happy again?" Her breath stuttered as she fought another sob.

He wiped her cheeks with his fingers before cradling her head, while his thumbs continued to chase stray tears. "I don't know how you'll find happiness again, but you will. One day you'll have a moment of joy. And then another. Until you know more joy than despair. You must believe those days are coming, Savannah."

"I can't see past the pain."

"I know, and you'll carry this pain with you always. Some scars you see. Others are written on our hearts. And you never know when those will bleed. But hopefully this scar will bleed less frequently."

She leaned forward, and Jeremy held her, cooing soft words in her ear.

***

"SAVANNAH, IT APPEARS you have a visitor," Sophronia said.

Savannah glanced toward the doorway with a frown, then found Lucas hovering behind the butler.

He beamed as he sidestepped the butler, Poole, earning a loud grunt of disapproval from him and a smirk from Sophronia. "Mrs. Chickering, I presume? Wonderful to finally make your acquaintance. Sav, Aunt Betsy," Lucas said as he approached them to embrace them both. He wore a tailored gray linen suit with no tie.

"Lucas, it's wonderful to see you," Savannah said with a broad smile.

He released Savannah and moved toward Aunt Betsy, winking at her. "When my favorite aunt is in town, I need to see her."

"I'm your only aunt, you rascal," Aunt Betsy said with a smile. She fanned herself, shifting the long skirts of her sea-blue cotton dress.

Lucas wandered toward the polished piano sitting to one side of the room. He traced the rosewood inlay, his fingers moving as though playing the keys.

"I've heard you're something of a decent player," Sophronia said. "My daughter had the distinction of abusing that poor instrument. Thankfully she decided to leave it behind when she married. Her daughters have decided to deafen me with the violin rather than the piano."

"Play for us, Lucas," Aunt Betsy urged.

"What would you like to hear?"

"Something soothing. I've had a few rough days, and, although I've come to enjoy the newer songs you're playing, I wouldn't mind something older. More familiar." Savannah smiled encouragingly, sharing a long look with Lucas. "I've missed your music."

"Hmm ..." Lucas said as he sat at the piano, raising the key cover. He played a few keys, warming up his fingers. "You keep this tuned and in perfect condition for an instrument that is never played, ma'am." He looked toward Sophronia with a raised eyebrow.

"If one is to have the trappings of wealth, one might as well maintain that which gives us our perceived sophistication," Sophie said with a grin. "Play for us, young man. Show me this talent of yours." She settled back in her chair with her heels crossed at her ankles.

"I remember you liked this song, Sav," Lucas murmured as he played a gentle piece by Chopin.

Savannah closed her eyes, the lyrical notes as though a lullaby, reminding her of the days before she married Jonas. By the time Lucas had finished, she swiped at a few of the tears trickling down her cheeks.

Lucas looked toward her with a grin that quickly faded as he noted her tears. He rose from the piano bench and strode toward her, kneeling in front of her. "Sav, I'm sorry. I remember it was your favorite piece years ago. When it was our secret that I played the piano."

"That's why I was crying, Lucas. It reminded me of the girl I once was. Of how innocent I used to be. It made me nostalgic."

Lucas's jaw tightened at the allusion to her life with Jonas. "Have you had any contact with Jonas?"

"No, nothing." Savannah sniffled. "And I know that should soothe me. But it doesn't. It only makes me more afraid of what's to come."

"Whatever comes, you are not alone this time, dearest. You have all of us and the McLeods," Sophie said.

Lucas raised one eyebrow as he moved to sit in a chair next to Savannah. "The McLeods? Clarissa's too far away to be of any practical assistance."

"I've befriended Florence and Gabriel's brothers," Savannah said.

"I imagine his brothers are as capable as Gabriel," Aunt Betsy said.

"Cryptic as always, Aunt Betsy," Lucas said.

"If I remember the story correctly, it was Florence and the brother Jeremy who ... rescued you, for lack of a better word, from your husband's house," Aunt Betsy said.

"It was. And saved her from another horrid beating," Sophie said.

"Another, Sav?" Lucas asked as he gripped his hands and flushed with anger.

"Please, Lucas, I'm fine. It's nothing," Savannah whispered as she reached out to stroke his clenched fist.

"Promise me that you won't ever return to him. Not for any reason," he said, urgency lacing his tone.

"I promise." Savannah shuddered at the thought.

"As for you, young man," Sophronia said, "what are you doing, wasting your life selling linen when you should be performing?"

"One such as I does not perform, Mrs. Chickering. Only those of the lower classes would do such a thing," Lucas said.

"Balderdash," Sophronia said with a *harrumph* for emphasis. "Whoever filled your head with such nonsense, and I have to assume it's either your misguided mother or insipid grandparents, should know that such talent as yours should not be squandered."

Lucas flushed, this time with pleasure. "I thank you, Mrs. Chickering. I'm content with the life I lead."

"Content," she hissed. "*Content* is for those who are in their dotage reliving their lives, thankful they have no regrets. Careful, my boy, for you will not be one of those. You will become a sad, bitter old man for all that you did not do."

"Sophie!" Savannah gasped.

"Someone needs to speak sense, and it's clearly not going to be a member of your family, Savannah." She gave a pointed look at both her and Aunt Betsy. "If you had, Mr. Russell would be performing with the symphony by now, rather than in my parlor on my decrepit piano to a tone-deaf woman."

"You are far from tone deaf," Aunt Betsy said with a sardonic turn of her lips.

"Be that as it may, you need to begin to concern yourself with your future, Mr. Russell," Sophronia said. "I hope to hear that things have changed the next we meet."

"Do you ever stop meddling in the lives of your friends?" Savannah asked.

"Of course not. What would be the purpose of my friendship and influence if I refrained from interfering?" she asked with a laugh.

CHAPTER 17

THE FOLLOWING WEEK, Savannah stood with hand raised, on the verge of knocking on Jeremy's door, as indecision and insecurity rose inside her. She stared at the worn wood, partially lit by the bright sunshine entering the window behind her. She leaned nearer to the door, closing her eyes as she listened to Jeremy's deep voice singing a lighthearted song. After a few moments, she took in a long breath, squared her shoulders and let her hand fall, rapping the door. She heard the gentle singing cease and then footsteps approaching the door.

"Ma'am," Jeremy said with a broad smile after he opened the door. "Please, come in."

She entered the workshop, moving instinctively toward the rocking chair. He stilled her movement with a gentle hand to her arm. "Would you like to see what I've been working on?"

"Oh, of course," she said, as she moved toward one of the workbenches. She traced the wood of the oval top of a table, noting the rosewood inlay.

"I thought you said the apothecary wanted maple," Savannah murmured.

"This is for a successful theater owner. He wants cherry with rosewood inlay. Many times in the past weeks, I've wished Gabe were here to help me, but I think the man will be pleased."

"How could he not be?" Savannah asked as she continued to trace the tabletop. "I like this shape." Jeremy nodded, seeming pleased at her approval of his work.

"Are you finding many customers then, Mr. McLeod?" Savannah asked as she moved toward the rocking chair and sat.

"Enough. I could live independently if I wanted to, although I have no desire to move away from Richard and Flo."

"How are they? I haven't seen Florence in a while," Savannah said.

"They're well. Slowly preparing for the baby," he said. He watched her as she stilled before she continued to rock.

"I hadn't realized they expected a baby," Savannah whispered. She forced a smile as she met Jeremy's eyes.

"Well, it's come as a bit of a surprise. A welcome one but still a surprise. It's hard to imagine Richard a father."

"Or yourself an uncle."

"Oh, I'll enjoy that well enough. That's the easy part, spoiling a child senseless without having to worry about discipline," he said with a wistful smile. "Are you all right, ma'am?"

"Of course. I'm very happy for Florence and Richard. How foolish of me. I thought she was merely putting on weight," Savannah said.

"I think she'd be happy for your help as she prepares for the baby."

"I'll try, although it will be very difficult for me." Savannah leaned back into the rocking chair and rocked for a few minutes. A harmonious silence enveloped the room, and Jeremy began to sing softly. After a while a chuckle interrupted his song.

"What amuses you?" Savannah asked.

He looked at her over his shoulder as he continued to sand a board. "This. You, here. Sitting in Clarissa's chair."

"Why?"

"It reminds me of the letters Gabe wrote me of his visits with Clarissa. I never thought to have the same," he murmured, as he turned away to face his work again.

"Why wouldn't you imagine someone visiting you?"

"I'm not like Gabe. Or Richard. They're gentlemen. Gentle men," he said softly, carefully enunciating the two words separately. "Though they might not fit your definition of a gentleman," he said with a rueful laugh.

"And you think you are nothing like them?"

"I know I'm not."

"Well, you fit my definition of a gentleman," Savannah said with a tender smile.

Jeremy turned to face her and moved to lean against the table near the rocking chair. He waited for her to continue.

"You help ladies in distress. Repeatedly. You listen, truly listen, to those around you. You care about the people in your life more than appearances. You're excited to become an uncle and eager to spoil your niece or nephew."

Jeremy flushed. "Thank you, ma'am." He sat on the bench facing her. "You seem more at peace now than the last time you were here a week ago."

"I will always mourn my daughter, Mr. McLeod."

"Jeremy," he murmured.

"Jeremy." A shy smile flirted around her lips. "I'll always miss her, and I know I will continue to have days when I'm sad."

"But you've begun to find joy again."

"Yes, moments of joy. Lucas visited us the other evening and played for us. He is so talented, Jeremy."

"I remember listening to him play last spring. What did he play for you?"

"A beautiful song by Chopin. It was one of my favorite songs before I met Jonas. It reminded me of a simpler time."

"But it didn't make you happy."

"Do you know how sometimes things are so beautiful they actually hurt? Or when you are so happy you want to cry?" At Jeremy's nod, Savannah smiled. "That's how it was for me. With that Chopin piece, he captured my mood. It was as though, by playing a song from before Jonas entering my life, Lucas had reminded me of all that I could be."

"He brought you back to yourself."

"Exactly. I'd forgotten who that Savannah was. I think I'll enjoy becoming acquainted with her."

"I know I have," Jeremy said with a soft smile.

"Thank you for always welcoming me. I don't know what I would have done without your friendship."

"Nor I yours."

"What do you mean?"

"Why do you think I recognized your sadness so readily? The darkness within?" He watched her with a guarded expression. "I have the same within me, Savannah. I know what it is to fight, every day, to find that moment of joy. Lest I be lost in a quagmire of darkness."

Savannah rose from the rocking chair and moved to sit next to him on the bench.

Two of his fingers clasped a loose strand of her hair and twirled it around his fingers. "I hope, every day, that you'll visit me. I know it is foolish of me, and yet I do."

Savannah bit her lip as she fought a broad smile. "I tell Sophie that I visit you because Florence is away from her house. I think she sees through me, but I want to be able to see you too."

"Do you think she'd prevent you from visiting me?"

"No, although I think she worries that my visits here could be construed as improper and any chance for a case against Jonas will lose merit."

"And when you tell her there has been no impropriety?"

"She raises an eyebrow and smirks at my rumpled state," Savannah said as she blushed rosily.

"Rumpled?" Jeremy's brow furrowed. "Oh, well, that was because you were crying."

"She has a vivid imagination," Savannah whispered.

"As do I," Jeremy said.

Savannah blushed a rosier red and dropped her gaze.

He raised her chin with two fingers to meet his gaze. "I mean no offense, Savannah. Please forgive me for teasing you."

"Does that mean you don't imagine ..." Savannah's voice faded as she met Jeremy's intense stare.

"Oh, I imagine," he whispered huskily.

Savannah took a deep breath and leaned forward, kissing him hard on the lips. Jeremy grunted as their noses bumped. He pulled away, a chuckle escaping him, as he caressed her cheek.

"There's no rush, sweet Savannah," he murmured. He canted forward, capturing her lips with his. On her sigh, he deepened the kiss. He stroked a hand over her hair, dislodging a few pins, before brushing his hands down her back, whisper soft. He scooted toward her, tangling his long legs in her skirts.

Many minutes later, Jeremy leaned away, dropping his hands from Savannah. She watched him with wide eyes, two fingers to her lips. "I should—" he began but was cut off as Savannah stopped his words with her fingers.

"—not speak," she said with a tremulous smile. She leaned forward and kissed him once more before standing.

"I must return to Sophie's," Savannah murmured, as she reached up to her hair.

"There's a mirror in the corner," Jeremy said as he pointed at the stove.

She moved toward it, unpinning her hair and finger-combing it. She pulled it into a ponytail and formed a loose knot at the nape of her neck before jabbing pins in place. "That will have to do," she said as she looked at herself in the mirror. "I just have to hope that Sophie doesn't remember how I had my hair fashioned before I left today."

"Doubtful. That woman seems as sharp as a hawk." Jeremy reached out to stroke her earlobe and the side of her neck. "I'm sorry if I've caused you any difficulty."

"I just hope your imagination was satisfied," Savannah murmured, raising her hand to hold his by the side of her neck.

"Oh, I'm far from satisfied, sweet Savannah. But this is a good beginning," Jeremy said with latent heat in his eyes.

"I'll try to call again soon." Savannah grinned at him. She released his hand and moved toward the door.

***

"IS THAT YOU, DEAREST?" Aunt Betsy called out. "I hope you had an enjoyable afternoon with your friend."

Savannah entered the parlor and leaned down to kiss Aunt Betsy.

"It's clear she did, Betsy," Sophie said as she studied Savannah.

"Are there any sandwiches left? I'm a bit hungry," Savannah said, as she reached for the cup of tea her aunt had prepared for her.

"I shouldn't be surprised, from the look of you," Sophie said.

"I look perfectly respectable, and you know it," Savannah said with a glower.

"Unless you look in your eyes," Sophie said. A smile bloomed as she studied Savannah. "I haven't seen you this happy, truly happy, since your arrival here three months ago. And don't try any insipid nonsense that you were with Florence cooing over baby patterns." Her aquamarine gaze dared her to tell the truth.

"Florence was out again—" Savannah said.

"I've never known a person needing to do so much shopping," Aunt Betsy said with an amused smile.

"Thus I visited with Mr. McLeod."

"I suspected as much," Sophie said. "Although this time I refuse to believe any claim to crying in his arms as the reason for your rumpled state, Savannah."

Savannah felt her ears reddening. "We had an interesting … discussion about imaginations."

Sophie cackled. "Ah, be careful, my dear. When you start that sort of discussion, they tend to lead to experiments." She raised and lowered her eyebrows in a teasing manner.

Aunt Betsy giggled. "I agree, although I don't know as I would warn caution. It seems to me you've lived your life filled with caution and have had very little pleasure for it."

Savannah sobered. "Yes, well. We all know nothing will come of my visits. It's nice to feel …"

"Yes?" Aunt Betsy asked.

"Anything," Savannah whispered as, in an instant, she was blinking away tears.

"Oh, Savannah." Aunt Betsy set down her teacup and reached out to clasp Savannah's hand. "Now I must ask your forgiveness as I had to ask Clarissa for hers. I'm sorry I didn't take a more active role in your life when you were younger."

"What do you mean?"

"The few times I attempted to give Matilda advice, she became very upset. I had no wish to cause a rift in the family and be separated from my niece and nephew, thus I kept my concerns to myself. I've known for some time that I was wrong, and I'm sadder than I can say."

"Nothing you could have said would have changed my decision," Savannah said.

"Well, there's no reason to reimagine the past, as it is done. Now we can only learn from it and ensure that the future is more to our liking." She patted Savannah's hand before releasing it.

"There is nothing between Mr. McLeod and me. He's a good friend. Besides, a relationship would be completely unacceptable."

"To whom?" Sophie asked. "To your snobbish grandparents or insufferable mother? What did their guidance bring you the last time? I'd think you'd have the sense to shed the prejudices that they attempted to instill in you and think for yourself."

"Clarissa's love of Gabriel is not unacceptable, Savannah," Aunt Betsy argued. "He's a good man, and he provides well for her. He might not be as wealthy as you expected, but money is a cold bedfellow. As I believe you know."

Savannah flinched from the gentle reproach in her aunt's voice. "I know," Savannah said in a small voice.

"Although I believe you have listened to too much advice in your life and have not learned to trust your own instincts, I'm going to give you more advice." Sophie's eyes twinkled with wry humor. "Take some time away from him. I'd hate to see you leaving one man, only to begin with another. Take time to know who you are first."

"Jeremy is nothing like Jonas," Savannah hissed.

"Jeremy, is it?" Sophie asked with a raised eyebrow. "I know he isn't, but you're missing my point. My hope for you is that you learn what it is *you* want from life and for your life, independent of the wishes and desires of a man or other members of your family. As long as you continue to see him, you will not have that opportunity. This is your chance for self-discovery, Savannah."

"Is that fair to him?" Betsy asked. "It seems Savannah's a regular visitor. If she disappears, he'll worry."

"Savannah's spent her life considering the concerns of those around her," Sophronia said. "Now is her time."

"What do you think, Savannah?" Aunt Betsy asked.

"I will consider what you both say," Savannah said. "If you'll excuse me, I wish for time alone."

She rose, ascending the stairs and walking down the hallway to her room at the rear of the house. She barely noted the paintings on the wall or the small tables with vases overflowing with fragrant flowers.

She collapsed onto the chaise longue, her mind filled with Jeremy. His voice. His quiet approval of her shining forth from his eyes. His touch. His passionate kisses. Her fingers stole to her lips and traced them, and she couldn't prevent a smile from bursting forth. She swallowed a giggle, curling onto her side.

She longed for Clarissa, for the days when they were each other's confidantes. How she needed to speak with her, gain her advice. Was it normal to feel a mixed-up jumble of emotions? Was it normal to dream of kissing Jeremy? Of craving his gentle touch? Of wanting even more with him?

In an instant she blinked away tears, realizing she could have lived her entire life without knowing any of the passion and pleasure from today's encounter with Jeremy. Maybe Sophie was right that she needed time away. But how was she to stay away from a man who finally made her feel like a desirable woman?

***

A WEEK AFTER SAVANNAH'S ENCOUNTER with Jeremy in his workshop, Savannah continued to battle her own vivid imagination. In an attempt to heed Sophronia's advice, she decided to visit Florence rather than Jeremy on a bright late-September day.

"Hello, Savannah," Florence said.

"Is this an inopportune time to visit?" Savannah asked, watching as Florence swiped at the sweat on her brow.

"No. Don't leave!" Florence grasped Savannah's arm and pulled her inside. "I could use the help." She moved toward a small room off the dark hallway. "I know this is improper, but I'm so tired I can't seem to mind."

Florence pushed open the bedroom door. Savannah jerked to a stop to find Jeremy on a bed, across the room, the sheets tangled around his waist.

"You're right, this is highly improper," Savannah stammered. She looked toward a wall, trying to focus on anything but Jeremy's prostrate form.

"You've been married. Nothing should come as a surprise to you," Florence said with a wicked smile. "However, I'm not asking you to do anything that will mortify you. Just help me care for him. Wipe his brow, talk to him when he starts thrashing about."

Florence moved toward Jeremy and stroked the hair off his forehead. "He's calmed by someone talking to him."

"What's wrong with him?" Savannah asked as she inched into the room.

"A malarial attack. I hadn't realized he'd suffer them, even though he was no longer in the Philippines, but the doctor told us that he must not have been completely treated and is having another attack."

"The doctor was here?" Savannah asked. "Florence, I don't mean to offend …"

"Although you probably will," Florence said with a wry twist of her lips.

"But could you afford his care?" Savannah asked with a gentle pat to Florence's shoulder.

"Barely. We're trying to put as much aside for the coming baby." Florence paused, absently patting her belly. At Savannah's nod of understanding, she said, "And a visit from the doctor ate into our meager resources."

"Would you let me help?" Savannah asked.

"Of course not." Florence's weak smile tampered the sting of refusal. "Whatever else we might be, we McLeods are mighty stubborn and self-sufficient."

"You're very proud of being a McLeod," Savannah said. She sat on the chair next to Florence, her worried gaze darting over Jeremy's still form.

"I finally belong, Savannah. I'm wanted. You can't know what that means." Florence met Savannah's gaze. "I've been up the past two nights tending to Jeremy. Can you watch him for a while so I can sleep?"

"Of course," Savannah whispered.

"Don't worry. Just wipe his brow with this." She held up a dry cloth. "Stroke his brow when he starts to sweat again. If he becomes agitated, talk to him about anything, and he'll settle. He's not due for another dose of medicine until Richard returns home, so you won't have to deal with that onerous duty."

"Onerous?"

"You've never seen a man fight you so hard when you want to put a spoon in his mouth," Florence said with a shake of her head. "I'm not saying I don't understand, but it makes the caring of him more difficult."

"I'm sorry not to spend time with you, Florence. I wanted to talk with you about your wonderful news."

"Oh, there's plenty of time for that. The best thing you could do for me is let me sleep." She squeezed Savannah's shoulder and rose. A few moments later Savannah heard a door creak shut down the hall.

Savannah glanced around the sparsely furnished room. Jeremy's single bed sat across from the doorway. A battered maple table next to the bed had a lamp with a chipped shade; a stack of books were beside the lamp. Chairs she recognized from the dining room had been placed next to his bed due to his illness. At the foot of the bed, a tall chest of drawers stood, with a few bottles on top. A glass and ewer sat on top of the bureau positioned to the right of the door, with a mirror above the pitcher.

She now sat with a chair between her and Jeremy, and she decided to move to sit next to him. She picked up two of the books. "*Tess of the D'Urbervilles.*" She shook her head. "No thank you. *An Ideal Husband.*" She smiled. "Seems a bit risqué to read Oscar Wilde, but why not?"

Savannah set the Thomas Hardy down and flipped open Wilde's book. She squirmed around in the hard wooden chair, attempting to find a comfortable position. After a moment of reading to herself, she glanced toward Jeremy. "I feel ridiculous reading aloud to myself, Jeremy. But I will, for your sake."

She used the cloth to mop at the small amount of sweat on his face, brow and neck before settling back to read. She read, giggling at times. To entertain herself, she tried to make up different voices for each character but then forgot which voice she'd given to which character.

"I had not thought to hear your voice, ma'am."

Savannah looked up from the book, gasping and dropping it. "Jeremy! You're awake. How do you feel?"

"Like I've been run through the ringer," he rasped. "Is there any water?"

Savannah rose to the bureau and poured a small amount of water from the ewer into a glass. "Here, sit up," Savannah said. She reached over to help him and found herself perched against the edge of his bed, one arm around his shoulder as she used her upper body to propel him into a sitting position. "Up you go," she urged.

"I hate being so weak," he said through chattering teeth. After slurping a little water, he collapsed again on his side, shaking uncontrollably. "Are there any blankets? I'm so cold."

"I thought you'd have a fever," Savannah said, as she reached out to touch his forehead, finding it burning to the touch.

"I do, but I wax and wane between very hot and very cold. Right now, I'm cold." He burrowed into the blanket Savannah placed over him, grasping her hand. "Please stay," he said.

"I will," she said as she squeezed his fingers. "Do you want me to keep reading to you?"

"I don't care." He closed his eyes. "Just keep talking to me. I love your voice," he whispered as his body shook uncontrollably.

Savannah reached a hand out and stroked his shoulder, tucking the blankets around him. "I've been thinking a lot about my life before I married

Jonas. About the girl I was before my grandparents took a great notice in me. Clarissa and I were always in trouble. Lucas and Colin too, although they always made it seem like Clarissa and I were the ones who started everything. Patrick, Clarissa's eldest brother, disapproved of everything and never took part in any of our antics."

Savannah chuckled before sighing. "One time I remember our old maid, Bridget, took in a stray cat. He was a feisty, mean thing, had a scar down the left side of his face from his eye to his cheek. It looked like it should be a friendly tabby, but it was vicious. The only person it had a soft spot for was the cook, because she fed him bowls of milk. Mother would have had a fit if she'd known how much milk went to that animal.

"One day it started yowling and hissing, cornering Clarissa and me as it swatted at us. We were freed only when Lucas took a broom to it. The four of us decided we were going to get that cat back. It had a favorite spot it liked to sun itself. Clarissa and I bought sturdy green ribbons and tied bells to the end of each. We then tied the ribbons to two long strings and gave them to Lucas and Colin.

"Clarissa and I stood in a corner of the kitchen, on the lookout for the maid and the cook. Lucas and Colin, who wore really long thick gloves borrowed from Clarissa and me"—Savannah chuckled as she acted out putting on long gloves—"crept toward the slumbering beast. They managed to attach one of the strings and tie it with a sturdy knot, although the second string brushed the cat's face and woke it up."

Savannah giggled as she covered her mouth with glee for a moment. "I've never seen two people jump so high so fast! They yowled as loud as the cat and scurried over to us. The cat rose and shook itself. As it did, the bells rang and scared it silly. It started to run, thinking it could escape the noise. However, the more it moved, the more of a racket it created. Soon it was running through the house, careening into the furniture and knocking over vases!"

Savannah brushed at her eyes as she laughed. "Oh, I'd never seen Mother so angry. Or Father try so hard not to join in the hilarity. I can still see that cat scurrying around a corner, trying to escape the noise."

She sighed again, reaching out a hand to wipe at Jeremy's forehead. "The cat received an extra portion of milk that night, so I shouldn't feel too sorry for it."

After a few moments of silence, Savannah felt Jeremy's forehead. "Oh, no. You're even hotter than before." She rose, finding another clean cloth on the bureau. As she turned toward the bed, she paused at the sight of Richard.

"You're the last person I would have expected to find in my brother's sickroom," Richard said as he entered. "That was a fine story, Mrs. Montgomery. Seems you're more like Clarissa and Colin than I'd given you credit for."

"I'll take that as the compliment it was intended to be," Savannah said, blushing. "I'm sure I've overstayed my welcome." She glanced at Jeremy, shivering on the bed. "He will recover, won't he?"

"He always has," Richard said. He reached out his hand for the cloth. "Thank you for visiting today and giving Florence a chance to rest. She's been run off her feet caring for Jeremy." He tossed the cloth from one hand to the other, his gaze flickering between Jeremy and Savannah. "Will you come back tomorrow? It would mean a great deal to know that Florence will have more rest tomorrow afternoon. I'll be able to work without worrying so much about her."

"Of course," Savannah said. "Please tell Florence and Jeremy I'll return in the afternoon." She smiled at Richard, brushed Jeremy's hand and moved past Richard to slip out of the room.

***

JEREMY AWOKE FEELING a deep ache in every muscle in his body. He groaned and a rough hand touched his forehead. "Is that you, Rich?" Jeremy asked.

"Yeah. About time you woke up," Richard said with a note of worried teasing in his voice. "I've about worn a permanent indentation in my backside sitting in this chair for so long."

"Sorry," Jeremy mumbled as he rolled to his side. "God, I feel awful." He buried his face in his pillow and groaned.

"Is it worse than usual?"

"No, I just keep trying to forget about how bad these attacks are. I've already got the damned memories. Why must I have the disease too?"

"As long as you're alive and well, Jer."

"I wouldn't call frequent bouts of malarial ague as alive and well."

"So he's awake then," Florence said as she walked into the room, holding a pitcher of water and fresh cloths. She set down everything and then reached for Richard's hand.

"I'm sorry to have caused you so much work," Jeremy said, as he opened his eyes and noted the dark smudges under Florence's eyes. "Especially when you should be caring for yourself and the baby."

"Jeremy, I'm fine. A few sleepless nights won't harm me. Besides I had help." Florence sat in the vacant chair next to Richard. She placed a hand on the swell of her belly, nearly six months pregnant now, and smiled as she felt the baby kick.

"Thanks, Rich. I can only imagine how hard it's been, having me ill and working at the forge too."

Richard grinned and shared an amused glance with Florence. "You don't remember, do you?" he asked Jeremy.

"You know I never remember what happens when I'm sick with malaria." Jeremy stretched and yawned. "God, I need a bath, but I think I'd fall flat on my face if I stood up."

"Savannah was here and helped care for you. Allowed Flo to rest," Richard said.

"Savannah? My … our friend?" he asked.

"Yes, showed up day before yesterday. I think she was here to talk with me about the baby, but I didn't really listen to her. Just thrust her in here and into the role of caring for you. I was so tired by that point, and she didn't seem to mind."

"How can I not remember she was here?" Jeremy asked.

"You just said you never remember," Richard said.

"I know, but …"

"But you think you should have remembered that the woman you're attracted to, for lack of a better word, was here tending you at your worst?" Florence asked. "According to Richard, you even missed a rather entertaining story about her youth."

"Yes, something to do with a cat and bells," Richard said with a laugh. "You should ask her about it some time. You were the calmest when she spoke to you."

"I hate that she saw me like that," Jeremy whispered.

"Well, it's part of who you are. Not worth trying to hide it," Florence said. "At some point you'd have to tell her." Florence shrugged.

"We're friends, Flo," Jeremy said.

"And I'm a Chinese monk," she said with a wry smile. "Would you like some soup? Mint's in season, and I remember you liking the cold mint soup last time after you were ill."

"That sounds wonderful," Jeremy said as he rolled onto his back.

"I'll leave Richard here to help wash you and to change the sheets."

Richard reached for the pitcher of water, pouring some of it into a bowl. He wrung out a cloth and handed it to Jeremy. "Do you feel up to bathing yourself, or do you need my help?"

"I'll do it," he said, grabbing the cloth. He sat up and swung his legs over the side of the bed, gripping the mattress edge with his free hand.

"I'll be back in a minute with the sheets," Richard said.

Jeremy began to wash, pausing every few moments to rest. Richard returned with a stack of clean towels, clean nightclothes for Jeremy, as well as fresh sheets. After Jeremy washed and put on fresh clothes, he sat on a chair huddled under a blanket while Richard stripped the bed, flipped the mattress and then remade it.

"I can't believe Flo is having you do this," Jeremy said. He canted to one side from his exhaustion, finally scooting the chair next to the wall so he could lean against it.

"She said that I had learned many important skills while I lived with Gabe, and there was no reason I couldn't continue to use them when we married. Thankfully she hasn't resorted to having me cook dinner."

"Thank God," Jeremy said with a snort of laughter. "You always were the worst of the three of us. When I knew it was your night to cook, I made sure I ate before coming home."

Richard pelted him with the dirty pillowcase. "You did not!" At Jeremy's laughter and nod, Richard shook his head.

"You don't mind one second, do you, Rich?"

Richard shared a small smile with Jeremy. "Not at all. I have Florence in my life, and she's content. If I need to change some beds or sweep a floor, I'm happy to do what I need. I got her back, Jer, and I'll do what I can to ensure she's happy."

Jeremy closed his eyes as he leaned his head against the wall. "Of course she's satisfied. She's a McLeod."

"Doesn't mean much when you're all alone," Richard said.

"Did I do anything to embarrass myself in front of Savannah, Rich?"

"Not that I know of. You were barely awake when she was here. She told you stories, read you part of that Oscar Wilde play you were reading. Flo heard her giggling a time or two over that one."

Richard tugged on Jeremy's arm, pulling him to his feet and then spinning him to the freshly made bed. "Ah, heaven," Jeremy said with a sigh. "Thanks, Rich."

"Before you fall asleep, take your medicine, Jer. I have no desire to force it down your throat again."

Jeremy opened his eyes and furrowed his brow in question, as he watched Richard approach him with a spoon and a bottle of medicine.

"You were a beast, thrashing and fighting as I tried to get this down you. More ended on your chest and neck than in you. I even had to sit on you once, although it only made you fight harder."

Jeremy flushed and looked away. "Sorry, Rich. I didn't know what I was doing."

"I know. I didn't fully understand what I was attempting or what you'd been through until now. Forgive me for not comprehending what you'd experienced."

Jeremy nodded, taking the spoon and shuddering as he swallowed the metallic-flavored medicine. "There's no way you could. You weren't there."

Richard raised his eyebrows and returned the medicine to the bureau.

"Thanks, Rich," Jeremy murmured as his eyes closed, and he fell asleep.

CHAPTER 18

SAVANNAH DESCENDED THE STREETCAR at Haymarket and walked toward Salem Street, long shadows falling in the late afternoon. The streets bustled with passing carriages and carts, and the sidewalks were crowded with women, many of whom carried bulging baskets after a day of shopping. Men were sweeping Salem Street, cleaning away the remains of the day's market.

As she approached the small alleyway that led to the McLeods' house, she stopped short. "Jonas," Savannah breathed.

"Hello, darling wife," Jonas said. He wielded a walking stick in his left hand, pushing away those next to him on the sidewalk. His brown eyes shielded by his hat did not prevent her from seeing a gleam of triumph within.

"I had not thought to find you in this area."

"Are you still searching for your long-dead daughter?" he sneered as he watched her. "I would have thought you'd have realized she'd died and given up the search. Although you always were without sense."

"What are you doing here, Jonas?"

"Have I no right to visit this part of town?" He glanced around at the other streetgoers dressed in work-roughened clothes. From his stylish hat and suit to his highly polished shoes, he stood out like an oasis of refinement, with those passing by careful not to jostle or mar his fine clothes.

"You've never expressed a desire before." Savannah stiffened as he leaned toward her. "I had thought you'd never leave the exalted environs of the Back Bay and commercial districts of Boston."

"This is why women will never be in business. They incapable of under-

147

standing the full extent that a man must go to in order to succeed. Even the most undesirable must be faced, Savannah, my love."

She paled at his endearment. "I wish you success with your business. I must go."

Jonas moved toward her, backing her up until she was pressed against a wall. "Do you think I don't know you visit those wretched McLeods? I find it nearly unforgiveable you have formed such a friendship as the one with Clarissa's schoolteacher friend. I will learn everything there is to know about you, wife. You are mine, and never forget it."

"I am no one's," Savannah declared. She stood on her toes in an attempt to escape touching Jonas in any way.

"No, you are mine until I deem you no longer desirable." He laughed mockingly. "You never were desirable. But you are mine until you are no longer worth my attention."

He leaned away, looking to his right and left, a charming smile aimed at the worried glances of those passing by. "I expect you at the house this evening, Mrs. Montgomery. You've been away for nearly four months, and I want you home. I'd hate for you to need too many lessons."

Savannah shivered, unable to hide her revulsion and fear at his words.

He nodded at her and spun, walking away.

Savannah's body shook, but she fisted her hands and forced herself to remain standing and not crumple to the ground. She tried to smile at those walking past her, but they were seen as though through a rain-drenched windowpane. Blinking her eyes only made the tears fall, and she paused to wipe them away before continuing her walk to the McLeods' home.

Savannah turned down the mouth of their alley, no men loitering at this hour. The air was thick, heavy with the scent of rotting vegetables and trash. She glanced toward the sky, wondering if the darkening clouds would lead to any relief of the overwhelming stench. On their doorstep, she took a deep breath and rapped on the door.

"Savannah," Florence said. "It's wonderful to see you. Our invalid is on the mend." Florence smiled, only to frown after a moment, perplexed as Savannah remained silent. "Please, come in. I'll make us some tea."

Savannah followed her, not sparing a glance for Jeremy's room. She slumped onto the couch, barely missing the cat. At its yowl in protest, she emerged from her dazed stupor. Florence sat next to her, the tea forgotten.

"Savannah? What happened?"

"I met Jonas a few blocks from here." Savannah gripped her skirts in an attempt to still her hands from shaking.

"Did he hurt you?" Florence placed one of her hands over Savannah's, her gentle touch imparting solidarity and comfort.

"No. But just seeing him terrifies me." She exhaled a stuttering breath. "He demanded I return to his house tonight."

Florence stilled, her jaw clenching for a moment before she relaxed into the couch. "Will you?"

"Of course not. I can imagine how irate he'll be, and it will be that much worse the next time I see him. I hate that merely seeing him reminds me of the power he once had over me. That he is able to instill fear in me with such ease."

"I don't know why you'd believe he'd have any less. You've never confronted him over his callous disregard and mistreatment of you."

"Only a suffragist would envision a woman could confront a grown man."

"It's how it should be. How it will be one day. Women will have rights, independent of those of their husbands, and those rights will be defended by the courts and law." Florence's passion-filled, purposeful gaze challenged Savannah. "Besides, you've barely been away from him. You need time to recover from what he did to you."

"Thank you, Florence." Savannah gripped her hands. "How is Jeremy?"

"Improved, although still weak. Most likely irritated you haven't gone in to visit him."

"His fever's broken then?"

"Yes. The doctor visited again today and thinks the higher dose of quinine will prevent any further relapses."

"I hope he's correct." She bit her lip as she stared toward the far wall. She squinted as she turned to face Florence. "If the doctor came again, the cost ate into your meager savings even more, didn't it Florence?"

Florence burst out into joyful laughter and then continued to smile broadly. She brushed aside a stray black curl and pushed her glasses more firmly onto the bridge of her nose. "No, it didn't. Richard had written his uncle, telling him our news, and Uncle Aidan sent us money for a baby fund. He was quite generous."

"Oh, that's wonderful!" Savannah gripped Florence's hands. "I couldn't be happier for you."

"Nor I. Richard tried to hide his concern, but he wasn't successful. I am so thankful for his generous uncle. I wish he would return to Boston. Aidan would have his reunion with Jeremy and see Richard again. He's never visited since we married, and I've yet to meet him."

"Did he mention visiting in his note?"

"He said something about the fall. He's quite busy with work, and he now has a home in Missoula. I try not to be envious of Gabriel, having frequent contact with Aidan. After all, Richard has Jeremy. But I know Richard dearly misses the support and guidance from someone who knew his father."

"I wish Clarissa and Gabriel would come home," Savannah whispered.

"I fear that's a dream that will never come to fruition. I doubt you'll ever see Clarissa in Boston again."

"I'm afraid you are correct." Savannah sighed before straightening her shoulders. "I should visit with Jeremy a few moments before returning to Sophie's."

Florence nodded and Savannah rose. She walked down the hallway and poked her head around the door frame. She smiled as she saw Jeremy lying on his back with his hands crossed over his belly, his head turned toward the door. His green eyes opened, and he grinned upon seeing her.

"I hoped you'd visit me. I could no longer hear your voices, and I feared you would leave without coming to speak with me first," he said.

Savannah moved into the room, sitting on the chair facing him, rather than her customary chair closer to him. She catalogued his features. He had a four-day growth of stubble that enhanced rather than detracted from his looks. The black beard, along with his ebony hair, made his green eyes appear an even deeper, darker hue. His cheeks were more concave, and the rigid control that he exuded was absent.

"You're still recovering," Savannah whispered as she reached out to straighten his sheets and blankets. She blushed, stilling her motion just as she was about to lean over him. "Forgive me. I know you have the strength to do this now."

"I'll never be saddened if a beautiful woman wants to care for me," Jeremy said with husky humor in his voice.

Savannah settled in her seat again but not before Jeremy grabbed her fingers and clasped her hand. He raised fatigued, thankful eyes to her. "Thank you for taking such good care of me while I was ill and giving Flo time to rest."

"It was my pleasure," Savannah whispered. "I'm glad you're recovering and will soon be back to work."

Jeremy groaned as he rolled onto his side, releasing Savannah's hand in the process. "I doubt I'll be working for a few days yet. The thought of walking there makes me break out in a sweat."

"How long does it generally take you to recover?"

"Up to a week. Generally not much longer."

"But this time the doctor thinks he has treated you so that you will not have a recurrence."

"I can tell you that, if I do have a malaria ague again, I'm not taking that wretched medicine." Jeremy shuddered at the thought. "It's part of the reason why I was never fully treated. I fought them so hard not to take it that they gave up."

"You mean you'd rather be ill, for years to come, than suffer through a few days of taking a horrid-tasting medication?" Savannah shook her head in disgust.

"You haven't tried it."

"And you're a fool not to take what might cure you. I wouldn't think you'd relish living through too many more bouts of malaria."

Jeremy sighed and then shivered.

Savannah frowned and raised his blankets up over his shoulders so only his head was visible.

"You're right of course. And thank you."

"I'm wearing you out. I should leave," Savannah said, unable to resist stroking a hand along his head and brushing the hair off his forehead.

"Come visit me when I've recovered. At the workshop." He reached up a hand from inside the blanket to grasp hers.

Savannah's eyes shone with pleasure. "Send word once you are recovered." He nodded, gripping her hand a moment before releasing it. She turned to face him as she opened the door and met his intense gaze before slipping into the hallway and departing for home.

CHAPTER 19

SUN STREAMED INTO THE HIGH WINDOWS of the workshop. Dust motes danced in the air as Jeremy stood at his workbench sanding a piece of cherrywood, humming an off-key version of "Ta-Ra-Ra-Boom-De-Ay" to himself as he worked. A drawing of a square table was tacked to the wall in front of him along with different design ideas for carving. A small pile of wood lay against the wall next to his workbench. Chisels, metal files and other tools hung from a board attached to the brick wall behind the workbench. In the corner of the room, near the stove and rocking chair Gabriel had created for Clarissa, was a small pallet on the floor for the nights when he worked late or didn't want to return home.

He studied the drawing of the design he wanted to carve into the wood. He took his pencil and tried to trace the design onto the wood, a faint line showing on the raw, unvarnished maple. He took out a chisel and began the slow process of carving.

Although he attempted to focus solely on his work, his mind continued to wander to Savannah. Nearly two weeks had passed since he'd last seen her, and she'd yet to visit him at his workshop. He grunted his displeasure as he nicked off an extra sliver of wood, causing the arch to be wider than desired at the corner of his design. He blew on the wood dust and extracted a smaller, finer chisel to carve more slowly but with more precision.

What did it say about him that she only wanted to see him when he was insensate? Had he acted in an improper manner when she had cared for him? He sighed, cursing the malaria and his inability to remember her ministrations while he was ill.

A gentle tapping at the door caused Jeremy to lay down his chisel. He glanced at the carving with a scowl before wiping his hands on his worn pants and striding toward the door. He pulled the door open and nodded at the sight of Savannah on his doorstep, the scent of a crisp October day clinging to her.

"Hello, ma'am. It's nice to see you again." He motioned for her to enter.

She hovered near the door as he moved toward the workbench. He rolled his shoulders a few times, as though in an attempt to release pent-up tension. As he picked up his chisel, she said, "If you're too busy for a visit, there's no need for me to stay."

He paused his motion before placing down the chisel. He stood facing away from her for a moment before turning to her, his expression carefully neutral. Savannah studied him, noting the healthy color on his cheeks.

"You didn't shave after you recovered," Savannah said with a small smile. Jeremy rubbed absently at his beard and shook his head no. "I like it. You look healthy." *Virile*, her mind whispered, and she looked away as she fought a blush.

"You look better too, Mrs. Montgomery, than the last time you visited me here at the workshop."

Anger flashed through her eyes, and a flush, brought on by irritation rather than embarrassment, limned her cheeks. "Never call me by that name again. Call me, ma'am. Call me Savannah, but never Mrs. Montgomery. Not you."

Jeremy let out a pent-up breath and relaxed a fraction at her anger. "I had hoped you'd call sooner. After caring for me while I was ill, I had hoped …"

Savannah shrugged her shoulders in response.

"I'm sorry if my discussion about imaginations frightened you away."

"No, no, of course it didn't," Savannah said. "I'm sorry I've stayed away for so long."

"Why did you?" Jeremy frowned at the faint longing he heard in his voice. "Why did you only come to see me when I was out of my mind with fever?"

"I was advised that a liaison, with any man, was not to my advantage at this time."

"Due to the divorce proceedings?"

"No. Well, not only because of that but mainly because I finally have the opportunity to learn what I desire from life free of the influence of a man or family."

Jeremy took a quick step toward her before stopping himself and attempting to hide the anger from his voice. "Do you think I would try to bend you to my will? To make you see things as I do? That I would be disappointed if you had your own thoughts and ideas?"

Savannah searched his gaze, and a wondrous smile bloomed. "No. I don't. It's why I decided to finally ignore that advice and visit you again. I've missed you." Savannah moved from the door and walked toward the rocking chair. She removed her coat and hat, sitting with a small sigh.

Jeremy tracked her movements, an intense longing in his eyes. "I've missed you, too. Not seeing you has made me nearly mad with frustration."

"Why?"

"I worried I had offended you in some way. That you had decided you no longer desired our friendship. Not being able to talk with you ..." He paused and shook his head. "I've taken to sleeping most nights here on the pallet, so that Florence and Richard don't have to contend with my black mood."

"I'm sorry, Jeremy. I was attempting to follow the advice of those who care for me. However, the more I did, the more miserable I became. I realized I was obtaining no further clarity remaining away from you than if I visited you."

Jeremy nodded with a half smile before becoming serious. "Any word on the divorce?"

Savannah jerked and stopped rocking. "None," she said in a dull voice. "I can't do what they say I must." She looked up, startled to find Jeremy crouched by her side.

"And what is that?" He took one of her hands in his, massaging her fisted hand until it relaxed in his.

"They want me to detail every episode of abuse at his hands. They say it's necessary for any proceedings to be successful." She stared into Jeremy's eyes, his calm acceptance encouraging her to continue. "And I can't! I can't speak of everything that happened."

"Why not?" He squeezed her hand gently in support. "As I said before, there's no shame in survival."

"If there's no shame, then why am I filled with it as I imagine the newspaper stories and their lurid headlines? Why do I feel as though it were my fault?"

"If you are unwilling to detail what you suffered for the sake of the court case, you may find there is nothing you can do, Savannah," he murmured. "You may find that there is no way to obtain a divorce."

"I can't accept remaining his wife," Savannah said as she attempted to blink away tears.

Jeremy reached toward her, pulling her onto his lap as he settled onto the floor.

At first Savannah stiffened, but soon she relaxed.

Jeremy whispered, "Why? Why does it bother you to remain his wife if you aren't living with him?"

"Because he may believe he still has some rights over me."

He crooned, rocking her and brushed a hand over her head and down her back. "Sometimes, even though we don't get what we think we want, it all turns out for the best."

"How can you say that?" She sniffled and leaned deeper into his embrace.

"Well, I'm sitting here, with you in my arms. And no matter what happens, it brought us together," he whispered into her ear, kissing the side of her neck.

"Jeremy," she breathed as she leaned her head to the side to allow him better access. "I am a married woman."

"In name only. In all the ways that matter, you are free. Free to decide what it is you want." She shivered at his words. "Tell me to stop. Tell me that you don't desire me, and I will …"

"No," Savannah protested, turning her head to kiss him. "No, I want … " She moaned as the kiss intensified. Jeremy carefully moved her up so that she was facing him, and soon they were kneeling in front of each other.

He leaned away for a moment, breaking contact.

"No, please," Savannah whispered as she reached out to twine her arms around his neck.

"I know things between you and your husband must have been difficult," Jeremy said as he kissed her under her chin.

Savannah shivered. "I don't want to think about him. About any of that."

"I know. I don't either." He leaned away and met her passion-filled gaze. "I want you to know I will only ever touch you with care. If at any moment I do or say something that you do not like, tell me."

Savannah leaned forward and kissed him for a long minute before breaking the kiss and nibbling on his ear. "The only thing that would make me upset is if you stopped. I never knew I could feel like this. That this was what it was supposed to be like."

Jeremy smiled at her dazed admission. "My love," he murmured, "let me lock the door." He nuzzled her cheek, caressed her shoulders and rose, striding purposefully toward the door to lock it. He turned to gaze in wonder at Savannah waiting for him.

"Let me," he whispered, moving toward a far wall. He opened a rusty trunk, extracting a few worn wool blankets and placing them over his pallet. He spread them on the floor and held his hand out toward Savannah. "It isn't nearly fine enough for you. I—" He broke off, glancing away with embarrassment as she continued to stare at him.

He returned his gaze to hers. "Forgive my presumption," he muttered, as he turned away to stare at the wall.

After a few moments, he heard her rise, and he closed his eyes in agony as he imagined her making her way toward the door and departing. Jeremy flinched as he felt her hands tracing the contours of his back through his thin shirt. He spun to face her. "I thought you'd leave."

"Never." Her luminous smile lit her eyes with joy. "Kiss me." She leaned toward him, and he clasped her against his chest.

"I don't want you to regret this." His worried gaze took in her exultant expression, and he half smiled.

"Never."

He leaned toward her, teasing her lips with his before kissing her deeply. They collapsed to the blankets, on their knees again, facing each other. "I promise to be gentle. To always treat you with respect."

"I know," she whispered as she kissed his neck. "Show me what I've missed all this time."

**

SAVANNAH NESTLED HER HEAD on Jeremy's shoulder, attempting to banish her anxiety and fear at his continued silence. She pushed herself up, deciding she should leave.

"No, don't go. Stay with me," he murmured, caressing her back. He curved his head down to kiss her tenderly.

"For how long?" Savannah teased.

"Forever." He sighed as he gathered her close. Savannah stilled, her tension mounting. "Shh, forget I said that. I'm sorry."

"You don't mean what you said?"

"Of course I do, but I don't want you to worry. I have no expectations."

Savannah pushed herself up, gripping a blanket to her chest as she glared down at Jeremy. "Why? Am I so unworthy?" Tears glistened in her eyes, and she moved to stand.

Jeremy sat up and grabbed her hips, pulling her onto his lap. "Not so fast." Savannah struggled to break free of his hold, but he clasped her firmly. "Don't fight, love. Don't hurt yourself."

She lowered her head, and he heard a soft sob. "Oh, God, don't cry, my Savannah," he pleaded in a tortured voice, tilting her face to his to kiss away the tears.

"Please listen to me. Please," he begged. "I'm not worthy of you. I should never have touched you."

"Don't say such things," she hiccupped.

"You look at me and have no idea the monster I was," he rasped. "These hands"—he held one out to the side to stare at it——"I've used them to hurt so many people."

"I don't believe you."

He let out a cynical laugh. "The things I've done make Jonas look like an angel." He closed tormented eyes. Savannah squirmed in his lap, and he released her. "Leave. You have every right to."

Instead, she leaned away to better study his face. She cradled it in her palms. "Tell me, Jeremy. Tell me why you would ever think that way." She leaned forward and rubbed her nose with his.

"I killed men, tortured men, when I was in the Philippines. I raided villages, helped to burn them to the ground, hurt innocent people." He shook his head with his eyes closed as though trying to quell the memories. "War is subjugating others to your will, and it is so ugly."

"Were you following orders?"

"Yes," he whispered.

"Then how are you to blame? You did what every soldier has to do."

"You don't understand, Savannah. When you're in battle, a sick appreciation for killing can come over you. I was so good at killing."

"Oh, my dearest," she murmured. She leaned into him, kissing his cheeks, his closed eyes and his eyebrows. "I can't say it doesn't matter, because it does. It matters because it hurts you still." She caressed his cheeks, waiting patiently until he opened his eyes and met hers. "Someday you will banish this agony. Let me help you." She continued to stroke his back, his hair, his arms, ending at his hands.

"I don't deserve you, Savannah." He groaned as he clasped her to him and pulled her more firmly to him onto his lap. He bent his head, resting it against the curve of her neck and shoulder.

"I think you do," she whispered before she kissed him softly on his head.

Jeremy held her tightly, lost in the moment and her.

***

JEREMY STROKED A HAND down Savannah's back. She lay sprawled on top of his chest. "Savannah, Savannah, my love. You have to wake and dress. It's already late for you to be returning to Mrs. Chickering's."

"I don't want to go," Savannah mumbled against his chest.

Jeremy sighed with contentment. "I don't want you to either. But the last thing I want is to lose any esteem in that woman's eyes. I would hate to be barred from you."

"She would never bar you," Savannah said, and he could feel her smile against his neck as she kissed him. "Though I don't want to test that theory." She leaned up, pushing away her disheveled hair. "Help me dress?"

"With the greatest reluctance," he said, stealing a quick kiss.

When Savannah was fully dressed, he walked her to the door. "Savannah …"

She held up her fingers to his lips, silencing him. "Come see me tomorrow? Take me on a walk, have tea with me, anything?" Her voice rose hopefully.

"With the greatest pleasure," he whispered, kissing her again. He opened the door, reluctantly released her hand and watched her walk toward the stairs. She smiled again as she paused at the head of the stairs, and then she was gone.

CHAPTER 20

"SOPHIE, I INVITED SOMEONE to have tea with us today," Savannah said. Bright sunlight streamed in through the bow-fronted windows. A tea tray sat on a low table in front of the chairs and settee, largely untouched.

"No need to look nervous, Savannah. Florence is always welcomed here," Sophie said as she settled into her chair.

"I didn't invite Florence."

Aunt Betsy sat, her cane falling to the floor with a loud *thwack*, and she leaned forward in her chair to study Savannah. "You're more like Clarissa than you ever let on, aren't you?"

"I think I must be," Savannah said. "Mother would be most displeased."

Sophronia squinted at Savannah for a moment. "You've invited that McLeod brother, haven't you?"

"Yes. And he should be arriving any moment."

"What do you hope to gain from such a liaison?" Aunt Betsy asked.

"I don't know. But he treats me well. Truly listens to me," Savannah said.

"You can't hope for marriage while you're still tied to Jonas," Aunt Betsy said.

"I know, Aunt. I'm trying not to think too much about the future," Savannah whispered.

"Is that fair to him?" Sophie asked. "Although I worry you are becoming entangled too soon after your separation from your husband, I'm also concerned for him. He seemed to be someone who needed ... to come back to himself after his misadventures in the Philippines. There are plenty of worthy causes to devote your time to, Savannah. I would enjoy having another friend and confidante at the weekly suffragist meetings."

"Thank you, Sophie, but I do not see myself agitating for the vote. I wouldn't know what to do with it."

"Think for yourself for a change, that's what. Be able to fight for your rights, rather than waiting on a courtroom full of men. Wouldn't you rather have had the ability to be seen as Jonas's equal in the eyes of the law rather than as his chattel?"

"I think you go too far, Sophie," Savannah said.

"I don't go far enough. It's about time you realized that, if you'd had more rights, rights that men take for granted every day, then you would not be in the predicament you find yourself in. You'd have the money your grand-parents set aside for you. You would not be a social pariah. You would be able to chart the course for your life as you see fit, not as the men of this world see it."

"Sophie, no matter how much you argue for the vote, I will not be swayed. I can only see harm coming from women believing they have the same rights as men. Women don't, and never will, have the same rights."

"Of course they will, Savannah."

All three women spun toward the doorway at Jeremy's voice. Savannah flushed at him overhearing their conversation.

"Mrs. Chickering, nice to see you again," Jeremy said. He nodded toward Aunt Betsy, "Mrs. Parker, nice to meet you. I've heard a lot about you."

"Sit, young man, and cease with the social niceties," Sophronia barked. "Are you saying that you believe that women have the same rights as men?"

"No, I'm not. They don't have the same rights as men. But they should," Jeremy said as he accepted a cup of tea from Betsy with a smile. "And with women like you, they will."

"Why would you believe that?" Sophronia asked.

"My mother was forward-thinking. I don't know if she would have called her-self a suffragist, but I'm confident, if she had lived, she would have joined the movement. She believed in education for all, not just for the wealthy or for men.

"I heard her and my da discuss politics regularly. He always listened to her opinion, argued with her as though what she said had merit. And the irony was, although she was the more educated of the two, she was the one who couldn't vote."

"Ah, so you had a good example," Aunt Betsy said with a satisfied nod.

"Yes, until they died unexpectedly. I was quite young, and yet I still remember those discussions. They believed their boys should be members of the world and of Boston, and should be aware of what occurred in the world as well as in this city—although I'm sure they sheltered us from the truly horrible news."

"As all parents should," Sophie said.

"I'm confused by you, Savannah. Why don't you believe women will have the same rights as men?" Jeremy asked.

"If the movement can't even convince me, who has as strong a reason as any woman to strive for more rights, that an increase in my rights will lead to an improvement in my life, then the movement will always falter," Savannah said. "Why should I believe that men such as my husband would ever allow women to vote?"

"Not all men behave as your husband or Cameron," Jeremy said, his mouth tightening with displeasure.

Sophie scowled. "I can never foresee a time when a woman is as strong physically as a man. But she can outsmart him. And when she has the same protections as a man under the law, can work the same professions as a man and is seen to have as much worth as a man, then she will be his equal. Not all strength comes from brute force or violence, dearest."

"I understand what you are saying, Sophie. But what you envision will bring discord and disharmony."

"Has the current situation brought you peace?" Sophie asked, unable to hide her impatience. "You must start to see your life in a new light. You can't continue to allow the old teachings to blight your future. Nor the future of the women of this country."

"I can't believe Clarissa had as radical ideas as you," Savannah said.

"You'd be surprised," Sophie said with a satisfied smile as her gaze became distant. "I shocked her regularly of course. It's one of my many talents." Sophie raised an eyebrow at Jeremy as he bit back a chuckle. "However, she knew that women needed more rights in order to live more fulfilling lives. Why should Florence have to lose her teaching position merely because she was seen in a tea shop with a man not of her family? Or Clarissa hers because she is now a married woman? Men can see whomever they choose and carry on any sort of lurid act they like and keep their teaching posts. Married men can teach. They aren't seen as a threat to the purity of the young minds they instruct."

At this Jeremy was unable to hide his laughter. "You are very forward in your thinking, and I know it will be some time before society believes as you do."

"That is true, young man. I'm afraid I am ahead of my time." She took a sip of her tea. "Your visit here today is fortuitous. I have news to impart that affects both of you."

"Does it concern the divorce?" Savannah asked.

"In a way. Because you are unwilling to detail the extent of your abuse at your husband's hands, it's impossible for the lawyers to put forth a motion for cruelty. They cannot depend on the testimony of third parties. Thus, I am now certain that any divorce proceedings against Jonas would only fill the coffers of the city's many papers and lead to an undesired infamy."

"So this means Savannah will be tied to Jonas forever," Jeremy said.

"Yes. She will continue to be perceived as his wife. She will remain Mrs. Montgomery." Sophie pinned Savannah with a fierce stare with her aquamarine eyes. "And, as long as you are, visits to a warehouse on Canal Street need to cease."

"You can't dictate what I do, who I'm friends with or where I go, Sophie," Savannah said with a defiant tilt of her chin.

"No, but I am willing to buy off only so many newspapermen. Do you know how much they are charging for their silence about your illicit visits?" Sophie asked.

Savannah paled as Aunt Betsy gasped.

"Who are they?" Jeremy asked.

"I will not tell you, as I enjoy your company and do not wish to see you act in an irrational manner," Sophie said. "However, those intrepid men know there is a story behind your defection and are intent on determining the exact cause as to your abandoning Mr. Montgomery. They would like nothing better than to have a reason to entice you to tell them the truth. Preferably in a serial format so that they could bleed their readers of more of their hard-earned money."

"What am I to do?" Savannah asked, rising from her chair and pacing to the front window.

"Cease your visits to see Mr. McLeod. If you must, visit Florence when he might be home. But do not give them a reason to continue their interest in you. There is only so much I can do to protect you."

"You've just added to my belief as to why women and men will never be seen as equal, Sophie," Savannah said, bitterness lacing her tone.

"Simply because you are unable to do as you please now doesn't mean the future must always remain as it is," Sophie snapped. "Don't become petulant. You've fought too hard for the life you are now leading."

"What do you think, Jeremy?" Aunt Betsy asked after an awkward pause.

"I believe Savannah should listen to the advice of those who mean her well, consider what it is she wants and then do as she believes is best for her. Advising Savannah on how she must act, and then becoming, well, petulant"—he gave a wry smile to Sophronia—"when she questions that advice, only undermines her faith in her ability to make her own decisions."

Sophie barked with laughter. "Well said, young man. Well said. However, it does not diminish the threat from the reporters."

"No. You also presume Savannah wishes to continue her visits to Canal Street." Jeremy clenched his hands in his lap.

"Do not insult my intelligence," Sophie said. "Savannah, come and join us again."

Savannah walked from the window area to her chair and sat. She gazed with a distant expression at the empty fireplace. "I want to continue to have the freedom to move about Boston as I choose. However, if I'm not pursuing a divorce because I don't want the infamy, I also have no desire for the newspapermen to take an interest in my personal life."

"Nor would I imagine you want Jonas aware of your interest in Mr. McLeod," Aunt Betsy said.

Savannah looked toward the windows. "He's been aware of my friendship with the McLeods for some time."

"What?" Jeremy asked.

Savannah met Jeremy's worried gaze. "When you were sick with malaria, I met him in the North End. He demanded I return to him that evening."

"That was a few weeks ago," Jeremy said. "Why did you never mention it?"

"I don't know. I'm tired of being afraid of him. Of having every conversation be about him. I had hoped he'd leave me be."

"It seems this is most likely his way of enticing you home," Sophronia said. She tapped the arm of her chair. "I wonder what business he, a businessman among the wealthiest of this town, would have in the North End."

"He said it was one of the reasons women would never be a man's equal. The fact I had so little understanding of business that I couldn't fathom his presence there," Savannah said.

"Pompous fool. Although I wish it were otherwise, I'm sure we'll know in time his business."

"Did he hurt you, dearest?" Aunt Betsy asked, reaching a gnarled hand out to stroke Savannah's arm.

"No, not at all. Although I hated seeing him. At the time, it seemed he only knew about my visiting Florence in the North End."

"Then it is even more imperative that he does not discover your visits to the workshop," Sophie said. "For no matter what you say, I fear he is far from rational. He sees you as a plaything, and he's far from finished toying with you—or your friends."

Savannah shivered and shared a worried look with Jeremy. "I'm afraid you may be correct."

"If you do not object, Mrs. Chickering, I would like to continue to call here," Jeremy said.

"You may, young man, but not daily. Perhaps you should come with a portfolio as though you are discussing a project with us?" She smiled. "That way, we will be able to tell the newspapermen that you are here on business."

"You may complete the commission your brother started but failed to finish when he departed nearly two years ago," Betsy said. "Why don't you return tomorrow to discuss it further? I find I'm too tired to consider detailing all I desire in the piece today."

Jeremy watched her, his concern fading as he noted her sly smile. "Of course, Mrs. Parker. It would be my pleasure."

"If you could come by around two, that would be most agreeable," Sophie said.

"Oh, I agree," Betsy said.

"Aren't you visiting your parents tomorrow afternoon?" Savannah asked Aunt Betsy.

"Exactly, dearest. Exactly," Aunt Betsy said with a triumphant smile. Sophronia cackled her delight, and Jeremy grinned at the conspirators.

He smiled at Savannah as he rose. "Thank you for inviting me to tea. I look forward to tomorrow." He nodded, his glance lingering on Savannah, before he turned and left.

"Well, my dear," Aunt Betsy said. "Now I understand why you ignored Sophie's advice. I'd be hard pressed to stay away from such a man."

Sophronia *harrumphed*, but Savannah noted a smile playing around her lips. "He seems a decent man. I hope he proves himself as worthy as his brother."

"So do I," Savannah whispered.

CHAPTER 21

"WHAT HAS UPSET YOU, sweet Savannah?" Jeremy asked. He reached out to trace the line of her jaw, hoping to infuse a bit of color in her ashen cheeks. He glanced around the small sitting room at the back of the house, noticing they were alone.

"Have you seen the papers?" Savannah asked. She thrust one at him and spun toward the door to lock it. "I have no desire for the maid or others to overhear our conversation and profit from it."

He noted the article's headline, "Back Bay Socialite Abandons Mansion for Carpenter's Dusty Warehouse." Jeremy looked up and met Savannah's stricken eyes. "Who talked to them?"

"I don't know," Savannah whispered. "If they know about you, then you're in danger, Jeremy."

"Don't worry about my safety, darling. I can fend for myself." He scanned the article, frowning and shaking his head as he finished it. "What a bunch of worthless twaddle." He tossed it onto a small side table. "They suspect you are visiting someone in the Haymarket area because you are seen frequenting the neighborhood and because your cousin married a cabinetmaker. They suspect you are conducting an affair after your defection from your husband's home four months ago. Although my identity has yet to be confirmed, if I even exist."

He reached out and stroked her shoulders. "You're not seeking a divorce. It doesn't matter, love. It's just idle curiosity." He caressed her cheek. "Although I hate to admit it, I think Sophie's right. You need to cease visiting me."

"I need to see you," Savannah said as she leaned into him. "I hate that this might keep us apart."

"It will only prevent us from having time alone at my warehouse. It won't prevent me from seeing you. You can visit Flo, and I can call here. We have the perfect excuse for me to visit, thanks to your aunt."

"If you come here too frequently, some might become suspicious," Savannah whispered. "You shouldn't need to discuss the design of a cabinet too many times or people will wonder about your competence. I'd hate for your business to suffer."

"I could claim that we are discussing our mutual relatives," Jeremy said. "And there's nothing that says you must remain in Boston."

"I enjoy travel," Savannah said as she nestled her head on his shoulder. "At least I did when I traveled first class. I don't know what it would be like if I would travel now."

"The seats won't be as wide or as plush, but you end up in the same place. With more coin in your pocket," Jeremy teased.

"I'm not ready to leave yet."

"Start over. Start over with me," Jeremy said, unable to hide the trace of pleading from his voice. He cradled her face with his large hands. "I know you have no reason to put your faith in another man, but I promise you that I will treat you well. I ..."

Savannah shivered at his words and pushed away from him, any color from his embrace leeching away again. "You don't know what you're asking of me, Jeremy."

"I know you're the woman I want to be with. Together we can face anything. Can't you see that, darling?"

"No, I can't," Savannah said, her arms wrapped around and hugging her waist. "Due to my actions, I'm in this predicament, Mr. McLeod. This is my fate."

"So, I am back to *Mr. McLeod*. What happened between us means nothing?" Jeremy demanded, as he clasped her arms and shook her gently. "Why are you denying yourself a chance at happiness?"

"I can't marry you!" She pointed to the paper taunting her on the side table.

"I don't care," Jeremy said but then closed his eyes on a long sigh. "That's a lie. I do care. I want you. I want you as my wife." He opened tortured eyes to meet hers.

"No, you don't. Not really."

"Do you think I make love to women in my workshop frequently?" Jeremy demanded. "Or was that acceptable behavior for one of your class?" His flushed cheeks and rapid breathing betrayed his anger.

"I'm not who you think I am," Savannah murmured. Tears spilled from her eyes, and, before she could wipe at them, Jeremy had raised his hands to brush them away.

"What do you mean?" he whispered, as he leaned forward to kiss her cheek and the tears that continued to fall. She cried, gripping him to her.

Savannah refused to let him go. She didn't want him to see her face. "I can't have another child. Never again."

He leaned away, clasping her shoulders. "Tell me."

"When I had my baby, the doctor told Jonas that I had injured something inside me that prevented me from having any more children."

Jeremy pulled her close, his breath rasping in Savannah's ear. "I imagine your husband took great pleasure in tormenting you with this fact," Jeremy whispered. At Savannah's nod, his hold on her tightened. "I will not lie to you and tell you it does not matter to me." Savannah was unable to stifle a small sob at his words.

He leaned away from her, wiping tears from her cheeks and wisps of hair away, tucking a strand behind her left ear. "I have dreamed, unwillingly, of seeing you heavy with our child. Of knowing that we were to share the dream of a child." Savannah nodded a few times, her eyes losing any vibrancy and becoming dulled with pain. "But listen to me and listen to me well, my love. My dream is to be with you. To wake with you by my side every day. To talk with you, knowing that no matter my demons or dreams, you will accept them and me.

"Understand me, Savannah. I want you, the woman. The woman who was strong enough to stand up to her husband. The woman who would fight to find her child. The woman who never became bitter or angry with the world but is still filled with sweetness and goodness. The woman who looks at me and does not shy away from what she sees. If we are not to have children, we will bear that. What I cannot bear is to be without you."

"You say this now, but you won't be content a few years from now. You'll want more and become dissatisfied with me," Savannah whispered.

"You must have faith in me, darling. Faith in my love for you. Has it been so long since someone has loved you?" Jeremy whispered, wiping away fresh tears.

Savannah closed her eyes before meeting his with her sorrow-filled eyes. "Yes. There has always needed to be a reason for someone to love me. My dowry. The prestige I would bring the family. My beauty."

"I can't lie and say I don't love your beauty," Jeremy teased. "But I love you, my darling. I hope someday you can believe in it."

"Help me to believe," Savannah whispered as she leaned into Jeremy, kissing him. He kissed her gently before moving to kiss her neck.

"Savannah," he whispered. "Let me hold you. I ask of nothing more from you," he whispered as he traced soft circles on her back.

She froze in his arms for a moment before relaxing again in his gentle embrace. He murmured, "Shh, don't fret so, love. I desire you. I will always desire you. But I don't want you to think that is all I want."

Savannah burrowed into him, seeking more of his comforting touch. "Thank you, Jeremy." She felt a whisper of a kiss against her head and stood there, for many minutes, in contented silence in his embrace.

Savannah whispered after a while. "What are we to do?"

"What do you want to do?" Jeremy asked.

"I want to run away from here with you," she said on a long sigh.

"No, you don't," Jeremy said with a tender smile. "The Savannah I know and love would want to face what is occurring here before embarking on a new life."

"Will you wait for me?" she whispered.

"Of course, my love," he murmured as he leaned forward and kissed her fleetingly.

"Will you visit again tomorrow?" Savannah asked as he moved toward the door.

"Of course," he whispered, grasping her hand to kiss her fingers.

**

SAVANNAH SAT IN THE REAR sitting room, contemplating Jeremy's visit. After a while, she heard raised voices coming from the front of the house. She rose, tiptoeing down the stairs and hallway to the doorway of Sophronia's yellow front sitting room. Angry voices emerged from there, and

Savannah paused in midstep as she recognized the voices. She peered around the doorway, awed by Sophronia and her lack of fear in the face of Jonas's wrath.

"How dare you continue to keep a married man from his wife?" Jonas intoned. "You have been warned, Mrs. Chickering, that I will take action against you for harboring her."

"And what exactly will be the charge, Mr. Montgomery? Do you truly wish the court to hear all of your vile escapades against your wife?"

"No one will hear anything of the sort," Jonas hissed. "The courtroom remains under the domain of men. It is one of the many ways men continue to shelter women from the harsher realities of the world."

"More likely it is one of the many ways you deprive us of our rights and then declare you do so out of your interest in our welfare. How dare you enter my home, and threaten me and my guest?"

"And how dare you enter my house and encourage my wife to leave me," Jonas snapped.

"If she had been content with your company and treatment, such an offer would never have been enticing. However, I fear that one too many encounters with your fist or your boot showed her your true colors."

"I want my wife back." Jonas stood in an attempt to make Sophronia cower.

"Never," Sophie said, standing and glaring at him. "You will never have her back."

"If you think she will find happiness with another man, I will find him and kill him. She is mine."

"No, she is her own person. She belongs to no one," Sophronia said.

"Damn your infernal meddling, woman!" Jonas roared, striking Sophronia severely across the cheek, sending her flying. Her head hit a side table with a resounding smack, and she collapsed onto the floor.

Savannah screamed for the butler and maids, and, within moments, the room was filled with Sophronia's staff. At Savannah's yell, Jonas turned to stare at Savannah, his eyes gleaming in triumph.

"Ah, so there you are, my lovely wife," he said in a cool, calm voice as he blocked her entrance into the sitting room.

"Jonas, let me help Sophie," she said, moving to rush past him.

"No, there are plenty to help her," he said. He gripped her arm and pushed her against the wall in the hallway. "I fear you are in need of many lessons, Mrs. Montgomery."

Savannah began to shake at the soft predatory tone he had always used before one of his "lessons."

"No, I have no need, ever again, for lessons from you," Savannah said as she struggled. He held onto her wrists, gripping them fiercely to the point Savannah thought they would snap.

"You think not? You dared to leave me. You failed to return home after you were instructed to. You have much to repent for," Jonas said.

"Not as much as you, Jonas," Aunt Betsy snapped, bringing her cane down hard on his foot. As he turned toward her, howling in pain, she raised it up, whipping him across the face. He spun away from Savannah and landed facedown on the floor. "Never touch my niece again."

"Come, Savannah. Let us see to Sophie. The police and doctor will be here soon. I rang them when I heard the commotion."

"Aunt Betsy," Savannah whispered with relief.

"Yes, dear, I know," she said, patting Savannah's arm. As she attempted to maneuver around Jonas's prostrate form on the floor, she slipped and the full weight of her cane landed on Jonas's lower back. He howled again in pain. "Oh, do forgive me, Jonas. You know how these things happen."

Betsy glanced toward Sophronia's butler. "Will you ensure Mr. Montgomery remains here to speak with the police?"

"Of course, madam," Poole said with a feral glint in his eyes.

Savannah turned from him, looking toward her friend. "Sophie!" she cried as she saw the blood-soaked cloth the maid was holding at her forehead. Sophie rested on a settee, her skin alabaster white in contrast to her navy dress.

"Don't make such a racket," Sophie barked, though her voice was less forceful than usual. "My head doesn't need to pound any worse than it does already."

"Well, Sophronia," Betsy murmured with wry shake of her head, "I did not believe you needed to go to such extremes to show this man's cruelty."

Sophronia attempted to raise one eyebrow but grimaced in pain. "I hadn't envisioned he would become so enraged as to actually do me bodily harm." She looked toward Savannah worriedly. "I am more thankful now than ever that you are out of his sphere of power."

"I'm so sorry he hurt you," Savannah said as she took the cloth from the maid and held it to Sophronia's head.

Sophie speared her with an intense glare. "This is not your fault. His actions are not a reflection of you. He is his own person, and his actions reflect solely on him."

"Do you think this will help Savannah?" Betsy asked.

"We can hear what my lawyer says, but I'm afraid they'll construe his attack on me as a man losing control due to a passionate desire to be restored to his wife. Or some such drivel."

"The papers should hire you to write for them," Betsy said.

"Don't even start on those newspapermen. When I think of all I've paid them ..." She broke off as she heard commotion in the hallway. "Ah, Doctor, thank you for calling."

Savannah rose, tiptoeing to the door to watch as the police handcuffed Jonas and led him away. She smiled bitterly as she heard him bellowing about how he had suffered at the hands of Aunt Betsy.

Savannah returned to the sitting room and held Sophie's hand as the doctor competently stitched up her head.

"It'll hurt worse than you can imagine come tomorrow," he said. "I'll leave behind a little something for the pain but don't take too much of it. I'd hate for the feistiest woman I know to lose her bark due to this medication."

Savannah rose and walked him to the sitting room door where he turned to her and said, "Don't let her overdo it. She must rest the next few days. I'll return to ensure she isn't concussed." Savannah nodded her agreement and watched him descend the stairs.

"Well, Savannah?" Sophie asked.

"I don't know what to do," she whispered.

"This might be a time for what the generals call a strategic retreat."

CHAPTER 22

"WILL YOU WAIT HERE, sir, while I determine if she is at home?" the butler asked. He turned and walked up the stairs in an unhurried manner. After ten minutes had passed, Jeremy was allowed to enter into the smaller sitting room where he had visited Savannah yesterday.

"Mr. McLeod," Sophronia said from a chaise longue placed near the window. A desk had been pushed to one side to make room for the chaise.

Jeremy barely spared her a glance as he looked for Savannah. "Mrs. Chickering," he said formally with a small nod. "I hope you are well."

"She's not here, young man," Sophronia said with a hint of humor in her voice. His gaze veered toward her, and he blanched at the bruising all along the right side of her face and the bandage over her left ear.

"My God," he whispered as he moved toward her. He knelt by the chaise, cradling her hand in his. "What happened?"

"Mr. Montgomery paid us a visit."

"Jonas? That bastard did this to you? I'll—"

"No, stop right there, young man. Do not say anything I may need to perjure myself over in the future." She smiled ironically. "He visited, showed his true colors and was taken away by the police. He is being held on assault charges. As I am not his wife, I refuse to let such treatment toward me pass. More important it sets a precedent in the court that he is a violent man and capable of cruelty toward his wife."

"You intended for him to harm you?"

"Nonsense. I expected him to shout and rail against me, but never to hit me so hard I was tossed across the room. I may seem foolish in the pursuit of my goals, but I am more cautious than I am given credit for."

"Savannah. Where is Savannah?" Jeremy asked, unable to hide the panic from his eyes.

"She is safe."

"Did he hurt her? Terrorize her?"

"Your concern is well meaning, but she is fine."

"I need to see her. Ensure she is well," Jeremy said, his tightening grip on Sophronia's hand betraying his agitation.

"Mr. McLeod, why would you think that I would want my good friend to go from one man to another? She needs time to decide what she wants, free from a man's influence."

Jeremy paled as he leaned away from Sophronia, dropping her hand. "I would never harm her. I know you don't know me well enough to believe me," Jeremy said as he looked down.

"Nonsense," Sophronia barked. "If you are anything like your brother Gabriel, and so you have shown yourself to be these past months, then I have no doubt for her future with you. However, what Savannah needs is time, free of mischief from men. And that includes you."

"How long are you asking for?" Jeremy whispered.

"How long are you willing to remain apart?"

Jeremy paused, sensing that he was being tested. He rose, pacing the small room. "You want me to voluntarily cease any contact with Savannah?" At Sophronia's nod, Jeremy sighed and pinched the bridge of his nose. "I can't do that. Not because you ask me to. I would only do it if she asked it of me."

Sophronia smiled with approval. "Well done, young man. I like that you refuse to be manipulated, even by me. It shows a strength of character, which I think Savannah is going to need. Why don't we see what she has to say?"

***

RICHARD TRAVERSED THE WEST END, wandering in and out of bars looking for Jeremy. He began to think that Florence had sent him on a fool's errand when, after over an hour of searching, he found his brother at a bar near Scollay Square.

"Jer!" Richard said. "What are you doing here?" He elbowed his way to a space at the bar next to Jeremy.

"Trying to forget about the day." He raised an unsteady hand, holding a glass of beer as though in salute. "October 19, a day to obliterate from my memory."

"Why?" Richard asked.

"Savannah doesn't want to see me," Jeremy rasped as he took a long swig from his glass of beer. He closed his eyes as though trying to banish the reality of the words.

"I find that hard to believe," Richard said.

"Jonas was at Mrs. Chickering's house yesterday. Knocked her around pretty badly." He turned to share a long look with Richard. "Mrs. Chickering, not Savannah. Seems, now he's shown his true colors to such a degree that they can't be ignored, Savannah might be able to obtain her divorce. Be free of all men."

"Surely that isn't what she said?"

"She wants time away from me to decide what she wants. What type of life she wants," Jeremy rasped. "She'd told me that she had overcome her fears of being with me after Jonas. I guess when he showed her again what a bastard he really is, she reconsidered her decision."

"Jer, she was brutalized by him. Don't you want her to be certain that she truly wants to be with you?"

"My love for her doesn't matter."

"You know that isn't true, Jer," Richard said as he shook his head to ward off the bartender offering Jeremy another drink.

"Just a few days ago I told her that I loved her, that I could bear anything but not having her in my life," Jeremy murmured. He dropped his head onto his crossed arms on the oak bar. "It seems she doesn't feel the same way."

"Jer," Richard said, his voice filled with compassion.

Jeremy laughed humorlessly as he tilted his head to look at Richard. "What would you have done had Florence said the same to you?"

Richard sighed. "Much the same. Just like Gabe did when he was banished from Clarissa's life."

"But she didn't banish him," Jeremy argued.

"No, she didn't." Richard thought for a few moments. "How long a separation does she want?"

"As long as she needs," Jeremy said. "What does that mean? It could be a year."

"I doubt that. She seems to be someone who's not happy alone. Once she realizes what she had with you isn't easily replicated, she'll come back to you."

"What is it the poets said about love? What did Mum read us when we were kids?" Jeremy asked as he closed his eyes.

Richard let out a long sigh. "*'Tis better to have loved and lost than never to have loved at all.*"

Jeremy shared a rueful look with Richard. "What a bunch of rubbish. I bet that poet didn't know what this feels like."

"Are you saying you would rather have not met Savannah?"

Jeremy shook his head. "Of course not. So I guess the damn poet is right. Doesn't mean it hurts any less."

"No, of course not," Richard said. "Are you ready to go home and face Florence?"

"No," Jeremy said with a hint of a smile. "But let's go anyway."

"She'll be irate, you know," Richard said. "She likes Savannah, but you are her brother, and she doesn't like anyone hurting you."

***

"JEREMY!" FLORENCE EXCLAIMED as they entered the house. "What has happened? Is Savannah all right?" She held the growing swell of her belly as she was now seven months' pregnant and lowered herself into a chair. Jeremy gripped her free hand and sat next to her.

"No, Flo, I don't think she is. I don't know if she ever will be all right."

Florence looked toward Richard in confusion. "Why is Jeremy here with us rather than comforting her?"

"She doesn't want me near her."

Florence stilled, her entire body tensing at Jeremy's words. She clamped her jaw and spoke with precision. "She forbade you from seeing her again?"

"Yes, for now," Jeremy said. "She needs time to determine what she wants from life."

Florence waited a moment, as though expecting him to rise and pace. When he remained seated with his head bowed and shoulders stooped, she leaned forward and pulled him into her embrace. "If she can't see what a wonderful man you are, the antithesis of that horrid man she married, then she doesn't deserve you."

"Don't think badly of her, Flo," Jeremy said.

"I can and I will. She's too blinded by fear to see the gift she's been given."

"I told Jer that she'll come around," Richard said as he sat on the couch.

"Why should he want her back? I'd look for a woman who doesn't need convincing that she wants to be with you," Florence said as she rubbed his shoulders.

"She's championed by your friend, Sophie," Richard said.

"Only because Sophie felt compelled to help because of Clarissa. And it's something she'd do. Help another woman in need."

"Like a good suffragist," Richard murmured. "Besides, I think she does want to be with Jeremy. She's just confused. Give her some time." He gave a pointed stare at Florence. "You gave me time to act like an imbecile."

"An idiot was what I called you," Florence said with fondness.

"Sav's neither," Jeremy said, raising his head and rubbing at his face. "She's a woman who hasn't known her own mind for too long. I need to respect her enough to give her the time to determine what it is she wants."

He shared a bleak look with Florence. "If it's not me, I'll survive. I've lived through worse."

Florence gripped Jeremy's face, cradling his head in her palms and forcing him to meet her eyes. "I want more for you than just surviving, Jeremy. I want you to be happy. Truly, outrageously happy. I want you to find a woman who never doubts how fortunate she is to have you in her life. That helps loosen the hold your demons have on you."

Jeremy sighed and leaned into Florence, resting his head on her shoulder as he battled tears. "You're describing Savannah. I have to believe she'll come back to me. Thanks for being the sister I always wanted." Jeremy squeezed Florence's shoulder as he rose and moved toward the hallway. He grabbed a book from the bookshelf. "I think I'll try to read. I don't need any more drink." He smiled sadly as he turned for his room.

Richard and Florence watched his departure before sharing a worried glance. "How long do you think she'll make him wait and wonder?" Florence asked.

"I have no idea. I fear this last altercation with Jonas really spooked her," Richard said. "I hate that she has the ability to hurt Jeremy."

"I'm not. It means he's coming back to us. No longer living just a half-life but able to envision a full life." Florence smiled. "I hate that she's hurt him, but, if he's anything like you, he'll forgive her."

"I hope he doesn't have to wait years like I waited for you, my black-haired beauty," Richard murmured as he leaned forward to give her a kiss. He then bent forward and kissed the growing swell of her belly.

Florence blinked away tears. "I sometimes can't believe we have this life, Richard. It's as though a dream to me."

He rose, grasping one of her hands and kissing her palm. "I wish I could provide a better home for you."

"This is *our* home. What more could I want?" Florence stood on her toes and kissed his chin. "I love you, Richard McLeod, and I will never cease giving thanks that I was brave enough to risk trusting you again."

"Nor I. Now all we must do is hope the same will occur for Jeremy and Savannah."

Florence sighed her agreement as she rested her cheek on Richard's shoulder.

CHAPTER 23

Montana, August 1902

I STOOD IN LINE at the post office on Main Street and waited my turn. I fanned my face with the letters I had written Savannah and Sophronia as no breeze entered the open windows and door. A large desk in the middle of the space separated the public from the private areas, with postmen working behind the desk to sort mail. To my right, small boxes fully lined the wall with a keyhole to open each box.

I inched forward and bit my lip in an attempt to hide my grimace as I heard Mrs. Vaughan's voice. When I'd entered the post office, I hadn't focused on the people in front of me, although she would have been unmistakable in her peacock-colored dress with matching hat. The feather hung limply around her left ear, withered in the heat.

"She has her purposes," a voice behind me whispered.

I jolted at Cameron's low silky voice in my ear.

"Are you willing to make a scene, Clarissa, to avoid speaking with me? For everyone, including the estimable Mrs. Vaughan, will see you rush away from me."

The muscles of my neck and back tightened at his taunt. I clamped my jaw together and looked forward, refusing to turn and engage him.

"Still not going to speak with me, Clarissa? You aren't afraid of me, are you?"

I jerked forward, bumping into the patron in front of me to escape the grazing of his hands along my elbow. My gaze met the exultant one of Mrs. Vaughan as she passed.

"Ah, so wonderful to see the two of you together again." I grimaced, both at her words and at her booming voice. "I imagine you have avoided Mr. Wright for so long due to your regrets, hmm, Mrs. McLeod?"

"I have no regrets, Mrs. Vaughan," I said through pinched lips. I forced a smile as I attempted to move away from Cameron.

She laughed with a hint of malicious glee. "Ah, so brave of you to put on a positive face now that you have no alternative." She turned around the post office to ensure she had captured everyone's attention. With her imperious voice, it wasn't difficult. "Mr. Wright, we look forward to your company at the family dinner this evening. It appears your loss, Mrs. McLeod, was my family's gain. I've never seen my niece so happy."

"Appearances can be deceiving," I muttered as I moved forward a place in the line. I looked around the post office, smiling wanly at the growing number of speculative looks.

As Mrs. Vaughan moved past me toward the door, she nudged me with one large hip, pushing me backward toward Cameron. I stumbled, reaching forward to grasp the person in front of me to no avail.

In an instant, I was in Cameron's arms again with the scent of bay rum enveloping me, and I fought panic. I struggled to free myself from his tight grip, but he maintained his hold on my arms. "I wouldn't want you to fall and harm yourself, Mrs. McLeod," he proclaimed to all who were watching the scene. In my ear he whispered, "I knew you missed me. That you still dreamed of my touch."

I stomped on his foot with my sturdy boot, the heel crushing his toes, and he grunted. I jammed my elbow hard into his side in my frenzy to free myself, earning another grunt. Finally I was free. Even though it had lasted only a few seconds, I began to shake.

"Reminiscing are we, dear Clarissa?" he whispered, leaning toward me as though helping to steady me.

"Trying to forget I ever met you." I stepped forward, separating myself from him and attempted to smile for the postman. I looked down, surprised to see my hands empty of my letters. I had dropped them at some point in my interactions with Cameron, and I didn't know where they were. I turned to look for them on the ground and grimaced at the thought of Cameron having my letters, even for an instant.

"Here, Mrs. McLeod." I looked up to meet the worried gaze of Sebastian

Carlin. "You seem to have dropped these."

"Thank you, Mr. Carlin." I reached out to grab my letters, clasping them to me for an instant before turning toward the postman. After a moment, I turned back to see Sebastian watching me from the side of the line. "Will you wait for me?"

"Of course."

I paid the postage for my letters and departed. Cameron moved toward me as I was leaving but backed away when Sebastian cleared his throat. I reached Sebastian and walked in front of him outside.

"Thank you for your help, Mr. Carlin," I said. I closed my eyes for a moment as I took a deep breath. I felt his hand under my elbow as he propelled me into motion.

"Let's walk a little, Mrs. McLeod. There are those in the vicinity who are a bit too curious about you."

I nodded my agreement as we strolled down the boardwalk. Even in the shade of the awnings, I had to squint against the powerful late morning sun.

"Why were you at the post office? I would think you'd be too busy to be away from the mill."

"I generally am. But I needed to send a telegram from the train station and decided to check for any mail on my way back to the mill."

We walked for a few moments, nearing the workshop. I slowed, wanting to speak with Sebastian before we reached Gabriel. "Why would Cameron back away when he saw you? He doesn't seem to care about anyone's good opinion."

"He cares for mine. Or at least gives the appearance of it." Sebastian grimaced as he looked down the boardwalk, nodding to passersby. "He's begun to work at the mill. Seems Mrs. Bouchard's husband wants him to prove that he's a good worker."

I snorted. "He doesn't know the meaning of the word."

"I'm afraid you're right. And I fear his laziness will end up hurting one of my men who needs the job. He's more concerned with impressing the owner so as to be able to wed the daughter."

"Will he cause you problems, Mr. Carlin?"

"When there's a man like that around, there can't be nothing but problems, Mrs. McLeod. I'd avoid him in the future."

I nodded my agreement, and we walked toward the workshop. "Does Gabe know yet?"

"No. I haven't seen him much since he reconciled with you."

I blushed and bit back an embarrassed smile.

"And that's as it should be, ma'am. A husband should want to be with his wife." He nodded as we approached the workshop. "Ma'am."

I smiled my good-bye before taking a deep breath and bracing myself to tell Gabriel the news. I entered into the well-lit workshop, light streaming in the open door and windows. Dust motes danced in the beams of sunlight, and a cacophony of sound enveloped me from Ronan's hammering to Gabriel's whistling as he sawed.

"Gabe!" Ronan bellowed when Gabriel failed to turn around after a few moments.

Gabriel spun to face me, his face breaking into a broad smile as he saw me. "Darling. I had thought you were to mail your letters and then go to the depository."

"I was, but something happened, and I wanted to tell you. I didn't want you to hear it from the gossips."

He set down his saw and motioned for me to sit on a bench near Ronan. "Should I shut the door?"

"No," I said. "It's nothing that serious." Ronan watched me from behind his worktable, and Gabriel gave me an encouraging nod. "Cameron and Mrs. Vaughan were at the post office today. I didn't want to make a scene, but it was put about again that I was upset in my choice of you. That I was morose over not awaiting the arrival of Cameron."

"The only thing that will stem the gossips is if we continue to show how happy we are in our choice of each other," Gabriel said.

"I know," I said. "Sebastian was there. With one look, he kept Cameron from approaching me again. He can be quite fierce, can't he?" I watched Gabriel and Ronan mull over my question, and saw Ronan's amused agreement. "Did you know Cameron's now working for Sebastian? That Mrs. Bouchard's husband wants him to work for him at the mill to prove his worth?"

Gabriel gave a hoot of laughter and clapped his hands together. "Oh, that's fantastic! Some of the best news I've heard in a long time."

"Someone could get hurt, Gabe!" I protested.

"Preferably that eastern idiot," Ronan said.

I gasped. "No one would intentionally harm him."

"Of course not," Gabriel said. "If nothing's been done to him by now, and I've promised you many times I will not be the reason we are separated …" We shared a long, intense look. "Then no one will act now. Doesn't mean he won't do something to hurt himself."

"Mills are dangerous places," Ronan said, as he shook his head with amused disbelief. "What has you worried, Clarissa?"

"Why does he continue to focus on me? I'm another man's wife."

"Some men can't admit defeat. Maybe he hopes he'll receive some of that money from your grandparents by demonstrating how hard he worked to bring you round," Ronan said.

"They've already given it away," I whispered.

"What?" Gabriel asked.

"My so-called dowry. In one of my da's latest letters, he left space for Mrs. Smythe to write, which he rarely does. I haven't heard from her in months. She took great pleasure in informing me that my dowry had been given to the group fighting the vote."

Gabriel reached forward and stroked my cheek. "Does this bother you, darling?"

"No. It was never my money. It was always theirs. Theirs to spend as they wished. I was merely to be another pawn, just like Savannah."

"Well, she paid a heavy price," Gabriel said.

"Yes, married to the likes of Jonas." Then I brightened. "Oh, I almost forgot. Here's a letter I picked up today at the post office. It seems a bit tattered." I fingered the frayed edges and tried to make out scrawled writing on the front beside the address. Gabriel moved us toward the rear of the workshop where he had a few chairs, only in need of varnishing. We sat close to each other, and Ronan began to hammer again at a shoe, singing a little ditty to give us privacy.

Gabriel smiled at the familiar handwriting and ripped it open. "It's a letter from Jeremy. Do you think your Mr. Pickens will mind if you are a few more minutes late?"

I shook my head as I leaned forward, anxious to hear the latest news from Boston.

Dear Gabriel and Clarissa,

I continue to work in your old workshop, Gabe, and I remember much of what you had taught me. With time I'm slowly improving my carving skills. I wish you were here to help me, although there are still many here who remember you and commission me to produce fine pieces solely due to your name. I wonder if you really did have to leave all those months ago or, if that storm, like so many caused by our aunt Masterson, would have passed, too.

Clarissa's cousin, Savannah, has visited us a few times. I never thought to have sympathy for one such as she, but I do. Even with all her trappings of wealth, she isn't happy. Has anyone written you that her daughter lived? Her lowlife husband lied to Savannah and kept her drugged on medication for months with the hopes of preventing her from remembering the truth. He placed her child in an orphanage rather than keep her, all because she was a daughter. I've never seen a more haunted woman than Savannah.

Florence and I will continue to aid Savannah in her search for her daughter, but, so far, there is no trace of her. As for Savannah, she is no longer living at the mansion in the Back Bay but with a formidable woman who is your friend, Clarissa. A Mrs. Chickering, and I believe Savannah is slowly recovering.

Thank you for your frequent letters. I know you are happy in Montana, but I dream of a day when we are reunited again.

Ever your affectionate brother,

Jeremy

Gabriel glanced up and met my worried eyes. "There's a postscript scribbled in here from Florence." He continued reading:

Clarissa, there is nothing more that could be done for Savannah. Jeremy and I will do all we can for her. She is safe with Sophie. - Flo

I took a stuttering breath and shared a horrified glance with Gabriel. "What can I do?"

"There's nothing to do," Gabriel said. "I'm sorry you've been worried."

"I needed to know. I've wondered, for so many months, why she's rarely written me."

Gabriel turned to stare at the letter, looking at the smudged date. "It's a month old, this letter. I wonder why it took so long to be delivered?" He flipped over the envelope and peered at the words next to Jeremy's hand-writing. "'Sorry for delay,' I think it says."

"What could have happened to Savannah since then?" I shared a frus-trated look with Gabriel. "I hate that I have so little news from Boston. I re-ceive letters weekly from Aunt Betsy and Sophronia, but very few contain anything of real import."

"What good would it do to know that Savannah had her baby taken away rather than the baby dying at birth?"

"I could have written her, let her know how concerned I am for her. I can't imagine Jonas giving away her child."

Gabriel snorted. "I can." He had a faraway look in his eyes as he fingered the letter. "It sounds exactly like something that man she married would do." He stared at me, and, for a moment, I saw a deep yearning in his eyes that was soon hidden. "Some men are incapable of recognizing the gifts they've been given."

"Gabriel," I whispered as I leaned forward and clasped his hand.

"I would have cherished a daughter, as much as a son. You know that, don't you, Rissa?" Gabriel asked with intense urgency in his voice.

His hand tightened around mine to the point of pain, but I refused to grimace.

"I know, Gabriel. And I continue to hope, every day, that we will be blessed."

Gabriel closed his eyes. "And I will continue to give thanks that you are here with me, healthy and happy." A smile lit his eyes as he leaned forward and kissed my forehead. "Now, you'd better go to work, or that Mr. Pickens will send out a search party."

"I doubt it. He thinks you've finally shown sense and are acting as a newly married man should." I blushed as I spoke.

Gabriel laughed and rose with me. "Well, for once, I am in agreement with that old geezer." He kissed me swiftly, and I departed for the depository.

***

THAT EVENING, I leaned against Gabriel on the overstuffed mauve camelback settee in Uncle Aidan's sitting room. Colin sprawled on the floor with Nicholas, playing with tin soldiers. Amelia sat in the rocking chair with little Anne, comforting her as a new tooth came in. Ronan and Sebastian remained in the dining room, nursing their cups of coffee.

"I hope this doesn't have to end when Aidan returns," Colin said.

"It will be different, Col," Ronan said. "It's his house. He's not going to want it overrun by the likes of us numerous times a week."

"It's not that I don't want to see him," Gabriel said with a tender smile as he kissed my head. "It's just that I don't want things to change either."

"I agree," Amelia said. "I worry how Nicholas will take it. He's become a bit free, roaming about where he shouldn't with Aidan away. Now that he's coming back, it will seem a bit cramped in the back rooms."

"You'll just have to come over to our place," I said with a smile that quickly turned into a frown as I looked at Ronan.

"Or you can come to mine," Sebastian said. "I have a decent home over by the mill."

"I'll talk with Mr. McLeod about having Sundays off. Or at least one of the meals on Sunday off. That way, the children and I would be free once a week."

I patted Gabriel's arm. "I'm sure you're all worrying for nothing. Aidan's kind and generous. He'll delight in having us over."

As the conversation moved on, Gabriel murmured in my ear, "Are you all right, Rissa?"

"I'm fine. Just a bit tired. I didn't sleep well last night."

I heard Colin snort and wished I were within kicking range. I opened my eyes at the sound of Ronan moving his chair to the living room and Sebastian walking to the chair next to our settee, near the fireplace and across the room from Amelia.

"I remember you mentioning you missed your cousin's music," Sebastian said. He pulled out a black case tucked in behind a chair. I hadn't noticed it on our arrival, and Sebastian must have placed it there in the commotion of helping Ronan into the house.

"Yes," I said. "Now would be the perfect time to relax and listen to something Lucas would play."

"Would you object to my playing the fiddle?" he asked.

I pushed away from Gabriel to watch Seb. "You play the fiddle? You've played all this time and never before performed for us?"

An abashed smile drifted over Sebastian's face as he nodded. "I was a bit rusty. Hadn't played in years, but I've been practicing the nights we don't meet up." He pulled the violin from its case and plucked at the strings before running his bow over it, as though tuning it.

"By all means, play, Seb," Gabriel said as I leaned down again, nestling into his side.

I closed my eyes, drifting to the lyrical music. The second song he played caused me to laugh as it reminded me of one of the songs Colin had said he was learning at the forge. Colin sung in his off-pitched voice. Soon we were all attempting to join in, with Ronan using a spoon on the metal of his wheels as a sort of drum.

The music continued on in that vein for nearly an hour. Finally Sebastian laid down the violin, stretching his hands. "I have to stop, or I'll have a permanent hand cramp," he said with a smile.

"Oh, you must play for us again," I enthused.

"I'll see about practicing new pieces for the next time we are together," Sebastian agreed. He picked up Nicholas, who had leaned against his legs, to hold him on his lap.

"Seb, now that you're done entertaining us, why don't you tell us about the mill," Gabriel said. I heard Ronan snort as he wheeled his chair farther into the parlor.

"Mr. Bouchard's being a darned fool," Sebastian said with a shake of his head. "How he can think that worthless easterner can work in a mill is beyond me."

"I heard from one of the men at the forge that he's hoping he'll run it someday," Colin said.

"He'd never!" Amelia sputtered. "Mr. Wright has no idea how to run a proper mill. That would be terribly unjust."

"Well, I'm not the one showing an interest in the owner's daughter," Sebastian said. "Now it seems Mr. Bouchard is trying to placate his wife by providing some sort of employment for Cameron. Seems they're willing to overlook the fact he's a beggared, albeit well-dressed, smooth-talking man due to his connections out East."

"Damn fools," Colin hissed.

"All I hope is that the fool doesn't lead to any harm to my men who need the work and know what they're doing," Sebastian said. "It's hard enough preventing accidents and keeping my men healthy when they're well trained and competent."

"When it comes to Cameron, I've learned to expect chaos," I said with a mournful glance in Sebastian's direction.

***

AMELIA ROSE TO CARRY Anne to the bedroom. Sebastian followed suit with Nicholas in his arms and joined her in the rear of the house, away from their friends who continued to discuss Cameron, the mill and whether his interest in the Bouchard daughter was feigned.

"It's all right, Nicky," Sebastian soothed as he settled the child on his bed. Seb undid his shoes, stripping him of his stockings, pants and shirt. Nicholas curled on his side, and Sebastian rubbed his back. "Is it all right, ma'am, if he sleeps in his underclothes?"

Amelia turned to watch Nicholas with exasperated affection. "Yes, it's fine. He's exhausted, and it's far too late for him to finally be going to bed. Tomorrow he'll be a bear to be around."

"I'm sorry, ma'am," Sebastian said, his shoulders stiffening. "I never meant to make your life more difficult."

She stroked a hand down Anne's back in the too-small crib, then turned to grasp Sebastian's arm before he could spin away. "No, you misunderstand me. This was a wonderful night, and I'm glad he could be a part of it. He loves his time with you and listening to your music. If he's grumpy tomorrow, it will be worth it."

Sebastian's eyes lit with tenderness. "I wish we were friends," he whispered.

"We are," she breathed.

He traced a finger from her hairline over her cheek to her jaw. "I'm a fool for wishing for more." His deep sigh resonated with regret as he backed away.

"No, you aren't," she whispered, leaning on the tips of her toes to brush a feather-soft kiss over his lips.

He jerked as though struck by a hot fireplace poker, watching her with a fiery intensity in his eyes.

"I've never been courted by anyone but Liam, and I ..."

Sebastian's smile bloomed like a desert flower after a gentle rain and quieted her with a soft shake of his head. He leaned forward and kissed her forehead. "Will you let me court you, Amelia? Show you what we could have?"

She bit her trembling lip, unable to prevent a tremulous smile from bursting forth, and nodded. Her eyes were filled with wonder as he leaned toward her and kissed her softly, his hands caressing the side of her neck. She gripped his arms, arching into him, but broke the kiss before he could deepen it when Nicholas grumbled in his sleep, interrupting their quiet interlude. Sebastian smiled again, a quiet contentment in his eyes as he stroked a hand from her shoulder to her hand, before turning to leave the room, his boot heels clicking softly so as not to wake the children.

Amelia ran a soothing hand over Nicholas's head, pausing for longer than was necessary. She stood for a few moments to collect herself and to calm her racing heart before rejoining her friends.

CHAPTER 24

I STOOD IN THE DEPOSITORY, proudly staring at the rows of book-shelves Gabriel had just installed. I ran my hand over one of them, smiling at the thought of organizing the books properly, rather than on tables.

"You plan on standin' there all day, Missy, and wasterin' this fine day, marvelin' at your husband's talents?" Mr. Pickens asked as he thumped his cane on the floor.

I laughed as I faced him. "Maybe I do. I'm so excited we finally have bookshelves, Mr. A.J.!"

I raced toward him to give him a quick hug. Then I assisted him to a nearby chair so he could continue to oversee my work but not overtax himself.

"I ain't as sick as I look, Missy." He attempted to take a deep breath, but ended up shaking from a deep, rattling cough.

"I know what the doctor said—plenty of rest and no exertions. That means you can watch me work and entertain me with stories."

"I ain't no circus clown," he grumbled. "Yer lookin' better, Missy. You an' that husband of yours finally make up?" Mr. Pickens wriggled his eyebrows at me as he watched me.

"We weren't fighting, Mr. A.J."

"You sure could've fooled me. Actin' like a pair of wounded wolverines, never seeming happy to be together. Didn't seem right, being newlyweds an' all."

"We've been married over a year, Mr. A.J."

"Well, when you reach the forty-year mark, like I did with my Bessie, then you'll understand yer still a newlywed now." He smiled his near-toothless grin. "How'd you get him to apologize?"

I rolled my eyes at him, then laughed. "It wasn't like that. Just a misunderstanding."

"I hope it didn't have nothin' to do with that useless deadbeat who followed you out here."

"A little."

"He'll leave you be, once you get with child." Mr. A.J. gave me a pointed look.

"Mr. A.J. Please." My voice broke, and I turned away for a moment before facing him again.

"Hmm. Well, seeing as you're newlyweds, I'd enjoy the time afore a little one comes along and runs you rugged." Again the wriggling of his eyebrows and a thump of his cane for good measure. "It'll give you more time to read and misinterpret those cookbooks you seem so fond of."

"Amelia's been very helpful. I just can't seem to cook anything away from her kitchen. I've been visiting with her most afternoons after work, and she continues to help me with cooking classes."

"Speakin' of that widowed friend of yours, I'd think you'd have plenty of stories from her."

"Amelia?"

"That be her name. Just yesterday Mrs. Vaughan stopped in to inform me—" At this he ceased talking as he heard the outer door creak and slam.

Heavy footsteps sounded on the stairs, and I raced toward the stacks of books to give the appearance of being busy at work. I didn't want to be caught in my ritual morning gossip session with Mr. A.J.

"A.J., Clarissa!" The deep voice of Mrs. Bouchard bellowed through the room. "I'm glad to see that man has finally finished his work. It's about time, when you consider all we paid him."

"You know as well as I do that you received a discount due to his fondness for the library," I said, unable to hide a flash of annoyance from my eyes. I attempted to always call it a library with Mrs. Bouchard and Mrs. Vaughan, to prevent any further irritation on their part. "And he delivered them a few days early."

"Hmmph." She walked toward the bookshelves, causing the floor to creak with each step. Her sapphire-blue suit gleamed in the midmorning light streaming through the windows. She reached out to touch the wood, frowning as she traced the simple contours of the shelves. "I had thought they would look more substantial. More decorative. I want our members to feel that there is no better place for them to borrow books in Missoula."

"There ain't, you daft woman," Mr. A.J. muttered but low enough she couldn't hear him.

"What was that, A.J.?" She turned toward him with an arched eyebrow. "I'm glad to see you were agreeing with me."

"And as for you, Mrs. McLeod." She paused for a long moment, taking in my faded indigo shirtwaist and old shoes. "I had hoped by now you would be able to present a more genteel face to our customers. I'd think that husband of yours would want you out in public with a bit more style."

"I'm perfectly comfortable as I am, Mrs. Bouchard. And Mr. McLeod has no concerns about my appearance."

"Hmm. Considering he had to marry you in such haste, I imagine there is little he can do about it now." She eyed me shrewdly. "I give thanks, daily if not hourly, for your mistake and thus allowing my dear daughter her chance with Mr. Wright."

I paled at the thought of having married Cameron but tried to hide my reaction to one of Missoula's biggest gossips. "I believe things turned out as they were meant to."

"At least you acted with more discretion than that disgraceful woman who traveled with Mr. McLeod from Butte. I've never heard the like." She paced around the bookshelves, picking up books from one table, tracing the binding of the book before dropping it on a different table with no concern for my attempt at sorting the books. She was in no apparent rush to depart.

"You got something pacific against the widow?" A.J. demanded.

I smiled as I realized he meant *specific*.

"Upstanding women of the community, trying to raise their children in good Christian homes, do not have single men leaving their homes late at night. It is not proper."

"Improper my boot," Mr. A.J. hissed, snapping his jaw as though clamping on a phantom pipe. "That lovely woman ain't never showed you no sign of impropriety. And it don't say much about the woman who goes around malingering another woman just trying to make her way in this world." He banged his cane down a few times with his anger.

Mrs. Bouchard watched Mr. A.J. in confusion.

"I think you mean *maligning*, Mr. A.J.," I said. "And I couldn't agree more.

Mrs. Egan is a good woman, and anyone who believes differently should hold their counsel."

Mrs. Bouchard sniffed once in disgust. "Well, I had thought you both were better at discerning one's character. Clearly I was mistaken." She turned to look around the room. "As for your work, Mrs. McLeod, I hope you will have more success at organizing now that we have bookshelves. For we would hate to have to search for a new assistant."

I gave her a stony nod while A.J. sighed.

"I bid you both good day." She moved toward the stairs, and, a few moments later, I heard the slamming of the outer door.

"Mr. A.J.," I whispered after her departure. "Is that what you were going to tell me?"

"I wanted to know if the young widow was soon to be a bride, was all. Seems that Mr. Carlin was seen leavin' her place a few evenings ago."

"I don't see why that would cause such gossip."

"There ain't much that's goin' on in this town right now, especially as fall's about to begin. When winter settles in and no one goes outside, there'll be no chance for much gossip for months. And those two biddies always want to stir the pot." He raised his eyebrows at me. "Asides, I hear tell he left with his hair all ruffled."

"Mr. A.J.! He was playing marbles with Nicholas."

"Well, it makes a man wonder if somethin' more 'n that happened. The widow is lovely." His eyes were teasing, although I sensed a warning in them too.

"I'll talk with Amelia. I need to speak with her about helping me with a project."

"What sort of project?"

"Although I hate to admit it, Mrs. Bouchard is correct. I need a few new dresses. I hope Amelia will help me."

"Don't you know how to pick out clothes yourself?"

I shrugged my shoulders as I moved toward one of the tables Mrs. Bouchard had rearranged. I picked out the books she had moved around and organized them again. "I always had someone to help me in Boston. I was never any good at discerning colors or patterns."

"Not very domestic, are you, Missy?"

"Not at all, Mr. Pickens." I began to place books in order on the shelves.

"Yer lucky that man of yours is so crazy 'bout you."

"I know," I said with a broad smile.

***

"AMELIA, I'M NOT AT ALL certain that is the type of fabric I should be considering," I whispered as we glanced at various types of cloth in the Missoula Mercantile. I had already waved off an overly eager attendant, instead choosing to rely on Amelia's expertise and keen eye for color. I moved toward the rear of the room where the cheaper fabrics were stored. "I think this is better," I said, fingering a navy wool. We stood behind a large display, our presence hidden from anyone who entered the room. I looked around at bolt after bolt of cloth, overwhelmed and feeling defeated before even starting.

Amelia had taken a few hours to help me pick out cloth. Nicholas and Anne were with Gabriel and Ronan at the workshop while we searched for fashionable clothes for me.

"Gabriel told me that he wanted you to start wearing clothes that highlight your beauty. Similar to the beautiful gowns you wore in Boston." Amelia grabbed the bolt of bombazine from my hand and placed it down with a thunk. "That color makes you look like an old woman."

"Amelia, what's going on with you and Sebastian?"

Amelia flushed before shaking her head. "Nothing, Rissa. He's fond of the children, and I'm thankful for that."

"Are you saying you only like him because he's good to them?"

"Of course not. He's a kind, generous, thoughtful man." She glared at me as she stopped speaking.

"I've always wondered why the two of you aren't married already," I whispered, lest there were others listening in.

"Hush that talk," Amelia whispered back. "I know the townsfolk think I'm fast for having him to dinner." She shared a sardonic smile with me. "A second time without everyone else. I had intended to invite you and Gabe, but the day got away from me, and then he was at the door."

"Amelia, I'm only teasing you. You know I'll stand by you."

"To have everyone whisper behind your back—people you'd once considered friends—it's terrible. I don't want to go through that again."

"Then, although I am in no way agreeing with the sisters, I wouldn't be seen with him alone again, Amelia. Not unless you want to acknowledge what you feel."

Amelia nodded and glanced around, focusing on the fabric again. "Why are we in the back with the uglier fabric?"

She was about to push me toward the front of the room and the more expensive, lush fabrics when I heard voices and my name being spoken. I hushed Amelia, and we turned to listen.

"I tell you, Hettie, that girl should not be allowed to work further at the library."

I stilled as I heard Mrs. Bouchard's loud voice, although not as booming as usual. It appeared to be her attempt at a whisper. "She spends her time with shameless widows. And we now know her reputation was in tatters when she arrived from Boston. But did she have the decency to tell us?"

"Of course not." I heard Mrs. Vaughan's voice join that of her sister's. "Women like her will never be forthcoming about their past indiscretions. It's no wonder her husband thinks so little of her that he cares not she is dressed in virtual rags. He must have been sorely disappointed on their wedding night."

I heard vicious giggling as I tried to take a deep breath and prevent fainting. I gripped the edge of a display, holding on so that I wouldn't collapse to the floor.

"You know that she must have acted in a shameless manner for a man to lose control of himself. No honorable man would have acted in such a way without provocation. And we know that Mr. Wright is to be held with the utmost esteem."

"Shameless hussy. Coming to our town with airs and graces form the East Coast when she should have taken up residence on Front Street," Mrs. Vaughan said.

I heard Amelia gasp at the implication that I was no better than a prostitute. Her arm came around my waist as though to shore up my strength.

"We shall have to speak with A.J. about having her removed from the library staff. I would hate to think what our customers would do should they learn the truth." Mrs. Bouchard continued to prattle, but her voice faded away as they moved toward another department, and I finally gave in and collapsed to the floor.

"Clarissa. Clarissa," Amelia repeated urgently. "You must ignore what they said. They are mean-spirited, jealous women who wished they had such a good man as Gabriel. A man as attentive."

"If that is what they're saying, soon most of this town will believe it," I whispered as I attempted to remain calm and to ward off any shaking.

"You have more people supporting you than you realize," Amelia urged. She put her hand under my elbow and propelled me to my feet. "I think our shopping expedition can wait."

"No. Gabriel wanted me to purchase cloth for a few new dresses, and it's more important than ever that I buy them." I glanced around realizing Amelia had been correct. The more inexpensive material was not what I needed. It had become imperative that I show a confident face to those who wished me ill, and, to do that, I needed to look the part.

"Help me find beautiful material?" I implored. I hastily swiped at an errant tear, stood tall, and moved toward the front of the room, in full view of all patrons and searched for material for five new dresses. I smiled wickedly, thinking that whether they liked it or not, the library and Mrs. Bouchard's brethren were helping to pay for my new clothes due to their hiring Gabriel for the bookshelves.

***

"HOW WAS THE SHOPPING EXPEDITION?" Gabriel asked. He sat in a rocking chair in the workshop, little Anne curled asleep on his chest. He stroked a hand down her back every few moments as she sighed in her slumber. Ronan was with Nicholas, who was hammering away at a pair of shoes.

"Enlightening," Amelia said. She raised an eyebrow to see Anne asleep in Gabriel's arms even though Nicholas was making so much noise.

Gabriel watched me. "Clarissa?"

"I've ordered material for five new dresses. They should be done soon."

"Good," Gabriel said, then he winked at me as he handed little Anne to Amelia. "We'll see you tomorrow night for dinner, Amelia. I'm looking forward to one of your home-cooked meals."

I elbowed him in his side but nodded my agreement. Ronan chuckled as Nicholas gave him a quick hug. "See you tomorrow, Uncle Ronan!" He bounced down from his seat and raced toward Amelia and the door.

When Amelia and the children had departed, I spun to face Gabriel.

"Will you come upstairs with me? I need to talk with you about something."

All amusement fled his expression, and he nodded. "Of course. Ro, can you watch the shop?"

Ronan nodded his agreement. He studied us as we ascended the stairs before he bent over his bench and began to work again on a pair of shoes.

We entered our living space, and Gabriel shut the door to give us privacy. "What is it, darling? The bloom's gone out of you again."

I flung myself into his arms and held him to me. "I ran into the sisters today."

Gabriel stiffened as he leaned me away. His hands came up to cradle my face in his palms. "What did they say, Rissa?"

"That you were ashamed of me because I'm so poorly dressed. That I should have waited a few more days, and I'd have had the good fortune of marrying Cameron." I hated how my voice broke on Cameron's name.

"Vicious harpies," Gabriel hissed. He pulled me into his arms again, and I pressed my face into his chest.

"I wanted you to know ... to know what others might say," I whispered. "They said ..."

"No one who considers me friend would ever believe their lies over our visible happiness." He leaned forward and kissed me, the gentle kiss soon giving way to a passionate embrace.

"Gabriel, they said ..." I lost my thought as he kissed me again.

"Their words are meaningless." He backed me toward our sleeping area, and I gripped his arm as I tripped on my skirts.

"Gabriel! It's the middle of the day. What would Ronan think?" I whispered.

"That we're showing some sense finally," he murmured as he nuzzled behind my ear. His hands were already busy at work unbuttoning and unfastening my gown. Soon it pooled at my waist. He pushed it down, and I stumbled on it as I continued walking backward.

He continued to kiss me as his nimble hands worked on the ties to my corset. "Dammit," he muttered. "I think I got it tangled." By this point I was standing next to the bed. He turned me so my back was to him, and he worked on the knot in my laces, all the while placing small butterfly kisses to my nape and back. After a few moments, my corset landed by the side of the bed.

I turned to face him and sat on the bed. I reached for him, tracing his face, the subtle black stubble on his cheeks, his dark eyebrows. "How I love you, darling," I whispered as I leaned up to kiss him. He moved to stand between my spread legs, kissing me all the while.

I giggled as he tried to kiss me, unpin my hair with one hand and unfasten his trousers with the other. I brushed aside his hand, unbuckling his belt and unbuttoning his pants. He moved from me to shuck his pants, and then he was lifting me, pulling my undergarments from me.

I scooted farther onto the bed, and he crawled up me, kissing me everywhere. "Gabriel," I rasped.

"Never doubt for a moment the joy I find in our marriage," he whispered. "Those women, they wish they had what we have."

CHAPTER 25

"ARE YOU TELLIN' ME you don't want Missy workin' here no more?" I heard Mr. Pickens's wheezy demand and the thump of his cane as I crept up the stairs to the depository. I remained in the shadows, watching the tableau as it unfolded. A.J. sat on his customary chair, a fierce scowl marring his expression. Mrs. Vaughan and Mrs. Bouchard stood ramrod straight, their tangerine and violet dresses clashing.

"We of the Missoula Library Committee feel that her behavior is reprehensible. Our customers should not be forced to associate with the likes of her." Mrs. Bouchard's bellow would have been heard by all who passed by on the street below, had the windows been open. Instead they ricocheted around the room, piercing my heart.

"An' what misbehavin' has my Missy done 'cept escape the net of that worthless easterner? Your daughter would do well to take a page from her book." Another dull thump of his cane.

"She presented herself to us as a respectable woman when nothing could have been further from the truth." Mrs. Vaughan had joined the conversation, her body quivering with indignation.

"And who do you have to take her place? Ain't no one 'round these parts who loves books like she does and who's willin' to work here for the poultry pay."

I half smiled as I silently corrected him—*paltry* pay—in my mind.

"That is none of your concern, A.J."

"Damn straight it is, you meddlesome women. My Bessie helped start this place and now you 'bout to run off the one girl dedicated to it. Don't seem right to me."

"You have no say," Mrs. Bouchard bellowed.

"You think not, mouthy?" he snapped. "I tell you this. You force Missy out, and I'm no longer workin' here. Find another caretaker."

"A.J." The surprise in Mrs. Vaughan's voice was authentic. "Think of Bessie."

"I am. And she'd be appaloosa'd at the two of you."

I fought tears at his show of loyalty, both to me and to his dear, departed Bessie.

"Where would you go? You enjoy seeing the townsfolk when they come to the library." Mrs. Bouchard had begun to wring her hands.

"Why, I'll set up calling hours at Mr. McLeod's shop. Thataway I can still see my Missy. Only one 'round these parts with any sense." He stomped his foot down, then heaved himself to his feet, tottering a few moments before finding his precarious balance. "Ain't that right, Missy?"

I froze for a moment before straightening my shoulders and entering the depository. "Hello, Mrs. Bouchard, Mrs. Vaughan. I am saddened that you no longer wish me to work here."

"You insolent hussy," Mrs. Vaughan hissed. "How dare you present your-self with your Eastern airs and graces? You are worse than the lowliest women. At least with them, we know what type of women they are."

"I am a woman worthy of respect."

"You are not. Any woman who entices a man with a dowry and then beggars him by reneging on that promise is shameless."

I paled, blinking to forget moments of mindless terror and helplessness. I took a deep breath and faced my tormenters. "My only hope for your daughter, Mrs. Bouchard, is that she never suffers as much of Mr. Wright's regard as I did."

"Suffer? How would you have suffered with his solicitude? His kind-ness?" Mrs. Vaughan asked.

"No, Mrs. McLeod, it is you whose charade is over. You who has been found out and do not have the grace to admit it." Mrs. Bouchard glared at me.

"I have more grace than you could ever imagine. There is nothing in my past that shames me." I fisted my hands at my sides and leaned forward as I prepared for battle. "I hope, when you come to your senses, you will be able to say the same."

Mr. Pickens's cane thumped loudly, reminding me of his presence. "Well said, Missy. I'm sure the patrons will miss your charm. And your knowledge." He frowned at the sisters as I nodded to him and turned to leave.

"Mr. Pickens, I'll speak with Mr. McLeod, but we will expect you tomorrow at the workshop."

"That will be fine, Missy. That will be fine," he said. He tottered toward the back, muttering about "Prattling Prisses."

I shared an intense, anger-filled glance with the sisters before I turned to the stairs.

***

"GABRIEL." I LOOKED AROUND the workshop and saw he was hard at work, carving an intricate piece of molding. I bit my lip, loathe to interrupt him.

"Gabe, your wife wants a word."

Ronan's bellow captured Gabriel's attention, and he spun to face me.

"My darling," he said with a wisp of a smile, the joy lighting his eyes easing some of my tension.

I glanced gratefully at Ronan for a moment, earning a wink before focusing on Gabriel. "Gabriel, can we talk?"

He set down the chisel and walked toward me, reaching out to trace the frown line between my brows. "Of course. Let's go upstairs." He clasped my hand with his, nodded toward Ronan and led the way upstairs.

Once there, I paced as Gabriel moved toward the living area in the center of the long room. He sat in his comfortable chair, easing into the lopsided cushions. After a few moments, he chuckled. "I enjoy spending time with you, darlin', and watching you pace is fascinating, but why don't you come sit by me and tell me what's upset you?"

I spun to face him, the thrust of my argument evaporating with the wry amusement I saw in his gaze. "I need a favor, Gabriel."

"For you?"

"Of course."

He reached out his hand, and I moved toward him. I had planned to sit on my rocking chair next to him. Instead he pulled me down onto his lap until I was settled comfortably. He kissed the top of my head and sighed.

"I love holding you like this," he murmured. "What favor do you need, darling?"

"The sisters Bouchard and Vaughan informed Mr. Pickens today that I'm no longer welcome to work at the depository." I gasped as Gabriel's arms tightened around me. "Mr. A.J. refuses to work there if I'm not allowed to."

Gabriel maneuvered me so that I leaned against the arm of the chair and could meet his worried gaze. "And?"

I took a deep breath. "He wants to sit in the shop downstairs and see his friends as they come by. That way he can still see them and me."

Gabriel closed his eyes for a moment and leaned his head against the back of the chair. "Mr. I-can't-understand-half-of–what–he-says wants to set up calling hours in my shop?"

I smiled at the incredulousness in his voice. "Yes, exactly. He's planning on coming by tomorrow. I didn't agree. I only told him that I'd talk with you. Well, and that we'd expect him here tomorrow."

Gabriel met my gaze. "I know he's your best friend here. I know he had a hand in helping us reunite. I know he's stood up for you against those awful women. I just can't imagine day after day of his incessant chatter."

"I think you've misunderstood him. You'll come to like him as I do." I smiled as I kissed his cheek.

"Are his friends any more intelligible than he is?" Gabriel asked, a small smile flirting around his mouth.

I laughed as I envisioned them. "Oh, no, they're worse! But you'll never lack for stories. Or company." When I met his serious gaze, I sobered. "I'm sorry, Gabriel. I know times like this will make you yearn for the peaceful days before my arrival." My voice broke, and I tried to rise from his lap.

His hold on me tightened, restraining me from rising. "Oh, no, my darling. You have it all backward. I was sitting here, thinking about my empty warehouse, devoid of Ronan's off-key whistling, free of his ribald jokes, and trying to envision what changes your Mr. Pickens will bring." He pushed a piece of my hair that had fallen loose from my bun behind my ear. "I was thinking how fortunate I was at last to have such a full life. To have people around me who love me, make me laugh and help me to appreciate every day. You've brought me that. You've filled my life with such joy." He leaned in to kiss me tenderly.

"Your Mr. Pickens is very welcome in my shop. For it will make you happy." He gave a small grimace. "Although I may need you there to interpret for me."

"Thank you, Gabriel," I whispered as I leaned into him. I inhaled the smell of wood, varnish and the sweaty-musky smell that was all Gabriel. "I worry I have brought you too much …" Here I stopped speaking, not wishing to give voice to the sisters' venom.

"What more did the sisters say that you haven't told me?"

"Mr. Pickens calls them the *Prattling Prisses*. I think he meant to say princesses, but I like the sound of prisses better." I felt Gabriel chuckle soundlessly.

"I may come to appreciate him. What did the Prattling Prisses say, Rissa?"

"Cameron is ingratiating himself with Mrs. Bouchard's daughter. He has told them that I had agreed to marry him, but that I cried off, running out here to find you and that I beggared him in the process. But that I … favored him before I left."

"Insolent fools!" Gabriel hissed. He met my eyes, his angry, worried gaze meeting my tired, resigned gaze. "They have no right … no right to judge."

"To society as a whole, Gabriel, I was … damaged. And you were a fool for ever marrying me." The weariness in my voice surprised me.

"Look at me, Rissa." He grasped my chin, forcing my gaze to his, intense with love. "Look at me, and tell me that you have ever thought I was disappointed in you. That I wished for more. What anyone outside of these four walls thinks of our relationship doesn't matter. The only thing that matters is what you and I believe. What we know to be true."

"What do you know, Gabriel?" I asked with a small smile, his love for me banishing doubts and hurt caused by unfeeling, self-righteous women.

"That I will only be completely happy when I'm with you." He leaned forward and kissed my forehead. "You've told me that my love for you is as a miracle. I wonder that you do not realize it is the same for me? All I care about, Clarissa, is that you know that what they say is a lie. And that it doesn't affect for a moment how I feel for you."

I nodded as he wiped away a stray tear. "It's difficult not to be hurt by their malice, Gabriel."

"As long as you never doubt what we have."

I met his adamant gaze and nodded.

***

"THANK YOU, AMELIA, for the invitation," Colin said. He took a bite of the roast, leaned back in his chair, and let out an appreciative sigh. "I heard you were buying fabric at the Merc."

"Why would that interest you?" I asked. I looked at Gabriel seated at my right, and he seemed amused by our conversation. Amelia had settled next to me with Nicholas beside Colin. Sebastian sat by Gabriel.

Colin speared me with an intense stare, before looking down toward his plate heaped with potatoes and peas. "And how are things at the depository?"

I paled, setting down my spoon with a clatter. "Slow. They've determined they do not need my help for the foreseeable future." I cleared my throat and blinked rapidly in an attempt to forestall any crying.

"Those wicked old biddies," Colin hissed.

"What have you heard, Col? Rissa was just told today that she wasn't welcomed there," Gabriel said.

"What happened, Clarissa?" Amelia asked. "I never thought they'd actually act."

I closed my eyes, a shuddering sigh escaping. "They, the sisters Vaughan and Bouchard, visited this morning." I reached down and gripped Gabriel's hand, our fingers lacing.

"I meant to tell you about everything. But I was … distracted." The tenderness in his eyes at the shared memory and his squeezing of my hand bolstered my lagging spirit.

"Yes, Clarissa, what did the sisters say this morning? What they had to say at the Merc yesterday was enlightening enough," Amelia said with a frown.

"The sisters visited this morning. They think I am a woman of loose morals and do not want one such as me having any association with the library." I attempted to speak in a neutral voice, but was unable to hide the desolation from mine. "They learned what happened in Boston, although it's a version of the tale spun by Cameron to make himself seem like he had been the one deceived."

"That's not all they said, Rissa, and word is spreading," Amelia said.

I flushed and looked down.

"Clarissa?" Gabriel asked. "I thought we'd spoken of this? What more could they have said that you wouldn't have wanted to share with me?"

"Gabriel, it made me so ashamed," I whispered.

"Nothing you have ever done should cause you a moment's worth of shame," Gabriel said with a great intensity. He turned toward Amelia. "Amelia?"

"That the correct place for her would have been on Front Street."

Sebastian interjected. "That whatever happened in Boston was Clarissa's fault because no honorable man would ever act in such a way. That she duped Gabe into marrying her. And that Gabe must have been sorely disappointed on his wedding night. It's all anyone wants to talk about at the mill. I suspect because I'm good friends with you, they hope I'll let slip unknown information."

"What?" Colin gasped.

"Idiots!" Gabriel roared as he rose to pace a few steps. He spun to face me, studying me for a few moments, crouching down in front of me. He took my clenched hands into his, gently massaging them until they relaxed. "Why didn't you tell me all of what they said, darling?"

I shrugged by way of response.

"The only one who need feel shame is Cameron. He is the one who grossly abused you. The only emotion you should feel is pride. Pride that you had the courage to live the life you wanted." He waited a few moments for me to again meet his eyes. He nodded before leaning forward to kiss me along the side of my head, whispering into my ear, "And you know that neither of us was disappointed on our wedding night." His husky, soft voice was like a caress.

"What am I to do? I can't address their horrible gossiping. Because, no matter what anyone says, it's true." I glanced around the room, hoping for guidance from all present.

"Bull," Colin snapped, "the essence may be the same, but it still smells like pure Cameron manure." He looked toward Amelia, smiling apologetically for his plain speaking. "Anyone who would believe him over you is an idiot."

"Which we know the two sisters are," Amelia said.

"The problem is, everyone in town enjoys listening to them," I said.

"What you must do, Rissa, is put it around that you wish to focus on Gabriel and your marriage. That you prefer now to provide a good home for him and that you no longer have time to work at the depository. Not the other way around," Amelia said.

"How would I do that?" I asked.

"Let's visit the seamstress tomorrow. If there is one person, other than those vile sisters, who can gossip, it's her. And then we'll visit a few stores and ensure we are talking about the same. Soon all will know it was your decision."

"A sound plan, Amelia. And have the seamstress work extra hard to have Clarissa's fall and winter dresses finished quickly," Gabriel said. "I want there to be no doubt of my tremendous pride and good fortune to have married Clarissa."

CHAPTER 26

"HOW ARE THINGS at the mill, Seb?" Gabriel asked.

I sat next to him in Sebastian's living room in his house near the mill. Curtains hung to either side of the front windows, a gentle light entering during the early fall evening. A fire in a brick fireplace against the far wall smoldered, battling the chill of an early October night, while bookcases lined the other cream-colored wall beside the entrance to the room. A large opening led into the dining room with an adjoining door visible to the kitchen. Mismatched, comfortable furniture filled the room.

Seb sighed and stretched his long legs in front of him in the rocking chair Gabriel had built him. "Fine, if you don't count that idiot who pursued you west." Sebastian nodded toward me. "He's not one to follow orders. Thinks he should already be runnin' the place. Nearly got Jimmy's arm lopped off last week being such a fool."

I grimaced, and Amelia murmured her distress. Sebastian gave a chagrined look in our direction for his blunt talk.

"What can you do, Sebastian?" I asked. "It seems that the wedding is to occur the week before Thanksgiving. Mrs. Bouchard talks about how he's such a bright young man and soon he'll take over the running of the mill."

"You know she's full of hot air," Gabriel said.

"And a whole lot else," Ronan said with a snicker. I giggled.

"Unfortunately Mr. Bouchard has agreed with his wife's plan. He wants Cameron to learn the running of the mill and to take it over for him. Seems to have forgotten how long it took him, or any of the rest of us, to learn things. Doesn't seem to believe that Cameron should have to work all the jobs, like the rest of us, to fully appreciate how a mill runs."

"And that can be dangerous," Colin said. "I'd hate for someone to come into a forge who hadn't any idea what was going on. And that's a much less complicated place than a sawmill."

Sebastian nodded his agreement.

Amelia rolled her eyes. "If you could have heard Mrs. Bouchard today at Allenstein's when I was buying groceries. Never came up for breath, singing his praises. How lucky they were to have gotten such a fine, upstanding gentleman interested in their daughter."

"As I told Mrs. Bouchard once, I hope she never has to suffer as much of his regard as I did," I said, unable to hide the bitterness from my tone.

Gabriel reached over and clasped my hand, giving it a gentle squeeze.

"She'll never have the sense to understand what you meant," Amelia said.

"Other than the man from the East, things are going well. We've never had so much business." Sebastian stifled a yawn as he shifted on his chair. "At times it's hard to keep up with the orders. I often work late in the office, just to keep up with the paperwork."

"That's a good problem to have," Colin said. "It's always better to be too busy rather than worrying if there'll be enough to cover your next paycheck."

"I agree," Sebastian said as he rose and moved toward a corner of his living room. He added wood to the fire, causing it to roar to life. I saw his violin case in the corner, but he didn't move to open it.

"How are things for you, Clarissa?" Sebastian asked.

I shrugged. "I've dedicated myself to becoming a better cook." I pinned Ronan with a severe glare as he choked on his coffee. "And I've cooked a few meals."

"I would even venture to call them delicious," Gabriel teased with a wink. "Although Rissa has a long way to go to match one of your pies, Amelia."

"Wonderful, Rissa!" Amelia clapped her hands together with joy. "I knew you just needed time to focus. What do you do when you aren't cooking or cleaning? I haven't seen as much of you as I thought I would in the month since you stopped working at the depository." Amelia pulled little Anne onto her lap and snuggled her as she began to fuss before falling asleep.

"As I had walked all over town talking about my wish to be at home, I thought I should remain there." I shrugged as I thought about my days. "I write a lot of letters. I'm trying to improve my knitting." I speared Colin with a fierce scowl as he guffawed.

"Do you think those shopkeepers believed your tale of a desire to become more domestic?" Amelia asked.

"I don't think they did in the beginning. But now that they see how happy Gabriel and I are, I think they've begun to."

Sebastian grunted. "Well, the only talk I hear about the two of you is how you've reconciled. Seems the townsfolk think you're boring now, not worth gossiping about. More interested in the upcoming nuptials and what outlandish outfit Mrs. Bouchard will wear."

"Her poor daughter," Colin said. "I've never met her, but can you imagine having a mother like that?"

"I bet she's just like her mother," Amelia said.

"Well, then I'll be interested to see her dress too," I said with a giggle.

"Any word from Uncle Aidan?" Ronan asked Gabriel.

"Yes, I received a letter today informing me that his business is keeping him much busier than usual for this time of year, and he doesn't know when he'll return."

"Thus we don't have to worry about being forced out of his house just yet," Colin said.

"In any case, I'm glad you all came to my house. It's nice to have some company here for a change," Sebastian said. We nodded our agreement, prepared to listen to music.

When Sebastian reached for his violin, I curled into Gabriel's side. We all settled into our seats as Sebastian tuned the violin. Rather than the riotous sing-along songs we'd become accustomed to, he played a melodious, moody song. I blinked away tears at the plaintive longing I heard and leaned more into Gabriel, kissing him on the cheek. He tilted his head, resting it on top of mine.

I saw Sebastian stare at Amelia intently when he finished playing, before he switched tempo and played an upbeat song. After a few moments, Colin and Ronan began to sing along. I watched as Amelia swiped at a tear, hugging Anne to her.

"Give them time, Rissa," Gabriel whispered in my ear before his harmonious baritone joined in.

***

I SAT UPSTAIRS, staring at a blank sheet of paper, Sebastian's violin music from last night playing through my mind. I hummed the first song he had played but couldn't remember the exact tune. I gave up trying to remember, raising the lid of the small music box Gabriel had given me for my birthday. It played "Fur Elise," a song he knew I liked and one that would remind me of Boston and Lucas.

I focused on the music until I heard a shout coming from the workshop. When I heard a second one, I dropped the lid to the music box, abruptly cutting off the lilting music, rose and crept down the stairs. Ronan leaned over at his waist, his shoulders jerking. At first I worried he was crying, until I realized he was laughing. Gabriel was swiping tears from his eyes and shaking his head.

I sat on the stairs, hoping to remain unseen.

"An' there I was, Sonny," Mr. Pickens said, "naked as a jaybird, sittin' in a tree, with an irate moose tryin' to get at me with his huge antlers. They say bears are mean. An' they are. But moose are just as ornery. 'Specially in the fall."

Ronan lifted his head, his shoulders still shaking. "What did you do?"

"What do you think I did? Froze my tail off, sittin' in that tree for hours till that beast got tired of pacin'. Probably smelled some nice female and took off. I scampered down out of that tree, bleedin' from the scrapes from the pine bark in my nether regions. Never did get in those warm springs. Decided I'd better hightail it home while I still had a chance."

I saw him swinging his cane around as he continued to speak. "My clothes were scattered all over the clearin'. Damn animal thought it was fun to paw and play with 'em as I sat as naked as the day I was born on a tree limb that seemed less sturdy the longer I sat on it."

I heard Gabriel hoot, and I leaned over to see him watching Mr. Pickens with rapt fascination.

"Took me an hour to collect my clothes and still had to make do with only one sock. An' my Bessie, do you think I got any sympathy from her? No sirree. She laughed as hard as Sonny here. Only wished she'd been there to see me jump near out of my skin and scamper up a tree. Did no end of teasin' as she tended my scrapes and bruises." He thumped his cane down, and I heard his whistling exhalation of a laugh.

"Ah, those were the days. Not many folk here, wild lands to be explored.

Animals everywhere." Mr. Pickens's voice was filled with nostalgia.

"I'd think it's pretty much the same now," Gabriel said. I heard him begin to sand wood from the far side of the room.

"Oh, no. Missoula's gettin' too big. You mind me, Sonny. Soon we'll have more people 'n we know what to do with." He sighed. "But it's still a glorious place for you young'uns to explore. Don't you agree, Missy?"

I gasped at having been caught before giggling and peering around the corner to smile at all of them. "Interesting story, Mr. A.J.," I said.

"Glad you didn't hear the first part of it," he said with a chagrined smile to Gabriel and Ronan. Ronan snickered.

"Have you heard the news, Missy?" Mr. Pickens asked. "We're allowed back to the depository. Seems they can't do without us."

I rose and moved toward him. "Really?" I paused, battling any excitement I felt. "Why should I return simply because they want me to?"

"There's the Missy I know," Mr. Pickens said with pride. "Give 'em hell, Missy. I told 'em we wouldn't work for their misterly pay but needed a decent raise."

"*Miserly*," I said as Gabriel shook his head in amusement and mouthed the word as I spoke it. "Did they agree?"

"Well, seein' as they've lost track of a good portion of the books that used to be a part of the so-called library"—he thunked down his cane—"it's why anyone with sense'd call the place a depository, they didn't have much choice."

"Oh, that's wonderful!" I said as I spun with glee, tripping on my long skirts and landing on a heap on the floor. Gabriel hauled me up, dusted me off and helped me to a chair near Mr. Pickens.

"Before you two get excited about returning to your old ways," Gabriel said with a mock-serious stare, "I want time away with my wife."

"Oh, finally takin' my advice, are you, carpenter?" He wriggled his brows up and down as he winked at me. "Finally goin' to have some canoodlin' time."

"I'd thank you to speak respectfully about my wife," Gabriel said.

"Ain't nothin' disrespectful about a man wantin' to have some time with his wife. Seems the most respectful thing a man could want," Mr. A.J. said in protest. "Why, my Bessie—"

"Old man, don't even start," Ronan said.

I studied Ronan, not having seen him this content since I had met him. "Mr. A.J., tell us about Hamilton."

"Oh, so your young man is finally taking you to see the Bitter Roots." He sighed as he closed his eyes for a moment. "I know some will argue there be prettier mountains, but I ain't seen 'em. Course, with the time of year and the planned activities, you won't have time to go into the mountains."

"Why would I want to go into the mountains?" I asked.

"To truly be alone, Missy," Mr. A.J. said. "To smell clean air. Nothin' like a pine forest to soothe the nerves and make the world seem right again." He nodded and had a distant look in his eyes. "Why, my Bessie 'n' me'd go into the woods as often as we could. And it wasn't often enough. But late fall ain't the time."

"We'll let you know what we think of those mountains," Gabriel said with a wink to Mr. Pickens.

CHAPTER 27

I STOOD AT THE KITCHEN SINK in Aidan's house a few evenings later, washing the dishes after another delicious meal served by Amelia. It had been a small group tonight, with only Gabriel and me joining Amelia's family. Amelia was busy putting Nicholas to bed, and I could hear her soft voice as she read him a bedtime story. Gabriel sat in the living room, whistling as he read the paper. Just as I recognized the song and began to hum along, he invariably switched to a different tune. I glanced out the kitchen door to see his dimple flash as he continued to whistle, his eyes meeting mine for a moment and flashing with humor at my inability to hum along.

I giggled and turned back to the dishes. After deciding to leave a large pan to soak, I turned toward the kitchen table and glanced out the side window. I saw Colin racing toward the door, and I moved to open it before he could pound on it and wake little Anne and rouse Nicholas. "Col!" I said.

He entered the kitchen, bent forward at the waist, gasping for breath. "Water, Rissa," he gasped.

I spun, poured him a glass of water from a pitcher on the table and thrust the glass at him. I pulled on his arm and dragged him into the living room area. Gabriel's joyous whistling had ceased with Colin's precipitous arrival.

"Colin?" Gabriel asked in his deep baritone.

"There's been a terrible fire at the mill," Colin said. "Seb's hurt."

"Mr. Carlin?" Amelia asked from the kitchen doorway.

I spun to face her, rushing toward her as she became more ashen. "I'm sure he'll be fine, Amelia," I soothed.

"What happened?" Gabriel asked. "Seb's fastidious in his desire to prevent a fire."

"No one has any idea. At this point, they're ensuring there's no chance the fire can come back to life. The windy weather we've had lately hasn't helped. They've brought him to the hospital," Colin said.

"I'll take you there," Gabriel said to Amelia as he noticed her agitation. "Rissa, will you stay here with the children?"

"Of course."

"I'll stay here too," Colin said. "We'll be fine, Gabe."

Gabriel and Amelia departed, rushing down the kitchen steps to head toward St. Patrick's Hospital.

After checking on the children in their room and preparing a plate of cold leftovers for Colin, which I left on the dining room table, I collapsed on one of the sofas in the living room. I hugged a pillow to my chest as I sat.

Colin crouched in front of me before settling onto a foot stool in front of me. "What's the matter, Rissa?"

"Who else was hurt in the fire, Col? I know Cameron works there now, and it seems unlikely he would be unscathed."

Colin reached forward and clasped my hand. "Rissa, Seb went into that inferno looking to save Cameron. He was trapped inside."

"So Cameron's at the hospital too?"

"No, Seb couldn't get him out. He died."

"What?" I stared at Colin with unseeing eyes. I shook my head as though I no longer understood English. "That can't be."

"It is, Rissa. Cameron died tonight. It's one of the reasons I raced here. I didn't want you to hear it through any of the gossips. I didn't want Mrs. Bouchard to say something vile to you when you had no idea why she would speak to you that way."

"Someone will tell Gabriel," I whispered.

"Most likely," Colin said. "I should have realized that Amelia would want to go to the hospital to see after Sebastian. Even though they're not officially courting, they sure do act like it."

"Give them time, Col," I murmured, my gaze distant.

"Well, in any case, I would like to have told Gabe before he raced off with Amelia."

I sighed. "It's fine, Col." I blinked back tears and turned into the sofa. Colin leaned forward, wiping at my cheeks.

"Rissa, you're not crying for Cameron," he said with absolute surprise in his voice.

"No matter how much I loathed him, no matter how much he hurt me …" I sniffled. "No one deserves to die like that, Col."

Colin shuddered. "I agree."

"And I feel so guilty. I had wished him gone so many times."

"I highly doubt you had wished him dead."

"You have no idea." I trembled. "After Boston, I imagined all sorts of vile things. But I never would have wanted them to come to fruition. That's not who I am, Col."

"You didn't cause this accident, Rissa. You didn't give him a job in a place any fool would have seen he was unsuitable to work in." He stroked a hand down my head and patted my back. "I called him friend once too."

"I know, Col," I whispered, gripping his hand. "What a sad ending to his tale."

***

I WOKE THE FOLLOWING MORNING in my bed, with only a vague memory of how I had returned home. I turned to snuggle into Gabriel and frowned to find his portion of the bed empty. I ran my hand over his side, noting it still held his warmth.

"Gabriel?" I called out. The privacy screen was up, and I couldn't see into our living area. I heard something ceramic set down on wood and then his footsteps as he approached. I leaned on one elbow, watching as he poked his head around the screen.

He wore a loose pair of pants and nothing else. "Why bother putting pants on?" I asked with a teasing smile.

"I should head to the hospital soon. See how Seb is."

At his serious statement, I blanched, and all teasing faded. "Darling, come here." I held out my hand to him, and he moved to join me on the bed.

He crawled under the covers again, pulling me into his arms. He sighed as I nestled into him. I breathed him in, feeling safe, cherishing this early morning ritual of being held in his arms.

"How is Seb?" I whispered against his throat. I kissed him once where his pulse beat steadily, then laid my head onto the pillow of his shoulder and upper chest.

"He'll recover. He's a severe burn on his hip and lower back. The doctor thinks it will heal, although it'll take time. He'll need a lot of nursing care. And he might always have a bit of a limp with his walk."

"But he'll live," I breathed. "Thank God. I don't think Amelia could survive losing another man she loved."

"I think she hadn't admitted to herself how much she cared for him until last night," Gabriel said. "And there's still the risk of infection."

"If he needs nursing, I'm sure Amelia will be there to see he's well taken care of." Gabriel's chuckle resonated in my ear. "Did anyone speak with you about Cameron?"

"Why would they?" Gabriel asked as he nuzzled the top of my head.

"Because he's the reason Seb went into that burning mill. He was trying to save Cameron."

Gabriel pushed me away from him, tilting my face up so our eyes met. "Ah, so Colin told you?"

I nodded, my anxiety increasing the longer he refrained from holding me in his arms.

He brushed a finger down my cheek, rubbing it back and forth as he appeared lost in thought before focusing on me again. "Why are you so tense, love? What's the matter?"

"What if he's not really dead?" I bit my lip. "And then I think, what if he really did die?"

"Which would you prefer?" Gabriel brushed at the side of my head, stroking his thumb over one of my eyebrows.

"I don't know." I met Gabriel's concerned glance. "And I hate that I don't know. I should never wish that something as horrible as death should befall him."

"It's a normal reaction, after how you suffered at his hands, darling. I'd think it abnormal if you hadn't at one point envisioned something miserable befalling him. He was a horrible man."

"I know," I whispered as I laid my head on his shoulder again. "But all I can imagine is his mother receiving the news. No matter how horrid they all were to me, believing themselves superior to me, I hate envisioning what she'll suffer when she receives the news."

"That's because you are a wonderful woman, my darling," Gabriel said huskily. I met his gaze, love shining from deep within. "You'd think of the pain she'll suffer rather than what you endured at his hands."

"Can I come with you to the hospital?" I asked.

"Of course, although I thought you hated the sickroom."

"I do, but I want to see Seb. Then I'll go over to Amelia's and tend the children while she's at the hospital."

"I doubt she'll spend much time there," Gabriel said. "It's a small town, and she won't want to engender more talk than's already circulating about the two of them."

I sighed, leaning into Gabriel for a moment before kissing his collarbone and then moving away to rise. He grasped my hand as I sat on the edge of the bed on the verge of standing. I turned to face him, my long hair cascading over my back to my hips, brushing the top of the bed.

"After Seb is better, why don't we finally take a small vacation together somewhere? Go to Hamilton on the train, see those Bitter Root mountains your Mr. Pickens talks about?" He brushed his fingers through the edge of my hair.

"We don't have the money for that, darling," I whispered.

"We've a little saved, and I'd like time with my wife. Time without friends and family always around us."

I smiled and leaned toward him, intending to kiss him but for a moment, yet the kiss deepened. I broke it with a groan, smiling with chagrin. "If we keep that up, we'll never make it to see Seb."

"And that's exactly why we need time away," Gabriel said. "Although we'll probably never see those mountains and that small town everyone is raving about."

I blushed and pushed away, rising. I moved toward the side of the bedroom area to the closet to prepare for the day.

Gabriel rose, caressed my shoulders, kissed my nape and murmured, "I'll make fresh tea." He moved past me, and I soon heard him rummaging around in the kitchen.

***

WE ARRIVED AT THE HOSPITAL, and Gabriel led me through the doors, down a well-lit corridor and up a flight of stairs to the room Sebastian was in. His bed was in the middle of a rectangular room, only three of the eight beds occupied. On his side of the room, the bed to either side of his was unoccupied. On the other side of the room, only one man lay on his side, staring out the window.

Sebastian looked flushed and was sweating. I approached him and touched his face, moving my hand from his forehead to cheek to neck. "He's no fever," I whispered to Gabriel. "Why's he sweating so much?"

"Pain," Sebastian gasped as his pain-dulled eyes opened. "'Lo, 'Larissa." He licked at his dried lips, grimacing with any movement as he inadvertently shifted in the bed.

"Don't scare us again like this, Sebastian," I said through tears as I gripped his hand. I eased my hold on them when I saw the white bandages and his grimace at my grip.

"I'll try not to," he whispered.

Gabriel picked up the chair from the other side of the bed and moved it beside where I was standing so we could both sit at Sebastian's side and face him. "Why don't they give you more to ease your suffering?"

"Don't want more. Don't want to become some addict." He gripped his teeth as he fought a shiver of pain.

"Sebastian, if it can help you now, that's what you need to consider," I urged. "How can you heal well while suffering such agony?" I pulled my clean handkerchief from my purse and blotted his forehead.

"Thank you," Sebastian said as his eyes closed. "Gabe, everyone at the mill got out all right, didn't they?"

Gabriel shared a long glance with me. "Well, Seb, everyone but Cameron. He never emerged."

"God dammit," Seb hissed as he opened his eyes.

"What happened?" Gabriel asked.

"You know as well as I do, I've been working late. Trying to finish orders, doing paperwork. I thought the men had left for the night but turns out some of them were slow to leave. And then I heard them screaming about a fire."

He sighed. "We could account for almost everyone. Except for Benedict and Cameron. I doused myself in water and ran in. Something landed on my back, and I must have blacked out. Next thing I knew I was outside with my men around me. Benedict had already gone home but came running at the sound of the bells."

"Seb, you did all you could." Gabriel reached out to grip his shoulder but stilled his hand, as though realizing any touch would lead to more pain. He patted the bed next to Sebastian instead.

"They assured me that they'd seen Cameron out, that he was fine. Are you sure he's dead?" Sebastian demanded.

"His charred remains were found a few feet from where the falling timber hit you," Gabriel said, meeting my shocked stare. "I spoke with Colin for a few moments this morning while Rissa changed."

I shuddered, curling into myself at the image Gabriel painted. He placed an arm around my shoulders, and I leaned into him.

"What's important, Sebastian, is that you will heal," I whispered. "We didn't lose you."

He nodded as his eyes drifted shut. "Tell Amelia …" he whispered but was asleep before he finished his sentence.

***

GABRIEL AND I LEFT the hospital and, for one of the few times in my life, I was thankful for my corset. Its stiff binding forced me to walk upright, rather than stooped over with the weight of my concern for Sebastian. I looped my arm through Gabriel's, and he gripped my hand.

"I should stop by the depository for a moment. I've just returned to work and now I have to take a day away. I should speak with Mr. A.J.," I said.

"Yes, and give him your version of events before he hears from the sisters," Gabriel said. He sighed and slowed our pace. "I wish you could have waited to return to work there until we'd had our time away."

"I didn't want to antagonize the sisters, after they had granted me a raise, by advising them I wouldn't return for several more weeks." I squeezed his hand. "And we'll find a way to travel."

We walked the short distance to the depository, and I grimaced as I heard Mrs. Bouchard's voice as we climbed the stairs.

"Did I not tell you that woman would bring disgrace upon this town? That she would be the reason for God-fearing Missoulians to huddle under their covers at night?" Mrs. Bouchard's bellows reverberated around the room.

I glanced toward the windows, thankful they were once again closed. She paced between the tables, bumping into the edges of them periodically with her wide hips. Her dress was a gray satinlike fabric that shimmered when she walked.

"Do you know that, due to her antics, the good people of Missoula will be deprived of the wedding of the decade? They will not see my beautiful daughter married. They will never have the good fortune to see the suit I purchased especially for the occasion. All of the planning ruined. Ruined, due to that wretched girl."

"I can hardly see how a fire in a sawmill could be construed as my fault, Mrs. Bouchard," I said. "I was never the one keen to have Mr. Wright employed in a place he was ill-prepared for and ill-trained to work in. I was never the one to interfere in my husband's business."

"You insufferable—"

"I'd watch yourself, Mrs. Bouchard," Gabriel said with thinly veiled menace. "I've heard all I care about the sisters' opinions on my wife and her previous relationship with Mr. Wright. He suffered a tragic death, a death that neither my wife nor I had any part in."

"Darn straight," Mr. Pickens said with a thump of his cane. "If you had any sense, mouthy, you'd know fire is one of the greatest dangers in one o' those mills. Either that or sawin' off a limb. Can't imagine why you ever wanted that pampered wasterel workin' there."

Mrs. Bouchard and Gabriel stared at Mr. Pickens for a moment, and then I half smiled. "*Wastrel.* You mean *wastrel,* Mr. A.J."

"Exactly. Useless, good-for-nothing rich boy. Thought he could come out here and impress all us townsfolk with his pretty clothes and smart accent. Well, most of us weren't fooled. Just his dumb bad luck you were, Mrs. Bouchard. Thinkin' you could put him to use in a sawmill. A sawmill of all places. If anyone's to blame, it's you." He thumped his cane so hard I thought he'd crack the ancient floor.

"Mr. Pickens, I expect you to show me the respect I am due as one of the leading townswomen. As a patron of this fine establishment." Her bosom heaved with her distress. "I have suffered greatly in the past few hours, all due to this … this abomination of womanhood."

"I repeat, Mrs. Bouchard, I had nothing to do with Cameron's unfortunate and untimely death. If you continue to speak about me in such a manner, I will consider suing you for slander," I said, my hands gripped at my sides, my nails gouging into my palms.

"I've never said an untrue thing in my life."

"You've built your life around half-truths," Gabriel said, "never caring who you hurt in the process. It stops now, Mrs. Bouchard."

"Oh, you think so? You think you're so cunning, acting the happily married couple when I know the truth. I know you can barely stand touching her. Soiled goods."

"That is enough!" Gabriel roared. I felt him next to me, vibrating with anger. His cheeks flushed, and I feared that he would lose control of his rage as he faced Mrs. Bouchard. "I understand your family has suffered a loss, and, for that, I am sorry. But you will apologize to my wife. For there isn't and never has been anything soiled about her." His eyes gleamed with sincerity and passion as he confronted Mrs. Bouchard.

She turned from him, then to me, watching us. "I refuse to be misled, unlike the rest of the townsfolk, that you are happy in your choice of wife."

"The only one who's a fool is you, mouthy," Mr. Pickens said. "Anyone could see there's not a happier newlywed couple around. Course yer not only deaf, you're blind to what's right in front of you." He shook his head at her.

"I suppose you'll now try to convince me that Mr. Carlin never intended to steal the money in the safe while he was manufacturing his attempt to save poor Mr. Wright?" She placed one hand on her gray suit, glaring at each of us in our turn.

"What are you talking about?" Gabriel asked. "Seb heard there was a fire and ran to help. Like anyone with sense would who works at a mill."

"You really are the most easily duped man," Mrs. Bouchard said with scorn. "I wonder what it's like to go through life trusting in those around you like you do."

"Mr. Carlin nearly died trying to save Mr. Wright," I insisted.

"So you think," she said. "Seems one of his cohorts took the money from the safe while he provided a suitable distraction."

"I wouldn't call nearly being burned to death a distraction," Gabriel ground out.

"Call it what you will, but those in the know understand Sebastian Carlin isn't worth trusting," Mrs. Bouchard said. "As I suspect few are who associate with the likes of you."

"Mouthy, you say any more against Missy, and I'll torch this place myself, Bessie or no Bessie," Mr. Pickens said with a thump of his cane. "I hear tell books burn almost as fast as sawdust."

Mrs. Bouchard paled before she spun on her heels and stomped down the stairs. I moved toward Mr. Pickens and collapsed on my stool.

"You all right there, Missy?" Mr. Pickens asked me. He canted toward me to steady me as I listed to the side with him nearly toppling off his chair. He caught himself with his cane and grunted his approval as Gabriel moved to kneel beside me.

"You showed that trumped-up bag o' air yer not gonna run away just because she's got it in her craw that someone other than herself's to blame for this disaster." Mr. A.J. grinned his approval.

"Is it true though, what she said about Seb and the money?" Gabriel asked, his hands lightly stroking my back and shoulders.

"Alls I've heard is that a goodly sum is missin'," Mr. A.J. said. "I wouldn't be surprised if they searched his home."

"Seeing as he hasn't been there, how'd they expect to find anything?" I asked, any feeling of lassitude evaporating with my ire at Sebastian's treatment.

"Well, see, Missy? Yer talkin' like someone who's usin' sense. That's sorely missin' right now." He shook his head, pursing his lips as though blowing out smoke from a cigar. "If I were that trussed-up friend of yours lyin' in a hospital bed, I'd be mighty worried."

CHAPTER 28

I STOOD IN ONE of the upstairs' bedrooms in Aidan's house, balancing on one foot and then the other, listening to the floorboards creak. I moved toward the small cupboard by the right side of the bed, placing a few pieces of clothing inside. A tree outside provided shade to this room, and it was darker than usual for midafternoon.

"Is everything all set, Rissa?" Gabriel asked as he poked his head in. He came in, shutting the door behind him. "It'll just be for a little while."

"I know, but I like our home," I whispered.

"I'd thought the rooms were bigger." He glanced around at the double bed set against the wall to the right of the door; two small tables sat on either side of the bed, and a bureau was at the foot of it. "Not much more would fit in here."

"Seeing as all we have to do is sleep, we'll be fine," I said. I giggled at Gabriel as he winked at me before sobering. "How is Seb?" I glanced behind Gabriel to ensure the door was closed.

"Determined to prove he didn't steal the money. But I don't know how he can. Only he and Mr. Bouchard had access to the safe."

"I'll never believe he stole it."

"Nor I. But those sisters have stirred up trouble again," Gabriel said, reaching forward to pry open my fisted hands, caressing one of my palms to relax me.

"I know, and that's why I'm willing to stay here until he's able to live at his place. I don't want Amelia to suffer more from their gossip."

"Nor do I, although I'm afraid they'll think we aren't the best chaperones for two unmarried people."

"Well, according to society standards, we suffice."

Gabriel bent down and met my eyes, before giving me a quick kiss. "Society can go hang. But, for Amelia and Seb, I'm glad we do." He squeezed my shoulder before turning toward the door. "I should return to the workshop. Will you be home today?"

"No, I'll stay here. I have what I need for now. I sent a note to Mr. Pickens explaining I wouldn't be in today. I'll see if I can help Amelia." I leaned into him, standing on my toes to give him another quick kiss. "I'll see you tonight." Gabriel traced my jaw, smiled tenderly, then opened the door and strode down the hall. I heard his boots on the stairs and then the front door closing behind him.

I walked across the hall and knocked on Sebastian's door. After waiting a few moments, I turned to leave before I heard his voice calling me to enter.

His room was almost a mirror of ours, although slightly bigger because two chairs were crammed inside, one on either side of the bed. In our room, no chairs would fit. I sat on the chair near the door because he lay on that side, facing me.

"How are you, Sebastian?"

"Fit as a fiddle." His eyes fluttered as though fighting sleep. "Thank you for agreeing to come here. To protect Amelia." His voice was weakened by pain and fatigue.

"Of course. I'm glad she was able to take you in." I reached forward, touching his forehead, and relaxed when I felt no sign of fever.

"Did you know she used house money to wire Mr. Aidan? Asking him if I could stay here?" He opened an eye and saw me shaking my head. "She received his permission, though I don't know what she would have done had the man said no."

"Aidan's not that type of man."

"You seem confident in who he is, when you barely met the man."

"I know his nephew well. He seems a man of integrity."

"If you're talking 'bout Gabe, I agree. The uncle, I don't know. But I'd have to be willing to think the same after he agreed with Amelia."

"How are you really?" I reached out again, unable to sit still, and straightened his blanket. His strong hand gripped mine, and I looked up to meet his eyes. Tortured, devastated amber eyes.

"Ruined, Clarissa," he rasped. "There's no way to prove I didn't plan the robbery. Only my good name, and there's too many here willing to believe the worst of a man."

"There has to be a way. I refuse to admit defeat."

"Mr. Bouchard will already have replaced me. Of that I have no doubt."

"With whom?" I cried. "You're talented, capable, reliable. I've heard how the men of your mill talk about you with respect."

"Oh, there are always those waiting in the wings, just biding their time." Sebastian closed his eyes. "Just like I bade mine, someone else's done the same."

"How did you become foreman?"

"The man I replaced died. Accident in the mill." He shook his head. "No need for you to hear any of the details."

"That's my point, Sebastian. You didn't die, and you didn't steal that money."

"I'm thankful you believe in me, but not many folks will." He moved a bit on his side, hissing in a breath of pain which the movement wrought.

"Don't give up hope," I said, gripping his hand. He blinked once before his eyes fluttered shut and his breath slowed with sleep. I watched him a few minutes before I rose, leaving him to his sleep.

***

A FEW NIGHTS LATER, I lay on my side, attempting to ignore the low rumble of deep male voices as Gabriel and Sebastian talked late into the night. Sleep eluded me, although I was bone tired. Dinner had been a tense, stilted affair with Amelia offering little more than one-word responses to our questions.

I heard Sebastian's door click shut and then ours open as Gabriel slipped inside. I rose up on my elbow and watched Gabriel creeping around the room, attempting to walk quietly in his boots. He stifled a curse as he stubbed his toe on the bureau, and I giggled. He glanced toward the bed and grinned at me.

"I'm sorry to wake you, darling." He quickly undressed and climbed into bed, wrapping me in his arms.

"I wasn't asleep. I have trouble sleeping when I'm not next to you."

He gave me a soft squeeze. "Thank you, darling."

"For what?"

"For believing in Seb. For wanting this life with me. For having patience with Amelia."

I traced his forearm, causing gooseflesh to rise. "I can't imagine Sebastian being guilty of what he's been accused. Something else must have happened."

"Seeing as he and Mr. Bouchard are the only two with the combination to that safe, and they were to make a large deposit at the bank the following day, it is highly suspect, Rissa."

"I still won't believe that of him. He's not that sort of man."

I felt as much as heard Gabriel sigh. "I just wish Amelia would say that as plainly to him as you just did to me. It's tearing him apart that she doubts him."

"She's never said ..." I sputtered to a stop, unable to voice the words.

"Not in so many words, but her actions show her doubt. She barely speaks to him as he lies in that bed, bored and in pain, day after day. She has Nicholas or one of us bring him his meals. She only visits him to change his bandages. I know we're here to act as chaperones, but that doesn't mean she can't have any contact with him."

"I'll talk with her."

"No, Rissa. That's the last thing I want you to do. Because then Seb would find out we'd meddled, and he'd be upset. He wants Amelia to determine what she wants without any influence from us."

"What can we do for them?"

"Nothing more than be here to stem any further gossip surrounding them. Sleeping on this lumpy bed is penance enough." He kissed the top of my head as I grumbled. "We can't make everything better for everyone, darling. But we can give them the chance to work it out on their own."

***

AMELIA CRACKED OPEN Sebastian's door and crept inside, her stockinged feet sliding silently on the wooden floor. His chest rose and fell in the soft cadence of sleep. She moved to the chair facing him and perched on its edge.

Her eyes roved over his face in an attempt to discern if he were improving. She raised a shaking hand and held it over his brow, a few inches from his skin, tracing the shape of his face in the air but never touching him. A deep, yearning sigh escaped, and she moved to rise, but she gasped as Sebastian reached forward and caught her hand.

Pain-filled brown eyes met her startled hazel ones. "Why won't you speak with me?" he rasped. "Every night you visit. Every night you do the same thing. And you never speak with me."

Amelia wriggled her wrist until he released her hand. She raised it, caressing his russet-colored hair and tracing her fingertips down his stubbled cheek until her hand cupped his face. "I hope, every night, that you'll be awake. But you always seem to be asleep." She dug the tips of her fingers into the side of his face as he turned his head into her hand.

"Why won't you visit me during the day? You send Nicholas to impart the news, as though he were the town crier, when all I crave is your company."

Amelia grimaced at the recrimination she heard in his voice. "I don't want there to be more gossip than there already is. I created quite a stir by insisting you remain here under my care. I'd hate for you to suffer due to my acting rashly."

He moved his face so as to kiss her palm. "You acted in such a manner to care for me. I'll never regret a bit of gossip." He raised worried eyes to her. "Gossip is the least of my worries."

"Sebastian." She leaned forward until she slipped off the chair and knelt beside his bed, her face even with his on the mattress. "I know you are innocent. We'll find some way to prove it."

A tenseness Amelia hadn't even realized had pervaded him eased at her words.

"Thank you." After a moment where they stared into each other's eyes, he whispered, "There is no possible way to show my innocence. I've no reputation past what Mr. Bouchard is willing to say, nothing to recommend me for another job." He closed his eyes for a moment. "I've nothing to offer you now. Forgive me, Amelia?"

She sniffled and chuckled humorlessly. "For what? For attempting to save another's life? For risking your own?" She nodded. "Yes, you should ask my forgiveness for that for, if you'd died, I don't know if I would have recovered."

She stroked his cheek. "Sebastian, remember, Liam was taken from me cruelly." She reached under the high neckline of her dress and pulled out a necklace. On it an oblong metal object hung. He reached forward and traced it, before looking at her with blatant curiosity.

"This was Liam's tag. When he didn't come out of the mine that day, they knew he remained trapped inside. When they realized he'd died, they gave it to me, and I've worn it, every day since I buried him, next to my heart." She blinked away tears. "If you had died, I would have had no right to mourn you. No right to such a talisman."

He raised a questioning eyebrow, the intensity of his expression fore-stalling any prevarication on her part.

"You were spared, and I daily give thanks for that. I don't know what will happen, but I will never cease being thankful you are a part of my life," Amelia whispered. "I will be forever grateful I don't need to fashion another talisman to wear next to my heart."

"I hope you continue to feel that way," Sebastian whispered, as he turned his face to kiss her palm again. "There are things you don't know about me. Things that others will be only too happy to repeat now that I'm injured and unable to defend myself."

"None of it matters to me."

"It does to me, because there are always shades of truth to it." Sebastian sighed deeply. "I was married before, Amelia. I had a wife who became dis-satisfied with this life and ran away."

"Why?"

"Said she never imagined living as a nobody, married to a nobody in a nothing town. Expected more from her life." His jaw hardened. "There are those who will say I was cruel to her. Treated her in such a manner as to force her away."

"Did you?" Amelia asked.

"We yelled at each other a lot. Especially at the end. When I knew she was unhappy and I couldn't figure out how to make her so."

"No one can make you happy, Sebastian. That comes from within."

"Well, they sure can make you miserable," he said wryly. "I want you to understand that I never raised a hand to her. Never threatened her in any way. But I did raise my voice to her."

"Do you think Liam and I never fought? That we had a blissful under-standing about everything? We argued fiercely at times, but there was always enough caring to bridge the distance of our misunderstandings."

"Thank you, Amelia." At her questioning look, he said, "For understand-ing. For considering me worthy of a talisman." A long pause followed as he stared into her hazel eyes. "For caring for me."

"That's the easy part," she murmured, leaning forward to kiss his cheek. She smiled, caressed his face one more time and rose, slipping out of the room as silently as she had entered it.

CHAPTER 29

ALMOST TWO WEEKS after moving into Aidan's house, I sat in Aidan's study, reading letters from Boston. There were two windows in the office at the front of the house and another to the side, allowing a generous amount of light in every day. Whitewashed walls made the room seem even brighter, and a few paintings of San Francisco hung on the walls. Aidan's desk sat in front of the two windows with a pair of comfortable leather chairs in front of them. A leather ottoman was shared between both chairs, and I propped my feet on it as I curled up to read my letters.

I had taken to spending a few hours each day reading and sending letters, as Amelia had no need of any help in the kitchen, and I had no desire to hold a conversation with myself as she continued to brood. A quick glance outside to the fading afternoon light indicated Gabriel would soon arrive to keep me company before dinner. Aidan's study had become our private retreat, and I relished the time we shared discussing our days or sitting in peaceful harmony, holding hands.

I looked toward the door as a gentle knock sounded. Amelia entered, a small yellow envelope in her hand "This was just delivered for you."

"Thank you." I reached forward, tracing my name scrawled in an unknown hand on the front. Amelia nodded and closed the door with a quiet click. I scanned the few words, rereading them twice in my confusion.

Unknowingly I let out a screech and fell out of my chair. I knelt on the floor of Aidan's study, rocking in place. I opened the telegram again, rereading the words but still disbelieving them. How could they be true? I wrapped my arms more tightly around myself in the belief that I could in some way hold myself together. And yet nothing worked. I rocked and rocked and rocked to the point I tipped over onto my side, unable to restrain a keening wail.

"Shh, darling, don't carry on so," Gabriel crooned as he entered the room and knelt beside me, caressing my back. He leaned over, kissing my exposed forehead, my nape. When he realized I was lost to my grief, he gently pulled me toward him as he leaned against the shut door. I came to rest on his lap, his arms and legs sheltering me, my face resting on his chest.

All the while, he continued to croon soothing sounds in my ear. The soft, repetitive motion of his hand over my scalp and upper back acted as a balm, and my sobs quieted. "Ah, darling, I hate to see you so sad," Gabriel murmured, kissing my head. "Can you tell me what happened?"

"My da, he's dead." My throat ached from all the crying.

I felt him stiffen and then relax. "How, darling?"

"A heart seizure. At the forge." My stuttering words were barely comprehensible, but Gabriel managed to understand.

"Oh, darling, I am so sorry." Another kiss to my forehead before he pushed me up to meet his gaze. He caressed my cheeks, rubbing away the tears that continued to fall. "When is the funeral?"

"Soon," I sobbed, fresh convulsions racking me as tears poured from my eyes. "I must be there, Gabe. I have to."

"Who wrote you, darling?" Gabriel kissed my head, swaying a bit from side to side in an attempt to soothe me.

"Aunt Betsy sent a telegram. She was afraid we wouldn't be informed in a timely manner. Says she'll try to postpone the funeral as long as possible." I met Gabriel's gaze with determination. "I know you've been frustrated due to our need to be here for Sebastian and Amelia and having to postpone our trip away. I know we don't have much saved, but I need to return to Boston. I need to be there."

He studied me for a long moment, a sigh escaping him as he looked deep into my eyes. "I understand, my darling. There's no better use for our savings than to ensure you are at your father's funeral."

"Thank you, Gabriel." I leaned against him, all my strength spent. "I still have most of the money Aunt Betsy gave me when I traveled here."

"I can only imagine how pleased she would be to know that it would help ensure you could travel home for your father's funeral."

"Not home," I whispered. I shook as the shock of the news became real.

"I hate that the last conversations I had with my da were either in anger or me misleading him." I shuddered in a breath. "I hope he knows how much I loved him."

"He knew, darling. No father loved a daughter more than he loved you. He was just misguided by that awful woman."

"Oh, Gabe! I knew I might never see him again. But to know there's no chance now, no hope …"

He held me closer, his big palm against the crown of my head. "I know, Clarissa. And nothing will ever take away this pain."

I pushed away, bracing my forearms on his chest. I reached up to trace his cheeks, and I saw decades-old sorrow reflected in his eyes. "Now I'm an orphan too," I whispered.

He groaned and coaxed me to rest again on his chest. "We have each other, darling. And our siblings."

"Although I haven't heard from Patrick in over two years. Ever since he moved to New York, he's failed to maintain any contact with us."

"Rissa, does Colin know?"

"No-o," I stammered. I snuggled back into Gabriel's arms, wishing I could remain in his embrace forever, ignoring the telegram heralding the death of my da. "I can't imagine telling him."

"We'll tell him together, before supper tonight. He's coming over to eat with all of us."

"Oh, Gabriel, I can't. I …" I broke off.

"I know you want to curl up in bed and hide," he whispered. "The pain's too fierce and how could you possibly sit through dinner?" He kissed my eyebrows. "But you'll be with friends who are as family. You need the support of those who love you at a time like this. Let them help care for you, darling."

***

I HEARD COLIN'S BOOMING VOICE as he entered the kitchen. I closed my eyes and inhaled deeply at what lay before me.

"I'll be here with you, love." Gabriel squeezed my shoulder before opening the library door to speak with Colin. I heard their deep voices, Colin telling some tale about an errant dairy cow's escapade through the city's streets as they approached.

"You sure have made yourselves at home," Colin teased as he entered the study. I saw him still as he looked toward me. He stood rigidly with his shoulders drawn together and his hands clenched at his sides as though preparing for a fight. "What is it, Rissa?"

"I had a telegram today, Col," I croaked out, sounding as hoarse as a bullfrog.

He rushed toward me and crouched beside me. "Is it Savannah? Has that bastard—"

"No, no, Col." I gripped his hand and patted it as a tear leaked out. "Da died. He had a heart seizure at the forge and died."

Colin fell backward until he sat on the floor, a dazed and distant look in his eyes. "He can't be dead. He was always so strong. So healthy."

"I know, Col. But Aunt Betsy wouldn't lie to us."

He nodded. "When's the funeral?"

"Soon." I bit down a sob. "I plan on traveling east for it. I hope to leave on the train tomorrow."

"I should have been there," he rasped. "I shouldn't have left him to run it alone. I knew how much work it was. How hard a time he was having finding someone he could trust. And I left him. I left him!" Colin banged his fist onto the wooden floor in his anger.

"Yes, to help me," I whispered, swiping at my tears.

"I need to go back, Rissa. I need to travel with you."

I looked toward Gabriel, standing near the doorway, a silent sentinel to our devastation. "Gabriel and I have enough saved for two to travel. We'd decided, if you wanted to come, you and I would go, and Gabe would stay."

"That's not fair to you, Rissa." Colin shook his head, and I could tell he was readying his argument.

"I want you with me as we face attending our father's funeral. You should be there too, Col," I whispered, unable to speak louder past the thickness in my throat.

"I can't believe Da's gone. I ... There's so much I wanted to say to him. So much I never said because I got so mad at him because he married that awful woman." Colin lowered his head, resting it on his bent knees as his shoulders shuddered with his sobs.

I reached forward to touch his back, uncertain how to impart comfort when I was in as much need for comfort. He took a deep breath, reining in his grief. "And we'll have to face her again."

He met my shattered gaze. "Most likely Mrs. Wright and the grandparents, too."

"I know. But I still need to be there."

Colin nodded. "We should pack if we are to leave tomorrow. I'll tell Amelia why I'm not staying for supper. I couldn't possibly eat." He rose onto his knees again and leaned forward, embracing me for a few moments.

***

"ARE YOU ASLEEP?" I whispered. I laid on my back staring at the ceiling, tracing patterns on Gabriel's arm wrapped along my middle.

"If I were, I'm sure you'd wake me up," he mumbled, his voice thick with fatigue. I turned my head, meeting his teasing eyes. "That whisper would've woken the dead."

I turned, rolling into him for a full-bodied hug. He grunted at my sudden movement before adjusting and holding me close. Our foreheads touched, and, if I arched my back, I could kiss him. For now, I remained in his embrace, breathing the same air, memorizing his touch.

"Are you all right, my darling?" He brushed his fingers up and down my back.

I shook my head, trying to blink away tears. "I know I need to go. I want to go. But I can't stand the thought of leaving you again. Of not having you next to me."

Gabriel stroked my cheek, causing me to meet his worried gaze. "I'll telegram Uncle. Borrow the money from him. I'll come with you."

"No, I know you should stay here. You've important commissions."

"Nothing is more important than you, darling. If you want me with you, I'll be there."

I blinked my agreement, plump tears escaping my eyes. "Of course I want you with me, but I know you should stay here. Even if it's borrowing from Aidan, I don't like being in debt." I turned, wiping my face on the pillow for a moment before moving again so I could see Gabriel. "I'm just being selfish."

"No, you're not. And it never hurts me to hear you need me. That you want me with you."

"Always, my darling. I'll miss you, more than I can say while I'm away," I said as I choked on a sob. Gabriel pulled me close as I cried on his shoulder.

"And I will never be happier than when you return to me," Gabriel said.

CHAPTER 30

"WHY DID YOU WANT to come to Quincy with me, dearest? You have been quite reticent of late, and I'm worried about you." Betsy sat in her back parlor, the sage-green wallpaper with silver filigree running through it lit up by lamps. The fireplace along the rear wall emitted a soothing warmth.

"I feel a fool, Aunt Betsy," Savannah whispered. "Jeremy scared me, and I ran."

Betsy frowned as she studied Savannah. "Jeremy doesn't seem the type of man to hurt you. He seems even gentler of a man than his brother Gabriel."

"We argued, and, when he moved toward me, all I could see was Jonas. The way Jonas ..." Savannah broke off and looked out the back window.

"Share this with me, Savannah. I fear, if you keep it inside, you will be prisoner to it forever. You need to know there is no shame in what happened."

"There is! I knew I shouldn't marry him. I knew I should listen to Clarissa. To you. But I wanted to believe I could belong in that world. The world that glittered and where I'd have many maids to wait on me. A fancy house with beautiful carriages. I was too stupid or gullible to realize I wasn't wanted."

"What do you mean?" Aunt Betsy asked, clasping Savannah's hand gently as she spoke.

"He wanted the dowry from my grandparents. Not me. Never me. He was embarrassed by me from the beginning. He loathed my parents,

Clarissa—everyone but you and the grandparents—because of their simple ways. He despised Clarissa for her spirit. When he saw what he called 'the Clarissa influence' in me, he became increasingly determined to beat it out of me."

Betsy gasped, gripping Savannah's hand tightly. "Which is why you were so frequently 'ill.'"

"He didn't want me to see my family. He desired me to be dependent on him. And he wanted me to beg for everything I wanted." Savannah closed her eyes as tears trickled down her cheeks. "If I disobeyed him, the punishments were severe. He broke my ribs and then took perverse delight in having my maid tighten the laces to the point I would faint if I did more than whisper."

"Oh, dearest." Betsy swiped at her cheeks, turning her head away for a moment.

"Forgive me, Aunt Betsy. I should never have spoken of such things. It's very uncouth of me."

"No, Savannah. You have nothing to ask forgiveness for. Although there are many who should be begging your forgiveness. Including me." She clasped Savannah's hand again, meeting Savannah's eyes. "I thought you no longer wanted much to do with us. We all did. I never suspected ..."

"It's what he wanted. I learned never to countermand him. I couldn't ... I didn't know if anyone would believe me. Mother was so happy with me marrying a man of such social respectability as Jonas. She never seemed concerned about the man beneath the veneer."

"Whatever you may think about your mother, she does love you, Savannah." Betsy watched her niece with concerned eyes.

"Not enough. She worried more about the scandal when I left Jonas's house than me. Not about what would it take to provoke me to leave his home."

"I find it interesting you call it his home, dearest. Not yours."

"It was never mine. I wasn't allowed to furbish it. I wasn't allowed to have friends call. I was to be present as an arm ornamentation for Jonas when he had business associates visit. To never have a thought of my own but to parrot what he wanted me to say."

"With all you have said about Jonas, I'm confused how you could compare Jeremy McLeod to Jonas."

"I made Jeremy angry. He reached for me, and it terrified me. For an instant, I envisioned him treating me like—"

"Like Jonas treated you."

"Yes. I also know Jeremy has demons, Aunt. He did terrible things in the Philippines. Things he now regrets and that haunt him."

"Savannah. I want you to think of Jeremy. Of how he has treated you. Of the man you know. Do you see him treating you poorly? Abusing you? For, if you do, no matter how much I might like his brother, I do not want you with him. I want you with a man who understands what a treasure you are."

Savannah closed her eyes, a frown furrowing her forehead. After a few moments, her countenance brightened, and a faint smile lit her face. "When I think of Jeremy, he is taking care of someone. Florence, Clarissa, me. It's as though he's trying to atone for what he did by being a better man now," Savannah whispered, her tone one of a revelation. "He wouldn't hurt me, Aunt Betsy." She smiled broadly as she returned Betsy's hand clasp.

"That was the impression I had, Savannah dear. In the end, it only matters what you think. For you are the one who will need to fight your fears and these memories forever." She patted Savannah's cheek. "The memories will fade, but they will always be there."

Savannah collapsed against the comfortable sleigh-back settee with rosewood detailing. She reached for a pillow, pulling it to her chest, as she forced herself to meet her aunt's direct gaze. "I don't understand. Why does my mother wish me such ill will? And why does Father try to placate her?"

"Darling, your parents were young once too."

"What does that have to do with now?" Savannah asked, nearly wailing the question.

"Everything. Your mother resents you and Clarissa because you are determined to live the lives you want. Not the lives others wanted for you." Betsy took a deep breath. "And because you were brave enough to give up everything for those lives."

"But she loves Father. Theirs was a love match."

"Ah, Savannah. There's so much you do not know." For a long moment, Betsy studied her with eyes made green from her jade dress. She reached out to push away a stray tendril of hair from Savannah's forehead. "I wonder if I have the right to tell you."

"Please. For if you don't, I'll never know. This anger will only grow, and I fear any hope I had for happiness will be devoured by it."

"That's a bit dramatic, dear, but I agree. There have been too many secrets for too long. My parents, your grandparents, instilled in all three of us girls the need to always give the outward appearance of decorum and calm. That, to forestall gossip, one must act as others expected us to act. And that, in the end, we had no rights to our own desires."

"I don't understand. Aunt Agnes married a man she loved. I'm sure of it."

"Yes, Agnes did. She was the only one of the three of us fortunate enough and intelligent enough to marry for love and not bow to the weight of expectations, thus providing a wonderful example for Clarissa. I married out of duty. I love your uncle now, although I had only met him a handful of times before we wed. I fulfilled my parents' expectations. As had been foreseen for Matilda. However, Matilda was always a little wild."

"Wild? Mother is the least adventurous person I know."

"You say that now. If you had known her then, you would have thought her more radical than Sophronia."

"Surely you exaggerate."

"I knew her well. I married Tobias to quiet the gossips. Believe me, I remember." Betsy tapped her fingers on the armrest of the settee, her motions belying her agitation. "Matilda wanted to travel to Paris. Meet the artists, live a wild, free life. And have our parents bankroll it.

"Our parents had other ideas. They arranged for her to marry a Mr. Fitzgilbert. A kind man, set to inherit a fortune. A man whose idea of adventure was eating dinner fifteen minutes later than usual. Matilda railed against our parents' choice and began to sneak out to Scollay Square. She met an actor there. I'm not even sure of his name."

After a few moments of silence, Savannah whispered, "What happened?"

"She thought she was in love. She was quite foolish and soon found herself with child. As you can imagine, our parents were furious. I was shocked and quite naive, as I had been the most sheltered of the three of us and had never imagined such a scandal. That sort of thing did not happen to our sort of people." Her tone perfectly mimicked Savannah's grandfather.

"As any hope of a marriage to the dour yet appropriate Mr. Fitzgilbert was now dashed, my father searched for another candidate. He knew he could not aim as high as before. One day at his tailor's, he met your father delivering cloth. Your grandfather's business was hurting as he was not importing the high-quality French linens he was famous for, due to the Franco-Prussian War.

"My father saw an opportunity. He offered your father's father a generous dowry in exchange for your father marrying his daughter with no questions asked. Mr. Russell agreed, even though your father was engaged to another. Matilda and your father met for the first time on their wedding day."

Savannah paled at Aunt Betsy's story, her sky-blue eyes unblinking as she thought through the story. "Why the lies? The deception about them marrying for love?"

"Appearances, dearest. Your father did not want to be accused of being a bought man, and your mother could not afford to have the truth of her situation come out. For her part, Agnes was furious. She encouraged Matilda to live with her, have the child and dare to live a life free of the restrictions instilled upon us by the grandparents. Matilda declined her offer."

"But I've never met an older sibling, other than Lucas. And Lucas's twin, Anita. And she died when I was very young. Are you saying they aren't my father's children?"

"No, Savannah. Your mother lost the baby. Less than two months after the wedding." Aunt Betsy smiled forlornly. "For what it's worth, I believe your parents do love each other now. It has taken time, but I think Matilda would be lost without Martin. He's a very good, calming presence for her."

There was silence for a few moments. "You must understand, Savannah. Times were different thirty years ago. Your mother and father asked everyone who knew their true story to refrain from speaking of it. Well, and when you speak of someone marrying for a love match enough times, you start to believe it a little yourself."

"Everything I thought I knew about them is a lie," Savannah said.

"One day you'll understand that you'll want the right to have others know only what you want them to know about your past. Not everyone has the right to know everything, dearest. Not even a daughter."

Savannah clutched the pillow tighter, almost bending it in half in her anxiety. "Even with all you've told me, I don't understand why Mother treats me as she does."

"She will forever try to regain the good graces of your grandparents. She desires that above all else. And, as I said before, she resents that you and Clarissa had the strength to defy your families. She bowed to their wishes."

"Oh, Aunt Betsy. She did what she had to do for her baby. As any mother would. Why can't she see that? Why can't she love me enough to see that I'm doing what I must so that I can survive?"

"Are you?"

"What do you mean? Of course I am. I'm away from Jonas, even though I will not be able to divorce him. I'll never be within his sphere of influence again."

"Is that all you want, Savannah? To survive? I would think, after all you have been through, you'd want more."

CHAPTER 31

"SAVANNAH, DEAREST, IT'S WONDERFUL to have you back from your aunt's, although I'm sorry for the reason you've had to return," Sophie said. She sat in her rear sitting room, long shadows on the wall. She reached toward a lamp and switched one on. A gentle fire warmed and partially lit the room. She'd once told Savannah dusk was her favorite time of day for quiet contemplation and that she preferred to watch the changing light without interference of man-made light.

"We were shocked to receive word that Uncle Sean had died," Savannah said. She leaned against the back of her chair, letting out a weary sigh. "I can only imagine how hard this is on Clarissa."

"Yes, especially as her last interactions with him were influenced by that horrid woman he married," Sophronia said. "I've had word that she is hoping to travel for the funeral."

"I can't imagine she'd travel so far."

"Wouldn't you for your father?" Sophronia raised an eyebrow, her aquamarine eyes lit with reproach.

Savannah blushed and nodded. "Of course."

"You seem to have thrived under your aunt's gentle care. It's good to see you looking healthy and at peace."

"Aunt Betsy is wonderful at spoiling me. And at making me face truths." Savannah sighed, her gaze roaming Sophronia's face. "You look much better too, Sophie."

"A few bruises and a trifling head wound aren't going to keep the likes of me down," Sophie said. "Although, having suffered as I did, most terribly according to the papers"—she raised a sardonic eyebrow at Savannah—"it still had no bearing on your case against Jonas. My lawyer suggested I settle with him on my case."

"I hope you gouged him for a horrid amount of money," Savannah said.

"Never you fear, I did," Sophronia said with a gleam to her eyes. "Now, on to more interesting topics. Did you write your young man at all?"

"No, I didn't believe it would be proper. Not after I'd asked him for time to better determine what I needed. It seemed hypocritical."

"Though you thought about him." When Savannah nodded her agreement, Sophronia said, "I think you would have been surprised by his letters. I know Clarissa enjoyed her Gabriel's letters and cherished all he sent her. Even though they were parted, it gave her the sense they were still close."

"I know. But she hadn't asked him for space. It's not at all the same situation." At Sophie's challenging stare, Savannah fidgeted. "I've realized I need to see Jeremy. I want to. I want him in my life. And I fear I have ruined everything by my absence."

Sophronia nodded her agreement. "I'm glad you took time away to determine your own mind. Now you'll have no doubts. As for Mr. McLeod, I've rarely seen a man as dedicated to his love's happiness. I was impressed by our conversation over tea and when he arrived the day you departed for Quincy. He appears the antithesis of Jonas."

"I agree. I continue to hope he'll give me another chance." Savannah sighed. "I won't contact him until after the funeral. It wouldn't be seemly."

"Well, I hope he doesn't hear of your return before you write him. Men have a tendency to misunderstand even the most simple of situations."

Savannah laughed at Sophronia and curled into her chair. "It's good to be back, Sophie."

***

THE FOLLOWING AFTERNOON, Savannah entered the formal front parlor and paused for a moment as she saw her father conversing with Sophie. "Father!" She rushed forward to hug him.

"There's my girl," he said. He pulled her to him and held her for a few moments. After he released her, he held onto her hand and eased her onto the settee next to him. "I've missed you while you've been with your aunt Betsy."

"I missed you too, Father."

"When you returned from Quincy, I continued to hope you'd return to us," he said.

Savannah flinched at the reproach in his voice. She nodded, acknowledging his concern. "This is where I should be, Father. I can't live under Mother's constant criticism. I'm glad Aunt Betsy will be with you for a little while."

"As are we, although we are all deeply saddened by the reason for her travel."

"I know. The funeral is in a few days."

"You will attend, Savannah?"

At her hesitancy, where she bit her lip and looked away, he reached forward and gripped her hand. "Savannah, what has you worried?"

"What if Jonas is there?" Her voice trembled at the thought.

"As if that man would deign to attend the funeral of a blacksmith," Sophie said with a sniff.

"I worry he'll surprise us. I can't see him. I need more time before facing him again." Savannah drew small circles on her dress in her agitation.

"Mrs. Chickering, do you mind if I have a few moments alone with my daughter?" Martin asked.

Sophie nodded, rose and closed the door behind her with a soft *click*.

"Why did you never tell me how he treated you?"

"I was ashamed. Afraid you'd believe it was my fault." Savannah looked down. "And then I'd truly have had no hope."

"Did you think I wouldn't believe you? That I wouldn't defend you against such a man?" he rasped.

"Mother said that I needed to accept my choices. That once I was married to him, I needed to believe as Jonas did and to not question him." Savannah blinked away tears and turned her face away from her father, casting her face in shadow.

"Dammit, I'm not your mother!" Martin roared. "I would have protected you. I would have ensured you left his house after the first time he hurt you. Why would you stay?"

"I thought it was expected of me!" Savannah gripped the edge of the settee, her fingers digging into the fine silk as she met her father's eyes, unable to hide the devastation in her gaze.

"To live with a man who brutalized you? How could you doubt me so?" Savannah flinched at her father's anguished whisper.

He rose and paced toward the mantel. As Savannah spoke, he held up a hand. He faced the crackling fire, staring into the flames. "Please, don't say anything. I'm again acting as though this is your fault. As though you have something to atone for. Whereas I'm the one who needs forgiveness."

He turned to face his daughter with tormented eyes. "Forgive me for failing you, Savannah. I realize now I chose not to see the subtle clues you showed us. I couldn't bear to believe you would be treated in such a way. And now I realize the reality you suffered was much worse than anything I'd imagined."

"How do you know how I was treated?" Savannah asked, tears trickling down her cheeks.

"Your aunt Betsy and I spoke late into the night last evening. She detailed the little you told her. It was enough to give me nightmares."

"Did you speak with Mother about what Aunt Betsy said?"

Martin sighed and nodded.

Savannah's breath hitched as she said, "So she understands now why I left." She saw her father wince at the hopeful tone of her voice.

"Don't become hopeful. She believes you ..." He paused as though looking for the words. He looked away, unwilling to watch the hope dim from his daughter's face as his words resonated.

"Fabricated the reason to abandon my good home and bring shame onto the entire family," Savannah said, her voice laced with dull resignation.

"Exactly," Martin said. He approached the settee and sat next to her. "I'm sorry for your mother."

"At least you understand. Thank you." She leaned into him. "Although I don't believe you need it, I forgive you."

"Thank you, my Savannah. I find I very much need it. It's like a balm to a festering wound. As for your mother, I don't know as she will ever change her mind." He handed Savannah his clean linen handkerchief, and she scrubbed her face.

"I'm trying to accept her as she is, although I know I'll never be close to her again." She turned to sit sideways and to better face him. "I'm sorry for you. I wish she were more understanding." At his inquisitive furrowing of his forehead, she whispered, "Aunt Betsy and I had plenty of time to chat while I visited. I badgered her into telling me about you and Mother."

"She had no right, Savannah. That was not her story to tell."

"Maybe not. But you were never going to tell me, and I needed to better understand Mother. I didn't want my disappointment and hurt to evolve into hate."

He nodded. "I can understand. It doesn't paint either of us in a good light." He squeezed her hand. "Whatever you imagine, however you believe what you have learned has helped you understand your mother better, never doubt what you knew to be true when you lived at home. We loved you and Lucas, and we love you now. We've come to care a great deal for each other. Never doubt the affection we've shown.

"The only time I've known regret since I married your mother has been recently. When I learned how you were treated by Jonas." Martin met her worried gaze. "I want you to know I plan on visiting Jonas and demanding he release you from this marriage. He has no right to continue to wish you home after how he has treated you."

"Please be careful. I know Jonas, and he'll be enraged that you believe you have the right to give him any form of instruction."

"I have failed in almost all aspects as a father once he was introduced to you. I refuse to fail you now."

Savannah blinked away tears. "Thank you."

"Is there any truth to the stories in the paper about you and a carpenter?"

Savannah blushed and looked away. Then she straightened her shoulders and met her father's worried gaze with a hopeful one. "Yes, there is. Did you ever meet Jeremy McLeod? Gabriel's youngest brother?" She watched as her father took a moment to think through the people he had met before he shook his head no. "He befriended me last summer. When I searched for my baby. We became close."

"I can't approve."

"Father," Savannah began but was hushed by Martin.

"I can't approve until I can meet him and see for myself that he treats you well. I need to take his measure. See for myself how he is and not be guided by your mother or anyone else."

"You liked Gabriel."

"I did, and that is something this Jeremy has in his favor. But he is his own man, and I will judge him for who he is. Not who his family is." He smiled at Savannah. "When can I meet him?"

"I'll see what I can arrange," Savannah whispered, fighting tears. "I believe you will like him."

"The fact you think so highly of him is in his favor." He gripped her hand as he rose to leave.

CHAPTER 32

"YOU SEEM TO BE LABORING under a misapprehension," Jonas said. He sat in a polished mahogany swivel chair behind a large mahogany desk. The desk filled a quarter of the room, as though its size alone proclaimed the importance of the man sitting behind it. Sitting across from double doors, large windows let in late afternoon sunlight onto the desk. Dark wood paneling covered the walls, and thick red-and-black Persian carpets covered the wooden floors. A faint scent of cigar smoke lingered in the room, mingling with the aroma from the hothouse roses sitting on a table near a window to the left of the door.

Jonas's navy jacket was slung over the back of a nearby chair, and he sat wearing a pristine white shirt, navy waistcoat and burgundy tie. Gold cuff links caught the sunlight. He crossed his legs, creasing his tailored suit pants, watching his father-in-law with thinly veiled contempt.

"I'll have you know that no man has the right to treat my daughter as you have." Martin Russell vibrated with fury as he watched his son-in-law. He wore an equally fine suit in a rich chocolate brown that highlighted his eyes. At this moment, they flashed with fury, appearing more black than brown.

"You fail to understand that, when I married her, she became mine, to do with as I wish."

"She's not a possession."

"No, she's of less value, as she causes me no end of expense for her upkeep. Nor does she fulfill her one purpose in this marriage," Jonas said.

"You have no basis for complaint with Savannah. She has been a perfect wife for you from the first day."

"Only a father could believe such about a daughter like yours," Jonas said as he steepled his fingers and watched Martin disdainfully.

"Accuse me of being proud of my beautiful daughter. I see no shame in that. Charge her of any crime against you, and you are a liar."

"Careful, old man," Jonas said. "I'd hate to sue you for slander."

"I wouldn't think you'd want any more scandal associated with you," Martin said on a deep exhale. He took another deep breath in an attempt to calm himself. "In whatever way you think you have been misused, I assure you my family's suffering is worse."

"She had one task. One!" Jonas said with a slight rise in his voice. He slammed his hand down on the desk as he leaned forward and glared at Martin. "And she couldn't fulfill the most basic task. I was assured she was the epitome of a refined woman. I couldn't have been more misled."

"You were the most fortunate of men to have married my Savannah."

"With the influence of women such as your rebellious niece, Clarissa, I count myself cursed. Mrs. Montgomery needed more guidance than a woman accustomed to my social standing should have needed to know her place."

"Beating her into submission would never convince her to your way of thinking," Martin hissed.

"After all I did for her, bringing her into my world and introducing her to the finest of society, how dare she produce a girl? Why would I want a daughter? I needed a son!" Jonas roared as he rose to pace the small area behind his desk.

"You are mad to believe she had any control over that outcome," Martin said. "If you truly believe my daughter acted to thwart you in such a manner, I'm glad she is free of you."

"Is that what you think?" Jonas asked as he turned to watch Martin with a possessive gleam in his eyes.

"Yes. We will always regret our liaison with you."

"Finally something we have in common. My associates tell me your business is thriving of late. After a little … hiccup this summer, it appears your shop is more popular than ever."

Martin watched him, the pursing of his lips the only sign of his mounting tension. "I have been fortunate to have loyal customers."

"Yes, I imagine that is necessary when one is in trade. Such a precarious position to be in, isn't it? Surviving solely on the whims of the customers and bankers."

"I repeat, we have been fortunate."

"All good fortune comes to an end," Jonas said with a hint of steel. "Unless your daughter returns to me, I will ensure your business loans come due in the next month."

Martin paled before flushing with anger. "If you think for one moment that would induce me to consign my daughter to even one more hour in your company, you don't know me." He watched Jonas with loathing. He rose, tugging on the tail of his jacket. "I wish you a good day."

"Enjoy your month," Jonas said as he settled into his chair.

***

"MATILDA, YOU MUST SEE that Savannah cannot return to that man," Martin said. He paced the upstairs parlor, moving toward the door to slam it shut. The paintings on the wall vibrated, one tilting to one side. He continued to march around the room, pushing ottomans out of his way as he made a circuit from the door to fireplace to piano and back.

"Martin, there is no reason to act as you do," Matilda said. She sat working on needlepoint, jabbing a needle with lilac thread in and out with precision. "You know as well as I do that Savannah's tales of abuse are fabrications. She envisions herself some sort of martyr to that horrid cause Clarissa espouses."

"Do you even listen to yourself, Matilda? This is your daughter, our daughter, we are speaking of. The beautiful, vibrant girl we raised."

"No need to be so dramatic. She married well, as the women of my family are expected to."

Martin banged his hand against a side table, rattling it so hard the lamp shook. Matilda looked up from her needlepoint to meet his irate gaze. "Don't tell me about socially acceptable behavior, Matilda. Don't tell me about doing what is expected. If I recall, you experimented with your freedom."

"Yes, and look what it brought me!" She rose from her chair, tossing her linen to the vacated chair.

"What did it bring you, Matilda? Tell me, after all this time, tell me." Martin watched her with hurt, passion-filled eyes.

"To a husband who will always see me as nothing more than damaged. To the decrepit South End." She took a shuddering breath. "The one thing

I could bring you, Martin, was social respectability. I think I fulfilled my part of the bargain."

"No, Mattie, no," Martin whispered. His anger left him as quickly as it had come. He reached out toward her, cupping her face with one of his large palms. "I've never seen you as damaged. I've always seen you as too good for me. Living above a linen store when you come from Beacon Hill. How could you possibly want a man like me?"

"I've done my duty," Matilda said, blinking rapidly to forestall shedding any tears.

"Is that how you see me, as a duty?" Martin asked, dropping his hand and flinching from her words.

She turned to watch him. "Savannah is our concern, Martin."

"Yes, she is. But I will not allow you to dissuade me from speaking with you of this. We've never resolved this between us, Matilda. I thought—" He paused as though selecting his words with care. "I thought it better to never discuss the reason behind our marriage. To instead work toward forging a successful union."

"We've had nearly thirty years together, Martin. There is no reason to speak of this now."

"I think there is. I think that because of your … choices, you feel compelled to show your parents that you raised an exemplary daughter. One they would be proud of. I see now that their influence has been harmful."

"My parents are wonderful people."

"Only if you do and act as they wish you to. I, for one, am tired of feeling as though a puppet to their bidding." Martin reached out and encased her slim arms in his large hands, gripping them gently. "Mattie, do you care for me at all?"

"This is unseemly, Martin."

"I don't believe it is. If you're willing to consign your daughter to a loveless marriage, to a man who brutalizes her for the sake of regaining esteem in your parents' eyes, I think you need to be frank with me. Is it because you've lived so long without knowing how I feel that you believe our daughter could live a similar life devoid of love?"

"You've never treated me poorly," Matilda said. "I would never have countenanced it."

"No, and I never will. I love you, Mattie. I have since I held you in my arms as you sobbed over the loss of your child."

She hissed in a breath, taken aback by his words. "Martin—"

"Shh ... I have, Mattie. I tried to tell you. I sang to you, songs about love. And every time I did, you turned away. I guess I was a coward and lost my opportunity to tell you how I truly felt." He sighed, squeezing her arms for a moment. "I've always loved you, Mattie."

"Martin," Matilda said as she shook her head and broke away from his gentle grip. She wiped at her cheeks, as her tears fell unchecked. "You have been a good man to me and a good father to the children."

Martin jerked his head back as though slapped. "I see. Yes, a good man. And, until now, a good provider." He turned from her and paced toward the fireplace. He pinched the bridge of his nose and took a deep breath.

After a few moments, he spoke. "You are right, Matilda. Savannah is our concern. You believe she is fabricating stories to prevent her return to Jonas. I disagree. I believe her stories of mistreatment to be true. Do you believe any of what Betsy told me?" He turned to meet her gaze, anger lighting his eyes.

"If you believe Betsy, you'll start espousing her notions for women," Matilda snapped.

"Well, she may convert me to her way of thinking now that I've come to realize all that she's done for our daughter." Martin's voice turned colder as he spoke with Matilda. "When will you accept that Jonas beat Savannah? That all of her so-called illnesses were to recover from his abuse?"

"Martin, I never knew you to believe in fairy tales."

"Damn it, Matilda, I'm serious!" Martin roared. "How can you not see that our only living daughter was subjected to such hell? How can you not care?"

"She married him. It is her duty to remain with him."

"If you truly believe that, then you aren't the woman I've thought you were. I will not consign Savannah to an early grave simply because you are unable or unwilling to see sense. That is *my* duty as her father."

"Have you spoken with Savannah about this purported treatment at the hands of her husband?"

"Of course. Did you never imagine, not even for a second, what it would take for Savannah to leave her husband's home?" Martin asked. When Matilda remained resolutely quiet, he took a deep breath. "As my wife, I feel it is my duty to inform you that in one month's time, there is every chance we will lose our living."

"What?" Matilda gasped, clutching one hand to her heart. She reached for her chair, nearly sitting on her needlepoint. She pushed it out of the way, thrusting it onto the floor.

"Jonas informed me today that, in one month's time, our loans will be called due."

"He can't. He wouldn't. He's not that sort of man!"

"He can. He will. And, Matilda, I think it's time you accepted that, yes, he is that sort of man. He will do whatever he needs to ensure that Savannah returns to his home."

CHAPTER 33

I STOOD IN SOUTH STATION, my head tilted back as I stared at the main terminal waiting area. Muted light filtered in through high windows although, on this overcast day, no shaft of sunlight brightened the cavernous interior with its multileveled-coffered ceiling. I heard the clicking of a multitude of shoes on the marble floors but remained rooted in place, overwhelmed by memories of the last few times I was here.

I closed my eyes, remembering the moments before Gabriel had boarded his train west. My heart clenched as I heard a conductor call, "All aboard!"—in an instant thrusting me back to that moment when Gabriel had left Boston. A cascade of images came: his piercing blue eyes studying me as though memorizing me; our last kiss; him walking away; Colin holding me in his arms as the train wended its way out of sight. I sniffled, and the strong scent of shoe polish reminded me of the day in early May last year when I had departed with Sophronia and Aunt Betsy. I had searched the crowd, hoping to find a familiar face before leaving Boston—for what I had envisioned was forever—only to find no one had come to see me off.

I jerked as Colin touched my arm, and I opened my eyes, returning to the present. "Rissa, I've found a porter. He'll help us with our trunks. Are you sure about where we should go?"

"Of course. I know we'll be welcomed." I blinked back tears. "I can't go to the house. Not now. Now that Da's not there. I couldn't live with her when he was alive, and it would be impossible for me to reside with her now."

"I've no desire to see her any sooner than necessary," Colin said. "I bought a paper. It will inform us of the upcoming wakes and funerals."

We boarded a horse-drawn carriage, and I settled into one side of the seat, closing my eyes to the rocking motion. I heard Colin rustling the papers as he read.

"Damn," he muttered.

I peered at him to find him poking his head out the window and yelling up to the carriage driver. The carriage veered to the right, and I held my hands out to brace myself against the wall and ceiling, to prevent falling onto the floor. "Col, what's the matter?" I asked.

"Da's service is right now, Rissa. If we rush, we might make the burial," he said. "It's in Dorchester at Saint Mary's."

"He can't be buried there. He won't be buried next to Mama." I blinked away tears at the thought of my parents not buried beside each other.

"Rissa, there's nothing we can do about it. I've told the man that we're in a rush, and all we can do is hope we arrive there in time."

After what seemed an eternity, but which I knew was really a very fast journey to Dorchester, the carriage jerked to a halt. Colin and I hurtled ourselves from the carriage. He held onto my arm, preventing me from falling into a puddle. "This way, Rissa," Colin said and began to walk with his long gait toward the crowd in the center of the cemetery.

"Col," I gasped. "I can't walk as fast as you."

"Then run," he said as he picked up his pace. I trotted next to him. We raced past rows of granite headstones, some listing to one side. My feet sank into the dampened earth, a reminder of a recent rain. The bare-limbed trees provided no relief to the solemn occasion.

As we approached those gathered, I heard disgruntled murmurings. All the mourners were attired in severe black mourning clothes, whereas Colin and I were in traveling clothes. As it was a cold November, Colin wore a dark gray overcoat with a bright green scarf. I had worn my warmest jacket, a burgundy wool with black scrollwork detailing.

I heard the priest speaking in a purposeful yet monotone voice and moved in that direction. We pushed our way forward until we were near the front, standing beside our stepmother, Mrs. Sullivan, who Colin and I continued to call by her first married name, Mrs. Smythe. I tried to focus on the priest's words, but all I could see was the deep chasm scarring the ground filled with my father's coffin. Soon it would be covered by dirt and all that would remain as a reminder of my da would be a headstone.

I stifled a sob and leaned into Colin. The priest intoned "Amen," and a chorus of "Amens" washed over us.

I heard someone gasp and glanced to my left. I met Savannah's huge eyes an instant before she shrieked. "Rissa! Colin!" She rushed toward us and enveloped first Colin and then me in hugs. "I never thought you'd make it." She returned her mother's frown as her exuberant welcome had momentarily paused the burial.

"We'll explain everything later, Sav," I whispered. "Stand with us?"

"Of course," she said, looping her arm through mine.

A moment later I felt a warm hand on my shoulder and heard Lucas murmur in my ear. "It's wonderful to see you, Rissa, although I'm so sorry." I leaned backward into him for a moment before standing tall and attempting to focus on the remainder of the burial.

As Mrs. Smythe moved forward to toss dirt on the grave, I knew I needed to also be a part of the ceremony. "Col?" I whispered.

"Yes, I agree," he said. We walked forward and each picked up handfuls of dirt. As I held mine over the open grave, I thought of my da and mama together at last, and said a prayer that they were reunited in heaven, even though they wouldn't be next to each other in the graveyard. I opened my hand, watching as the dirt fluttered down to coat the top of his casket.

I rejoined Savannah and Lucas and, with Colin, we formed a small circle of sorrow. After the final blessing, I waited for other mourners to pay their respects. However, they spoke with Mrs. Smythe and then departed, without speaking with either Colin or me. A few nodded their heads in deference, but most filed past without acknowledging us.

"You aren't properly attired, Rissa," Savannah whispered.

"We just arrived on the train this morning. How were we to change our clothes and make the burial on time?"

"Many see it as disrespectful to your father to come dressed as you are," Lucas said as he nodded to an acquaintance. "And many haven't forgotten the scandal from last year when you ran away to marry a man who'd been banned from your father's house."

"If they were truly concerned about courtesy and respect, they would be upset with Mrs. Smythe for having the ceremony on the day we informed her we were to arrive," Colin hissed but then cleared his frown with a vague smile at a passing couple.

"She knew you were to arrive?" Savannah asked.

"Of course," I said. "We cabled her the minute we made our plans."

Savannah sighed and said, "Here comes Mother."

I looked around Savannah and nodded toward Aunt Matilda and Uncle Martin. "Clarissa, you are a sight for sore eyes," Uncle Martin said and pulled me into his loving arms. "It's good to see you."

"And you, Uncle," I whispered. My throat thickened at smelling his familiar scent and for feeling, for an instant, sheltered in his strong arms again.

He held out his hand and shook Colin's. He looked at the two of us with a deep sadness in his eyes. "I'm terribly sorry about Sean. It came as a shock to us all."

I gripped his arm in acknowledgment, my eyes filling with tears and throat thickening, unable to speak.

"I can't believe you would disgrace your father in such a way by arriving as you did," Aunt Matilda seethed. "Your mother would be appalled."

I glanced around the site to realize very few people remained. I cleared my throat and blinked away my tears. "Mama would be appalled, Aunt, that our stepmother did not have the decency to hold the ceremony one day, even though she knew we were coming. She'd be appalled that her husband is not to be buried next to her. Our appearance would be the least of her concerns."

"Well, I can see you've only become less refined in that horrid town you live in out West," Aunt Matilda said.

"Yes, and I'm thankful for it. I'm able to decipher what truly matters," I snapped.

"Mattie, you know the girl has the right of it," Aunt Betsy said.

"Aunt Betsy!" I exclaimed. I saw her standing near Lucas and moved toward her to embrace her. "Thank you for all your letters."

"I promised you that we'd have letters," she said, as she wiped away one of my tears. "Have you spoken with her yet?" she asked as she nodded toward Mrs. Smythe. I shook my head no. "I'd speak with her and end your agony now, dearest."

I nodded and turned toward my stepmother. I signaled to Colin that I needed to speak to her alone and approached Mrs. Smythe, who had turned to leave with Mrs. Wright. "Mrs. Smythe," I said.

"How dare you? Have you no shame?" She spun to face me, her blond hair hidden under a black hat. She wore a stylish, flattering black dress and jacket that highlighted the curves she'd never lost after she had Melinda.

"I beg your pardon? I believe you are again asking questions that you should answer. I can't believe you didn't have the decency to hold the funeral for Colin and me."

"Why should I have felt compelled to do anything for you and your feck-less brother? You are nothing to me, and were nothing but a source of pain and disappointment for your father." Any of the singsong sweetness she had used when my father was present was now absent, replaced with a grating, purposeful voice that no longer hid her cunning or ambition.

"Why would you think that statement would shock me? I've never been anything to you, other than a means to an end. And I chose my own path," I said with pride.

"You deceitful girl. Your father despaired of you, and it's your fault he was brought to an early grave."

Colin had joined us after watching the heated exchange from a few feet away. She spun to him. "And you, you ungrateful leech. Learning all he had to teach you and then abandoning him to run the forge on his own. I'm not surprised he died such an early death with the likes of you as his children."

"Why not look in the mirror, Mrs. Smythe, and realize that your endless harping and spendthrift ways were just as likely to have led to his early death?" Colin said with a vicious snarl. "You only wanted him for security and for the prestige he could bring. You never cared for the man nor his family."

"You see, Mrs. Wright?" Mrs. Smythe simpered into her handkerchief, her voice taking on the sugary tone I despised. "These are the remaining members of Sean's family that I'm to look to for comfort in my grief. I must find solace and strength on my own."

"I am only thankful that such a woman never became a member of my family," Mrs. Wright said as she glared at me. "Shameless, useless girl, only bringing pain and heartache to those around her."

"The feeling is mutual," I snapped.

"Was Patrick informed of Da's death?" Colin asked as he gripped Mrs. Smythe's elbow. She glared at him, but he refused to release her. "I'm shocked he wouldn't travel the short distance from New York City."

"I cannot recall who I informed in my state," Mrs. Smythe said as she cried.

"Save your tears. We know you for the conniving woman you are." Colin glared at her with eyes the color of glowing blue ice. "You purposefully held the ceremony on a day when you thought we wouldn't be able to attend. You didn't tell our brother of his father's death. Why, Mrs. Smythe?"

"You left!" she hissed. "You left. You have no right to any consideration after the way you treated your father and me. The three of you, all ungrateful children, abandoning your home and your duties. Always your duty to your family first. But, clearly your mother, such an unprincipled, wild woman, incapable of raising children, failed to instill that basic tenet in you. Thus, you deserve to suffer, knowing your father died missing you and was buried without you."

I gasped, and Colin shook with rage. "How dare you bury him away from our mother."

"Do you honestly believe I was to have him buried next to her, with no place for me? Besides, when I spoke with your grandparents, they were only too pleased to have one more space in their plot for a deserving member of their family, not an upstart blacksmith who had no right to marry their daughter."

"You vile woman. I will forever rue the day you married my father," Colin said.

"You may call me what you like, Colin. It does not bother me. I know what it takes to survive in this harsh world, much more than you do." She glared at the two of us before pivoting and storming away, Mrs. Wright on her arm.

I shook and reached out to grasp Colin's steady arm. "What did we ever do to deserve her?"

"Nothing," Colin said. "Just had the misfortune of having a misguided da." He noted my shaking. "Ignore her, Rissa. Nothing she says is true."

"I know. But seeing her fills me with rage, Col. At the way she attempted to ruin my life and never feel any regret about what she did."

"Never fear. She'll receive her comeuppance."

"It can't occur soon enough," I said as we moved to rejoin Savannah, Lucas and the rest of the family.

***

"WELL, DEARS, HOW WAS IT?" Sophie sat on a settee in her front living room, a roaring fire adding ambiance to the room.

"Sophie?" I said from the doorway.

Her head jerked toward me, and a satisfied smile flitted across her face as she rose. "Ah, my girl. You arrived in time, I hope?"

I nodded as I fought tears and rushed into her arms for a long embrace.

"There, there, no tears on my account," she murmured.

I shook my head no and backed away. "Forgive me," I whispered. "Sophie, I don't know as you remember Colin."

"Mr. Sullivan, welcome to my home. I hope you find it as comfortable as that luxurious hotel in Minneapolis." She waved to the furniture around the room and Colin, Savannah, Aunt Betsy and I settled.

"How was the weeping widow?" Sophie asked with a raised eyebrow.

"Attempting to appear sad but failing on all counts," Colin said.

"I'd think she'd be terrified of what will become of her now that she doesn't have a husband again," Sophie said.

"Why? You do fine on your own," Savannah said. She smiled to the maid who delivered fresh tea and poured cups for all of us.

"That is my point, Savannah. My husband left me plenty of money, and my tastes were not of the exorbitant kind. She doesn't appear to have the sense to know she must curtail her ways."

"I'm sure Da left her plenty," Colin said. "He'd want to look after Melinda."

"Did you see your sister?" Sophronia asked.

"No, she wasn't there. I thought it was because she was so young, Mrs. Smythe didn't want to expose her to the ceremony."

"Hmm ... Well, I'm sure we'll know in time." She pinned a stare on Colin, her aquamarine eyes shining with curiosity. "Are you returned to take the helm of your father's blacksmithing shop?"

"It's what I should do," Colin said.

"Hmm ... I wouldn't spend too much of my life worried about what I should do, young man. I'd determine what it is I want to do, and then endeavor to do it. Life's too short for the shoulds in life."

Colin shrugged with feigned nonchalance. "It's what my da would have expected of me."

"Humbug. Your father would want you and your siblings happy, wherever you live and whatever you do. He wouldn't want you to martyr yourself to a forge you had no desire to run."

"I need to honor him in this way," Colin murmured.

Sophie began to speak but settled back in her chair when she met Aunt Betsy's severe stare. Aunt Betsy said, "I knew Sean well. I know what he suffered after the death of your mother, and I'm confident he would want both of you to follow your dreams. If you have no desire to live here in Boston, Colin, then don't," Aunt Betsy said.

"It's not that simple, Aunt," Colin said.

"I don't understand why not," Savannah said. "I'd think you'd have the sense to find your happiness and fight to keep it."

"That's your battle, Sav, not mine," Colin said. "The truth is that, if I'd been here, there's a good chance Da wouldn't have died. That he wouldn't have had to work so hard."

"Don't even think of giving that woman's words one moment of credence," I hissed, my face flushing with anger. "She only speaks words of poison to induce pain and promote disharmony."

"There's truth in her words, Rissa. You know I've wondered the same," Colin said.

"It's just as likely your father would have died at the same time whether or not you were sweating away next to him in the forge. The only difference is you would have had the distinction of watching your father die without the ability to render any true aid. Would you then feel you had done your duty as a son? Would you feel free to live the life you desired?" Sophronia demanded.

Colin rose and paced about. "I just buried my father today. Talk of what is to be done with the forge is premature."

Sophie sighed. "My boy, it's premature to anyone with a modicum of decency. However, we all know your stepmother hasn't a decent bone in her body. She'll do what she sees fit with what has been bestowed upon her. I suggest you learn quickly what your father's true wishes were, not what she wants you to believe they were."

"Sophie?" I asked.

"I've heard rumors that she has debts due to her delusions about her grand house in the South End. Debts your father was attempting to repay at the time of his death," Sophronia said, her words sending a chill of foreboding down my spine.

"She wouldn't do anything precipitous with her means of income," I said.

"We know she shows the world the appearance of an eminently ridiculous creature but do not underestimate her." Sophie shared a fierce look with me.

I nodded. "No, never underestimate what she will do to obtain her desired goal," I whispered.

***

AFTER A LIGHT DINNER, Aunt Betsy departed to return to Uncle Martin and Aunt Matilda's home. I wished she could stay with us at Sophie's, but I knew that, with our arrival, Colin and I were using most of Sophie's spare rooms. I attempted to calm my racing thoughts as Savannah poked her head into my room.

"Rissa, do you mind if I join you?" she asked.

"Of course not."

She shut the door behind me, walking soundlessly to the chaise longue set along the far wall of the room. I tucked my legs under me, giving room for Savannah to join me. My night clothes were on my bed, with the covers turned down. Lamps on the low tables throughout the room were lit, many in front of mirrors to give the impression of more light.

Savannah glanced around the room for a moment. "I'd forgotten this room didn't have any windows," she said.

"Sav, are you all right?" I asked, not caring about my room.

"Rissa, there's no reason we should be speaking about me. You've just arrived from a long trip across country and buried your father today."

"I know, and I'm exhausted, but I'm worried about you. I thought you were finally happy now that you were free of Jonas."

"I thought I was. Happy, I mean. But I doubt I'll ever truly be free of a man like Jonas." She glanced at me, and I saw a glimmer of fear in her eyes. "A man like him doesn't accept a woman's wishes."

"He can't hurt you anymore, Sav." I clasped her hand.

"He hurts me every day by being my husband. And it's a wound I inflicted on myself. You can't know what that's like, Rissa. Knowing that all this pain and misery I brought on myself. Why didn't I listen to you? Why didn't I pay attention to my own doubts?"

"Sav, I've learned the fastest way to make myself miserable is to try to change the past," I whispered.

"What in your past would you want to change?"

"What if I had gone to Gabriel sooner? What if that had prevented ... events from that spring with Cameron? My life would have been very different." I blinked away tears.

"Would you be happier now?"

"I have no idea. Because those events did happen. And there's nothing I can do to change them. Wishing it were different only gives me a headache, causes Gabriel pain and leads to sleepless nights."

"I told Jeremy I didn't want to see him for a while," Savannah whispered.

"Why? Did he frighten you? Harm you?"

"No! Never. I imagine he's a bit like Gabriel." Savannah half smiled. "Jonas visited Sophie, hurt her and then tried to force me to leave with him. He terrified me, Rissa. Reminded me of everything I had lived through and escaped. It made me doubt my ability to make decisions for myself. Besides, I'm not free. I'll never be free. It's not fair to Jeremy."

"I imagine that's for Jeremy to decide. If he wants to be your ... friend, then that's his decision, isn't it? Does Jeremy think you're afraid of him?"

"I worry that he does. He went through so much, Rissa, and now I worry I'm just bringing him more pain. He deserves to find some peace."

"Being separated from you, the woman he cares about, will hardly bring him peace. Especially if he believes you fear him. On top of that, if he's concerned about your safety with regard to Jonas, I imagine he's beside himself with worry. I've rarely met a more determined person than a McLeod, especially when it comes to protecting those they care about." I gave Savannah an ironic smile.

"What is it, Rissa?"

"As we speak of Jeremy, all I want is Gabriel. I wish he'd walk through the door right now and surprise me." I gave a half shake of my head. "Isn't it ironic? I've always thought of Boston as my home, but I miss Gabriel so much. I feel homesick for him, and I'm eager to return to him."

"Don't leave too quickly. You just arrived. I need some time with my favorite cousin," Savannah urged.

I smiled my agreement. "I also realized today how much I've changed. I never cared for all of society's rules, but to be snubbed because I wasn't in the proper attire at Da's funeral was beyond anything I could have imagined."

"Wearing a red jacket at a funeral is highly irregular, Rissa."

"It's burgundy," I said with a half smile before sobering. "I would think people would understand I'd just arrived on a train from the west and hadn't had time to change. Instead there was immediate judgment." I sighed my frustration.

"It's how things are, Rissa," Savannah said.

"I know. And I understand that there would have been murmurings in Missoula too, but I think people would at least have paid their respects. It just made a horrible situation that much worse." I rubbed at my face.

"You look exhausted. You should rest." Savannah squeezed my hand in support.

"It doesn't seem real, Sav. I can't believe he's gone," I whispered. "How can both of my parents be gone?" I lowered my head to my forearm resting on the back of the chaise longue, tears leaking from my eyes.

"I'm sorry, Rissa," Savannah said as she took my hand.

"I know. I'm so glad you're staying with Sophie. That we're together." I leaned forward and cried on her shoulder. She rubbed my back and held me but refrained from saying any of the useless platitudes about death and my da being in a better place.

I leaned away from her and swiped at my cheeks. She handed me a clean handkerchief, and I blew my nose.

"Will you be all right?"

"I'll have to be. I'm filled with such regret, and I don't know how to live with it," I whispered.

"Why? Your father was very proud of you. Delighted in the news you sent home. Thankful that you were a faithful letter writer, unlike Colin." She stroked her hand down my arm, as my mother had when I needed comfort.

I blinked back tears as I said, "I left here, disappointed in him. Convinced he would care more for Mrs. Smythe and little Melly than me. I couldn't reconcile the man he'd become to the father he had been. And all the time I hugged my disappointment to me, I knew I was unfair. He never knew what occurred with Cameron. He never understood my desperation to escape. How could he? I refused to speak of it."

"Why, Rissa?"

"I feared I would be forced to marry Cameron to save face. Due to the fact, as Cameron said, 'Now no one will want you but me.'" I shuddered as

I said the words and fought the onslaught of the memory. "I refused to be tied to such a man. I was determined that I would forge my own destiny."

"You're so brave, Rissa."

"But I never spoke with my da again after I was happy with Gabriel." I choked on my tears.

"Surely you wrote him all this," Savannah said.

"Of course. But I never looked into his eyes and saw the da I knew from when Mama lived. I left, with such anger inside me, Sav, and he must have sensed it."

"I'm confident your father knew he'd married a woman who had only brought disharmony among his family. That was his great mistake. He never begrudged you your ability to escape and find joy with Gabriel. I remember once, before I had the baby, I visited my parents for dinner, and your father was there, regaling us of tales you had written. I've never seen a father more proud than when he spoke of you, Rissa. He rejoiced in you, your letters, your tales of that wild place you had settled in. I think he wished he could travel to be with you."

I snorted. "Mrs. Smythe would never have borne traveling to Montana!"

Savannah giggled. "No, she wouldn't have, although I would have loved to have received your letter describing her misadventures."

I shuddered. "Not even in jest. I'm thankful knowing there is a place I can go where she has no interest." I smiled, gazing distantly over Savannah's shoulder before focusing on her. "Thank you for sharing that story with me. After what Mrs. Smythe said today, I worried he didn't receive the letters I had sent to the forge."

I studied Savannah for a moment before asking softly, "Sav, what did he do to you?"

"It doesn't matter now, Rissa."

"I think it does. You're allowing fear, learned from horrible treatment, to prevent you from imagining a different sort of life with Jeremy."

"What if I were to tell you Jeremy isn't as you imagine?" Savannah challenged.

"Then I would trust your judgment. You know him much better than I do."

Savannah's shoulders stooped as she exhaled, and she bowed her head. "I'd be lying anyway. He's a wonderful man. Though he is tormented by everything that happened in the Philippines."

"I know. He told me a bit about it when I visited him in his workshop one day." I traced an intertwining circular pattern on the pale-peach-colored silk coverlet.

"He thinks he'll harm me. That he'll lash out in some way. But …"

I waited a few moments for her to finish, but she remained silent. "But …"

She raised her eyes to me, glistening with unshed tears. "I know … deep inside, I know he would never intentionally hurt me. Unlike Jonas, who seemed to plan in that office of his the ways he could inflict the most bodily harm."

"Sav," I whispered.

"Do you know I think he even consulted with doctors on how long it should take me to recover from my injuries so he knew when he could inflict the next round?"

My eyes widened in horror.

"For the doctor was never called for my benefit."

"Why didn't you leave?" I asked.

"He told me that he'd hunt me down and kill me. That he'd lowered himself to marry one such as me, and I should be thankful for any sort of attention from him." She looked away, blinking at tears.

"I'm sure Uncle Martin or Lucas had their doubts." Savannah nodded as I added, "Never underestimate the strength it took to leave, to not waver and to refuse to do what your mother or Jonas wanted. To continue to do what *you* wanted and needed. You should be proud of yourself."

"Thank you, Rissa." She sniffled as she leaned forward for a hug.

"Have you stopped looking for your daughter?" I asked, biting my lip as I saw a deep despair flash in Savannah's eyes for a moment.

"I looked everywhere I could imagine. I sent letters and visited orphanages, and I failed to find her. I console myself that she is with a good family, who treats her well."

"Oh, Sav," I whispered, unable to blink away my tears as they trickled down my cheeks. "I'm so sorry I wasn't here to support you. I'm so sorry I didn't know what you had suffered."

She leaned into my embrace, clutching me for a moment. "I needed you.

I won't deny it. But your absence forced me to find my own strength. And I learned that there are others who support me and care for me too, and that is a wonderful gift."

She pulled away, rubbing at her cheeks. "And now I really think we should go to bed," Savannah said.

I hugged her again before rising with a slight groan. "Remind me not to travel across country with any frequency." Savannah smiled as she left. I crawled into bed, dreaming of Gabriel.

CHAPTER 34

THE FOLLOWING MORNING, after breakfast, Savannah and I decided to walk to the Public Gardens. Although it was mid-November, the sun shone brightly, and the air was calm. I had donned my burgundy jacket, and Savannah wore a thick blue-gray coat that swirled prettily at her ankles as she walked. We walked arm in arm the short distance to the gardens, entering through the Beacon Street gate to stroll along one of the curving walks. The flower beds were covered for winter, and the bare tree branches swayed in a soft breeze with few birds remaining to serenade us.

"I imagine it's quite a shock to be here rather than in Montana," Savannah said as she squeezed my arm.

"It's not as provincial as you would make it out to be, Sav," I said. "Fashion isn't nearly as advanced, but there is electricity."

"Is there anything you miss about living here?"

"My family." She squeezed my arm in agreement. "The smell of the ocean, the heavy humid air after a fierce rainstorm. The museums, the music." I gave a wistful sigh and shared an ironic look with her. "The library."

"I thought you had a library where you live," Savannah said.

"There is one, although the elderly man I work with insists on calling it a depository until we have a proper building."

"What is it in now?"

"A room over a storefront, with books piled high on tables. Gabriel just built us beautiful bookshelves," I said.

"You say it's not provincial but it sounds terribly rural to me," Savannah said. She nodded to an acquaintance as we turned down another path.

"I imagine anything would, after Boston."

"Are you planning to visit my parents while you're home?"

"Of course, although I don't relish the tongue-lashing I'm sure to receive from your mother. I can already imagine what she'll say." I thought back to the tea I had with her after Gabriel left when she admonished me to marry a man from a similar class. "How she'll say it." I raised an eyebrow to Savannah.

Savannah looked at me with mild embarrassment. "Did you know that my parents' marriage was one of convenience?"

"Who told you that?" I demanded. "You know as well as I do that it was a love match, like my parents'."

"It seems they fooled us all and, for those who did know the truth, had trammeled them into a veil of silence."

"Why would they do that? Why would Aunt Betsy lie to us?"

"Loyalty to her sister. An ingrained training to follow the mandates of her parents. She had been told to repeat that my parents married for love until it would be believed as true. I think they had hoped, if it was said enough times, the lie would become truth."

"What really happened?"

Savannah gripped my arm. "It seems my mother might have been even more shocking than you or me in her day. She frequented the theaters in Scollay Square and became pregnant with an actor's child."

I stopped walking to stare at Savannah with my mouth agape. "Now I know you must be joking."

"Aunt Betsy told me in strictest confidence. I wanted you to know because I know how Mother likes to torment you and act as though she is perfect and that you and I are not living up to her standards."

"Why would your father marry her?"

"I guess for the dowry. To keep the business going during a conflict in Europe when they had trouble obtaining the fine linen from France. As Jonas discovered, the dowry was quite substantial. And I imagine the grandparents were willing to pay whatever was necessary to prevent further scandal. They wouldn't have wanted an out-of-wedlock grandchild."

"And the child? I don't remember ever meeting any older sibling of yours besides Lucas. Unless you're telling me this child is Lucas?" I gripped her arm.

"No, of course not. He's the spitting image of father. A few months after their marriage, mother lost the baby."

"I can't take this in. I can't believe that, for over twenty years, they've lied to all of us. Why aren't you angrier?"

"I've had more time to adjust to the news than you, Rissa. And, I must admit, I found the news freeing. My mother, who has always seemed so perfect and as though she's never set a foot out of line, so much so that I was afraid of doing anything wrong, is a hypocrite. And it seems she was a hellion."

"You come by it naturally at least," I teased. I bit my lip, deep in thought. "What worries you, Rissa?"

"I've been told since I was a child that my parents also married for love. Was that a lie too?"

"I don't believe so. What Aunt Betsy told me was that your mother was irate at the grandparents for forcing the match between my parents and invited my mother to weather out the storm of scandal at her house with your father. It seems Aunt Agnes didn't care much for social standing as long as she was with the man she loved. She thought my mother should strive for the same."

I smiled, relieved. "That sounds like Mama."

Savannah nodded, and we continued walking. Suddenly Savannah jerked beside me. I glanced at her to see Jonas standing next to her, one hand on Savannah's arm.

"Jonas," I said, as I attempted to maneuver Savannah away from him.

"Clarissa," he said with a menacing lift of his upper lip. "I had hoped your reported return was erroneous."

"As you can see, I'm healthy and happy to again be in the company of my cousin." I tugged on Savannah but she grimaced as Jonas's hold on her arm tightened further.

"My wife will be returning home with me," Jonas said. "I have endured quite enough speculation and gossip surrounding your absence from the house."

Savannah pulled on her arm again before yelping in pain. "I will not. Unhand me this instant."

"Do you want me to make a scene? Call over that policeman and have you in jail for accosting me?" I nodded toward a policeman watching us. "I can, Jonas, and with no regard to my reputation. For those who really matter to me realize it is meaningless when it is based on the standards set by the likes of you." I glared at him as I leaned toward him as I spoke.

"If you think that I'll allow my wife to spend one more moment in your company, you're mistaken," Jonas said.

"You have no right to decide what you will or will not allow me to do," Savannah snapped. She raised her booted heel and kicked him in the shin. Jonas grunted and released Savannah, who massaged her wrist.

I stepped toward Jonas. "Do you believe that you're impervious to justice?" I asked. "You aren't. You'll pay for what you've done, and then you'll wish you could repent."

"Do you dare to threaten me?" Jonas asked.

"No, Jonas, for I'll never be your physical equal. But I know, someday, you'll need someone to help you, and there'll be no one eager to come to your aid. Such is the measure of you as a man."

I turned away, and we continued our walk. I felt Savannah shaking next to me, and I tilted my head to study her. "Sav, are you all right?"

"I'm better than all right. For the first time in my life, I've stood up to him. You can't know how that feels, Rissa."

I smiled at her before laughing. "It's liberating learning to defend oneself, isn't it?" I asked.

"Yes, and it's helped me see things in a whole new way."

***

I STOOD OUTSIDE the McLeod house in the North End in the late afternoon and glanced around the alleyway. A group of men congregated on the steps at the mouth of the alley, waving arms and speaking in booming voices as they argued in Italian. I closed my eyes, remembering the times I'd visited this house, reminding myself that, when I knocked on the door, Gabriel would not answer. I turned back toward the door and rapped soundly with my knuckles.

I heard loud footsteps, and then the door opened. "Jeremy?" I asked as I peered up at him, noting the trimmed, attractive black beard that highlighted his bright green eyes.

"Yes?" He watched me with a curious expression, although he did not open the door farther to allow me inside.

"It's me. Clarissa."

"Clarissa?" He opened the door, and I flung myself into his arms. He grunted as I knocked him back a step and then chuckled. "Yes, it's you," he said as he leaned away, studying me. "You look very different. Not nearly as polished as when you left."

I blushed. "Well, things are different in Montana."

"Better, I hope."

"For me they are, because I'm with Gabriel," I said. He closed the door and led me down the hallway.

"Flo, look who's decided to return to Boston," Jeremy said as he entered the kitchen area, largely unchanged except for a few feminine touches. White eyelet lace curtains covered the back window and checkered red-and-white towels sat next to the sink. An emerald-green cloth covered the table.

Florence looked up from tallying a set of figures and dropped the pencil with a thud. "Rissa!" she screeched, and then rose as fast as her pregnant belly would allow her. "Oh, I never thought to see you again so soon."

I held her for a moment before releasing her. "Oh, Flo! I'm so excited for you and Richard. In the midst of all the travel and worry, I forgot about the baby. How long until the baby arrives?"

She sat with an appreciative groan and rubbed to her lower back. "I've about two months to go. Although it can't come soon enough," she said with a smile. After a moment her smile faded. "Why are you in Boston, Rissa? Where's Gabe?"

I saw her share a worried glance with Jeremy. "I thought Gabriel would have written you by now," I said.

"You haven't had a falling out," Jeremy said with a glower.

"Of course not," I said. "My da died." Florence gasped, and Jeremy nodded his understanding as I blinked away tears. "Colin and I decided we had to come back. We needed to be here for the ceremony."

"Of course," Florence said, reaching out to take my hand. "I imagine the trip was expensive."

"Gabriel and I had some money saved, but thankfully my aunt Betsy had given me money when I had traveled west. I'd saved most of it. I'm glad I did as it ensured Colin could travel with me."

"I'm sure your family has been glad you're here, Rissa," Florence said.

"Not everyone. Aunt Matilda still believes I'm a bad influence on Savannah and wishes I'd remained in Montana." I noticed Jeremy stiffen at Savannah's name. "Mrs. Smythe was not happy to see us."

"Well, we're your family, and we're delighted you're here," Florence said. "I'm just sorry for the reason for your need to travel."

"Thanks, Flo." I glanced around the room. "What time does Richard arrive home? I was hoping to speak with him too."

"Why?" Jeremy asked.

"I'm worried about what Mrs. Smythe has planned for my father's business. I doubt she'll content herself with allowing Colin to run it. Knowing her, she has a different plan."

"She is your father's widow," Florence said.

"I know. That's what concerns me. I worry she has the right to do as she likes with the business. I wish Colin were the one to decide." I tapped my fingers on the table top.

Jeremy laughed. "You surprise me, Clarissa. Here I thought you'd rejoice that a woman would have the right to decide what happened to her husband's property upon his death, rather than having to rely on the counsel of men. Instead you'd like the laws to change to suit your desires."

I flushed. "I know. Sophie would be appalled. I just can't imagine Mrs. Smythe having Colin's or Melly's best interest at heart."

"Nor do many men," Florence argued. "It's the way of things, Rissa. You'll have to see what happens and then do what you can so that it is just."

"Flo, I'm home!" Richard's voice boomed down the hallway, and the sound of a door slamming shut reverberated.

"Good. There's a surprise for you!" she yelled.

"I hope it's your famous Indian pudding," he said just before he paused in the doorway. "Or it could be Clarissa." He beamed at me as he strode toward me. I had just enough time to stand before he enveloped me in a huge hug.

"Hello, Richard," I said as I blinked away tears.

"I heard about your da today. I'm sorrier than I can say, Rissa," he said as he swiped my cheeks with his thumbs, smearing away the scattered tears that had fallen.

"Where's Gabe?" he asked as he looked around the room.

"In Montana."

"Why wouldn't he travel with you?" Richard shared a worried glance with Florence and Jeremy.

"Richard, sit and have a cup of tea, and we'll bring you up-to-date," Florence said.

After I repeated my reason for traveling east without Gabriel, Jeremy asked, "And the other one? That Cameron fellow? What happened to him? Gabe just wrote that he died, and you no longer needed to worry about him. Seemed to happen months after you traveled to Montana."

"I forbade Gabriel from harming Cameron in any way," I said.

Jeremy watched me, stupefied. "Are you serious? After the way he threatened and scared you? Following you halfway across a continent like a deranged lunatic? He deserved to suffer and at Gabriel's hands."

"Not if it meant I'd be separated from Gabriel. Nothing, not even some notion of justice, warranted that." I sighed with relief upon realizing Gabriel had never explained to his brothers all that I had suffered by Cameron's actions.

"And Gabriel agreed with you?" Richard asked, sounding equally surprised.

"I think he'd spent enough time alone to know he wanted no reason for further separation." I paused. "And nothing he could have done would have changed what had happened." Jeremy seemed unconvinced, although he appeared to be considering what I said.

"At any rate, he and Gabriel had sporadic verbal sparring matches. Sometimes at the bar, at other times on the boardwalk. I avoided him as best I could, although I couldn't always evade him. Cameron began to woo a wealthy businessman's daughter. Her family was ecstatic that a refined, eastern gentleman had taken an interest in their daughter, and they were determined to have him as a son-in-law."

"Gullible fools," Florence said.

I nodded my agreement. "Be that as it may, he worked at one of the local sawmills as his father-in-law-to-be owned it. There was an accident, and he died."

"How?" Richard asked.

"Fire is very common in a sawmill, with so much sawdust and sparks, and a large fire broke out one day. He was trapped inside."

"Poor man," Florence said. She glared at Jeremy. "I know he was awful to you, Rissa. I can't bear to imagine all you suffered due to him. Yet I still can't envision dying like that."

"Nor can I," I admitted. "I had nightmares for days. We almost lost one of our best friends, the foreman at the mill. He ran into the mill, trying to save Cameron, but he couldn't find him. He barely made it out alive."

"Brave man," Jeremy said.

"Yes, and a very good one," I agreed. "Now Mrs. Wright believes I brought her son to an early death, all because I wouldn't marry him. If I had done my duty and had walked down the aisle with him, none of this would have befallen either of us."

"Well, she needs someone to spew her venom at, and you're alive and present. She'll never find fault in her dead, now sainted, son. She can't look to herself for her failings, so she must look to blame others," Florence said.

I nodded. "I'm just thankful there's no chance of mischief in Montana while I'm away."

"How long will you visit Boston?" Florence asked.

"I don't know. A few weeks at the most, I hope. I promised Gabriel I'd be home for Christmas."

"When is the funeral, Rissa? We'd like to be there to support you." Florence poured more tea into my cup.

"Oh, I forgot. When Colin and I arrived yesterday, he read in the paper that it was all occurring as we were boarding the carriage to take us to Sophie's. We had to rush to the cemetery. We barely made it there in time to hear the priest's final prayers."

"Surely you had telegrammed that you were coming and to hold the ceremony?" Richard asked.

"Of course. But Mrs. Smythe didn't want us here. Wanted us unable to take part in the ceremony or the burial."

"Vile woman," Florence said. "How dare she treat you like that?"

"We caused quite a stir arriving in our traveling clothes rather than in mourning garb," I said, chuckling before gasping in an attempt to swallow a sob. "Oh, Lord, why does any of it matter? My da is dead. That's all anyone should care about. Not the color of my coat or Colin's scarf." I wiped at my cheeks as tears fell. Richard leaned toward me, and I welcomed his brief embrace.

"Well, you've shown society you care very little for their conventions a time too many. I imagine there were some quite happy to snub you for it," Florence said as she patted my hand.

"I know you're right. Thankfully, Sav was there, and she didn't care." I shook my head in amazement. "Which is extraordinary, as she had become the most rigid of them all before she married Jonas."

"How is Savannah?" Florence asked with a quick glance toward Jeremy.

"Recovering from the trauma of a marriage to one such as her husband," I said. "She continues to blame herself for marrying him."

"No woman would ever imagine such a reality," Richard argued. "We don't know much of what occurred, but from what Florence told me of the day they rescued her from Jonas, it's enough to know she was treated abominably."

"Thankfully she heals. She's finding her inner strength one day at a time." I smiled at Jeremy. "And she asked me to give this to you." I held out a letter. "I know Gabriel would say I'm meddling, but I agreed to act as mailman."

"Why didn't she come to visit with you?" Jeremy asked. He stroked his name written in her penmanship.

"I believe she was worried about her reception here."

"Savannah is always welcome in our house," Richard proclaimed although Florence gave a sniff of disapproval.

"Flo?" I asked.

"I don't approve of how she treated Jeremy. I've tried to understand what she has suffered. I've attempted to imagine that kind of terror. And yet, how she could think, for one second, that Jeremy would ever hurt her is beyond me."

I frowned as I saw Jeremy flinch at Florence's words. I reached out and gripped his hand for a moment. "I know you'd never intentionally hurt her, Jeremy. We never intentionally hurt those we love, although that doesn't mean we don't cause them pain at some point. The difference is that you work to soothe it once the hurt is known."

Jeremy watched me with intense green eyes for a moment.

Richard watched Jeremy and me, his expression one of guarded optimism. He reached forward and clasped Florence's hand. She held it over her belly.

"How's Gabe, Rissa?" Richard asked. "I wish he were here."

"I think he would have preferred to travel with me, but he needed to remain in Montana for his business. He has many projects, and he would have lost work had he traveled. And we only had money for two fares. We thought it best for Colin to come with me."

"Work can't be more important than you, Rissa," Richard said.

"It's not. But, because I'm not allowed to work as a teacher, I have to work at a small library, earning very little. I can't add much to our income, and Gabriel is determined to provide a good home for us."

"As he should," Richard said with a smile toward Florence.

"Well, I'm happy he wants to be a good husband and provider, but I'd like to contribute more than I do," I said.

"I'm sure you do plenty, Rissa, with all the work you do around the house," Jeremy said.

I flushed and looked away as Florence snickered. "I doubt it, Jeremy," Florence said. "Clarissa never knew how to do any of the practical aspects of running a home. Isn't that one of the reasons your stepmother wanted you at home?"

I replied, "She was more interested in me sitting in the parlor wearing a provocative dress and enticing would-be suitors than learning anything of value. If you're interested, I've been learning to cook."

"Even a year later? Is it that hard?" Richard asked, sharing an amused grin with Jeremy. "Gabe and I used to do well enough with simple meals. Maybe you should have him teach you a few of the tricks that he learned when he was a bachelor."

"I'm not going to ask my husband for cooking advice, Richard."

"I would, if it meant you'd eat a decent meal," Jeremy said. "Nothing worse than being hungry."

"Anyway, we have a wonderful friend who is helping me," I said.

"Does she feed you too?" Florence asked.

"We're often invited to dinner after I have a lesson," I said and blushed as Jeremy, Florence and Richard laughed.

After a moment Florence calmed her laughter and watched me with serious eyes. "You're happy, Rissa?"

"I am. We've had some difficult times, but I never knew I could be as happy as I am. I believe Gabriel feels the same."

"Never doubt it, Rissa," Richard said. "In his letters to us, all he writes about is the wonder of that place and his joy in sharing it with you."

"How is Uncle Aidan?" Jeremy asked. "I can't believe I haven't seen him yet."

"He's well. He travels frequently for his business, although he has purchased a lovely home in Missoula."

"Why don't you live in it?" Richard asked. "Sounds nicer than living over the workshop."

"It's your uncle's home. I think Gabriel would like us to live in a place that is ours. And I support Gabriel. I don't want to live in a place that is beyond what we can afford."

"I'd think Aidan would want you there, rather than have the house empty for months at a time," Florence said.

"It's not empty. The woman who's helping me with my cooking, Amelia Egan, she lives there with her children as a housekeeper." I turned to Jeremy. "I wouldn't be surprised if Uncle Aiden were to travel here at some point. He's been invited to invest in an overseas shipping venture with Jonas, and I believe he wants to come east to speak with him. I'm uncertain as to what he will decide."

"I'd hope he'd have better sense than to have any dealings with that man," Jeremy hissed.

"He's often said that he shouldn't mix business with family, but I hope you're right," I said.

"If one is as successful as Uncle Aidan is purported to be, he should be able to decline dealings with anyone he chooses," Jeremy said.

"Jer," Richard said with a warning glance. "You know that he has to think about his business too. It's not just about how that businessman treated the woman who intrigues you."

"It's not like I'm playing some game, Rich," Jeremy said as he rose. "I'm not intrigued by her. I love her. If I had my way, I'd marry her tomorrow." He flushed as he turned to face the empty back lot abutting the rear of their house.

I shared a knowing glance with Florence. "I should return to Sophie's." I began to rise before sitting again. "Wait, I forgot." I reached over and gripped Richard's arm. "Richard, what's happening with my father's forge? Colin came back earlier this afternoon boiling mad, and I couldn't get a coherent word out of him. He stormed off before he explained anything to me."

Richard took a deep breath as regret flitted across his face. "I hadn't realized until today that your da had died, Rissa. The man who took over for

Old Man Harris, Mr. Wade, works us much harder than Old Man Harris did and doesn't like to catch us chatting while we work. Thinks we'll be more productive if we get into a routine."

"He treats you like you're a bunch of automatons," Jeremy grumbled.

"Well, anyway, I haven't kept in touch with my friends at your da's forge. I work hard and want to come home to see Florence. Spend time with Jer. I don't want to spend my time and money at the saloons. So I just learned today about your da. And about your da's forge."

"What about my da's forge?" I asked.

"Mrs. Smythe is already planning to sell it to Mr. Wade," Richard said. He flushed. "In fact, he talked to me today about having me take over the running of it."

I sat back in my chair, becoming paler by the moment. "Mrs. Smythe is selling Colin's birthright?"

"I think it's all but finalized. Mr. Wade was contacted two days after your da's death. Something about maintaining profitability and the goodwill of customers." Richard shook his head. "The problem is, I know that woman thinks she's cunning, but I doubt she has the head for business Mr. Wade has. He'll convince her that he's giving her fair value when in truth it's worth triple what he's paying her."

Richard sighed. "And I shouldn't have told you any of that because, if Mr. Wade finds out that I'm undermining his negotiations, he'll be furious. He took over after you ran away to be with Gabe, so he's unaware we're related."

"I don't want you to lose your job on account of me, Richard," I murmured.

"If I do, I'll find another. I know I'm a good smith. And I know I won't run your da's shop the way he would want me to. I can't be that type of a manager." He rubbed away a chagrined smile. "I can't say, just for a moment, that the thought of running my own forge wasn't very tempting. But, when I realized who I'd be taking it away from, I don't know if I could do it."

"I'd think Col would rather have you running it than anyone else," I said. I rubbed at my temple. "No wonder Colin was so furious."

"I can only imagine what he thinks of me," Richard said.

"That you are a good, loyal friend," I said. I squeezed his arm again and rose. "I should head home."

I walked down the hallway with Richard. As the front door opened, I gasped to find Colin on the front step, his hand raised as though to knock. "Col!" I gasped. I reached forward and clasped his arm. "I've been worried since you stormed out of Sophie's."

He nodded, and I hated the desolation I saw in his gaze. "I'm sorry, Rissa. I needed to think." He tried to smile, although no joy entered his blue eyes. I stepped aside, allowing Colin full sight of Richard. "Hi, Rich. It sure is good to see you again."

He reached out his hand, but, instead of clasping it, Richard pulled Colin into a quick embrace. After a pat on the back, Richard slung his arm over Colin's shoulder and tugged him into the living room area. I shut the door, following them.

As we entered, I saw Jeremy and Florence pause in the midst of what appeared to be a deep conversation. "Is there any more tea, Flo?" Richard asked as he ushered Colin to one of the chairs. Colin collapsed into it, smiling a vague hello to Florence and Jeremy. I shared a worried glance with Florence, and I again found myself sitting around the table with another mug of tea warming my hands.

"I visited Mrs. Smythe today. She wants money, and she wants it as fast as possible. I don't understand her haste," Colin said. "The forge runs well, will earn her a steady income as long as she has a good, reliable man at the helm. I don't know why she wants to sell it." Colin shook his head in dazed confusion.

Florence cleared her throat. "Word has it that she is quite extravagant in her purchases. I wouldn't be surprised if she's in acres of debt."

"Sophie mentioned much the same recently, but Da would have kept a tighter control than that," I argued.

"It makes sense, Rissa," Colin said.

"Sophie often spoke about what a ridiculous woman she was and of how she was beggaring your father," Florence said.

"What can we do to stop her?" I asked.

"In truth," Colin said, "I would love for you to run the blacksmith shop, Rich. I just don't want it sold to Mr. Wade."

"I agree," Richard said. "I mean, I don't want it sold to him. I'd have thought you'd want to run it."

"I've been here two days, and already I can't wait to leave," Colin said on a groan. "I may not be my own boss in Missoula, but it's where I want to be."

Jeremy, who had been pacing, paused and leaned against the counter. "Where's Uncle Aiden now?"

"He's at his office in San Francisco," I said. "Well, at least he was when we left."

"Why doesn't he buy the forge? He has the money, and it sounds like it will be a good investment, especially since it seems like this man is offering less than its value. Uncle Aidan wouldn't have to pay full market value. He'd earn a good profit if he ever chose to sell it, and Richard could run it knowing that it's now the family's forge."

"Col?" I asked him.

"In the end, it doesn't matter, Rissa. Nothing I do will bring Da back. Nothing will change the fact that I wasn't here when he needed help." He took a deep breath. "If Richard can be helped, that is good. I'll know that the forge will go to someone deserving."

CHAPTER 35

MY DARLING JEREMY,

I know I asked for time away from you. You were very upset with me when last we spoke, and I fear my request caused you both confusion and pain. I have returned to Boston and much has occurred. My uncle Sean has died. I have seen Jonas again. Clarissa has returned to us for a short time.

So much has happened, Jeremy, and, through it all, one constant emotion fills me: a deep and abiding need to see you. I miss you. I miss sharing my life with you. There is much I would like to say, if you will let me. Will you meet me at your house tomorrow at 1:00 p.m.?

Savannah

Jeremy sat in his room, fingering her letter. Anger and hope bloomed in his chest, and he sighed. He thought of the past month without her, and although he had promised himself he would not run to her the minute she asked it of him, he knew he would meet her.

He turned toward the door at the gentle knock. "Jer?" Richard asked as he poked his head in. "Is everything all right?"

"Fine, Rich." He held up his letter. "She wants to see me again."

"I told you that she wouldn't be able to stay away from you for long," Richard said with a sardonic smile.

"I just wish I were able to stay away from her."

"Why? For how upset you were with me earlier, it seems as though you still want to be with her." Richard moved into Jeremy's room, his face cast in half shadows by the bedside lamp.

"I know, but I want her to want to be with me."

"I'd think that letter would prove that to you."

"No, it just shows she's lonely, and she doesn't like to be lonely. I'm not certain it truly has much to do with me." He scrubbed a hand through his ebony hair before meeting Richard's gaze.

Richard watched him with a curious tilt to his head. "You don't value yourself as highly as you should, Jer."

"In the end, I don't know as it matters, Rich. We can't marry, and I have little to offer her."

"You've shown her that you value her opinions. That you are capable of respecting her as a woman without subjugating her to your whims. That is a remarkable gift for a woman who has suffered from the treatment bestowed upon her by her husband. When she asked for time away, did you try to force her to change her mind?"

Jeremy sighed and rubbed at his beard, pulling at individual hairs as he recalled the last time he'd seen Savannah. "I tried to reason with her, but, when I realized her need to leave, I accepted it."

"Did you intimidate her to make her change her mind?"

"Of course not." He glared at Richard.

"Then why can't you see that she has come to recognize that you are a man to be trusted? That you are a man she'd be a fool to lose?"

Jeremy watched him with an arrested intensity.

"Well then," Richard said. He straightened from his position leaning against the door frame. "Flo has dinner ready, and we should know better than to keep a pregnant woman waiting." He smiled and winked as he turned away. Jeremy laughed and rose to follow his brother.

***

SAVANNAH KNOCKED ON THE DOOR, brushing a hand over her hair in nervous agitation. Her smile dimmed as Florence opened the door with a frown.

"Why are you here, Savannah?" Florence asked, the door only partially ajar, barring Savannah entrance.

"I need to see Jeremy."

"If you remain uncertain how you truly feel, go home. If you don't know the measure of the man you turned away from you, you should leave now."

Her cheeks flushed from her agitation.

Savannah stiffened her shoulders, meeting Florence's firm stare. "This is between Jeremy and me, Florence."

"Jeremy is as a brother to me, Savannah. When you hurt him, you hurt me. You hurt Richard. Remember that," Florence said with a glower, concern shining in her eyes.

"I know. Please allow me to enter to begin to make things right, Florence."

"I will. Only because it would hurt him more for you to leave again." She stepped back, opening the door wider, allowing Savannah to squeeze inside. Savannah walked down the hallway, coming to a halt in the entrance to the main living area. The click of a door shutting behind her heralded Florence's entrance into her bedchamber, leaving Savannah to face Jeremy alone.

Jeremy stood stiffly beside the counter, with his hands behind his back, staring out the back window. He held himself as one does awaiting bad news, and she longed to grasp his large hand to soothe him. "Jeremy," she murmured, attempting to impart comfort with her soft voice.

"Ma'am," he said as he turned to face her. His gaze roved over her face, taking in her hair in a tidy chignon, her unbuttoned blue coat, opened to reveal a plain red wool dress underneath, and then returning to study her eyes. He said nothing further, waiting for her to speak.

"Thank you for agreeing to meet with me today." She gripped her hands in front of her and tried not to focus on him calling her "Ma'am" again.

"I had nothing pressing."

Savannah winced, paling at his words. "I see. Well, that helps me know where I stand."

"Is everything settled with your husband?" He watched her with inscrutable eyes, the green so cold they appeared black.

"No. It never will be. I've decided that I must content myself with being a disgraced woman among high society."

He cocked his head to one side and watched her curiously. "Does that matter?"

"No. It doesn't. It never should have mattered. It took me traveling to Quincy again to realize the truth." Savannah sighed as she shook her head.

"And what truth was that?" He clenched and unclenched his hands as he leaned against the counter, his jaw flexing.

"Aunt Betsy has a way of showing her nieces and nephews what is truly important in our lives. I didn't heed her advice before my marriage to Jonas. I thought myself wiser than my sage aunt." She closed her eyes as she continued to speak. "I've been angry for so long at my family, my mother especially, for encouraging my marriage to Jonas. I had plenty of time in Quincy for introspection, and, if I'm honest with myself, I'm as much to blame as she is. I knew what I was agreeing to, and I ignored all my reservations. I married the man. I am the only one to blame."

"There is no blame in wanting to see yourself married well." Jeremy reached out to grip her hand for a moment before releasing it. "I doubt any of you could have imagined what he would become."

"I've paid for my folly. I've paid for my desire for social acceptability. Now I know what is truly important to me."

"And what is that?" Although he tried to mask it, he could not hide the yearning from his voice.

"My sense of personal esteem. And my dreams for the future." She met his gaze, unable to hide the longing from hers. She canted toward him as though hoping for an embrace.

"What are your dreams, Savannah?" He watched her with guarded eyes, fisting his hands at his sides so as not to reach out and touch her again.

She smiled at his use of her name. "To be with you. To surround myself with those who care for me."

"There will always be those who shun you because you are separated from your husband."

"Yes, and those who will scorn you if you decide to associate yourself with me."

"Do you think I would care what those people say?" Jeremy asked urgently as he moved toward her and framed her face with his hands. She sighed, tilting her head slightly to kiss one palm.

"I hope not." She paused for a moment before meeting his eyes. "A part of me worries that our separation has shown you that you can have a better life without me."

"How could you possibly think that?"

"You've begun to find peace again, Jeremy. I have no desire to bring you any more strife." She reached up to stroke his hands still cradling her face.

Jeremy dropped his hands and turned away. He stared at the bare clotheslines strung between the adjoining buildings. Savannah waited as he took a deep breath and faced her again. "You are correct in that I have begun to find peace here. Living with Richard and Florence has been like a balm to my wounds."

"They are wonderful people," Savannah murmured.

"Yes, they are. And they are about to have their first child. The last thing they need is me in the house. I've known for some time that I needed to find my own place, but I haven't wanted to leave."

"Why?"

"Because if I left, you wouldn't know where to find me," he whispered.

Savannah nodded, blinking away tears. "Jeremy."

He reached for her and pulled her into his arms, caressing her head with one hand. When he spoke, he could not hide the urgency from his voice. "I want you, Savannah. I don't care if we never marry."

"What are you saying?"

"I want us to have a life together. A life like Richard and Florence are building."

"You want me to live with you?" She was unable to hide the incredulity from her voice. "I ... I don't know Jeremy. That's a very large step."

"If these weeks apart have taught me anything, it's that I don't want to be separated from you again. Not by society. Not by Mrs. Chickering. Not for any reason."

Savannah stepped away, one hand at her temple, staring dazedly over one of his shoulders. "You ask for quite a bit."

"Yes." He reached for her hand and raised it to his lips. "Please tell me that you'll consider it."

"Will you give me time?"

"As much as you want." He stroked her cheek. "Will you visit me soon at the workshop? I'd like time alone with you."

Savannah's smile bloomed even as she blushed. "Yes. I'll try to visit tomorrow."

***

SAVANNAH SAT IN HER CHAIR, attempting to read her book, another play by Oscar Wilde, as Sophie muttered over the latest headlines. Numerous lamps lit the room with a gentle glow. The front curtains were closed, and a fire crackled in the grate. "What's the matter, Sophie? Has someone written another disparaging article against the cause?"

"No, the King of Belgium was almost assassinated by an anarchist. I'd think people would know by now that violence never leads to any lasting solution." Sophie shook her head at the thought and turned the page. She lowered the paper at a soft knock on the door.

"Could this be your young man?" Sophie asked Savannah. Savannah shook her head no.

"Excuse me, ma'am, but there is a Mr. Russell who is inquiring if he might join you this evening. I know you are having a quiet evening at home, and I'm sorry for the interruption."

"Please show him in, Poole," Sophie said. "I wonder if it is you father or brother?" Sophie asked as she looked toward the doorway. "Ah, Mr. Russell, I know Savannah takes great delight in visits from her father."

"Father," Savannah said as she rose to embrace him, and Sophie moved to rise.

"I'd rather you didn't," Martin blurted out to Sophie as he took the proffered chair next to Savannah. "I'm in need of advice, and I've been informed by Betsy that you often provide some of the soundest advice to be had." He tapped his fingers on his knees, belying his agitation. "I've waited until now to ask you for it, what with the funeral and Clarissa's and Colin's arrival. But I'm running out of time and need your help."

"It is flattering that some are aware of my talents," Sophie said with a self-mocking smile. "What is bothering you, sir?"

"After I visited Savannah a few days ago, I called on Jonas. I hoped he would be amenable to freeing Savannah from her marriage now that there is no hope for reconciliation."

"I imagine he wasn't pleased with your visit," Savannah said.

"You're correct. He was affronted at my presumption in making such a request. He believed he would still be able to entice you to return to him."

"How?" Savannah asked in a small voice.

"It appears he is an even more influential businessman than I knew. He advised me that my business loans will be due in thirty days, to be paid in full, if you are not returned home."

"Have you had any trouble paying your loans up to this point?" Sophie asked.

"Never. I've always paid on time. However, I do not have the capital to pay the full amount in the time requested, as I'm sure he knows. He's a sly man, willing to do whatever he deems necessary to obtain his desired outcome."

"Who is your banker?" Sophie asked.

"I work with Mr. Searle at Temple and Searle."

"Ah, Mr. Searle," Sophie said with a satisfied smile. "We are old friends."

"I'm surprised such a stodgy man would be—" Martin broke off what he was going to say.

"Acquainted with one such as me?" Sophie said. "Although he seems a dour, sensible banker, you must realize that all men have their weaknesses. He married a woman fifteen years his junior. A flighty thing, although she has the sense to be a suffragist. I've known them for years. I knew him before he remarried, and there are certain … interludes from his past I'm certain he doesn't want to come to light."

"Do you believe you could aid me in postponing the loan payment?" Martin asked.

"Let me see what I can do. It's been some time since I've had the pleasure of visiting a bank," Sophie said with a wry smile.

***

"MR. SEARLE, I have need of your assistance," Sophronia said as she sat at the swivel chair in front of his desk. She wore a severe eggplant-colored brocade suit and drummed her gloved fingers on the edge of his desk. Dark paneling and thick green rugs covered the wooden floors.

"Mrs. Chickering. I was unaware I was to have the pleasure of seeing you today." He steepled his hands, resting his forearms on his paunch. His gray waistcoat bulged, and the silver buttons appeared on the verge of bursting. A silver watch chain gleamed as it trailed into his waistcoat pocket.

"As was I, but the need arose." Sophronia pinned him under her stare. "Do you have any dealings with a Mr. Jonas Montgomery?"

"As I am sure you are aware, Mrs. Chickering, I am unable to discuss my clients or their affairs with you."

"Just as I am sure you are aware that when one man asks another to intentionally ruin another man's business, it is not only illegal but unethical. I'd hate for the stodgy, moneyed people of Boston to lose faith in one of its oldest banking families."

"You have no right to accuse me of such things."

"Don't I? I've heard your wife boast often enough of your acquaintance with Mr. Montgomery and of his connections to New York City. Thus deducing who would aid him with his nefarious plan was rather simple." She sat even straighter in her chair, her bosom heaving with her pent-up fury.

"These are my terms, Mr. Searle, as I want you to be fully aware of all you will gain and lose if you attempt to cross me. You will cease any and all actions toward Mr. Martin Russell and his store, Russell's. You will inform your business associate, Mr. Montgomery, that you did what you could but were unsuccessful. If I hear differently, your standing in society and your perception as a discreet, reliable banker will be destroyed. Do we understand each other?"

"That's not all I will lose. I'll lose esteem in Mr. Montgomery's eyes, and he'll take his profitable business elsewhere. I gain nothing from your terms, Mrs. Chickering."

"What you gain, Mr. Searle, is the ability to continue as a banker in this city. To continue to live in that monstrosity of a mansion on Commonwealth Avenue. To hold your head high as a man worthy of esteem. For, if you cross me and carry out your plan, you will be forced to leave Boston. And be thankful to run a five-and-dime shop in Tulsa."

Mr. Searle blanched as he met Sophronia's fiery aquamarine eyes. "You're an unnatural woman."

"You think words like that will dissuade me from my goal? Do you believe that men haven't said words like that for years, in an attempt to keep me in the place they believe I belong? You don't know me at all if you believe I'd heed anything you say."

Mr. Searle leaned back in his chair, a gentle creaking sound rending the air. "You ask for more than you can imagine, Mrs. Chickering."

"I ask for you to act with the honor you claim you have." Sophronia squinted at him when he appeared lighthearted after he sat in contemplation for a few moments. "I expect you to dissuade any of your minions from acting in your stead. Simply because you do not act does not free you of your responsibility as the manager of this bank."

After a tense moment, Sophronia smiled with feral intent. "You know the influence I have attained through the years among those of good standing. As well as the knowledge of your ... peccadilloes, shall we call them. It would be a shame for those to come to light."

Mr. Searle frowned again, his momentary joy doused by Sophronia's threat. He met her eyes, subtly nodding his head and smiling wryly. "Fine. I will meet your terms. Not because I agree with you or believe in having any dealings with women. I will agree because I want to continue to work here in Boston, and my Bertha would loathe Tulsa."

"I'm glad we are in agreement. Good day to you, Mr. Searle." Sophronia rose and marched from the room without a backward glance.

CHAPTER 36

"JEREMY?" SAVANNAH SAID as she opened the workshop door that squeaked as she pushed it open. She looked toward the workbench, but he was nowhere to be seen. She bit her lip, on the verge of leaving when she heard a gentle snore from the pallet near the stove.

"Jeremy," she whispered as she walked toward him. He appeared restless in his sleep, a frown on his face. She reached out to brush a lock of black hair off his forehead and gave a small yelp as he gripped her wrist.

Savannah screeched as Jeremy opened wild, unfocused eyes. He reared up, grasping her shoulder with his other hand and tumbling her onto her back. He loomed over her, gasping. "You won't succeed this time."

Savannah shivered at his low, menacing voice and wriggled in an attempt to break free from his punishing hold. "Jeremy, please." Tears formed in her eyes, and, in an instant, she was released.

He pushed away from her, a look of dawning horror on his face. He rose, moved toward the table and sank onto one of the benches. "Savannah. Holy God, Savannah." As he lowered his face into his hands, his shoulders shook.

"Jeremy? What happened?" She straightened her gray-blue jacket, setting the plumed hat that had tumbled off her head onto the table, and approached him, caressing his back.

"I'd think you'd run screaming from this room, thinking good riddance to be done with the likes of me."

Savannah pulled out a chair and sat next to him. "Never. You told me that you had demons. I never realized they were as great as my own. Forgive me."

She leaned forward and clasped his face with her hands, forcing him to look up to meet her gaze. "Look at me, my love. I will not turn away from you because you are tormented by your past, Jeremy."

"I could've hurt you. If I hadn't realized … I could have …"

"You didn't and you wouldn't, Jeremy. I have faith in you and in our love for each other."

"Then you're very foolish."

Savannah paled and dropped her hands from his face. She looked away, toward the workbench. "Are you saying you no longer envision a future with me, Jeremy?"

He reached out reflexively, stilling her movement as she began to rise. "Savannah, I want to protect you from me. Nothing and no one will stop me from loving you."

A tremulous smile bloomed. "That is all I need to know." She leaned toward him, and he pulled her into a tight embrace.

"Are you all right, my love? Did I hurt you?" He stroked her hair, dislodging pins with each pass of his palm.

"No, although I was frightened for a moment."

"I'm sorry if I reminded you of Jonas."

"You didn't. Jonas knew what he was doing and relished harming me. I knew you had no idea what you were doing." She paused for a moment, leaning away to meet his gaze. "I'm sorry you continue to be so tormented." Savannah reached forward and traced her fingers down the side of his cheek, studying him for a long moment. "What are you afraid of?" She rubbed her thumb over his furrowed eyebrow.

Jeremy closed his eyes before meeting her patient gaze. "My greatest fear is that you will decide you do not want this life with me. That my dream for a future with you will be as elusive as the morning mist on the Charles River."

Savannah beamed at him. "That is one fear you need to banish, Jeremy." She stroked her fingers through his beard as she met his now-exultant gaze.

He grinned before leaning forward for a quick kiss. He backed away almost as soon as his lips touched hers. "Forgive me again."

"Why? I've been waiting for you to kiss me. I've dreamed of your kisses, of your touch, every day I was away from you."

Jeremy exhaled a rueful laugh. "I've promised myself I won't touch you. Not until you're certain what you want." He rose and walked toward the workbench.

Savannah watched his movements for a moment before she stood. He spun to track her as she walked toward the door. "Savannah, please don't go."

She glanced at him with a saucy look over her shoulder as she locked the warehouse door. "You seem to believe you have the right to make all the decisions between us, Jeremy."

"I don't want you to regret, ever, anything that happens between us. To wish things had been different."

"Do you really think I'm so fickle?" She watched him with curious eyes.

"No. I just can't understand why a woman as fine as you is standing in front of me."

Savannah beamed at him. She reached up and unpinned her hair, allowing her thick strawberry-blond curls to cascade over her shoulders.

Jeremy reached out as they fell to her waist, running the ends that curled into ringlets through his fingers. At his abrupt movement Savannah flinched. "I'll not harm you, Savannah. At least not in that way. I'm sure I'll do something at some time that disappoints or hurts you. But I promise you, I'll never raise a hand to you." He watched her with solemn eyes as he lifted steady hands to trace her long hair from the crown of her head to her waist.

"I know. It's instinct."

"It's fine, love. He'll never come between us." He leaned forward and kissed her. "I've missed you more than I can say. Let me love you, Savannah." He kissed her neck and brushed a kiss along her collarbone as he unbuttoned her dress.

"Yes," Savannah murmured, leaning away to gift him with a smile. "As long as I can love you too."

His chuckle resonated through her as he kissed his way down her cloth-covered back, unfastening her corset. "I wouldn't want it any other way."

***

SAVANNAH LAY SPRAWLED on Jeremy's chest, her head tucked under his neck, half awake as she traced circles on one of his arms. Jeremy kissed her head gently and caressed her back, the soft strokes of his hand provoking a shiver of pleasure from Savannah. He paused after a moment and moved to scoot out from under her. Savannah gave a gentle moan but rose up slightly so he could move with more freedom and then laid back down on her belly. Jeremy moved to her side and brushed aside her hair to better trace and to massage her back.

At Jeremy's hiss of an indrawn breath, Savannah stiffened. She moved to rise, but his firm hands held her in place. "Let me look, love," Jeremy coaxed. He removed his hands, and Savannah settled, although her body shook with nervous energy.

He traced a small indentation at the base of her right shoulder blade. "How did this happen?" Jeremy asked.

"A buckle," Savannah rasped. "I didn't move fast enough, and he hit me with the full force of it." She flinched and then relaxed as he kissed it.

"And this one?" Jeremy asked. He stroked a ragged white line along her left hip.

"A bottle broke," Savannah whispered. "It was one of the few times a doctor had to be called to see me. Shards of glass were stuck inside, and it had to be sewn."

"The bastard hit you with a bottle?" Jeremy asked.

Savannah turned onto her back and met his irate eyes. "He thought it kept me more docile, because I never knew what could be used against me."

"Why would you ever trust me? Any man?" He brushed the hair away from her brow.

"Because I saw how you treated Cameron," Savannah whispered. "I was at my parents' house in the spring of 1901, before Clarissa traveled west to reunite with Gabriel, and he was there, taunting Clarissa. I almost came in, but then you ... you forced him from the room." She blinked away tears. "I'd been married to Jonas for nine months at that point, and I'd lost my belief that a man would come to a woman's aid. And then you helped my cousin. I had to go to my old room and cry for a few minutes because I knew there was no one who could protect me from the man I'd married."

"All you had to do was ask," Jeremy vowed. "Your brother and father would have helped you in an instant. As would have Richard and I."

"I didn't know how," Savannah said. "The most powerful thing he took away was my confidence. I lost the belief that I mattered. That anyone truly believed I mattered enough to be concerned about me."

"Which you have regained. And you now know just how much you matter. To your father, your brother. To me," Jeremy said. He kissed her gently.

"I can't promise I won't bring you pain. But I will promise never to raise anything against you."

"I know. I trust you." She smiled fully. She reached up to run her fingers through his hair.

"I know this is a bit late to voice this concern," Jeremy said with rueful humor.

"Yes?"

"Do you think Jonas could have lied to you?"

"About many things, yes."

"Do you think he could have tried to convince you that you could never have children in an attempt to bind you further to him?" He watched her with cautious, hopeful eyes.

"Jeremy, I don't know. He might have."

"Shh … please, Savannah, don't fret. While you were away from me, I thought about our conversations. I had conversations with you. Although you didn't want contact with me, you were never far from my thoughts."

"Nor you from mine," she said as she arched up to kiss him.

"And it struck me that, if he lied about the baby's death, he could just as easily have lied about you never having more children. It's something he would have done because he relished provoking as much pain as possible."

"You can't have this false hope that I'll become pregnant," Savannah whispered. "I can't survive each month if you become more and more upset because I remain just me."

He chuffed out a laugh. "I'll never be upset that you remain just you, my sweet Savannah. I think you should see a doctor, one not bought off by Jonas, to confirm or contradict what you were told."

"And if he says I can have a baby?"

"Then we need to be more careful, unless we want a little bundle sooner rather than later," Jeremy teased. He held a finger to her lips. "And if he says the other doctor was correct, it will never alter my love for you. I couldn't love you more than I do."

"A part of me likes living with that hope, Jeremy. The thought of having it taken away is difficult."

"False hope can leech away happiness, my love, and prevent you from enjoying what you have." He raised her hand and kissed her palm. "I know if the doctors say there is a chance we can have a child, we will live with that hope. More than anything, I want the reality of a future with you." He watched Savannah with a guarded, hopeful expression.

She raised her hand, cupping the side of his face. "As do I, Jeremy. I want nothing more. Please be patient with me. I must decide if I can endure the infamy of living with you outside of marriage first." She smiled ruefully. "If it is determined Jonas lied, then the decision might be made for me. For now, I need time to consider what you are asking."

"I'll be as patient as you want, my darling. As long as you're a part of my life"—he kissed her shoulder—"I will never ask for more than you are willing to give."

CHAPTER 37

TWO WEEKS AFTER DA's FUNERAL, Sophie and I decided to visit the Museum of Fine Arts. As I descended from her carriage, I marveled anew at the splendor of Trinity Church to my right and the grandeur of the Boston Public Library to my left. Trinity Church stood with its grand French Romanesque design, its Dedham granite a perfect counterpoint to its brownstone trimmings. The public library's red tiled roof was enhanced by the green copper detailing clinging to the roof, like decorative icing on the edge of a cake, while the white brick gleamed in the sunlight. The museum's Gothic Revival red brick exterior, with numerous arches highlighted in white granite, complemented the majestic Trinity Church and the Boston Public Library.

"What has you sighing, my girl?" Sophie asked as she alit.

"I was studying the library, wishing Missoula had such a place. There is a library of sorts, of course." I shared an amused glance with Sophie. "Even when we have a formal library, it will never rival the Boston Public Library."

"How could it? Boston is one of the most learned cities in the nation, if not the world. Of course we would have a renowned library. I'd be thankful you have any sort of library in that backwater you call home."

"Sophie, it's a wonderful little town. I think you'd like Missoula."

"I think the two important words there are little and town," she said with a *harrumph*. I noted she leaned more heavily on her walking stick, although she still wielded it to push those out of her way who she viewed as an impediment to her forward momentum.

"I believe you are looking forward to seeing the exhibit," Sophie said as we moved into the darkened interior.

"Yes," I said. "It's been some time since I've been to an art exhibit."

"Well, they've some beautiful new pieces recently acquired from Europe. I think you'll enjoy them. And, while you're here, we should go to the symphony. I doubt you're able to hear such music in Montana."

"There's an opera house in Missoula, Sophie."

"And is there opera music?" Sophie asked with a raised eyebrow.

I shook my head and giggled. "No, the last performance Gabriel and I saw was a play. Although the Chicago Symphony performed at our opera house last winter."

"My point exactly, my girl. You are in sore need of culture. One decent performance in nearly two years does not render a place hospitable." We walked side by side into one of the galleries. "This exhibit opened only a few weeks ago."

I nodded as I became entranced by the artwork. I tried to imagine how I would describe each piece of work to Gabriel, before giving up and becoming lost in my enjoyment of the beautiful paintings. "Sophie," I said as I turned to find her. I blanched as I stood face-to-face with my grandmother.

"Clarissa," she said as she leaned heavily to one side on a cane. "I'm disappointed to see you have returned to us."

"Grandmama," I said. "Grandpapa." I nodded at my grandfather standing behind her like a silent sentinel.

"I had hoped, after your unfortunate defection to that worthless worker, that you would remain there. I assume you returned to Boston for your father's funeral. Such a scandal that one such as he was ever aligned with our family. It's regrettable you have yet to see sense and have remained here in Boston." My grandmother looked me up and down, sniffing with disdain at my simple clothes. "It appears the manners of the West are more to your liking."

"You are correct in that I returned to honor my father. I remain to spend time with friends and family." I lifted my chin in defiance of her words, my eyes flashing with ire.

"Honor him? You don't know the meaning of the word. Had you had any regard for your father, you never would have acted as you did last year. Not only have you brought your father's house under a cloud of ill repute, one that your sister will never recover from, you've forced another estimable family to suffer the loss of their son."

"I've done no such thing," I said. "Cameron's death was not at my hand."

"He would never have been in that godforsaken place had you not traveled there for your illicit liaison with your disgraced laborer. You enticed a well-intentioned, suitable gentleman to travel halfway across a continent and then proceeded to jilt him. Your shame knows no bounds."

"And yours knows no decency. You, who should have loved and protected me, were only ever worried about your standing in society. You, who should have cared more for my happiness than for any perceived alliance, wanted me to further enhance your social status. I refuse to accept any blame for believing I deserved more than sacrificing my happiness at the altar of your ambition."

My grandmother turned a bright red and began to shake. I sensed Sophie standing near me and turned toward her. "Imagine my surprise to find my grandparents also visiting the museum today."

"How … fortunate," Sophie murmured. "I continue to find myself disappointed in the prognosticative abilities of physicians. Although, if you see your granddaughter with any frequency, she may aid in proving them correct."

"I am not going to die any time soon, you insolent woman," Grandmama hissed.

"Well, as we are to be denied such an event, Clarissa and I must continue our tour of the museum. If you will excuse us?"

Sophie and I strolled away at a leisurely pace, and I knew the nonchalant air was intended to irritate my grandparents further. "Sophie, what did you mean about physicians and prognosis?"

"Your grandmother had an apoplexy earlier this year. The physician who attended her assured me that we were soon to be relieved of her presence among us. However, as you can see, that has not been the case."

"She looks quite strong."

"If you ignore her leaning heavily on one side of her cane and talking mainly from one side of her mouth."

"Her words are just as sharp," I murmured.

"Ah, you did well, my girl. They've never known what to do with you. It's been a joy to watch you flummox them."

"Has Savannah seen them?"

"No. I spared Savannah the necessity of listening to her grandmother's vitriol. Suffering through a visit from her mother and your Mrs. Smythe was enough penance for anyone to bear." We shared a sardonic smile.

I turned for a moment to watch my grandmother's shuffling gait. "I thought she'd be angrier with me about Cameron than she is. She and Mrs. Wright are friends."

"From what you told me, I'm surprised Mrs. Wright wasn't more vehement in her fury toward you when you saw her at the funeral."

I shared a worried glance with Sophie before I looped my arm through hers, intent on enjoying the rest of the exhibit.

***

"I'D HOPED TO SEE YOU more appropriately attired," Aunt Matilda said as she sniffed in disdain at my clothes.

I glanced down at one of the new dresses I had purchased in Missoula, an evergreen wool walking dress with ivory embroidery at the wrists, hemline and neck, and shook my head. "I'm not as concerned about style and the latest fashion in Missoula, Aunt. And there's only so much black I have in my closet. Gabriel encourages me to buy what I need, but I'm unable to purchase as extensive a wardrobe as when I lived here."

"You fail to show your father the respect he's due." Aunt Matilda sat in a stiff chair, her posture rigid and straight. She wore a severe navy tea dress that failed to highlight her figure.

"I disagree. He'd far more appreciate my presence than concern himself with the cut or color of my dress. He never worried about that sort of thing. It's one of the many reasons Mama loved him."

"She desired him because she wanted to defy her parents. I highly doubt she ever truly loved him."

"How can you be so cruel?" I blinked away tears. "I remember them together. I remember their tender looks, the love that shone in her eyes when she spoke of him. His desperation when she became ill. His devastation when she died."

"Believe what you like, Clarissa. It's time you faced reality."

"Such as the fact you married Uncle Martin to forestall a great scandal? Such as the fact you were an even greater scandal than Savannah or I could ever have imagined being? Such as the fact that you failed to have faith in love?" I gripped the arm of my chair in my anger, fearing I'd rip the delicate, decorative finial off in my agitation. "How dare you sit in righteous indignation, passing judgment on us when you acted much the same?"

"How dare you speak to me in such a manner in my own home?" Aunt Matilda fanned herself furiously, before whacking it closed with such a force on the edge of the table she broke the delicate ivory backing.

"I dare because I'm tired of you believing you have the right to ridicule the decisions I've made in my life. You, you of all people, should understand why I acted as I did."

"You brought shame and ridicule upon our family again!"

"Then all I did was continue a family tradition. Started by my mother and you," I snapped. "I'd think you'd have the sense to know by now what really matters in life, Aunt Matilda."

She glared at me. "Don't look at me like that."

"Like I'm disappointed in you?" At her nod, I said, "Well, I am. I'm disappointed in the fact you didn't have the sense to cherish your daughter and niece enough to support us in our decisions. That you'd continue to look to your parents for approval." I shook my head in confusion. "How could you ever have wanted a better man than Uncle Martin?"

"You'd never understand."

"No, I never would."

"And that disappoints *me*, Clarissa," Aunt Matilda said. "I'd hoped you, of all of them, would understand my deep disappointment. You who were brave enough to defy us all and live the life you wanted, rather than the life your family compelled you to succumb to. I'd thought you'd be able to understand my deep disillusionment and regret."

"If you'd married a man such as Cameron or Jonas, then, yes, I would have," I argued. "But you didn't. You married Uncle. A kind, generous man who's been able to provide well for you."

"The heart is not always logical. And, sometimes, what is lost becomes more precious than anything that could ever be."

I blinked away tears as I studied her. "How tragic," I whispered. "I can't imagine such a life. Why cling to the past when you were gifted with a wonderful future? Most women, most men for that matter, aren't that fortunate."

Aunt Matilda stared at me with haunted eyes before turning away but not before I saw her blinking away tears. She clamped her jaw firmly shut, and we sat in an uncomfortable silence until I rose to leave.

CHAPTER 38

"HOW LONG ARE YOU going to live with Mrs. Chickering?" Jeremy sanded a piece of wood, his gaze tracking Savannah's movement as she wandered his workroom. Nearly two weeks had passed since their reunion, with November nearing its end.

"I don't know. As long as I need to. Sophie doesn't seem to mind my company."

"I know I promised I wouldn't push, but, now that you're back, I can't seem to be patient. I want us to have more than a stolen hour here and there. I want us not to care that a newspaperman might be lingering behind a horse cart. I want to come home to you at night. That's what I want."

Savannah flushed red and trembled as she sat on the bench near the table. He moved toward her and sat next to her. "What I don't know, is what you want. Is this the way you want your life to continue? Clandestine meetings, furtive kisses in a workshop or in one of Sophie's parlors, always hoping we aren't interrupted or discovered?"

"They know we are in love," Savannah whispered.

"Is this enough for you, darling? If it is, I'll temper my impatience."

"Why?" She watched him with curiosity.

"For you, I would do almost anything. I love you, Savannah, and I don't want to cause you harm. If living with me, without the protection of marriage, will only bring you shame, then I don't wish that upon you. But I want you to know what is my dream."

"Tell me your dream," Savannah urged.

"To come home to you every day after work. To hold you in my arms every night. To no longer have to wonder when I'll next see you. To no longer

311

fear that those around you have changed your opinion of me."

She turned to face him fully and clasped his face between her palms, rubbing her fingers in the whiskers of his beard. "They could never change how much I love you, Jeremy. You've treated me with compassion, honor and respect. You've shared your darkest secrets and scars with me, and not shied away from mine. Never fear that I'll run from what we have again."

"I try to trust in this, Savannah," he said. She stroked his cheek and waited. "But every good thing I've ever known has gone wrong. I have difficulty having faith in us."

"I have enough faith for the two of us," she said as she fought tears. "I refuse to live in fear of Jonas. He had his chance to hurt me. To … kill me, and he didn't."

Jeremy smiled wistfully at her show of bravado. "Ah, but he could find other ways to hurt you, my love. And that I could not bear."

"I have no need of his money or of his social prestige," Savannah said. "I refuse to allow him to have such a hold over my life."

"Will you move in with me?" Jeremy asked, hope lighting his eyes. "It won't be nearly as grand as the places you are accustomed to."

Savannah took a deep breath and nodded. "I will. Although I have one condition." He watched her curiously, nodding for her to continue. "I want you to meet my father."

Jeremy's eyes shone with surprise and pleasure. "I'd be honored to."

"I know my coming here today was reckless, and I shouldn't be seen at the workshop with any frequency. I know there are still some newspapermen who are curious, although my absence last month aided us."

"I'd rather be discovered than suffer any further separation," Jeremy said, raising her hand to kiss her palm. Savannah freed her hand, tracing his bearded jaw, smiling in agreement.

"Can you call this evening at Sophie's? It's not unseemly as Clarissa is there, and she is your sister-in-law."

Jeremy pulled her into his arms, sighing with contentment as her head came to rest in the crook of his neck. "I've been looking for places to live. They're all quite expensive, but I found a small pair of rooms that should suffice."

"Where, Jeremy?"

He looked down. "It's near the school where Clarissa used to teach."

"We're going to live in the West End?" Savannah asked, her flush paling at the thought.

He nodded. "I can't afford much more. I'm starting to sell my work, and it's selling at a decent price, but—"

She held her fingers up to his lips. "It doesn't matter. Wherever we are, it will be home because we are together."

***

"CLARISSA," SAVANNAH SAID as I sat reading a newspaper. "I have to talk with you."

I set my feet on the floor, uncurling from my comfortable position on the settee in the back parlor, a throw rug over my legs. I had made myself at home since I'd arrived at Sophronia's almost a month ago. I sat up, watching Savannah as she sat in a chair next to me. Faint light entered into the back windows, dusk falling early on this late November afternoon. I reached over to turn on a light to better see Savannah, the light limning her face as she looked at me.

"What's the matter, Sav?" I tossed aside the paper.

"I'm afraid you're going to be very disappointed in me."

"I'm not your mother," I said as I watched her rise from her seat and pace the room. She moved from shadow to light, making it difficult for me to see her expression. "And I like to believe I am nothing like the grandparents. Please tell me what has you so agitated."

"I've agreed to move in with Jeremy." She turned to face me, straightening her shoulders with determination, as though preparing herself for my censure.

I gaped at her, my mouth ajar as a flush rose on her neck toward her cheeks. "What?"

"I'm never going to be completely free of Jonas, Rissa, as I'm not pursuing a divorce. I want to be with Jeremy."

"If I understood correctly from the discussion we had when I arrived, you said you didn't want to seek a divorce because you didn't want the infamy that it would bring. How is moving in with another man while still married to your abusive husband diminishing the possibility of an uproar among Boston's elite?"

"Rissa, please understand," Savannah said as she sat next to me and clasped my hand.

"Why would you, who has always ensured that you were never subjected to vicious gossip, wish to court it now?"

She glared at me and released my hand, nearly throwing it at me. "What has social standing ever brought me except bruises, broken bones and disillusionment? I desire a life with a man who esteems me for the woman I am, not the woman he attempts to mold me into. Any uproar will pass, while I will remain with the man I love."

"And how will you survive? You certainly won't be able to live in a well-to-do neighborhood on what Jeremy can earn. What will happen to your love as you become more disillusioned with the life he can provide for you?"

"Is that all you think I care about? Money? Social prestige? My address?" Hurt entered her sky-blue eyes, and her indignant blush paled with each question.

"It's all you used to care about," I countered.

She blinked away tears as she watched me with disappointment lighting her eyes. "I want a life I can be proud of. A life that I know will bring me joy. Even if I'm living outside the bounds of what is deemed proper by society, I want a life with Jeremy."

"What happens when you want a new coat or dress, and you aren't able to afford it?" I asked.

"Do you really think me so shallow?" Savannah asked in a hurt whisper. I raised my eyebrows, waiting for her answer. "I'll remind myself that my life with Jeremy is more important than any material item."

"Good, because you'll have to remind yourself, frequently, just that. You'll have to be content with the simple life you build." I beamed at her. "Finally the Savannah I know, the Savannah of my youth—before the grandparents' took notice of you—has returned."

She gaped at me for a moment before tears poured down her cheeks. "You did this on purpose? Doubting me? Pushing me?"

"Of course. For what I just asked and did will be nothing compared to what everyone else will do to you. You need to believe, without a shred of doubt, that your decision to be with Jeremy is what you want. And not allow anyone to persuade you otherwise."

"It scares me how much I want to have a life with him, Rissa," Savannah whispered. "It's nothing like what I thought I felt for Jonas. With Jonas, it was all about what I had hoped to gain by being his wife."

"And now?"

"Now it's what I hope I can bring to him," she said with a shy smile.

I gave a small whoop and hugged her tight. "Now we'll be sisters-in-law, as well as cousins. Sisters," I said, releasing her. "I couldn't be happier for you or for Jeremy." I bit my lip as I studied Savannah. "Do you plan to continue to live in Boston or will you move somewhere new?"

"I think, for now, we are going to remain here. Jeremy is receiving good commissions, enough for us to survive on. I can't imagine too many changes in my life at once."

I attempted to smile bravely, but knew I failed when Savannah frowned at me. "I was hoping you'd say you were planning to move to Missoula. To be near Gabriel and me. It was a foolish notion."

"No, it wasn't, Rissa. I hate that you'll leave again." Savannah swiped at her cheeks and at her tears. "Will Gabriel approve?"

I settled against the settee, a faraway look in my eyes for a moment. "Of course. He's noticed how much Jeremy has improved in the letters he's sent him and has suspected that a good portion of his improvement has been due to his association with you. It's worried Gabriel, but he'd hoped you'd changed after your escape from Jonas."

"I have, Rissa."

"I know," I said. I paused, biting my lip and blushing before I looked at her again. "Sav, what happens if you become with child? Do you want your child born with such a stigma?"

Savannah paled, the happy bloom fading at my question. "I'll most likely never have any more children, Rissa."

"Oh, Sav," I whispered. "Why?"

"I can't explain it, but I guess the birth went so badly that I'll be unable to carry another child."

"And this has been confirmed by other doctors, by doctors not working for Jonas?"

"The doctor I visited with Aunt Betsy's urging yesterday said it was 'Difficult to be certain, although very likely, that my womb was an inhospitable place for new life to thrive.'" Savannah mimicked the clipped tones of the doctor in an attempt to lessen the hurtfulness of the words.

I grimaced at the words.

"Yes, not the most tactful man. I thought Aunt Betsy was going to cane him for his lack of sensitivity," Savannah said with a small smile. "It was the only amusing aspect of the visit."

"I doubt Aunt Betsy acted like that to bring levity to the situation."

"Of course not. She was irate." Savannah met my eyes, unable to hide her despair at the prospect of a childless future. "I don't fool myself, Rissa. I know there is a very small likelihood I'll have another child." She pleated her skirt. "And, if I'm fortunate enough to have Jeremy's baby, I'll cherish our child, no matter if it is sanctioned by the church and society or not. The previous blessings did little to aid me."

"Sav," I whispered. "I'm sorry you suffered so terribly."

"I don't want to continue to focus on the past, Rissa. I must focus on my future."

I forced a brave smile. "Well, if you want to focus on your future, you should think about how you're going to live with Jeremy. You won't have a cook or maids to help you when you live with him. I'd recommend purchasing clothes that are easy to don without aid. Can you still cook?"

"I think so."

"I never understood why your mother stopped you from learning from your cook when you were a girl. Why would she think it was beneath you to learn to prepare meals for yourself? And it will be especially important now." I paused for a moment. "I wonder if Sophie's cook would mind you spending time with her?"

Savannah flushed. "I know she wouldn't. I've spent many afternoons with her recently. I remember much of what I had learned, and, the rest, I'm finding easy to relearn. I love spending time in the kitchen."

"I wish I could say the same," I said with a wry smile.

"What is it you wish you liked?" Sophie asked as she entered.

"That I liked working in the kitchen," I said.

"I hope there are restaurants you can frequent," Savannah said with a giggle.

"There are," I said.

"I know there's been momentous news as the door was shut," Sophie said. She turned from Savannah to me, as though she were uncertain which of us had the news. I blushed but nodded toward Savannah.

"I've decided to move in with Mr. McLeod," Savannah said.

"Even though this will bring down as much, if not more, infamy than any divorce proceeding?" Sophie raised an eyebrow. "You take after Mrs. Woodhull."

"Mrs. Who?" Savannah asked.

"Really, don't you know your history?" Sophie glanced from Savannah to me. "She's the first woman to run for president of the United States. She's also one of the earliest proponents for women to practice 'free love.'"

"Free love?" I sputtered.

"You laugh, Clarissa, but the time will come when women can live with whom they choose without worrying they are defying their families. And they will be able to decide if they want to marry the man or not."

Savannah blushed. "I believe you are reading too much into this, Sophie."

"As you always say. I'm glad you're finally coming to your senses and realizing living with me isn't how you want to spend the rest of your life."

I curled my feet under me again as I settled onto the settee. "I've warned Savannah about how hard it can be with the limited income Jeremy can earn."

Sophronia smiled mischievously. "I'd think you'd sell your story to the papers. Rather than have me buy them off. Why not approach them and sell it to the highest bidder? It would make a nice nest egg for whenever you needed it."

"I couldn't," Savannah whispered.

"Why not?" Sophie asked. "Someone at one of those papers will discover your story and exploit it for the good people of Boston. I don't see why you don't make a profit from it."

"I'd have to discuss this with Jeremy," Savannah said.

I could see her thinking through the possibilities and shared a small smile with Sophie.

"As I said before, dear, try for a serial format," Sophie said. "Bleed them for all they're worth, just as they'll try to receive as much as they can from their readership."

CHAPTER 39

THAT EVENING I SAT in the casual rear parlor, attempting to read *The Wings of the Dove*. My gaze continued to rise to Savannah. She fidgeted with her needlepoint, and I saw her grimace a few times as she pricked her finger rather than the cloth with the needle. "Sav, are you all right?"

"I'm fine, Rissa," Savannah said, setting down her needlepoint with a sigh. "Jeremy is going to call tonight."

"That's wonderful! I haven't spent nearly enough time with him since I arrived."

Sophronia glanced over from the desk, tapping the tip of her pen on a sheet of paper. "Something else has you a bundle of nerves. Is it that man?"

"No, I've had no word from Jonas. I know that should worry me, but all I feel is relief." Savannah took a deep breath. "My father is also coming this evening. I wanted him to meet Jeremy."

"Why didn't you inform me before now?" Sophie asked as she reached for her cane and rose. "Let's move to the larger sitting room. With any luck, your brother will join your father and entertain us with his piano playing."

I stood, holding my book in one hand, reaching for Savannah and giving her a one-armed embrace as we moved to the front of the house and the larger sitting room. "Don't worry, Sav. I know Uncle Martin will approve of Jeremy."

Savannah smiled at my attempt to bolster her nerves. We had barely settled when Poole knocked on the door.

"A Mr. McLeod to see you, ma'am," he intoned.

"Please bring him up. And when Mr. Russell arrives, he is welcome too," Sophronia said.

I set aside my book as I heard Jeremy's footsteps approaching the doorway. When I saw Savannah merely nod at him in welcome, I jumped up from my chair to embrace him. "Jeremy, it's wonderful to see you again."

He gripped me tightly for a moment before easing away. "And you, Clarissa. I hope you are enjoying your stay."

I sat, motioning for him to sit on the settee next to me. He watched Savannah as though attempting to gauge the reason behind her reticence. "I am. I've been to the museum, and I'm hopeful to attend the symphony soon."

"I imagine those are events not enjoyed in Montana." Although he spoke with me, his gaze remained on Savannah, and I sensed a rising tension in him at her silence.

I smiled my agreement as Sophie *harrumphed* at the mention of Montana. "There is culture and art there but not of the same quality."

"I hope I can add to your enjoyment," Lucas said as he strolled into the room, a breathless Poole glowering at him in the doorway.

We all rose to greet Lucas and Uncle Martin. Savannah gripped her father's arm as she turned toward Jeremy. "Father, I'd like to introduce you to Jeremy McLeod. He's Gabriel's brother. And my friend."

"I've heard quite a bit about you. It's nice to finally make your acquaintance," Uncle Martin said as he held out his hand.

Jeremy clasped it, a hint of a smile present before he sobered. "And yours, sir."

"I'm Lucas. If you hurt her …"

"Lucas," Savannah hissed as she jabbed her elbow in his side.

"It's only fair he knows where he stands, Sav. We failed you once. We won't again." He watched Jeremy intently, a satisfied gleam entering his eyes as Jeremy nodded his understanding.

"A fine sentiment, young man," Sophronia intoned. "Good to see you have sense along with an ear for music."

Lucas settled on the stool in front of the piano whereas Uncle Martin sat on the settee next to Savannah. Jeremy sat next to me, and I could sense the nervous energy running through him. Sophronia watched us with amusement from her comfortable chair closest to the fire.

Lucas played random, yet harmonious notes on the piano, as though tinkering away at a new song. He watched Jeremy with avid curiosity. I bit back a smile as Lucas's made-up song veered from a sweet romance to a dark tragedy to a soothing lullaby as he continued to study Savannah and Jeremy.

"How are things with your dreadful son-in-law?" Sophronia asked, breaking the uncomfortable silence. "We are all united in our concern for Savannah, and I hope you're willing to speak frankly."

"I would hate to burden Mr. McLeod with our family concerns," Uncle Martin said.

"I never have, and never will, consider Savannah's safety or happiness a burden, sir," Jeremy said. "I would be honored if you would include me in your discussion and confidence."

Uncle Martin watched Jeremy with grudging respect. "Jonas informed me last week that, due to unforeseen circumstances and influences out of his control, the original terms for the loans would be honored. Thus, my business is in no danger. Thank you for your aid, Mrs. Chickering," Uncle Martin said with a nod to Sophronia.

"It was nothing. I've rarely found anything to be as diverting as disrupting that pompous man's plans," Sophronia said with a cackle.

Uncle Martin sighed as he traced a pattern on the settee's fabric. "I've rarely seen a man as irate."

"He nearly tore Father's office door off the hinges when he stormed out," Lucas said as he played a discordant note. "His bellowing could be heard throughout the store as I attempted to persuade our customers there was little to interest them from the back rooms."

"I'm certain they ignored you," Sophronia said with an amused lift of one eyebrow. "It's rare to find such entertainment when shopping for linens."

"I'm sorry, Father," Savannah whispered.

"Don't be. I'm thankful he's realized that he's been living under a false perception of the power he wields." Uncle Martin clasped her hand and squeezed it.

"Unfortunately I doubt that man has truly come to that conclusion. He's been thwarted, thanks to our collective endeavor, but I doubt he will give up on his objective," Sophronia warned.

"Why would he continue to want me back?" Savannah asked. "I've given him no indication that I would ever return. He suffered one spate of negative press after his attack on you, Sophie. I shouldn't think he'd relish more."

"That is a mystery to me as well. He exhibits no regard for you or your well-being when he refers to you. Yet he doesn't waver from his desire to have you returned to his home." Uncle Martin released her hand. "Something I will never countenance."

"I'm thankful you're no longer within his sphere of influence," Jeremy said in a near glower.

"A sentiment I can't agree with heartily enough," Lucas said.

"I do fear he would only become more irrational if he were to learn of your liaison with another," Uncle Martin said with a pointed glance at Jeremy.

"I would never wish to bring more shame upon you or mother, but I must live my life," Savannah whispered.

"Although it is a half-life?" her father asked. Savannah recoiled as though she'd been struck.

I felt Jeremy stiffen next to me, although he remained silent. He clenched his hands on his thighs, creasing and uncreasing the fabric of his pants as he listened to Savannah's exchange with her father.

"The life I would like to live would never be a half-life, Father. It would be a much fuller life than any I could ever have imagined with Jonas." Savannah squared her shoulders as though readying for battle.

"What is it that you envision, Sav?" Lucas asked.

"I plan to live with Jeremy. Share a home with him. Build a future with him," Savannah said.

"Even though you would be living outside the sphere of acceptable behavior? Inviting ridicule and scorn?" Uncle Martin's brown eyes were clouded with concern.

"I refuse to spend the rest of my life as a virtual shut-in, as though I were embarrassed by my actions. I'm proud of what I've done. I escaped the reality of a life lived with a man who only wished to shower pain and torment upon me." Savannah's eyes lit with passion.

"I will only ever feel grateful for your strength, my darling daughter," Uncle Martin said before turning his attention to Jeremy, a challenge in his brown eyes. "Is this enough for you, Mr. McLeod? Living with my Savannah, out of wedlock, free of any obligations to her?"

Jeremy squinted as he studied Savannah's father. "Since the moment I met your daughter, I have desired for nothing more than to care for her. To show her that she is cherished. I do not need a piece of paper or a man in a robe intoning a prayer over our joined hands for me to feel a responsibility to protect and to provide for her. She never has been and never will be an obligation, sir."

An agitated flush highlighted his cheekbones, and I stroked a hand down one of his arms in an attempt to calm him.

"And when that man seeks her out? Because I know, without a doubt, someday he will. What then?" Uncle Martin demanded.

"I will do anything necessary to protect her," Jeremy said.

Uncle Martin smiled, nodding with satisfaction.

"What are you doing to thwart the newspapermen?" Lucas asked as he continued to tinker away on the piano. "I would think they'd relish the telling and retelling of your story."

"We're going to sell our tale to the highest bidder," Savannah said with a glance of entreaty to Jeremy. He met her gaze and frowned for a moment, before smiling and nodding his silent agreement.

Uncle Martin frowned as he watched Savannah and then gave an assessing glance at Sophronia. "This has the markings of your idea."

"One way or another, their story will become known. Too many people, including the customers of your store, are aware of her defection and are curious as to the real reason behind it. Rather than line the pockets of the newspapermen, I see no reason why Savannah and Jeremy shouldn't benefit from it. And control to some extent what appears in the papers," Sophronia said.

"This isn't something to proclaim to the world as though rejoicing," Lucas argued. "It's as though you're baiting the man."

"Why not?" Savannah demanded. "I rejoice, daily, that I am away from Jonas. That I dared to love again and find a man like Jeremy. Why should I be forced to feel a moment's worth of shame?"

"Not shame, Sav, but caution," Lucas said. "You don't know what he could do. He …"

Savannah laughed mirthlessly. "You're telling me, the one who lived through his beatings and brutality, that I can't conceive of what he could do?" She looked from her father to Lucas. "It's because I know exactly what he can do, and what it means to live a life devoid of joy or hope, that I refuse to ever be forced to live that way again. After living a lie and creating an illusion of a perfect life to hide the reality I suffered, it's why I must now live a fulfilling life. An authentic life."

"Savannah, he could still hurt you," Lucas warned.

"I know, but I can't live my life controlled by fear. I can't allow him to have that victory over me. I suspect the only reason he's left me alone for so long is because he believes I've continued to be the mousy little woman he converted me into."

"All that will change when the articles come out," I said, finally joining the discussion. "He'll be publicly shamed, not by sly gossip, but directly by you, Sav, and will want to find a way to save face."

"I would think you'd seek divorce rather than infamy," Lucas said. "Be fully free of him."

"Every detail of abuse would need to be known, Lucas. I can't abide that. With the newspaper stories, they will only learn what I want them to," Savannah argued.

"I think Savannah also fears there would be those who would construe her a madwoman for believing her daughter lived when her husband and a physician claim she had died," Jeremy said.

"Few would believe me or my maid over Jonas and a physician." Savannah blinked away tears. "They'll always side with the viewpoint of men."

"For now, Savannah dearest. For now," Sophie intoned. "But times will change. And I believe you aren't giving the public the benefit of the doubt. I'm certain there are many who would be sympathetic to you."

"Which is why you want her to divulge everything to the newspapers?" Lucas asked in confusion.

"Love is a wonderful thing, Lucas, but you still need money to live on," Sophie said.

"A suffragist who's a pragmatist," Lucas said with a smirk.

"I'd caution you, Sav, to not seek too much notoriety. I'd hate for you to attain it through these stories even though you'd attempted to avoid it with a divorce," I said.

"I know, Rissa. But this is something I have to do. For me. For my sense of worth." Savannah shared a long glance with Jeremy before smiling fully.

"Tell me, Mr. McLeod, what sort of business you have," Uncle Martin said after a long moment. "How do you plan on supporting Savannah?"

I smiled, rising from my seat next to Jeremy to sit on the piano bench next to Lucas. "Quit taunting us with wisps of songs, Lucas. Play us something."

"I wouldn't want to interrupt their getting to know each other," Lucas said with a nod to the room. "Besides, if I concentrate too much on music, I won't hear his answers, and I won't learn what type of man he is."

"Then why are you sitting over here, rather than among them?" I asked, watching as Jeremy leaned forward, resting his elbows on his knees as he discussed the nascent success of his business.

"Playing the piano, even just a few notes here and there, calms me. Helps me think better. It also makes those in the room think I'm not focusing on what they're saying or doing, and I can see how they truly are."

"And what have you discovered about Jeremy?" I whispered as I watched Jeremy motion with his hands as he talked about carpentry before discussing his family.

"He's a man in tune with the emotions of others. I've rarely seen someone able to hold their counsel and listen as he did. He has a singular focus on Savannah and her welfare, and yet he's aware of the room. Every time I hit an off-key note, he flinched."

"Lucas," I chided, "you shouldn't have toyed with him."

"At first I wasn't, but then I wanted to see if he'd ever turn his attention away from Savannah. He never did."

"So you approve of him?" I asked.

"For now. Savannah's been through too much for me not to be concerned about her moving on too quickly."

"You'll soon come to realize he's a good man," I said.

"You're biased because of Gabriel," Lucas said with a half smile as he now played "Fur Elise."

I closed my eyes as his music flowed around me. I listed from side to side gently as he played, my concern for Savannah and Jeremy momentarily eclipsed by the joy I found in his music. When he finished, I sighed, opening my eyes.

"Don't cry, Rissa," Lucas said with a tender smile. He swiped at my tears and then played a bawdy song, causing me to laugh. He nudged me with his shoulder as he whispered, "It's called 'The Bouncer at the Blazing Rag.'"

"Oh, Lucas, I miss this. I miss living near you. I wish we could all live near each other," I whispered.

"All that matters is that you are happy, Rissa. I can see, by the way you speak about Gabriel, that you are."

"I am, Lucas. I just hope that Savannah will find such happiness," I whispered.

"It appears that she will," Lucas said. "Father likes Jeremy, and, although it's unconventional what they are planning, I know he will support her."

"Will you?"

"Of course. Convention never brought her peace. Or joy. If this will, then I will champion her."

"But you doubt it will bring her the joy she envisions," I said, exchanging a worried glance with Lucas.

"I fear she's yet to fully understand the extent to which she is going against societal norms and how much that could affect her. She claims she no longer cares about good society, but she's never had to live under the brunt of its censure."

I shivered. "She'll learn not to care."

"It doesn't mean it didn't hurt you though, does it?" Lucas asked with an insightfulness that startled me.

"No," I said. "It always stung. But, when I realized I could live a proper life, with little future hope for joy, or leave it all behind for Gabriel, there really wasn't much choice."

"I missed you when you went away," Lucas said, raising sad eyes to me. "I always wished there was more I could have done to help you before you left."

I leaned into his side, and he ceased playing for a moment to sling an arm around me for an embrace. "You'll never know what it meant to me to have you accept me into your home, with no questions asked that spring. I needed a safe place, and you and Uncle Martin ensured I had it. Thank you," I choked out as I battled tears, resting my head on his shoulder.

"As long as you are safe now, Rissa. Loved as you should be," he whispered.

"I am." I raised my head and sniffled, watching as Uncle Martin and Jeremy laughed over some tale Savannah told. I smiled as I watched fragile bonds form between them that would strengthen with time. "I continue to wish you would find the same joy in your life, Lucas."

"My life is as it should be. Working at the store with Father is what I've been raised to do." Lucas looked at the piano keys, fisting his fingers to prevent playing them.

"But it's not your heart's joy, Lucas," I argued. "You should perform. Write your own songs. Travel around the country and share your remarkable talent with others."

Lucas's eyes flashed with eagerness and desire for a moment before dimming. "I know you wish the best for me, Rissa. But I know I'm to remain here, working at Russell's."

"Be brave like Savannah, Lucas. Break the bonds of expectations set upon you by your mother. Fight for your heart's desire and let nothing separate you from it."

Lucas watched me with guarded hope. "You've encouraged me for years, Rissa, and your faith in me has brought tremendous solace when it appeared no one supported me. I don't know if I can do what you encourage."

I gripped his arm, hoping to have his full attention. "You're brave, Lucas. As brave as Savannah or I. Have faith in that."

Lucas nodded, and embraced me. I heard him stutter out a breath. "Thank you for your belief in me, Rissa."

CHAPTER 40

"WHEN ARE YOU GOING to announce your news?" Sophie asked as she sat next to me on a settee in the back parlor. The bright light of an early December day lit the back room, although a cold wind blew outside, with harsh gusts rattling the windows.

I turned to face her, lowering my pen. "I'm afraid I don't know what you mean."

"Don't act innocent with me, my girl," Sophie said. Her expression turned cautious and concerned. "I know a pregnant woman when I see one."

"Sophie! Hush," I said as I rose to shut the sitting room door.

"Ah, so it is true." She smiled with a satisfied smirk.

I glowered at her before sitting next to her. "Yes. As you somehow discovered, I'm with child. I ... I haven't told anyone yet."

"Not even your young man?"

"Especially not him," I said. "He'd worry about me so far away and want me either to stay here to have the baby or to return immediately. I have plenty of time to travel yet."

Sophronia watched me with nostalgia. "My fondest memories of my marriage were when I was expecting. My husband would rub my back when it ached and spend hours with me, touching my belly to feel the baby move. We'd spend time together, with no need for words."

"Sophie," I whispered as I fought the need to see Gabriel. To be held by him. To share with him our wondrous news.

"Don't deny yourself those memories with your husband out of some sense of duty to your family here. Go home. Be with him. He has every right to spoil you properly now that you're to have his child."

"He spoiled me, even when he thought there was no hope of us having a child."

"Why would he believe that?"

"I doubted for months my ability to have a child. After the tea, I bled heavily. I think I made it too strong. A doctor in Missoula said there was no way to determine if Gabriel and I were unlucky or if it were due to what had happened that spring." I shared a long look with Sophie where she nodded her understanding.

"Of course you presumed it was due to your drinking the tea."

I nodded and took a deep breath. "But when I found the courage to tell Gabriel, he was more upset I hadn't trusted him with my fears. He was unconcerned with the possibility we might never have children."

"Perhaps he doesn't like them."

"No, he's very fond of them. However, I think he remembered his friend's near death from childbirth in Butte. Amelia, the miner's widow? She'd had a baby girl right before her husband died, and Gabriel was there. I heard Gabriel muttering to Ronan once about how hard the birth was and that he would rather have no children than have me suffer the same."

"Ah, a good man then," Sophie said with a smile. "Don't take too long to return to him, my girl. These are moments you'll never regain."

***

I WALKED FROM SOPHIE'S house toward Russell's to visit Aunt Betsy. She planned to leave tomorrow, and I wanted to see her again. Savannah had refused to come with me, unwilling to suffer her mother's disdain. I walked through the Back Bay and into the South End. Although I wouldn't visit Mrs. Smythe today, I wanted to walk by my parents' house.

As I turned onto Union Park, I paused to stare at the oval-shaped park. I walked slowly down the sidewalk, finding solace in the unchanged bow-fronted brick homes that faced the park. I closed my eyes for a moment as I faced my da's house, memories washing over me of Mama, Da and Gabriel, coming and going through the front door. I blinked and continued walking.

After a few steps along the cobbled walkway, I stumbled on the uneven bricks. A man sitting on a stoop in the cold midafternoon watched as I righted myself. I blushed and smiled at him as I resumed my walk toward my uncle's store. After a few steps, I stopped and froze in place before spinning to stare at the man.

He watched me with an amused expression. "I wondered if you'd recognize me."

I shivered at his voice and took an automatic step backward as he rose and approached me. "You're dead."

"No, my darling Clarissa, I'm not. It was meant to look like I'd died in that wretched fire." His arrogant smile made my heart stutter. "I'm glad my ploy was successful."

I hit him on the arm before jerking my hand away. "Mr. Carlin almost died trying to save … to save …" I shook my head as I stared at him.

"To save a dead man's corpse?" Cameron threw his head back and laughed. "I knew if I were to be successful, they'd need to believe I'd died. I knew no one would miss one of the drunks from Front Street."

"How could you?" I asked as I stared at him with dawning horror.

"Do you really believe I was going to spend my life living in that pathetic little town married to such an inconsequential woman?" He shook his head. "If so, you never really knew me, Clarissa."

I hugged my arms around myself, dazed. "On that we agree."

He took a step toward me, and the cloying scent of bay rum overwhelmed me. I shuddered and exhaled through my nose, attempting to dispel the scent. I tried to back away but he gripped my arms. "I knew I needed to return to Boston, but I wasn't going to return a pauper."

"You stole the money," I said. "Not Mr. Carlin." I glared at him and tried to wrench my arms free. However, he had a firm grip and spun me, propelling me backward until I was pushed up against one of my neighbor's side walls, near their servants' entrance. I was hidden from passersby as he loomed over me.

"Maybe I did. You'll never be able to prove it." He grinned at me as I tried to shrink away from him and his touch. "What, Clarissa? Not so brave now that you don't have that lumbering laborer around to protect you?"

His taunt made me shudder, and I tried to struggle against him. "Imagine my joy to realize it was you walking down the street. Alone. I thought to myself that, finally, we could have our time together that we've been so sorely deprived of since you moved to Montana."

"If you think for one moment that I'd relish spending any time with you—" I gasped as he gripped my hair and tilted my head back. A tear leaked out as I again realized I was at his mercy.

"I know you would. You're that type of woman. Passionate. Thirsty for adventure." His breaths along my ear caused me to shudder uncontrollably. "And now we don't have to worry about any interference from that husband of yours."

At the mention of Gabriel and my life with him, one that I'd struggled so hard to build, a rage filled me. Cameron had me pressed against the wall, but he leaned away from me a moment to study my face. I remembered a lesson Colin had taught me years ago and jerked up my knee, hitting him squarely in his groin. Any pleasure leeched from his face, and he doubled over in agony.

"Don't ever touch me again." I stepped around him toward the walkway. I glanced back to see him on his knees, grimacing in pain before I began a hasty walk toward Washington Street.

I wanted to see Aunt Betsy, but knew I wouldn't be able to handle an afternoon verbally sparring with Aunt Matilda. I approached Washington Street and ascended the new metallic steps that brought me to the elevated railway stop. When the train approached, I boarded and headed toward the North End.

However, rather than visit Florence today, I headed toward Gabriel's old workshop. I knew Savannah was to visit Jeremy this afternoon, and I needed her. I rode the train to North Union Station, descending the stairs near Canal Street. I was too agitated to note any of the local charm that had always made my walks to Gabriel's workshop interesting.

After climbing the stairs to the workshop, I leaned in with one ear against the door, but didn't hear noise from inside. I remembered the few times I had visited Gabriel and then blushed at the thought of what could be occurring. I knocked loudly and heard low voices before footsteps approached the door.

"Clarissa," Jeremy said as he watched me with frank curiosity. "Savannah told me that you were to visit your aunts." He opened the door farther, and I walked in. Savannah sat on a bench by the table, papers spread out in front of her. The stove heated the room to a comfortable degree. The only thing missing was a pot of tea. And Gabriel.

I turned toward Jeremy, blinking away memories and a tear as I attempted to focus on him. "You kept the chair," I whispered. I touched his arm, and he nodded with a shy smile.

Rather than sit in my rocking chair, I moved toward the table and sat on the opposite side of Savannah on another bench. Jeremy joined us, settling next to Savannah.

"Somehow I don't believe you're here for nostalgia's sake," Jeremy said as he studied me.

"I remember telling you that Cameron died," I said, pausing to clear my throat as my voice broke at Cameron's name. They both nodded. Savannah set aside the papers and pencil, paying full attention to me.

"I thought I'd walk to see Aunt Betsy and Aunt Matilda. It's not that cold today, and I wanted to stroll past my old street." I smiled as I shared a rueful smile with Jeremy. "I wanted a bit of nostalgia, remembering my walks with Gabriel, reliving our conversations. Remembering Da."

"What happened, Rissa? Why aren't you at my parents' house?" Savannah asked. She reached across the table, and I grasped her hand.

"I saw a ghost," I whispered.

Jeremy squinted at me and cocked his head to the side, a move so reminiscent of Gabriel that I had to look away for a moment. "Not Cameron."

I nodded.

"How?" Savannah breathed. "He died in a fire."

"He made it look like he died. Instead a drunk from Front Street was incinerated in that blaze. And Sebastian nearly died trying to save him." I closed my eyes and whispered, "I'd reconciled myself that he'd only torment me from my nightmares. I never imagined I'd see him, alive, talking to me again."

"Rissa," Savannah murmured.

"What did he do to you?" Jeremy demanded in a low, dangerous voice.

I shook my head dazedly, the memory of today intermingling with the memory from the sitting room nearly two years ago. I attempted to quell a shudder but failed.

"Did he touch you?" Jeremy asked. I felt him near me, but he refrained from getting closer.

I met his worried gaze. "Yes, he did. He intimated that, since I had managed to separate myself from Gabriel, we could have a reunion of sorts." I half smiled at Jeremy's growl of displeasure before I sobered. "He pushed me against a wall, and all I could smell was his cologne. And feel so weak again."

"Rissa," Savannah whispered. Her quiet entreaty brought me back to the present.

"I finally remembered one of Colin's lessons to me when I was younger."

Jeremy watched me, a hopeful, wicked gleam in his eye. "Please tell me you did more than stomp on his foot."

I laughed at his wry words. "Yes, I kneed him in his ... in his ..." I waved my free hand but didn't know what to say.

"Delicate zone," Jeremy said as he nodded his approval. "Good. I hope you left him flat on the pavement, ruing the day he ever dared to speak with you again."

"I did," I said with pride.

"Good for you, Rissa." Savannah bit her lip. "But why was he in your old neighborhood?"

"I have no idea," I said. "It was such a shock to see him, I never thought to wonder why he was there. The only person he knows is Mrs. Smythe."

"He couldn't have an interest in her," Savannah breathed.

"They're two sides of the same coin," Jeremy said. "I think they'd be perfect for each other."

I snickered my agreement.

"Wasn't there some sort of scandal involving money surrounding his death?" Savannah asked.

"Yes. When he died, the company safe was breached at the same time as the fire. Everyone accused Sebastian, the mill foreman, of stealing the money." I shook my head in consternation. "Anyone with sense would know he would never steal from his employers. He's loyal and smart and wouldn't do that. Besides, at the time he was supposedly busy stealing the money, he was in the mill, trying to save who he thought was Cameron. And nearly dying in the process."

"Maybe they thought there was some sort of conspiracy?" Jeremy said. "That he would look to be aboveboard when he was really working with others to rob the company."

"Whatever you say, I'll never believe Sebastian had anything to do with the missing money. He's a good man." I shuddered. "Besides, Cameron admitted today he wasn't going to return to Boston a pauper and mentioned the money from the safe. I'm sure he stole it. I just never thought he'd resort to murder."

"Well, it's your word against the town opinion in Missoula," Jeremy said. "What are you going to do about it?"

"I don't know," I whispered.

"I think we should have a gathering of minds," Savannah said. "Let's all meet at Sophie's tonight. Jeremy, come with Florence and Richard. I'll telephone Aunt Betsy, and we'll concoct a plan."

"I agree," I said as I rose. "I should leave. I'm interrupting." I waved, indicating the pile of papers in front of Savannah.

"Oh, I'm just trying to determine what we'll need in our new home. Delusions of grandeur as I know everything we'll have will be secondhand," she said with a contented smile.

"I'll escort you home, Clarissa. I don't want you walking around with Cameron lurking about." Jeremy rose, heading toward the small coat rack.

"I'll come too," Savannah said. I looped my arm through Savannah's for the trip to Sophronia's.

***

THAT EVENING, I SAT in Sophie's parlor, attempting to smile bravely as everyone slowly trickled in. A fire crackled, emitting a gentle heat. Scattered lamps lit on side tables provided a welcoming glow to the room, in contrast to the stark brightness that would have been provided by an overhead chandelier. I had moved nearly every chair and settee in Sophie's parlor so that they formed a large half circle, facing the fireplace, a low black walnut table in the middle. All seats were occupied. I sat nearest the fire, although I wished I had sat closer to the windows, as I felt a trickle of sweat run down my back.

"Well, my girl, you've gathered us together for some purpose. I hope you'll soon share it with us." Sophie's voice was scratchier than usual as she tried to puzzle out why we were all assembled.

"A few of you know what happened today, so please forgive me for repeating myself. I was to visit Aunt Betsy and Aunt Matilda this afternoon. However, on my walk to Russell's, I met Cameron."

Colin jerked in his chair. "That's impossible. He died in the sawmill fire. He's buried in Missoula."

"It wasn't him who died, Col. Some poor drunk from Front Street. Didn't it seem odd to you at Da's funeral that his mother wasn't angrier with me?

At the time I was focused more on Mrs. Smythe, but, now that I think about it, I should have expected his mother to be distraught at seeing me. And she wasn't."

"What does he want?" Aunt Betsy asked.

"An illicit affair with Clarissa," Jeremy said as I paused too long to answer.

"No," Sophie gasped. I had rarely seen her shocked, and this was one of those moments. "The insolence!" Sophie said as she fanned herself. Her eyes flashed her displeasure.

"What can we do?" Florence asked.

"I don't know. I have no desire to see him again, but a good friend of Colin's, Gabriel's and mine was accused of stealing the company money from a safe during that fire. I believe, and Cameron intimated, that he stole the money. I doubt I can obtain a binding confession from him. But I'd like some proof that he's alive."

"Have someone take a photograph of him," Jeremy said. "That would prove the man is alive and help your friend in Missoula."

"Would we have to hire a photographer?" Florence asked.

"No, we'll buy one of those Brownie cameras from Kodak. One of you"—Sophie gazed with meaning at Jeremy, Richard and Colin—"will keep yourselves hidden as Clarissa is speaking with him."

"If we splurge, we can buy one of their new pocket cameras," Aunt Betsy said. "It would be much less obvious."

"But how will we prove that she is speaking to him now and not when she used to live in Boston?" Savannah asked.

"The first picture taken should be one of the day's newspapers so it dates the photos," Jeremy said.

"Maybe I could also carry the same paper with me," I said.

"Exactly," Sophie said.

"We have to be close to them to obtain a decent photo of Cameron, Mrs. Chickering," Jeremy said. He frowned as he envisioned the scene. "If there's one thing I learned in the war, the best information you receive is that which the person freely supplies. We want him to feel relaxed with Clarissa, and, if he sees one of us, he won't be."

"Does he know all of us present?" Sophie asked.

"I'm afraid so," I said as I glanced around. "We could meet in a coffee or tea shop. They're always crowded, and one of you could easily hide."

"The problem is that we'd need to be at the next table, Rissa," Jeremy said. "The camera won't take a good picture, probably not even at that distance."

"He barely knows me," Florence said. "He saw me when I was at your house for tea once, and then when I was in Richard's arms at your uncle's house. I doubt he paid me any mind, a poor, penniless schoolteacher. And I doubt he'd look twice at a pregnant woman."

"I couldn't ask you to do this, Flo," I said.

"You're not asking. I'm offering. Besides, it's dreadfully dull being alone in the house all day." She smiled. "I can act as though I've just received a new present from my doting husband, and I'm learning how to use it. That way I can sit next to you and take photographs."

"You'll have to be dressed a bit better," Savannah argued.

"It seems a waste buying a new dress when I'll soon be two sizes smaller," Florence said with a pat to her belly.

"Savannah, you and Florence work on obtaining a dress. Colin, you can buy the camera," Sophie said. "As for you, my girl," she said with a tap to my knee with her fan, "I'd become accustomed to letter writing. You're not leaving this house without an escort again until that man has been dealt with."

CHAPTER 41

COLIN AND I STOOD on our old front steps, waiting for one of the maids to answer the door. I gripped my hands in front of me, pulling on my gloves with such force I tore off a button at the cuff. The black wrought iron handrail gleamed, as did the gold knocker on the door.

"Relax, Rissa. We have every right to want to visit our sister," Colin said.

I nodded as I pasted on a smile as the door opened. Bridget barely spared us a glance before attempting to shut the door without acknowledging our presence. Colin stuffed his foot in the small opening, grunting with pain as the heavy door met his instep.

"Come on, Bridget, you know you have to let us in sometime," Colin said. He leaned against the door with all his strength, and it burst forward as I heard a shriek and a *thunk*. I peered around Colin to see Bridget sprawled on the floor, her apron askew.

Colin entered, with me on his heels, and held out his hand to pull Bridget off the floor. "Loyalty is an admirable trait, as long as it's not misplaced or misguided," Colin said with a meaningful look.

She glared at the two of us and turned toward the back of the house, using the rear stairs to descend to the kitchen. Colin and I crept toward the door of the parlor and glanced inside. Colin couldn't help grunting in surprise, and I gasped at the changes in the room.

At our slight noise, Mrs. Smythe turned toward us and glowered. "How dare you intrude upon my quietude," she snapped. "You have no right to enter here."

"We disagree. This was, after all, our home," Colin said as he strolled into the room with feigned nonchalance. "Interesting choice of wallpaper."

"It's one that only the most esteemed of Boston society has been able to purchase. When I saw it, and realized the prestige it would bring our family, I knew I needed to have it installed."

"Even though it beggared you and Da?" Colin asked.

"It's done no such thing. And there isn't a more desirable drawing room in the area." She flushed as she slammed down her teacup.

"That wouldn't be hard as you are now in a working man's neighborhood. It's not as though you are in the Back Bay," I said. "Where did the piano go?"

"I thought a sitting area was more to our needs, rather than a decrepit old piece that constantly needed tuning."

"So you sold that too? Even though you knew it was one of our mother's favorite pieces?" Colin asked.

"One such as I will always look to my future rather than cling to the past. I'd suggest you do the same." She eyed Colin. "It's how I managed to receive more than I ever expected for the forge."

"You stupid woman," Colin growled. "If you had even a tenth of the intelligence you think you have, you would have spoken with me or someone with any knowledge about a forge. You would have known that, over time, you would have earned a handsome income. That selling was the last thing you should have done. Instead, you were on the verge of parting with it for a bargain to a fortune hunter."

"I did no such thing. I received half again what I had originally expected to receive. A wealthy businessman offered more than Mr. Wade had been willing to pay. I think I did quite well for myself."

"Did you never wonder why a wealthy businessman, one who has no previous experience in blacksmithing, would—all of a sudden—take an interest in your forge? He paid you half what it was worth, but because you'd been led to believe it had such little value, you thought yourself cunning. You're a fool, Mrs. Smythe." Colin paced in front of the fireplace.

"I fail to see how any of this is your business, Colin. It was mine to do with as I please. As your father's widow, I inherited his estate. You and your siblings were entitled to nothing as you had all left home, and no will was formally written."

"Did our da tell that you he'd like to leave us something?" I asked, my voice cracking as I looked around the sitting room, devoid of any of my mother's warmth or charm. I fought the inclination to strain for my da's booming voice; to listen for his heavy footsteps descending the stairs; to imagine, at any moment, he'd enter the parlor and enfold me in his strong arms.

"He made no specific bequests to any of you," she snapped. "You ungrateful children are entitled to nothing! All you brought him was pain and heartache with your defection and inability to show him filial loyalty."

"Mrs. Smythe …" Colin growled.

"And I would thank you to give me the respect I am owed as your stepmother. My name is Mrs. Sullivan, not Mrs. Smythe." Her bosom heaved as she spat out her first married name.

"It was my birthright!" Colin roared. "And you stole it from me. And still you don't have the decency to thank Clarissa and me for intervening, for advising Gabriel's uncle to buy the forge for more than you were to receive from Mr. Wade so that Richard could run it. You continue under your delusional belief that you were a successful businesswoman."

"How dare you interfere in my negotiations!"

"How dare you believe you could negotiate with a pair of sharks and not come out mauled!" Colin snapped, watching Mrs. Sullivan with unmitigated loathing. "If you'd had any sense, you would have kept the forge and offered it, if not to me, then to Richard to run."

"I refuse to have any further contact than is strictly necessary with that family." Mrs. Smythe glared at Colin and me, her back ramrod straight. "Any other foreman would have been preferable to a McLeod."

"You are such a fool," I whispered, filled with such a rage I couldn't speak any louder. "You have no idea what you've lost. What you've forced, each of us, to lose. We lost Patrick due to your meddling. Colin lost the forge. I almost lost Gabriel. And you wonder why we never welcomed you into our family? Why we insisted on calling you by your first married name? Because you never wanted us. You never wanted to be a part of our family. You just wanted Da and whatever material gains you could receive from him. And now none of it matters. Because you don't have Da, and you have no income." I blinked away tears as I stared at her, feeling my antipathy bleed into a numb indifference.

"I have no need to discuss my business transactions with the likes of you. I would like you to leave my house," Mrs. Smythe said.

"No. We want to see Melinda. We haven't seen her since we arrived in

Boston. We need to ensure that she is well."

"Of course she is well. How dare you intimate otherwise! When I think of all I've had to suffer at the hands of such ungrateful stepchildren ..." She glowered at us but did not finish her sentence.

I stood, my gloves twisted in knots in my hands. "We know the way to Melly's room. Good day, Mrs. Smythe." I turned and walked toward the parlor door.

"Good riddance!" she shrieked at my back. "If I never again see the likes of such malicious people who were supposed to be my family, it will be too soon."

"Save your tears for someone who actually believes your theatrics," Colin said as he followed me out the door. We walked up the stairs to the third floor, noting the furniture becoming more sparse in the hallway as we left the public areas. The wallpaper had bright patches, highlighting where pictures used to hang.

"Col?" I asked.

"I have a bad feeling about what's going on. Let's find Melly."

We reached her door and pushed it open. She sat in a corner, playing silently with a rag doll. She turned toward the door with wide, fearful eyes that became curious as we entered. I moved toward her, sitting on the floor next to her to be more at her eye level. Colin pulled over a small chair, his knees near his shoulders, looking ridiculous.

I giggled. "Col, you look a buffoon."

He winked at Melly. "I know." He watched her with serious eyes. "We're your brother and sister, Melinda. I'm Colin, and she's Clarissa. I doubt you remember us, as we left a long time ago. But we've never forgotten you and wanted to visit you when we were home."

She watched us wide-eyed, glancing from Colin to me, but not speaking. "Do you think she can speak, Col?"

He shrugged his shoulders in response and pulled out a wrapped present from his pocket. "We know you just celebrated your second birthday the end of November and wanted to bring you a present."

"Present?" she whispered in a childish lisp, reaching out to touch the box before grabbing her hand back.

"It's all right," I said, softly touching her arm. She pulled her arm away from me, although she sat in the same place. "Here. Open it, Melly."

She bit her lip, tracing the paper and pink ribbon. I nodded encouragingly, and she smiled shyly. When she pulled off the pink ribbon, she tried to pull the paper away, little by little.

"No, Melly. Like this," Colin said as he ripped the paper and made a loud tearing sound.

She shook her head with her eyes going round. She darted a glance toward the door and whispered, "No noise. No noise!"

I frowned, reaching out to rub my hand down her head and over her shoulders, while sharing a worried glance with Colin. "A little noise is all right, Melly," I whispered. "Let's see what the box holds."

She leaned forward, pulling off the lid and clapped her hands together without making any sound. As she bounced in place in excitement, I helped her pull out the small porcelain doll. "We thought you might like this. I had a similar doll when I was your age," I said.

She turned eyes filled with wonder and delight to Colin and then me. "Mine?"

I blinked away tears as I nodded and again stroked her head. "Of course. You are our sister. Although we haven't seen you since you were a baby, we wanted you to know we miss you and love you."

She smiled, and it looked like she was giggling, but again she made no noise. She traced her doll's dress, and I picked up her rag doll. Soon we were having a doll tea party. Although my greatest desire was to make a racket, I knew that would not help Melinda, as she was trapped in this house.

I turned as the door opened, and Bridget entered. "It's time for the little miss to prepare for dinner. You are asked to leave."

I watched all the joy and spirit leave Melinda at these words. "We'll try to come back," I whispered. She nodded, staring at the floor, her rag doll clutched to her.

I leaned forward, kissing the top of her head. "Take good care of yourself, darling sister."

Colin ruffled her hair and then followed me out the door. We descended the stairs and exited onto the front steps. "We have to see her again," Colin said with thinly veiled anger. "She shouldn't be living like that."

"I know, Col. We have to do what we can, although I don't know as there's much to be done. We won't be here that long. It's already the beginning of December, and I want to be in Missoula with Gabriel for Christmas."

We walked toward Sophie's, worrying about Melly, and what we could do from Missoula. "As to that, Rissa, I think I'll stay here for a bit to help Richard run the forge. I'd like to work with him, and I need to do this before returning to Montana."

"But you will return?" I asked, unable to hide my anxiety.

"That's my plan."

I frowned, because I knew how quickly plans changed, especially for Sullivans.

"Come. You need to focus on your meeting tomorrow with Cameron," Colin said. I shivered, and all thoughts of Melinda fled as fear and trepidation filled me.

CHAPTER 42

I ENTERED THE TEA SHOP and glanced around. Nearly every table was filled, and waiters scurried from table to table, carrying empty plates, teapots or heavy platters of sandwiches. The dark wood paneling, high coffered ceilings and orbed light fixtures lent the room a European feel. I saw Florence seated at a table next to Cameron, fiddling with a camera, acting the part of a vapid society matron. I bit back a nervous smile as I approached Cameron and avoided glancing in Florence's direction. The seat open to me was the one that put my back to Florence, allowing Florence to have a decent view of Cameron.

"You've finally seen reason and decided I am your better option," Cameron said. He asked the waiter to bring tea for me and coffee for him. "I was most gratified when I received your note."

"I wasn't certain where to send it as I did not know where you are staying."

"My mother passes along any messages she deems important." Cameron clasped my hand, and I hoped he failed to note my instinctive flinch at his touch.

I nodded at the waiter as our tea, coffee and cakes were delivered. I prepared my cup, tapping the spoon with such agitated force I worried I'd chip the fine china. "How did you do it?"

"Ah, you are curious about the most inconsequential details. All that should matter to you is that I'm adroit enough to escape the net of one such as Mrs. Bouchard."

"And turn a profit." I heard a clicking sound behind me and hoped Florence was taking photos.

"You wouldn't think I'd return a pauper? My family was in need of funds."

"And the poor man you killed?" I asked.

"I shouldn't think he would have survived the winter, what with the amount he drank every day. He would most likely have died of exposure at some point." Cameron grinned, appearing satisfied with himself. "I'd always thought that Sebastian Carlin was too honorable for his own good. And then, when he entered the mill in an attempt to save who he thought was me, it was perfect."

"Why?" I asked with a bright smile. I leaned forward, loosening my hand from beneath his and stroking the top of his hand. His eyes flared, and I had to battle my inherent fear at being near him.

"Because he left his office and I had easy access to the safe. Just that week, Mr. Bouchard had given me the combination to it. I couldn't have found a better way to distract the people of the mill and have access to the mill's safe."

"You killed a man and intentionally ruined the reputation of another."

Cameron shrugged. "It allowed me to come home. Not as triumphantly had we married."

"Had you obtained my dowry." I was unable to hide the bitterness from my voice.

"Of course. It's why men like me would ever be interested in women from your class." He studied me. "I would have kept you in much better style than that laborer. Look at what he's made you. A frumpy woman in last year's style, with little to no hope of betterment. It's rather pathetic."

"You're pathetic," I said as I leaned away from him and gripped my hands together on my lap. "You who think that the pursuit of money at any cost will bring you happiness. I loathe you."

"Think what you will, Clarissa, but I'm here, sitting in a tea shop with you rather than rotting in some jail in Missoula."

"As I told Jonas, you too will receive what you deserve, and when you do, no one will come to your aid," I hissed. I rose, bumping the table and sloshing the tea and coffee, spilling a bit of both onto his suit. At his hiss of displeasure, I smiled with bitter satisfaction. "All you hold dear is nothing but a mirage, and someday you'll rue the time you've wasted."

I marched out of the tea shop without a backward glance.

***

FOUR DAYS LATER we gathered again in Sophie's sitting room. I waited for Florence and Richard to arrive, as they were coming with the developed pictures. Jeremy and Savannah were already present, seated on the settee. Colin paced in front of the fireplace while Sophie and I sat next to each other in matching lady's chairs.

"Florence, show us the pictures," Sophie demanded as a breathless Florence entered the sitting room. "Once you are settled," Sophie amended, taking in Florence's flushed face and labored movement.

Florence eased herself into a chair and took a few moments to calm her breathing. She smiled in gratitude at the proffered cup of tea from Savannah, taking a small sip as she relaxed fully. Richard stood beside her. He fidgeted from foot to foot and waved away the offer of a chair.

"I'm afraid not many are any good. They're very grainy. However, I do have a decent one, when he is leaning in." She extracted the photos from a brown paper wrapping and handed the top one to me. I blanched as I stared at it. In it, Cameron was staring at me intently, holding my hand.

I handed the picture to Sophie. "Well, this looks a bit … intimate," she said as she raised quizzical aquamarine eyes to me.

I flushed and lowered my gaze.

Richard stopped fidgeting and placed a hand on Florence's shoulder. "Care to tell us what was going on in that?" Richard demanded.

I flinched at his cold tone.

Colin walked behind the settee and he, Savannah and Jeremy looked at the picture at the same time. Jeremy glared at Richard. "Are you all right, Rissa? I know it couldn't have been easy for you to be near him, and, to have him act like he was, it must have been difficult."

I let out a pent-up breath of air on a gasp. "Thank you, Jeremy." I rubbed at my temples. "It was awful to be so close to him. To be expected to act like I was interested in him."

"He's a fool to ever think you would be," Colin said.

"I think he thought I'd want him now. Now that I was away from Montana and Gabriel," I whispered. "That I'd come to realize all I was missing by living there."

"The only problem with the photo is it doesn't show the newspaper. We can't date him," Sophie said.

Colin cleared his throat and spoke. "Well, I'd heard all the trouble Sav's been having with the newspapermen here, so I thought I'd visit one of the more intrepid ones. He seemed intrigued by the story I spun, and wanted to come and witness what occurred. Didn't seem to believe what I could be saying was true."

"Why would you do such a thing without discussing it with all of us?" Sophie asked, her eyes flashing.

"The idea didn't come to me until early on the morning Rissa was to meet with Cameron. I also knew that a picture of Cameron alive wasn't going to condemn him and exonerate Seb."

"So you took it upon yourself to meddle with our plan?" Sophie asked.

"Yes." Colin matched her steely glare.

"Good. I always knew that boy would be hard to trap. I'm glad you had the initiative to turn our bad plan into a better one." Sophie cackled and the tension in the room dissipated.

"What did he say, Col, afterward?" I asked.

"Did you not see a man sitting near you, writing?" Colin asked.

"I … no," I said. "I was focused on getting through this. On what Cameron would or wouldn't do. I had no ability to be aware of anything else. If I hadn't seen Florence on the way in, I would have thought she'd forgotten about the entire thing."

"Well, as it turns out, he heard everything you spoke of. Thought it fascinating. Plans on writing an exposé in an upcoming article, after he writes the newspaper people in Missoula."

"He only has our word that the man I met was Cameron," I said.

"No, there were others there who recognized him. Cameron's not worried about being seen for who he is here. Thinks Montana is a backwater and that he'll not be brought to justice." Colin smiled triumphantly.

"Thank you, Col," I said. "Thank you, everyone." I took a deep breath. "Now I can return to Montana, knowing that this is as resolved as it can be."

"Rissa!" Savannah cried. "I thought you'd remain here for a longer visit."

"I'd hoped you'd stay until the baby's born," Florence said as she patted her stomach.

I shook my head. "No, I need to return. Although there is always more that I would like to do, such as visit my sister Melinda again, I must travel home. I promised Gabriel we wouldn't spend another Christmas apart after the Christmas when he lived in Butte. I need to return now so we can prepare for our second Christmas together." I blushed at Sophie's satisfied smirk.

CHAPTER 43

Montana, December 1902

I STOOD ON THE PLATFORM at the Northern Pacific train depot, watching as the crowd thinned. Unlike my arrival in June last year, a breathless Gabriel did not appear. I smiled at the porter, handing him the tags to my trunks and explained where they were to be delivered.

As I emerged onto the boardwalk in front of the station, I paused. The hills were covered in a light covering of snow with the wild grass protruding from it a burnished gold, glimmering in the sunlight. I smiled as I realized, with Christmas only five days away, we'd have a white Christmas this year. Puddles and muddy patches marred the dirt streets, and the horses riding by had muddy splotches on their legs and haunches. I shivered as a cold breeze blew from the Hellgate Canyon and began my short walk toward Main Street and home.

I pushed open the workshop door, shivering with appreciation at the blast of warmth that emerged from within. I tiptoed in, glancing toward Ronan's workspace, which was empty. My gaze swept the room and saw Ronan, his back toward me, as he sat near the rear of the workshop, facing a stooped over Gabriel.

"You know there's a good reason for her not writing you," Ronan argued.

"You'd think she'd have the decency to write more frequently. Does she really think a letter a week is enough?"

"I'm sure I saw you receiving more letters than just once a week," Ronan said. I watched him lift himself up with his arms in an attempt to settle himself again in his chair.

"That was until a few weeks ago. Now they've trickled down to nothing." Gabriel leaned forward and pinched the bridge of his nose. "It's like before, when she was so far from me. It's like that Boston society gets ahold of her somehow and changes her. Changes us."

Ronan snorted, hiding my dismayed gasp. "I doubt that, Gabe. I bet there's a good reason she's more silent than you'd wish."

Gabriel sighed. "I just want her home, Ro. Or I need to go there. I can't handle being separated from her. These past six weeks have been hell."

My eyes filled with tears as I watched Gabriel. I took a cautious step into the workshop, and I must have made some noise because his head jerked up. After a moment, where he stared at me as though I were an apparition, he gave a whoop of joy and moved toward me.

"Clarissa!" he said as he pulled me into a tight embrace, pulling me off my feet and twirling me around for a few moments. After setting me down, he held my face between his palms, gently swiping away my tears with his thumbs. "Darling, are you all right?"

"I'm fine," I whispered, leaning into him and breathing in his musky, woodsy scent. "I missed you so much, Gabriel. I'm sorry I didn't write more. I ... I couldn't."

He kissed the side of my head before he pushed me away to study my eyes. "You couldn't?" His puzzled tone matched the confusion on his face.

"Gabriel, I need to talk with you," I whispered.

He paled, and I gripped his arm, afraid for a moment he would faint. "Of course," he said. "Ronan, Clarissa and I will be upstairs." He clasped my hand and pulled me behind him.

I smiled a hello to Ronan as I followed Gabriel upstairs to our living space.

"Rissa, tell me now what happened in Boston. Please." He held me close, and I felt a tremble go through him.

"Oh, darling. Everything is fine in Boston," I whispered. I stood on my tiptoes and kissed him. His arms clasped me tightly to him, and he groaned as he deepened the kiss.

After only a few moments, he pushed away, our foreheads still touching, and he looked into my eyes. "Then why didn't you write more? Why did you write about the weather and all the things you knew I'd never care about?"

"I wrote you about Richard, Florence and Jeremy," I protested.

"Yes, but never about you," he murmured. "I felt like I'd lost you."

I closed my eyes for a moment and stepped away from him. "You didn't lose me, Gabriel. I knew the minute I arrived in Boston, disparaged and frowned upon because I was not in the proper clothes for my father's burial, that I had no desire to live there again. I didn't want to worry you with how poorly things were going for Colin and me."

"There's more you aren't telling me."

"And there is news that needs to be told in person, darling." I reached forward and grasped one of his large hands, kissing his palm. I took a deep breath and then held it to my belly. "We're going to have a baby."

He stared at me blankly for a moment. "What?"

"I realized, not long after I arrived in Boston, that I was with child."

"Why didn't you write me?"

I hated the hurt I heard in his voice. "I didn't want to tell you in a letter. I wanted to see you, be held by you when I did. Thus, every time I wrote you, I felt like I wrote around the most important news."

At his persistent silence, I began to ramble. "Please try to understand, darling." I reached up and pushed a lock of ebony hair off his forehead. "Sophronia advised me to return to you, even though I worried that Savannah needed me."

A brilliant smile bloomed on his face. "A baby?" I nodded as he gave a whoop of joy, picked me up and spun me around again. When I had settled, with my skirts swirling at my ankles, he asked, "You're certain?"

"Yes. I had the best doctors in Boston examine me. On Sophronia's orders. And all three of the experts agreed I'm to expect a child in early summer." I grinned, unable to hide my joy.

Gabriel tugged me with him and sat with me on his lap, and I felt him trembling gently. "Never scare me like that again," he said urgently. "I thought you'd been harmed again. And the thought that I hadn't been there to help you once again was too much to bear."

"I wished for you every day," I whispered into his neck. "I hated not being able to talk with you about what was happening, about why people were being so mean. About Colin losing the forge. I needed you, more than I can ever say."

Gabriel's arms tightened around me. "You're so strong, my darling, that I often fear you don't need me."

"Never doubt that I do. Knowing you are beside me, supporting me, gives me strength." I kissed his neck. "I missed you, Gabriel."

He groaned. "You have no idea how much I missed you."

I peppered him with kisses along his jaw, neck and upper shoulders.

"Rissa—" He pushed me away, and I frowned at the serious expression in his eyes. "I don't want to do anything that could harm the baby."

"As you can imagine, I was mortified to ask about marital relations," I said with a blush. "But one of those experts Sophie had me see said there would be no harm to the baby."

I shrieked as Gabriel stood, carrying me in his arms and strode toward the bed. "Well then, in that case, I'll put my faith in that expert. I've missed you, my Clarissa." He placed me on the bed and leaned forward, kissing me, as his nimble hands worked to free me from my clothes.

As I squirmed out of my dress, he paused, resting his forehead against my belly. He kissed it once, then again, before holding me close for a moment. I threaded my fingers through his hair as he trembled.

"Gabriel?" I whispered.

He raised tear-brightened eyes. "I want this baby. Never doubt that, Rissa." I nodded in understanding. "But I can't lose you."

"Darling." I reached for him, gently tugging at him until he moved up the bed and lay next to me. I kissed him and pulled him into my arms, holding him as he shuddered. I inched backward so I could meet his eyes.

"I can't promise you everything will be all right. I will promise I'll do everything possible to have a healthy birth. To have ten more children if that's our desire," I teased as I kissed away a tear.

I felt as much as heard his laugh, before I was lost to his kisses and being in his arms again.

***

"GABRIEL, THERE'S SOMETHING ELSE I must tell you," I whispered. He lay with his head on my sternum, and I feared I had waited too long to speak as I heard a soft snuffle sound.

"Mmm, give me a moment," he said with a sigh as he rolled to his side and settled my back along his chest. "Why is it you always want to talk afterward?"

I heard the teasing in his voice and smiled. I twisted until I faced him and saw the amusement fade as concern filtered into his eyes.

"I'm fine," I whispered with a tender smile. I leaned in for a quick kiss and had to force myself to back away before I forgot what I needed to tell him. He groaned as I settled again, still facing him, his hand playing in my long hair and tracing it down my arm.

A contented smile played on his lips, and his eyes closed.

"Darling, please," I whispered.

He opened his eyes and nodded. "Whatever it is, Clarissa, it'll be fine."

I shook my head slightly. "Cameron didn't die in that fire."

"What?" Gabriel asked. He half rose, leaning on his elbow as his free hand gripped my shoulder. Fury kindled to life in his eyes.

"I saw him in Boston. He's very much alive."

"There was a body, Rissa. Seb almost died saving him. And now Seb's lost his job because they thought he stole the company money."

I shook my head. "I swear to you, Cameron is alive. As alive as you and me. And he boasted to me about taking the money."

"Although he'd deny it if confronted," Gabriel said. He sighed in disgust when I nodded in agreement to his statement. "Dammit." He closed his eyes on a long sigh. "I should have traveled with you. I should never have let you travel alone, let you face that by yourself."

"How were you to know?" I asked with a tender smile. At his hesitation, my smile faded. "What aren't you telling me?"

He met my gaze. "I've had my suspicions for a while that he didn't die. A man well known on Front Street disappeared at the same time as the fire. A well-liked man. More often than not he was drunk as a skunk, but he was amiable, and folks sought out his company."

"And?"

"And I heard from a porter that a man with a striking resemblance to Cameron had boarded the train east the morning after the fire. No one would have been looking for him, and word wasn't out yet that he'd died. I thought the porter mistaken. But as we learned this other man had disappeared and that all the money from the company safe was stolen during the fire, it made me wonder if he hadn't been correct."

"Why didn't you tell me about your suspicions?"

"What was I to say?" He flushed with chagrin and anger. "You were finally finding peace after his death. You didn't have to worry that, every time you left the house, you'd be tormented by him or by something someone said about him as you were out. You were blossoming, and I couldn't bear to take it away on unfounded suspicions." He stroked my cheek, his earnest gaze entreating me to understand. "And then your da died."

I nodded my agreement, turning my face to kiss his palm. "Why didn't you tell anyone else?"

"Well, Seb, Ronan and I thought about talking to the police, but we knew they'd brand us as a group of fools, trying to pin the allegations against Seb on a dead man."

"But he's not dead, Gabriel."

"We have no proof." He held up his fingers to my lips to still my words. "Even if you were to speak to the police, it wouldn't matter. They wouldn't take you seriously because you're a woman. They'd think you were saying these things because everyone knows you had a falling out, and this would be your way to pay him back."

I glowered at Gabriel. "I hate that you're mostly right."

"Only mostly?" he asked with a small smile.

"We endeavored to have a picture of him taken."

"Anyone could say it was when you were still in Boston before you came west last year."

"Yes, but the first picture on the roll is of a newspaper dated on the day I met him at a tea parlor."

"You met him? Alone?" Gabriel asked, his eyes fiery with concern and anger.

"Yes, it was the only way he'd speak with me. And, unbeknownst to me, Colin had arranged for a newspaperman to be there too. He's now investigating the entire sordid affair."

"Why?"

"Cameron wasn't shy in his boasts to me about what he'd done," I whispered. "Seemed to think anything he had to do to leave Missoula with money was justified."

"You're all brilliant," he said as he swooped down and kissed me quickly on the lips. I nodded my agreement. "I can't wait to tell Seb."

"How has he been?"

"Despondent. He lost almost everything due to Cameron. It's been hard for him to have the townsfolk look at him with suspicion. Even if we exonerate him, I think it'll be some time before he feels welcomed here. Trusted."

"I never thought I could hate a person, but I really think I hate Cameron."

Gabriel's eyes clouded. "What did Cameron do to you?"

I blinked away tears. "Nothing. Just scared me. But I kneed him in his delicate region and left."

"Delicate region?" Gabriel smirked, pride shining from his eyes.

"It's what Jeremy called it." I waved my hand around and blushed as red as a beet. At Gabriel's laugh, I giggled.

He reached forward and traced my eyebrows, my cheek and then my collarbone with reverence. "Did he threaten you, my darling?"

"I'm fine, Gabriel," I whispered.

"Share this memory with me, so that the burden of it will not torment you." He leaned forward and kissed my nose.

"He pushed me against a wall, hid us in a servants' entrance and said it was fortuitous we were together in a city so far from you," I whispered. "I tried to escape him, right away, but he's very strong. Well, at least stronger than I am. And I couldn't break free.

"I was terrified I was going to relive my nightmare from the last time I was with him in Boston." I closed my eyes, unwilling to meet Gabriel's worried gaze. "I wake at night, tormented by dreams where I can't break free of him."

"But you did, darling," Gabriel said as he kissed my forehead. "You didn't need me or Colin. You only needed yourself."

I smiled through my tears at his pride and faith in me. "I remembered this life we are building here. I thought of our baby. Of how hard we have fought for it. And I was filled with a rage that he would ever think he had a right to harm us again."

Gabriel's satisfied smile bloomed. "That's my Clarissa."

"I don't care if Cameron lives. I never wanted him to die," I said.

"Didn't you?" Gabriel asked me with a raised eyebrow. "I wished it every time I saw you flinch. Or watched doubt enter your eyes when you should only have known joy. As you stiffened and pretended indifference as those around us spoke of him."

"Gabriel," I said as I held his knuckles to my heart. "I used to imagine him dead and what a joyful place the world would be without him in it. Instead, everything went wrong. Sebastian lost his job, Amelia the hope for her future, and I had no more peace than when Cameron lived."

I took a deep breath. "He's away from us. He might not be dead, but he's away from us and unlikely to cause us any harm."

"You have more faith in his nature than I do," Gabriel said.

I shook my head with haunted eyes. "No, I have none where it concerns Cameron. But I have faith in us and our life."

CHAPTER 44

"AMELIA, YOU LOOK TERRIBLE," I said as I entered Aidan's kitchen.

"Clarissa!" Amelia said as she rushed toward me. "Oh, it is good to see you. How was your journey? Your father's funeral? I hope you had time to visit everyone." She pushed me toward a chair in the kitchen and moved toward the stove to put on the kettle.

"Amelia, I'm fine. It was lovely to be in Boston, but I'm happy to have returned home."

"Lovely?" Amelia asked with an amused smile. "It seems to me, you always use that word when you aren't really delighted but are trying to act as though you are."

I laughed. "You've seen through me. I liked seeing my family, but I missed Montana. I missed my life here."

"You missed Gabriel."

"Of course." I played with the edge of a fraying napkin. "How are things with Sebastian?"

"You've just returned, Clarissa. There's no need to worry you."

"I think there is. I'm concerned about him. What is he doing now that he's no longer the foreman?"

"He's still recovering from his wounds, although he's about healed. I think he'll soon move away. He'll want to start fresh after what has happened here."

"Oh, Amelia. But what about ..."

"About?"

"About the two of you?" I asked hesitantly.

"There's nothing but friendship between us, Clarissa."

359

I watched her with sorrowful eyes as she moved with agitated movements around the kitchen. "I know that's not true."

"That's all that can be true," she snapped before exhaling a deep breath. "Forgive me. I'm a bit short-tempered just now. He told me that he was to leave here right after New Year's." She sat across from me with stooped shoulders. I'd never seen her with such little spirit. Even when she was battling for baby Anne's life, she had a determination to continue to fight. Now a deep resignation seemed to have settled over her.

"I'm sorry, Amelia," I said, reaching out to grip her hand.

"I told myself not to care for him. Not to become attached. But the heart's not logical." Amelia blinked away tears. "He's wonderful with the children, and I don't know how Nicholas will survive the loss of another ..."

"Man who's like a father?" I whispered.

"I tried to keep them separated, but it was impossible. Nicholas was constantly in Mr. Carlin's room, and I didn't have the heart to separate them when Nicholas sounded delighted and happy. And Mr. Carlin always showed such interest in him, even when Nicholas's great accomplishment was finding a colorful leaf."

"I know this is more than just your concern about your children." I gripped her hand.

"I'd begun to hope for a future too," Amelia admitted. "I'd already lost one with Liam, and, to lose the hope of another, it's almost too much to bear." She let out a stuttering breath as though she were stifling a sob.

"But you don't have to lose anything. You could go with him."

"And live on what? He has no job, no income. I survive solely due to the charity of Mr. McLeod. I have to think about my children, more than myself. For I'd never forgive myself if they were to know hunger or suffer due to my selfishness."

"But you love each other," I whispered.

Her eyes glowed a brilliant blue. "Yes, Rissa. And he and I know it's not enough."

"You believe he's innocent?" I bit my lip as I watched her flush with anger.

"I've always known him to be wrongly accused. Although I've learned that means little when those who are vindictive are set on obtaining their version of justice."

I smiled. "I have news that might help, although I don't know how much it will change things. I had hoped Mr. Bouchard had yet to find a new foreman."

"I've never seen a more vengeful pair, Clarissa. Mr. Bouchard—rigid in his righteousness in hiring a new foreman. And Mrs. Bouchard—marching around town in her outlandish clothes, proclaiming how her family has suffered at the hands of the unrighteous. It's enough to make me want to slap her."

"What do the townsfolk say?" I asked.

"In the beginning, they were sympathetic. Now many hide when they see or hear her coming."

I giggled. "Which wouldn't be hard."

"I know. What's the most difficult is her inability to admit that she has any part to play in any of this," Amelia said. "She's the one who wanted Mr. Wright to work there."

"I imagine she's also the one who convinced Mr. Bouchard to give Cameron the combination to the safe," I said.

"What?" Amelia gasped.

"Cameron didn't die, Amelia. He's alive and well in Boston. I saw him and spoke with him while I was there. He even boasted about leaving Missoula with money. I know it's the money from the mill. He even mentioned receiving the safe's combination that very week, although he never plainly said he took its contents."

"Although he intimated it?" a deep voice growled behind me.

"Sebastian!" I exclaimed. "It's wonderful to see you up and about again."

"Tell me all, Clarissa. I'll board the next train and …"

"There's no need," I said as I patted his hand once as he sat between Amelia and me. I began, telling them an abbreviated version of my interaction with Cameron while in Boston, finishing with "A newspaperman is looking into Cameron's story. He's contacting reporters from *The Daily Missoulian*. I hope there's an article soon to vindicate you."

I studied Sebastian, his lanky frame filled out and looking healthier than when he'd been working. "I'd hoped to see you looking the picture of health after weeks of Amelia's care, and I'm glad to see I'm not disappointed."

He scrubbed his cheek and a fine layer of red stubble. "It's hard not to eat such delicious food when surrounded by it."

He half smiled and rose, limping as he moved to leave. "It's not just good cooking that I need but exercise." He paused in the kitchen doorway. "I'm going to take the doctor's advice and go out for a bit."

"Don't overexert yourself," Amelia admonished. Sebastian and Amelia shared a heated, intense look filled with longing before he nodded toward her, and I heard the front door click shut.

"Did Colin come home with you?" Amelia asked.

"No, he didn't. He decided to stay and work at the forge with Richard. I don't know when, or if, he'll return."

"Oh, Rissa," Amelia murmured. "I can only imagine how hard that will be for you."

"I just want him to be happy. Although it didn't seem like he wanted to remain in Boston. In fact he said he couldn't wait to leave soon after we arrived. Later he changed his mind about staying. He feels tremendous guilt he wasn't with Da."

"Did your horrid stepmother have anything to say to influence him?" Amelia asked as she filled my mug.

"Of course. She said we were ungrateful, and my da wouldn't have died had Colin been there to help him work at the smithy."

"What a bunch of mean-spirited rubbish."

I smiled bitterly in agreement. "She didn't even want me to see my sister, although Colin and I managed to visit her once. Mrs. Smythe feared I'd influence her, if I spent any time with her."

"Horrid woman. We heard about Aidan buying the smithy for Richard."

I let out a long sigh. "Yes, it was the best solution and allowed the forge to stay in the family. Colin decided to remain in Boston for a while to help Richard with the transition and to run the smithy when Richard and Florence have their baby. It will allow Richard to have a few days at home with Flo."

"That's very thoughtful of him. It's such a comfort to have your husband with you after a baby is born."

"I agree, although I'll continue to hope he returns to Montana," I said.

***

"GABE, RONAN," SEBASTIAN SAID as he entered the workshop. He nodded to a man speaking with Ronan and wandered over to Gabriel on the far side of the workshop.

"Seb," Gabriel said, "I imagine you saw Clarissa and are curious." He flicked a glance to the man next to Ronan, indicating their need to speak of other matters for a few minutes.

"She looked well. I know you'd hoped she'd return for Christmas. I'm glad she did." Sebastian moved around the back area, with only a slight limp to hint at the accident.

"How's your leg?"

Sebastian stomped his foot, nodding to indicate all was fine. "Better, although it'll never be as strong as it was."

"Give it time, Seb. It's only been a few months, and you haven't challenged yourself at all."

Sebastian gave a chagrined smile. "I've grown lazy, eating Amelia's delicious food, having her fuss over me."

Gabriel glanced toward the front of the shop, seeing the other man leaving, but stopping from saying any more until Ronan rolled to the door and latched it shut. He then rolled toward them and settled his chair. "What brings you by, Seb?" His alert gaze looked Sebastian up and down, taking in his freshly laundered brown pants, cream-colored flannel shirt and tan jacket. "You seem more at ease today."

"I imagine it's because of something Clarissa said. I haven't been able to speak with you yet today, Ro, as the shop's been busy with customers," Gabriel said. "She told me late last night that Cameron didn't die."

Ronan stilled his movements in his chair, and Sebastian watched him with a fierce frown. "I just spoke with her, but it seems too fantastical to be true. She's certain?" Sebastian asked.

"As she told you, she had tea with the man," Gabriel said. "Bold as could be, he sat next to her and conversed with her in a tea shop in Boston. Wasn't even trying to hide. Thought he'd outwitted all of us out here."

Sebastian slammed down his hand on a piece of raw wood as he paced, his limp making it more of a lumbering, stuttering movement due to his agitation. "That son of a—" He broke off, closing his eyes and taking a deep breath. "Why did he kill a decent man like Tommy?"

"He saw a way out, a way to make money, and took it. He wouldn't concern himself with the fact he had to commit murder in order to obtain his goal."

Ronan scowled. "We know the kind of man he is, chasing after a woman who doesn't want him." He met Gabriel's gaze. "Did he harm Clarissa?"

Gabriel's face lightened, the frown replaced with a hint of a smile as pride shone from his eyes. "No, she freed herself from him when he surprised her, hitting him where it counts."

"Good," Ronan and Sebastian said at the same time.

"What does this mean for Seb?" Ronan asked. He traced his mustache and then scratched his beard.

"Colin arranged for a reporter to listen in, and he's going to contact people here in Missoula. I'd imagine he's already done that, as Clarissa met with Cameron over a week ago. Soon the townspeople will know what a charlatan Cameron was."

"It won't get me back my job," Sebastian said.

"I'd think Mr. Bouchard would be honor bound to restore you to your previous position," Gabriel argued.

"And if I were to take it, I'd rob the post from a man who moved here specifically for it and turn him out of a job. He's a wife and children to care for." He vibrated with anger and frustration.

"One could say you do too," Ronan murmured.

"Don't start, Ro," Sebastian hissed.

"It's about time someone did. Are you planning on playing with Amelia's feelings, having her children become attached to you and then simply leaving?" Gabriel demanded. "She deserves better than that. Hell, you do too. Look at you." Gabriel waved a hand, going from Sebastian's feet to his head. "You've never looked better. You've finally lost that scrawny, in-need-of-food look. Amelia's good for you."

"No one has to convince me of that. Hell, I've known that for months. I've known she'd be good for me since the moment I met her. I have no job to offer her. When I was foreman at the mill, I had a proper income. I had a home I could offer her. I've nothing now, Gabe." He sighed, the frustration and fight leaving him, as his shoulders stooped, and he became more dejected. "I'm living off your uncle's charity and her good graces."

"You'll find something again," Ronan argued. "You're a good foreman. They'll want you back."

"I'm a half-crippled ex-foreman," Sebastian said. "Anyone'd be a fool to hire me."

A loud knocking on the door caused Gabriel to start and turn toward it, opening it. "Yes?" He frowned quizzically at the paperboy standing in front of him, holding out a paper. "How can I help you?"

"I wasn't sure if you'd read the paper, sir, and I know you were connected with the man." He held out a copy of *The Daily Missoulian.*

Gabriel scanned the headlines, reaching into his pocket to extract a coin. "Thank you. Much obliged." He nodded halfheartedly to the boy before closing the door in his face and latching it again.

"Gabe?" Sebastian asked.

"Look what we have here. Redemption!" Gabriel held the paper high, moving toward his friends so they could huddle around the paper and read it together.

***

"MR. PICKENS, I'M BACK," I said as I climbed the stairs. I paused as I noted the books out of order and not in their rightful place in Gabriel's bookshelves.

"Everythin' all right out there in that big city, Missy?" he asked as he thumped out of the back room before collapsing into his chair.

"As settled as it's going to become," I said. "What's going on here?"

"Oh, they've been spendin' all their time arguin' over the wordin' for an application"—his eyes twinkled at the big word—"for a library from Carnegie himself."

"Do you think he'll grant us the money?" I gasped, holding my breath.

"Seein' as this is a too-small space for the likes of the townsfolk, I think we'll have a chance. The Prattlin' Prisses haven't had as much time to spend here keeping things orderly."

"We need a full-time librarian," I said as I set down my purse, took off my hat and gloves, and moved to the books that were out of place. "These are in the correct section, just need to be placed in order. At least it's not as bad as when I started here," I grumbled.

"Now, who'd be needin' a book when all they need to do is read the newspaper or listen to one of the sisters for anything more interestin' than you could find elsewhere?"

"Don't you start, Mr. A.J.," I said with an inelegant snort.

"I'd thought by now that man you'd married would've seen a way to help his friend."

"He's doing what he can," I said. I grimaced as I heard the raised voices of the sisters as they climbed the stairs to the depository. I moved toward Mr. Pickens and faced the doorway.

"Ah, so you've returned. To gloat after your trip to the East," Mrs. Vaughan said.

"Although you are as shabbily dressed as when you left," Mrs. Bouchard sniped.

"I'd thought you'd be able to visit a decent modiste while you were in that big city," Mrs. Vaughan said, holding her palms out at her sides as though to exemplify such in her shimmering satin dress with pearl buttons in a rich pumpkin color.

"I traveled to Boston for my father's funeral. I had little time to worry about the latest fashion." I clenched my hands at my side and attempted to speak in a calm tone.

"Your shame knows no bounds," Mrs. Bouchard said. "Returning here, continuing to perpetuate the falsehood that you have a happy marriage when anyone can see it is a lie. You ruined my daughter's chances to have a successful future because you couldn't bear to see anyone else happy."

"If you truly believe that, you are devoid of any compassion or goodness," I rasped.

Mr. Pickens thumped on his cane and leaned forward as though he were going to speak. However, he was forestalled at the sound of boots running up the stairs.

I looked toward the door as Gabriel entered. He paused as he noted the sisters. "Rissa, I had to show you this." He thrust the newspaper at me, and I gasped as I read. I held it so Mr. Pickens could read it with me. "*Dead Man Rises from the Ashes to Reunite with Family in Boston.*"

Mr. Pickens hooted with glee and thunked his cane down a few times with his pleasure. "Seems you were too busy for fashion all right, Missy!" he chortled as he looked at the picture Florence took of Cameron leaning in toward me. "What do you have to say about this, mouthy?" Mr. Pickens said, grabbing the paper from my hands and waving it toward the sisters.

I took it from him and walked toward the sisters, holding it so they could read it. Mrs. Bouchard gasped and became so pale I worried she would faint.

I looked around for a chair for her to sit on, but Mr. Pickens sat in the only available chair. "Lies, all lies," she rasped, although her voice lacked conviction.

"I saw him when I was in Boston. He relished speaking of his escape from the meddling mothers of Missoula," I said.

"Rissa," Gabriel said in a soft warning tone as he placed a gentle hand on my arm.

I took a deep breath, biting back further bitter words as I saw hurt and bewilderment flash across Mrs. Bouchard's face. I reached for Gabriel's hand, refusing to unleash the pent-up words stored within—to become like the women who had tormented me.

"You can make this right, Mrs. Bouchard," Gabriel said. "You can speak with your husband and insist that Mr. Carlin be given his job back."

"It's not that simple," she rasped. "But I'll discuss this … turn of events with him."

"And then you can inform the townspeople that you were misled by Cameron," I said. "And stop blaming Amelia, Sebastian and me for all your misfortunes."

"Come, sister," Mrs. Vaughan said, grasping Mrs. Bouchard's elbow. They turned and descended the stairs.

I moved over to a stack of books and lifted them aside to clear my stool. I collapsed onto it and gripped Gabriel's hand. "I can't believe it will now turn out well for Sebastian."

"There's no guarantee, Rissa," Gabriel said.

"If they don't give that man, who was injured tryin' to save another man's life, his rightful job back, the townsfolk'll have plenty to say. We've spent enough time listenin' to the wrong done to ol' mouthy. Now she can eat a little crumble pie."

"I think you mean *humble* pie," Gabriel murmured as he fought a chuckle.

"Darn straight," he said as he thunked his cane. "Well done, Missy. Although you looked a bit friendly with that rascal." He raised his eyebrows at me as he stared at the photo of Cameron leaning in toward me.

"How'd you know it was me?" I asked.

"'Cause you were the only one able to get that man to admit to what he did. Always seemed to puff up like a rooster 'round you." He sighed. "Good riddance."

"I agree, old man," Gabriel said. "Although I wouldn't be too quick to believe he'll never return. If they find reason to suspect he harmed that man from Front Street, they might put a warrant out for his arrest."

I groaned. "I just want him out of our lives."

"If he's convicted of murder, he will be," Mr. A.J. said with an ominous stomp of his boot.

***

"AMELIA," SEBASTIAN WHISPERED as he entered the living area. The lights were turned down, and a soft glow lit the room. She sat on the settee, her feet curled underneath her, darning on her lap, her head to one side as she slept.

He knelt beside the settee, reached forward and caressed her hand, his hand lingering over hers. His thumb traced a pattern over knuckles as he watched her sleep.

"Liam," Amelia murmured, her eyes flickering open with a warm, expectant glow.

"No, not Liam," Sebastian whispered, releasing her hand. He moved to rise but stilled when she traced his jaw with her fingers.

"Sebastian," she breathed. "I've been so worried about you."

"I'm fine, ma'am. No need to concern yourself for me."

She sat forward on one elbow, her darning falling to the floor as she came fully awake. She gripped his shoulder for a moment, noting the tension within. "Talk to me," she urged.

"Forgive me, Amelia. I came in and saw you asleep. I meant no disrespect when I touched your hand."

"Why are you upset with me?" Her brow furrowed as she tried to recall what had happened in her half-awake state. "Did I call you Liam?" At his terse nod, she sighed and stroked Sebastian's long hair. "Forgive me. Liam used to wake me by stroking my hand. No one's done that since … since he died."

"There's nothing to forgive. I'm a fool for being jealous of a dead man," Sebastian said with barely veiled rancor.

"You've no need to be jealous of him, Sebastian. He's dead. He's never coming back. I've begun to learn the importance of living in the here and now." She stroked his cheek and studied him. "What is it? What news do you have?"

"They have Cameron in custody. They've charged him with the murder of Tommy and with stealing the money." His eyes flashed with triumph.

"Oh, thank heavens!" Amelia sat up and threw herself in his arms. He clasped her tightly to him, cradling her head with one of his big hands. She leaned away after a moment and sat on the edge of the settee. "This means you'll get your job back."

"As you can imagine, the Bouchards are embarrassed and want to make amends for their accusations against me. However, they've already hired another man, a capable man. I don't feel right taking his job away from him."

"That's not right either, Sebastian. They fired you under false pretenses, accusing you of theft and destroying your reputation, when you acted honorably. With more bravery than most in such a situation. How dare they not insist you have your job returned to you?" An irate flush highlighted her cheeks.

"Amelia, what would you have me do? Turn out a man, who did nothing wrong except accept a job from Mr. Bouchard? That doesn't seem fair to me."

"What does that mean? What will you do?" Amelia paled, balling her hands in her lap.

"I'm taking a post at one of his sawmills outside of Missoula."

"You're leaving Missoula?" Amelia whispered. "Leaving …"

"Yes," Sebastian rasped. "It's the only way, Amelia. I'll have a good position. Build this new sawmill up almost from the very beginning."

"I see. We'll be sorry to see you go. But I understand a man's ambition," Amelia said as she rose. "Now, if you'll excuse me, I should check on the children and go to bed." She'd lowered her head, preventing Sebastian from seeing her eyes.

"Amelia." Sebastian gripped her arm, preventing her from sliding past him. "Look at me. Please."

"If you please, sir, there are things I must still do this evening." Her voice shook as she stared resolutely at the floor.

Sebastian held one of her arms but used his other hand to tilt up her chin. Her shattered gaze met his. "Amelia, love, I'm going away—"

"And you'll never return to me. Yes, I understand. Please let me go. I thank you for your kind friendship to my children. They will miss you."

"Will you miss me?" Sebastian asked, his brow furrowed with confusion as he studied her shaking form.

"As I would any friend." Her defiant tone sparked his temper.

"Oh, really? As you would any friend?" His irate gaze clashed with her resolute one. He swooped forward, his lips claiming hers in a passionate kiss. His hand traced along her cheek, then into her pinned hair, scattering pins as he kneaded her scalp. Her long hair began to tumble free, and he clasped her head in a gentle, yet unyielding hold, kissing her with months of pent-up longing. She raised her hands, gripping his shoulders, tugging him toward her, wanting him as close to her as possible.

After many minutes Sebastian broke the kiss and backed up a step. She instinctively followed him, not wanting to break her contact with him. "That is what I think of being just any friend to you, Amelia."

Tears trickled from her eyes, and soon a silent stream coursed down her cheeks. He caressed her cheeks, scrubbing the tears aside, but was unable to forestall more from falling.

"Sweetheart, don't cry. I'm leaving, but I'll come back for you. I need time to become established in Darby, and then I'll return for you and the children." He kissed each cheek as he made his vow.

"I can't bear for you to leave," Amelia rasped. "I can't handle losing another man I …" she choked on the word.

"I can barely manage to go," he whispered. "And I have no desire to become another man you've loved and lost." His teasing failed to ease her torment. "Hush, love," he crooned as he pulled her into his arms.

"Darby?" she asked. "Where is that?"

"It's down the Bitter Root Valley. There's a lot of timber in those mountains, and Mr. Bouchard wants to have a sawmill there." He kissed her head. "He's got the bare bones of one now, but, come spring, he wants a proper one built."

"When do you have to leave?" Amelia wrapped her arms securely around him, holding him tightly to her.

"I've told Mr. Bouchard I won't leave until after Christmas and until after the trial."

"I have you for a little while yet," Amelia said, kissing the pulse at the base of his neck.

He leaned away, framing her face with his large hands, his thumbs tracing over her cheeks in a soothing caress. "You'll always have me, Amelia. I might be down the valley in Darby, but I'm yours. I have been since I met you." He leaned forward and kissed her softly on her lips. "The passenger train goes all the way to Grantsdale. However, I won't be able to visit you on my day off because it would be too long a trip. You and the children could come to Hamilton for the day on the train, and I'd meet you there. We won't have to wait until I've established a home to see each other."

He bent forward and kissed her forehead and then her cheeks. "I know I have nothing to offer you right now. But I want you as my wife. As the mother of my children. I love you."

"Sebastian," Amelia rasped. "I love you too. So much."

"I know you'll always love your first husband. That's right and proper. From all accounts, he was a good man and a good father. I hope I can be the same to you."

"As I hope I will be the woman you want to come home to each night."

"Never doubt how much I want that, Amelia," he whispered, leaning forward to kiss her again before he pulled her close, a deep sigh of contentment escaping him as he held her.

***

I LAY IN BED, curled up against Gabriel, in that state between wakefulness and sleep, content to the tips of my chilled toes. Gabriel nuzzled my head and breathed deeply as though echoing my sense of well-being. "I hope Seb'll be able to recover his job," he murmured.

"Although it seems the man who's working there now is competent."

"And has a family to support," Gabriel said.

"But, if they no longer suspect Sebastian of theft, he could work someplace else," I argued.

"Yeah, although he was partially maimed. He'll never be as strong as he was with that lame leg."

"He's not lame, Gabriel. He just walks with a limp. I bet you that he's as strong as before."

"Well, let's hope the mill owners are as understanding as you."

"I wonder why they no longer wanted us there to act as chaperones?" I asked on a yawn. Gabriel settled his arm around the upper part of my waist under my breasts.

"Amelia gave up trying to please the likes of Mrs. Bouchard and Mrs. Vaughan. She realized that those who knew her understood she was caring for an injured man who was a good friend." I heard his voice begin to even out and knew he was on the verge of falling asleep.

"Gabriel?" I said as I picked up his hand and pulled it toward my mouth. I kissed his palm.

"Yes, my darling?"

"I felt the baby move today," I whispered as I placed his palm on my belly.

His grip on me tightened, and I heard him stutter out a breath. I rolled so that I faced him and hugged him.

"Thank you, Rissa," Gabriel whispered as he shuddered. "Thank you for your bravery. For daring to have our child.

"Shh … Gabriel," I murmured as I put two fingers over his lips. "I'm doing nothing different than any other married woman desirous of a family."

"But you're not any woman. You're my Rissa, and I'd be lost without you," Gabriel said as he pulled me closer. This time, it was as though he were trying to burrow into me.

"And I you," I said as I leaned away and caressed his face. "Have faith, darling. Life won't be cruel again."

Gabriel sighed again, tucking me against him. "I'll borrow some of your faith, my darling," he whispered as he fell again into sleep.

I laid awake, rubbing my hands through his hair and over his shoulders in an attempt to alleviate his fears and thus my own. After a while, when his breathing had deepened, I sighed, settling into him and sleep.

CHAPTER 45

I WALKED DOWN THE STREET holding onto Gabriel's arm, careful to watch each step. A cold snap had arrived the previous day, bringing with it a biting wind that howled out of Hellgate Canyon, turning the muddy roads into a large icy crevice-filled challenge. I gave a startled, delighted yelp as I dodged snow falling off otherwise naked tree branches. Gabriel kept a firm grip and prevented me from falling.

I shivered appreciatively, and Gabriel muttered, "Finally," as we turned up the short walk to his uncle's home. A small pine wreath hung from the front door. Gabriel gave a perfunctory knock and entered, ushering me into the welcoming warmth. I shed my coat, hanging it on a coat stand in the hallway before moving to the living room.

"Mr. Pickens!" I rushed toward him, sitting on a comfortable, overstuffed leather chair dragged out of the office and set by the fire. "How did you get here?"

"The missus's fine lad, Sebastian, picked me up," Mr. Pickens said. "Came 'round in a carriage an' delivered me here."

"How did you travel from the carriage to the house?" I shared a worried glance with Gabriel.

"He carried me like a sack of potatoes!" Mr. Pickens chortled with glee. "Said I didn't weigh more 'n' the little tyke." He patted the arm of the black leather chair. "Don't know as I've ever sat in as comfortable a chair."

"We should see if we could obtain one for the depository," I said as I looked around for a lap blanket.

"Or I'll build you one," Gabriel murmured, smiling at my nod of agreement as I tucked the blanket around his spindly legs.

"Stop your fussin' an' warm yourself by the fire. You look about chilled through." He slapped his hand against his thigh in glee. "Woowee! It's been some time since I heard that canyon roar like it is tonight."

"Mr. Pickens, here is the mulled cider I promised you," Amelia said as she entered with a tray of steaming mugs. "I thought you'd all like some after the cold walk here."

I mumbled my thanks a moment before taking a sip of the warm liquid. Heat began to pervade me again, banishing the chill. I moved toward the fire in an attempt to warm my feet, smiling at Gabriel's amused grin.

"Thank you for inviting us tonight, Amelia," I said. "It's been some time since I celebrated Twelfth Night."

"For me too and I thought it a good excuse for us all to venture out on a cold evening."

As the back door was thrust open, we heard a grunt from the kitchen area and then a crash. I heard a muttered, "Dammit," and then the slamming of a door. Gabriel and I rushed to the kitchen to find Ronan sprawled on the floor with Sebastian standing over him, hands on his knees, his breath sawing in and out.

"Ro, you all right?" Gabriel asked as he reached down and picked him up.

I pulled out a chair, and Gabriel sat Ronan there at the kitchen table. "Where's his wheelchair?"

"Strapped to Mr. Aidan's carriage," Sebastian said.

"You shouldn't have attempted so much," I scolded, earning a fierce glower from Sebastian. Gabriel rolled his eyes and slapped Sebastian on the back as the two men headed outside to collect the wheelchair and stable the horse. They detoured via the front door so Gabriel could don his coat and hat.

"Ronan, can I get you anything?" I asked.

"My pride?" he asked with a wry grin.

I squeezed his arm in reassurance and then moved toward the large pot on the stove filled with cider. I ladled out a mug for him and handed it to him. "I don't have a tonic for pride, but I found this warmed me up."

"Thanks, Rissa," Ronan said. "Seems odd not having Colin around."

"I hate that he's so far away, but I know he's where he wants to be. That brings some comfort." I gripped Ronan's arm again and rose to clear a space for the wheelchair. Gabriel and Sebastian returned, placed it next to Ronan, and he maneuvered himself from chair to wheelchair with no help.

I bit back my praise, knowing it was unwanted, but marveled silently at his ability to function as well as he did. He put the wheels in motion and maneuvered to the living room to greet Mr. Pickens.

"Hello, old man," Ronan called as he entered the room. "Glad you could join us."

"My Missy didn't like hearin' I'd spent Christmas and New Year's alone. When this celebration was planned, she insisted I come, although I think she was surprised I managed to travel on such a night."

"I'm glad you did. What stories do you have for us tonight?" Ronan asked, leaning forward with keen intent. "I've missed you since you left the workshop."

"Well, I like to work with my Missy, and she'd have a difficult time sortin' the books without my aid." He glared at me as I coughed to cover my laugh.

"I don't have a story for tonight, son. Least, not right now. Let me see how I feel after supper," Mr. Pickens said. Ronan smiled, patting him on the shoulder, and they began to chat about mutual acquaintances.

I sat on the settee while Amelia continued to work in the kitchen. Gabriel and Sebastian had a quiet conversation in the dining room. Nicholas was relegated to the back room until supper, due to misbehaving during the day.

After a delicious meal of roasted ham, pickled beets, boiled onions and mashed potatoes we returned to the living room. Sebastian pulled out his fiddle, plucking at strings as he warmed up. I sighed, leaning into Gabriel with contentment.

"Missy, any word on that worthless scallion?"

I looked at Mr. Pickens for a moment before Gabriel laughed.

"I think you mean *rapscallion*, old man," Gabriel said.

"Exactly. Any word?" He leaned forward, and I knew, if his cane were nearer, he'd thunk it on the ground for good measure.

"I've learned little more than what's been in the papers. I can't imagine they'd talk with me."

"I'd think the lawyer and those making the case would seek you out," Amelia said. "You saw him. You're the only one here who can verify he was in Boston."

"Yes, but now that he's been returned here, and all can see he's alive, my word isn't needed. Everyone can see for themselves and come to their own conclusion that they were misled." I hid my shaking hands in my skirt.

"I've heard they're pressuring him to plead guilty and spend his life in prison rather than risk being hanged for murder," Sebastian said as he paused in his soft playing.

"Why would one preclude the other?" I asked perplexed. "He killed the man. Why should pleading guilty prevent him from ..." I blushed and couldn't continue.

"Swingin' from a rope?" Mr. A.J. asked with a touch of glee.

"Mr. A.J." I shook my head in exasperation.

"Justice would be served. That man seems to elude it with too much ease," Ronan said.

"Well, he's in a cell here in Missoula, and, if he pleads guilty, he'll be moved without much fuss to the state pen. Seems there are a few who'd relish doing him harm, and the authorities want little fanfare surrounding him," Sebastian said.

"Appears they're not succeeding with the newspapers," Ronan said. "Headlines like 'East Coast Arsonist Returns for Reckoning' keeps the story in people's minds."

"It's the best story they've had in years!" Mr. A.J. proclaimed. "For once it's nothin' to do with the goin's-on with one of the Copper Kings or Butte. It's a home-grown scoundrel."

I corrected him. "*Scandal.*" Mr. Pickens didn't even acknowledge I had spoken, he was so enthralled by the topic.

He stomped his foot due to the absence of his cane. "Don't seem right to me an upstandin' man such as Mr. Carpin has to be forced away, due to those sisters."

I choked back a laugh. "Mr. *Carlin*, Mr. A.J."

He waved his hand at me. "However, maybe now you'll get my Missy down to see the Bitter Roots. Have her in those mountains."

"Mr. A.J., areas where they're clearing forest is no place for nontimber people," Sebastian said.

"The whole forest can't be under a saw," Mr. Pickens argued. "You'll see, Missy. You'll see."

"Once our child is born, I think we'll be close to Missoula for a while," Gabriel said with a frown.

"Ain't no easier time to travel than when the young'un is too little to walk. When they start walkin' is when they start havin' a mind of their own, and all peace is at an end. No, go early, when the baby's swaddled tight."

"We'll consider it, Mr. A.J.," I murmured, gripping Gabriel's hand to forestall any further argument.

"When will you leave, Sebastian?" I asked.

"I'm not certain," Sebastian said. "I think it may be a few months, in April or so."

"Good," I said as I watched Amelia relax imperceptibly.

***

SCANT LIGHT ENTERED the windows by the desk even though the curtains were tied back. I peered out the window at the unrelenting gray clouds, with little hope for the sun to break through on this dreary late-January day. Picking up my sheet of paper, I blew on it in an attempt to dry a letter I'd just completed to Colin.

"Rissa!" I heard Gabriel bellow from the workshop below. I rose, thankful for the reprieve, as I still had many other letters to write.

I descended the stairs but came to a full stop at the base of them. "What is that?" I pointed to a large crate filling the previously empty space near the doorway. Ronan's workspace was quiet today as he was at his apartment awaiting a home visit from the doctor.

"I have no idea, but it was just delivered, and it comes from Colin." Gabriel handed me a letter which came with the crate. He held up a crowbar with one hand and raised an eyebrow. I nodded absentmindedly as I ripped open the letter.

I read aloud. "*I found this at a shop selling secondhand furniture and thought you'd want it. I hope it arrives in one piece. The man in charge of packing it assured me that he would deliver it to you in as fine a condition as I purchased it. I'll visit Sophie soon to see if she can provide any further insight. More to come. Colin.*"

I raised my gaze, perplexed, watching as Gabriel used his crowbar on the crate. I winced at the squeaking noise made as the nails fought being separated from the wood, until finally the wood lay scattered on the floor.

I gasped, walking as though mesmerized toward the piece of furniture. I brushed away packing dust, scattering a fine sheen on the floor. "How can this be? This sat in my room." I raised my confused gaze to Gabriel. "This was my mother's. It was her vanity."

"It's very fine," Gabriel said, tracing his hand over the wood, helping to rub away the packing dust. He moved to a rear part of the shop and picked up a clean cloth, returning to swipe gently at the vanity. The wood shone after his gentle ministrations. His worried expression reflected mine. "Seems as though your stepmother hasn't completed her fund-raising efforts."

"She's already sold Colin's birthright. Now she's selling the fine furniture from our house. What more could she do?" My breath caught at the thought of all my parents' beautiful furniture lost to me. "I knew something was wrong when we visited, and already pieces were missing."

"It's only furniture, love," Gabriel said, gripping my fingers. "I'll make you whatever you want."

"I know. It's just that I've lost my parents. And now I'm losing everything that was theirs. I'll have nothing."

"You have your mother's vanity." He rubbed a thumb over my cheeks. "And they can never take away your memories of them, darling. No matter how hard they try, they can never do that."

I met his gaze, seeing understanding and concern. "I know," I whispered. "It's so hard to realize they'll never see our home. Never meet …" I broke down on a sob, and Gabriel pulled me to him for a tight embrace.

"Hush, my love," he whispered in my ear.

"I'm sorry, Gabriel," I stammered. "Forgive me."

"There's nothing to forgive. I want all there is of you, the happy and the sad." He smiled with unspoken tenderness. "Come. Let me make you a cup of tea."

I smiled as I remembered him telling me how his mother believed most things could be made better with a cup of strong tea. He led me up the stairs and to my rocking chair. I sat, still shuddering out a few errant sobs. He knelt by my side, holding my hands. When the tears continued to fall, he leaned over me, laying his head on my lap. I ran my fingers through his hair, finding my distress eased while I comforted him.

His deep sigh of contentment filled me with a tremendous sense of peace. "I'm better now, darling," I whispered.

"I'm glad," he said. "I was just having a conversation with our little one. Asking her to be gentle with you. To let you sleep at night and not give you indigestion."

I smiled. "And what did she respond?"

"That she'd enjoy her time as she saw fit but hopefully not give you too rough a go," Gabriel raised his head and winked at me. "I love you, my darling."

"Gabe," I whispered as another tear leaked out.

"Thank you, Rissa, for sharing all of yourself with me, including the sadness. This is what I always dreamed of. A full life, shared with you."

"I'd think you'd be tired of the trials I've brought to it." I continued to thread my fingers through his silky black hair.

"Never." He smiled as he leaned up for a kiss. "Whatever we share together is my greatest dream."

I sighed with contentment before my eyes clouded again. "What is occurring in Boston, Gabe?"

CHAPTER 46

SAVANNAH STOOD AT THE STOVE in the McLeods' home in the North End, stirring a fragrant pot of mulled cider. She glanced at her watch and opened the oven, covering her hand with a cloth. She shook the cake, and it didn't wiggle. The top was a light bronze color, and she knew it was time to remove it from the oven. After lifting it carefully out, she placed it on a rack by the side of the stove.

"Mmm, that smells delicious," Jeremy said as he entered the kitchen.

"I hope you enjoy it," Savannah said. "It needs to cool for a bit, and then it will be ready to be iced and eaten."

Florence sat at the table, setting plates and silverware around while she remained seated. "I wish I could help more."

"You're helping plenty," Savannah said. "And this is good practice for me to see that I've learned all I can from Sophronia's cook."

"What are we eating for dinner?" Richard asked. His hair was damp, and he'd donned clean clothes after returning from the forge.

"I thought we'd try something simple for tonight. A roast with vegetables and potatoes. Bread. And, for dessert, a spice cake with frosting." Savannah turned toward the stove, stirring the pot of mulled cider.

"I wanted to make dinner for tomorrow, but Sophie forbade it. She wants us all to eat at her place," Savannah said.

"I'd think she'd be with her family," Florence said.

"She'll be with them tonight. She says she often spends Christmas Day alone, so this will be a nice change for her."

Jeremy sat at the end of the table so he could watch Savannah as she worked. "I'm thankful she is considerate enough to not want you to cook on Christmas. Or you, Flo."

"Any word from Clarissa and Gabriel?" Savannah asked. "I know Rissa was eager to return home and be with Gabriel for the holiday."

"We just received a letter yesterday, and we decided to wait to read it until we were all together," Richard said as he sat next to Florence. He pulled it out of his pocket and began to read.

Dear Richard, Florence, Jeremy and Savannah,

I know by now you are preparing for Christmas, and I wish you a very happy holiday. I'm sorry I won't be with you, but it's wonderful to be home with Gabriel and preparing for another Christmas together.

I arrived home before the winter storms struck, although the journey seemed endless at times. Even though this was my third journey, I still marveled at the miles and miles of prairie. Just as I felt as though I would forever be in a flat land with golden stalks shooting through the snow, I saw mountains in the distance, and I breathed a sigh of relief. As you can imagine, I was never so happy as to see Gabriel when I walked into the workshop. I surprised him with my arrival, and the homecoming was all I could hope for.

Our exciting news is that you will be aunts and uncles by early summer. I feel well, although I battle a daily bout of nausea each morning. Gabriel is thrilled, although he reminds me of you, Richard. Excited and nervous at the same time.

There are no holly trees here in Montana, so I will string up a piece of pine along our makeshift mantel and remember fondly all the Boston Christmas traditions. The stockings are strung, one on either side of the stove, and I'm trying to knit one for the baby for next year.

I miss you all and wish you a very happy Christmas.

Clarissa

"Oh, isn't that wonderful news!" Florence said as she held a hand to her belly. She wiped at her cheeks with her free hand.

Savannah moved toward Jeremy, still seated at the table, and leaned against his side. He turned into her, stretching up to kiss the side of her neck. "I couldn't be happier for them," he said. He pulled Savannah until she sat on his lap, where she sniffed and nodded her agreement.

"I just wish we'd be with her," Savannah whispered. "I hate that we're separated."

They all jerked at a loud knock on the front door. Richard rose and strode down the hallway. At his whoop of joy, Savannah, Florence and Jeremy shared curious glances.

"Set another place at the table, Flo, Savannah," Richard called as pairs of heavy footsteps approached.

"Mr. McLeod," Savannah said. She attempted to rise off Jeremy's lap, but his strong arm across her midsection kept her in place. She turned until she could look into Jeremy's eyes, and he whispered, "It'll be all right, my love. You'll see." She kissed him softly on the cheek and then pushed against him once more to rise. He helped her up and stood behind her.

"Uncle," Richard said, "I'd like you to meet my wife, Florence."

Aidan nodded toward her as she remained seated. "Ma'am, I'm delighted to finally meet the woman who has brought such joy to my nephew Richard."

"And you must be Jeremy," Aidan said as he turned toward Savannah and Jeremy, a fierce joy lighting his eyes. He moved forward past Savannah and clasped Jeremy's hand before pulling him into his arms for a long embrace. "Oh, how I wish Ian could have lived to see his boys, all grown up. He'd be tremendously proud of you."

"Uncle," Jeremy said, a dazed expression in his gaze.

"Forgive me," Aidan said, turning to Savannah. "It's a delight to see you again, Mrs. Montgomery, although I had expected to see you at your home on Marlborough Street when I visited last week."

Savannah paled. "My circumstances have changed, sir."

Aidan gave an assessing look at the casual intimacy between Jeremy and Savannah, murmuring, "Apparently."

Savannah remained ashen but lifted her chin in defiance.

"I can't believe you're really here. I thought I'd never see you again. That you'd always spend your time in California or Montana," Jeremy said, ignoring the exchange between his uncle and Savannah.

"Oh, no, I knew I needed to see you again. When my business drew me to Boston, I endeavored to return. However, I had meant to be here weeks ago. Delays in Washington and New York City prevented me from arriving until now."

"Why didn't you contact us when you arrived?" Richard asked, motioning for Aidan to sit down at the dining table. "When do you have to leave?"

"Thankfully this is a quiet time for business, and I have no set schedule." He removed his coat, handing it to Richard—who tossed it onto the couch—and sat at the table. "I wanted to settle my business and then meet with all of you."

"I hope your business was concluded to your satisfaction," Florence said.

"Most of it was," Aidan said as he glanced toward Savannah. "I've had a more difficult time than expected with my negotiations concerning Mr. Montgomery."

Savannah turned toward the stove and stirred the pot again in such an agitated manner that contents began to spill onto the stovetop. She took a deep breath and began to slow her movements.

"He seemed much more unreasonable this visit than when I was here two years ago," Aidan said.

"That's because you're finally seeing the true man," Jeremy said. He frowned as he glanced toward Savannah and watched as she virtually churned the cider in her distress. He moved toward her, placing a calming hand on her arm. She stilled, leaning into him for a moment.

"I've become accustomed to bargaining for what I want, but he was most interested in bartering. He seemed to believe that my family had something he wanted, and he would negotiate favorable terms once his missing property had been returned to him."

"What exactly are you looking to acquire with Mr. Montgomery's help?" Jeremy asked. He stood with his back to the counter, one hand linked with Savannah's, her back to the room.

"He has many contacts in New York City, including influential banker friends and investors, whom I'd like to meet. I'm looking to further expand my business, and I'm searching for financial investors." Aidan studied Savannah's rigid back for a moment. "When I was here a few years ago, I believed he would be a good business associate and partner."

"Are you saying you're uncertain now?" Richard asked.

Aidan stared from one person to the next in the room and shook his head in confusion. "I feel like I walked into the middle of a play, and I don't know what happened in the first act. Would anyone care to explain to me what I should know?"

Savannah turned to face Aidan, ashen faced. "I'm here because I will never again live with Jonas. I would be thankful if you would refrain from calling me Mrs. Montgomery ever again. It may be my legal name, but I refuse to think of myself in those terms."

"Are you divorced?" Aidan asked as he studied her. He frowned as she gripped the back of a chair in an attempt to still her shaking.

"No, and I'm not seeking one. Although I'll be infamous, living away from my husband, loving another man, I cannot care about that."

"I'm afraid I do care," Aidan said. "My brother and sister-in-law would want more for their son than a flighty woman who abandons her husband for no apparent reason."

"How dare you?" Savannah rasped. "I've marks all over my body proclaiming my husband's esteem for me. I had my child stolen from me and given to strangers to raise because she was a girl rather than the coveted son. I'm not some object he misplaced and can barter with his business associates for its return. I'm worth more than any amount of money you might possess."

Aidan rose, a harshness lighting his eyes. Jeremy moved to stand between him and Savannah. "Please, Jeremy, let me speak with Savannah," Aidan said. Jeremy nodded, moving to the side but remained standing next to Savannah.

Aidan reached forward, touching Savannah gently on her shoulder. "Your husband beat you?"

She nodded jerkily.

"Took pleasure in tormenting you? Took your daughter from you?"

"Yes," Savannah rasped.

His hand tightened for a moment on her shoulder before releasing it with a soft caress. "I'll ensure to never undertake any business with him, and I'll endeavor that no one with any association with me does either."

Savannah gasped, and a sob escaped before she turned away, covering her face with her hands. Aidan watched as she leaned into Jeremy, sobs racking her. He shared a solemn look with Jeremy and turned to face Richard and Florence.

He took a deep breath and attempted a smile. "When will you make me a great-uncle?"

"Soon," Richard said with relief. "In a few weeks."

"A few days, if God be kind," Florence said with another soft pat to her belly. She shared a rueful glance with Richard and Aidan. "I'm not looking forward to the birthing of the baby, but I'm excited at the prospect of no longer feeling like an overripe pumpkin."

Aidan laughed. "It's a joy and a time of absolute terror." His smile dimmed as his gaze became distant.

"Uncle?" Richard asked.

"Ah, just memories, Richard. I might remain in Boston until the baby is born, if that is acceptable. I'd like to meet my grandniece or grandnephew before returning to the West."

"We'd like that very much," Richard said.

"I'm sorry to have interrupted your Christmas," Aidan said. "I know I should have written, but I've always enjoyed surprises, and I thought seeing me might bring you joy."

"You can't know what it means to have you here with us, Uncle," Jeremy said, Savannah still cradled in his arms. "To have family with us again on Christmas." Jeremy shook his head. "It's like a miracle."

Richard leaned back against his chair. "Do you remember all those Christmases with Aunt Masterson where we were relegated to the bedroom we shared, with no presents?"

Jeremy nodded. "Yeah, and often no food. We were always fighting with our cousins, and she loved to punish us."

"Even on Christmas?" Savannah asked.

"Oh, it was her favorite thing. To tell us for weeks about the special treats we would eat, the presents that would be waiting for us and then to deny us everything," Richard said. "That first year was the worst."

"For some reason I always believed she'd change and it would be different," Jeremy said, stroking a hand down Savannah's back as though soothing her would ease the pain of the memory. "But it never was."

"Things only improved because Gabe found ways to buy us little gifts. He'd barter a piece of whittled wood for chocolate. After that first year, he always ensured we had something to open on Christmas morning," Richard said.

"Do you remember the time he sweet-talked Kathleen Cleary into knitting him a scarf?" Jeremy laughed. "She made him one to match his eyes. But seeing as he and Rich have the same coloring, more or less, he gave it to Richard. I'd never seen a woman on the verge of murdering a man until that point."

Richard laughed. "I had no idea. She came up to me, tried to rip it off me, nearly choking me in the process. And Gabe, acting all nonchalant, as though it were perfectly natural."

"Ah, the poor girl. He didn't mean any harm, but he hadn't been able to think of another way to obtain a gift for you that year," Jeremy said.

"What did you give Gabriel?" Savannah asked, easing out of Jeremy's arms and turning to fully join the conversation.

Richard and Jeremy flushed.

"I'm embarrassed to admit the first few years we didn't think to get him anything. Then, even though we wanted to, Gabe insisted he needed nothing and that we see to ourselves," Richard said.

Florence smiled sadly. "That sounds like Gabe, protecting you even to his detriment."

Aidan glowered. "If I ever see that woman again, I cannot be held responsible for what I'll do."

Savannah moved toward the stove and pulled out a well-done roast. "I'm afraid this is a little bit overcooked. With your arrival, Mr. McLeod, I didn't take it out on time."

"It will be delicious," Aidan said as they settled at the table for dinner.

After dinner, Savannah and Jeremy rose. "I must return to Sophie's," Savannah said. "I live with a friend of mine, near the Boston Common."

"I can escort you home. I'm staying at the Parker House which is not too far from there."

"I always escort her in the evening, Uncle," Jeremy said.

"If you wouldn't mind my company, I'd enjoy spending more time with you, Jeremy," Aidan said. They rose to don their coats before emerging into the cold evening air.

***

"WHY DON'T YOU JOIN me for a drink?" Aidan said as they approached the Parker House Hotel after escorting Savannah to Sophronia's. Jeremy nodded his agreement, and they entered the hotel. Electric wall sconces lit the foyer, and paintings of Boston and New England were scattered along the walls. The mahogany paneled walls gleamed as though recently polished. When Aidan and Jeremy moved toward a side room off the foyer into a gentleman's bar, their boot heels sounded on the marble floor.

The bar was largely empty, with only a few men ensconced in overstuffed wingback chairs near the roaring fire. Dim lights mounted on the dark mahogany paneled walls did little to alleviate the shadows of the room. Jeremy followed his uncle toward a pair of chairs in an unoccupied part of the room.

"You can't know what it means to see you again, Jeremy. Have you fully recovered from the malaria?"

Jeremy flushed. "Yes, I think this last doctor's advice to give me a larger dose of quinine was correct. I haven't been ill for three months."

"Thank God," Aidan said. He nodded his thanks to the bartender who brought them their drinks. After taking a sip, he said, "Tell me about Savannah."

"I love her, Uncle. Divorce or no divorce, she's the woman I want to spend my life with."

Aidan sighed. "If you don't sound like Ian. It's extraordinary how the trait he passed down to you three boys, besides loyalty, was obstinacy."

"What was Da like, Uncle? I've so few memories of him."

Aidan smiled, a distant look in his eyes. "Loyal, kind, determined. He was a man who knew he'd do whatever he needed to ensure those he loved were well cared for. Even if that meant digging in the dirt for years on end, he'd work without complaint. He believed hard work could lead a man to a successful, meaningful life. He took such joy in his boys and his wife."

"Did my mum ever regret marrying him?"

"Well, I can't say I was privy to the secrets that come with marriage. And there are things that are only known between spouses. But I can tell you from everything I witnessed, your parents loved each other deeply. Your mother was content in her life with your father."

Aidan shook his head with impatience as he added, "Content isn't a strong enough word. She loved the life she created with him. The home she helped to provide for her three boys. She never tired of writing me about you, of all your triumphs. I never had reason she doubted her decision to marry your father."

Jeremy nodded. "That's how I remember her too. She was always so proud of us, even when the most amazing thing we'd done was learn the alphabet."

"Ah, but she knew—when you learned that—she'd have the chance to shape you into tremendous thinkers and readers. She always wanted her boys to be men of the world. To help shape it for the betterment of mankind."

Jeremy flushed and looked away.

"Jeremy? What is it?"

"I know she would be disappointed in me. Hearing you say that only confirms it."

"Because of what you did in the Philippines?" At Jeremy's nod, Aidan lowered his head for a moment as though deep in thought. "I can't lie and say that your mother wouldn't have been confused. She'd have hoped you'd use your talents in a different way. However, I refuse to believe the woman I knew would ever have ceased loving you."

He waited until Jeremy met his eyes. "And when she saw how you'd suffered, she'd have done everything in her power to ease your torment. She would only have known joy to have her Little Pop home."

Jeremy's eyes flashed at the use of a nickname not spoken since the death of his parents.

Aidan studied him, nodding his understanding at Jeremy's emotions. "Whatever you do, don't let your doubts about what you've done tarnish your memories of your mother and father. They would have been proud of their son."

Jeremy nodded, taking a sip of his drink.

"And never forget, Jeremy, if they had lived, you'd never have been in a position to need to go to the Philippines. You'd never have been desperate to leave. Life would have been very different."

"I try not to expend too much energy imagining how different my life could have been, Uncle. Instead, I'm trying to focus on the good fortune I've found recently."

"Very wise, Jeremy, very wise." Aidan glanced into the fire, that distant look in his eyes again.

**

SAVANNAH PAUSED AT THE ENTRANCE to Sophie's dining room, taking in the polished black walnut table set with crisp white linen. The silver next to each place sparkled in the light. The pair of candelabras lit with a half-dozen candles each were set in the two windows. Savannah moved into the room to take her seat next to Jeremy. Florence, Richard and Aidan sat across from her, with Sophie at the head of the table.

"Mrs. Chickering, it's a pleasure to meet you at last," Aidan said. "Thank you for including me in your Christmas festivities."

"It's a pleasure to have the McLeods with me to celebrate," Sophie said, including Savannah in her statement. She watched as two of her maids set out large platters of food. She nodded and they left. "Due to it being Christmas and that I would like the staff not to work too much today, we will dine à la française. I hope this offends no one?"

Richard shook his head with an amused smile. "I'm sure the food will be delicious, no matter how it is served, ma'am."

"You must call me Sophie, as your wife does." She took small portions of the food off the platters in front of her, passing them on to the person to her left. Richard nodded his agreement.

They ate for a few moments before Sophie spoke again. "It was generous of you, Mr. McLeod, to purchase the Sullivan forge for your nephew."

"It made good business sense," Aidan said. "And when I learned there was something I could do for Richard, there was little that would have stopped me."

"Although you stripped your niece's brother of his birthright?" Sophie asked.

"Yes, Clarissa is my niece by marriage. I like to I think Colin came to understand that, if I hadn't acted as I did, the forge wouldn't have remained in the family, no matter how distantly." Aidan watched Sophie with a curious expression. "As I'm sure you are aware."

Sophie nodded her agreement. "Tell me, Richard, about the forge. How is it now that you are running it?"

"More work than I could ever have envisioned. I'm glad Colin decided to remain, and we have the running of it together. I don't know how his father did it alone."

"How was it after his father died?" Savannah asked.

"Thankfully a loyal man named Jameson remained and kept everyone in line. He ensured no one robbed the forge blind. It would have been very easy to do with so much equipment, especially the hand tools."

"Seems you were quite fortunate," Sophie said. Richard nodded his agreement.

"Is Colin settling in?" Aidan asked.

"As well as can be expected. My mother wasn't keen on having him live with them, but Lucas and Father were, so her protests were ignored," Savannah said.

"I was concerned about my girl traveling such a great distance alone without Colin or a companion." Sophie took a sip of water.

"Well, she made it home fine, Sophie. And she has the most wondrous news!" Florence said.

"Ah, so she's finally told Gabriel she's expecting," Sophie said with a smug smile.

"How did you know?" Savannah demanded.

"I pay attention to the signs, dear," Sophie said. "It's one of the reasons I encouraged her to return home and not wait for the first little baby McLeod to be born."

"That was thoughtful of you, Mrs. Chickering," Aidan said.

"I thought so," Sophie agreed with a self-mocking smile. "As for my girl, I'm sure she'll bloom with impending motherhood. I only wish I could see her and the baby once it's born."

"I'm sure you could travel to her, Sophie," Savannah said.

"I've never had much desire to travel to the uncivilized zones of this country."

"You may find it more to your liking than you envision," Aidan murmured.

"I highly doubt that, Mr. McLeod." She leaned back in her chair, finished with her meal. She looked from Jeremy to Savannah. "When do the articles come out?"

"Articles? What articles?" Aidan asked.

Savannah flushed before speaking. "I've spoken to a reporter about how I suffered while living with Jonas."

Aidan raised his eyebrows for a moment before furrowing them in confusion. "Who thought that would be a good idea?"

"I did, Mr. McLeod," Sophie said. "Rather than have the reporters learn of the affair and exploit it for their own profit, while also bantering about misinformation, I advised Savannah to approach them and tell her story, in serial format. While, of course, selling it to the highest bidder."

"What good comes from such notoriety?" Aidan asked, perplexed.

"A bit of financial freedom," Savannah said. "And, like Sophie said, the ability to tell my story truthfully."

"Why not seek a divorce if you are going to do all this?" Aidan asked.

"Because with a divorce every mistreatment would need to be detailed. This way, I can choose what I wish to reveal," Savannah said. "I can keep some of my dignity."

"You'll always have that, Sav," Jeremy said, a fierce pride shining from his eyes. He met his uncle's worried gaze, entreating him silently for support.

"I wish you well with this, Savannah. I hope my worries are unfounded." He raised his glass of wine to Savannah in a silent toast, and the conversation moved on to the imminent arrival of Florence and Richard's baby.

CHAPTER 47

RAIN LASHED THE WINDOWS, and a strong wind howled, causing the curtains on either side of the windows to billow slightly into the room with each strong gust of wind. Savannah sat at the desk facing the windows, watching the pattern the rain created as though mesmerized. A pencil and a stack of papers, both long forgotten, lay in front of her. She bolted at the soft knock on the door and the intruding footsteps into the back parlor.

"I see I'm interrupting," Sophronia said as she moved toward the chaise longue and sat with a grateful sigh. She settled her wine-colored worsted wool skirt at her ankles.

"You aren't interrupting at all. I'm attempting to put together a list of things I'll need to bring with me when I move with Jeremy to our apartment. We are hopeful to move in March."

"Seems like a lot of dillydallying when you're determined on your course of action. I'd think you'd move in sooner with him."

"I want to wait until the first articles are released before undertaking any further changes."

"If there's one thing I've learned in life, Savannah, it's don't dawdle when action is needed."

A blast of wind struck the windows, and Sophronia pulled her thick taupe-colored shawl around her shoulders. She then glared at the window as cold air leaked in.

"Perhaps you should sit by the fire," Savannah said with a half smile.

"I'm settled now, and I'm of an age that energy should be conserved. I have important news to impart, and I fear I will change your relaxing plans for the day."

Savannah moved from the hard-backed oak chair in front of the desk to a tufted wingback chair near the roaring fire. Lamps lit throughout the room lent an inviting glow to the sitting room.

"Have you heard the news about Clarissa's stepmother, Mrs. Sullivan?" Sophronia asked, extracting a letter from a hidden pocket in the side of her skirt.

"No," Savannah said. "I've been focused on the home I'm moving into with Jeremy and the articles that will soon be released." She waved toward the pile of papers on the desk. "I haven't thought much about her since Clarissa left. Why?"

"It seems Mrs. Sullivan's nonsense has come back to haunt her."

"What do you mean?" Savannah leaned forward in an attempt to grasp the letter, but Sophie held it out of her reach.

"Do you know she outspent her husband's decent earnings two to one in the extravagant refurbishing of that home? I knew she had bought exorbitant furnishings, but I had never imagined she had gone that far."

"She's always had delusions of grandeur, but I can't imagine she would have spent to the point of impoverishment. Uncle Sean made a handsome living."

"Well, gold leaf wallpaper does tend to beggar a person. Nonsensical woman. Wasting her money on such frivolities."

"What will she do?" Savannah asked.

"Her good friend"—Sophronia *harrumphed* her opinion—"Mrs. Masterson won't accept her calls. I've heard Mrs. Sullivan's about run through every penny she received from Mr. McLeod for the forge."

Savannah nodded. "Thus her haste to sell articles from the home. Clarissa told me things were missing."

"Exactly. She needed a large influx of cash for her creditors. However, I've heard even that wasn't enough."

"What do you mean? What else can she do?"

"Besides learning to live within her means?" Sophie asked with an acerbic smile. "I suppose she could always have found another man to marry, and maybe she had hoped to with Mr. Wright, but, seeing as he is now jailed in Montana awaiting trial, that plan won't come to fruition. In today's post, I received a letter from Clarissa's maid, who was let go recently, asking if I had any work for her or knew of anyone. Of course she was dismissed without a reference, due to her attachment to Clarissa."

"Horrible woman."

Sophie grunted her approval. "I'll find something for the girl. At any rate, she wrote about the goings-on in the house, especially as regarding Melinda."

Savannah paled, gripping the wooden armrests of her chair as she watched Sophronia with dawning horror.

"It appears your Mrs. Sullivan is considering placing her daughter into the Home."

"She can't. She wouldn't." Savannah gripped the mahogany armrests with such vigor that her fingers whitened. She shared a look of despair with Sophie.

"Your cousin Melinda's abandonment is imminent, I'm afraid."

***

SAVANNAH SHIVERED as she sat on one of the two remaining chairs in the large formal parlor. The walls bare of any ornamentation looked as though dappled by the sun's rays due to the varying highlights on the golden wallpaper, a reminder of the hangings that used to be displayed. Her shoes scuffed the bare floors as she moved her feet underneath her skirts, the Turkish carpet nowhere in sight. Savannah stared longingly at the empty fireplace, imagining warming herself in front of a roaring fire for a moment.

"Savannah, I am surprised you would consider it appropriate to call on me," Mrs. Sullivan said, sniveling into a black lace handkerchief.

"I'm sorry I was unable to offer comfort after my uncle's death, Mrs. Sullivan."

"You would understand all there is to know about difficult circumstances, wouldn't you?" She fisted the piece of lace in her hand, tapping her closed hand against the arm of her chair. "How could Sean do this to me? He knew how important the refurbishing of this home was to me. He knew I expected to live with an expectation of a better future. How could he have died? It's so selfish!" She glowered as she glanced around the empty room.

"Mrs. Sullivan, I doubt Uncle Sean planned his death. He died while at work, hammering a heavy piece of metal at the smithy."

"I told him, again and again I told him, to have the younger men do the heavy work. Would he listen to me? No. He always knew better. He never took my advice. Always tried to thwart me."

"I'm sure that's not true, Mrs. Sullivan."

"I know it is! He was late to take my advice regarding Clarissa and look what scandalous behavior she wrought, running off to Montana, unmarried, to reunite with that worthless carpenter. If Sean had listened to me, she would have married that Mr. Wright months before she would have considered leaving Boston."

"Mrs. Sullivan—"

"Did he take my advice when it came to this home? To the number of staff we needed? To the proper running of his smithy? No, no, no!" She slammed her fisted hand again onto her chair's armrest. "If he had taken my advice, I wouldn't be in such an impoverished state."

"Of course not. You would have had your money from Cameron for helping to coerce Clarissa into marrying him." Savannah eyed her, unable to hide her scorn. "After all, your stepmotherly love and concern was limitless."

"Ah, so the kitten has claws." Mrs. Sullivan glared at Savannah. "You wretched girl. You're just like her, shameless. Although you seem improved from the last time I saw you." Mrs. Sullivan looked Savannah up and down, noting the healthy color on Savannah's cheeks.

"I am much improved. Thank you for your concern."

"I've never had much concern for you since your impetuous actions brought scorn upon your poor mother's head. Do you know what shame she has had to endure, listening to the gossip and ridicule from those she once called friends? Do you know how your actions have harmed your grandparents?" She sniffed in disdain. "If you had any regard for anyone other than yourself, you would never have acted as you did."

"I'm no longer interested in all that nonsense, Mrs. Sullivan. I've discovered what is truly important."

"And what would that be? Acting like a shameless hussy? Gallivanting about in a workman's warehouse unchaperoned? Consorting with the likes of Mrs. Chickering?"

"My actions are none of your concern. I hope someday you will discover that all those pretenses toward good society are an illusion. That love, true honor and loyalty are more important than any perceived social standing."

"I thought naïveté was Clarissa's forte. Now I see it's a familial trait."

"At least I have friends who will stand beside me through thick and thin, Mrs. Sullivan."

"Why are you here, Savannah? You've never shown me any of the regard that was my due in the past."

"I heard you were considering bringing Melinda to the Home. I would like to offer to care for her instead."

"As though I would consider you an acceptable alternative to my fine mothering abilities. You who were incapable of having a child and then who takes up with the firebrand suffragette who fails to know the limits of propriety?" She gasped for a moment. "You think I would want my daughter living with the likes of you?"

"I'd think you'd rather have her living in a fine home on Beacon Street on Beacon Hill, well-clothed and well-fed, rather than living as an abandoned child in a home for undesired children."

"How dare you speak to me about my daughter in such a way? You have no right."

"I have every right. She is my cousin. She deserves to be raised in a place knowing she is wanted and loved. I may no longer be with my husband, but I can offer her a good home."

"I could not countenance her living with you. The thought of my beautiful Melinda, who already knows not to cry or act out in any way, living with you, who has no sense of common decency? It's too much to be borne."

"Where is Melinda?" Savannah demanded. "Is she still here?"

"Of course not. I couldn't have her eating away at my meager savings. I couldn't have her expecting I'd squander any more on a Christmas present for her. I brought her to the Home over a month ago."

"How could you? And not inform anyone in the family?"

"I am her mother, and it is my prerogative to do as I choose with regard to her welfare. As I am unable to care for her, I found a place that would."

"Unwilling, you mean. You continue to live here, with a maid to open your door, and yet you'd consign your daughter to an orphanage?"

"You will find, Savannah, that motherhood is not for all women. I should never have had a child. Such messy, noisy creatures. My home is much more peaceful now she is away."

"Away. Banished to an orphanage." Savannah rose. "I hope you enjoy your remaining days in your home, Mrs. Sullivan." She smiled as her barb struck. "For, if the rumors are to be believed, you'll soon be on the streets, and this"—she waved a hand around the empty room—"will soon be just a distant memory. As will your liaison with my family."

***

SAVANNAH ENTERED the New England Home for Little Wanderers, the heavy oak door squeaking as it swung shut behind her. A lemony antiseptic scent pervaded the hallway, the wood floors shining as she approached the head matron, Mrs. Maidstone's, office. Savannah paused at the open door, tapping on it to gain the matron's attention.

Her head jerked up from a pile of papers on her otherwise spotless desk. "Ah, Mrs. Montgomery. You've returned to visit us again."

"Yes, I was hoping to discuss with you a situation that I only just learned about. If I may have a seat?"

"For a few minutes only. I have many meetings today, and I must prepare."

"Of course," Savannah said as she sat with her back straight and feet curled under her seat. She folded her skirts around her and laced her fingers together, resting her hands on her lap.

After a moment, Mrs. Maidstone spoke in an impatient tone. "This matter, Mrs. Montgomery?"

"I have learned that my cousin, Melinda Sullivan, has come into your care. I would like to bring her home with me and care for her."

"My dear Mrs. Montgomery, I'm afraid I don't see how this pertains to you." Mrs. Maidstone held herself with rigid control, her starched coal-gray dress without a visible crease. Her salt-and-pepper hair was pulled back in a severe, unattractive bun while her almond-shaped hazel eyes were devoid of any warmth.

"She is my young cousin. I can't allow her to be here. She needs to know she has family who wants her."

"Do you think I am so naive that I haven't heard of your infamous behavior? Do you honestly believe I would place a young, impressionable girl in my charge into the care of a woman who fails to honor her own marriage vows?"

"I would have thought you eager to find a home for one of your charges." Savannah stiffened her shoulders and firmed her jaw, glaring at the older woman.

"Her welfare must be of my utmost concern. Thus, I refuse to allow her into your care. What would my patrons say if they knew I consorted with women the likes of you?"

"The likes of me?" Savannah rasped. "The kind that finds a way to survive the brutality of her marriage? I'd think you'd rejoice with me rather than disdain me."

"You took vows, and it was your obligation to comply with them. I will not allow young Melinda to have her spirit warped by such an unnatural woman, even if you are her cousin."

"I am not unnatural. I merely demand more from my life than the pain and humiliation my marriage wrought."

"You desire my sympathy, Mrs. Montgomery?" She sneered as she looked Savannah up and down. "You'll have none from me. I know your type of woman. Spoiled and pampered. Nothing is good enough for you. Not your mansions in the Back Bay. Not your stables full of carriages and basements full of servants. You'll never find satisfaction in your life because you'll never learn to be grateful for what you already have. Melinda Sullivan will never be given into your care. A spoiled, disgraced woman who fails to have the decency to feel shame at her situation."

"You have finally spoken a truth. I will never feel shame for escaping my marriage." Savannah rose, patting a trembling hand over her skirts as she glowered at the seated Mrs. Maidstone. "You may sit there in your righteous indignation now. I hope, if you are ever in need, as I was, you will find someone compassionate and understanding. Someone who will be the antithesis of who you are right now." Savannah took two steps out of the door, preparing to storm down the long hallway.

"Did you ever find your baby, Mrs. Montgomery?"

Savannah spun to face her, gripping the back of the chair she had just vacated. "You knew where my baby was? All this time you've known."

The matron rose, and sauntered toward Savannah, a taunting smile on her lips. "I know many things, Mrs. Montgomery."

Savannah flushed red while the hand gripping the back of the chair whitened. "Tell me where she is. Tell me she is with good people."

"Accept that your daughter is lost to you forever. There is no possibility of ever recovering her." Mrs. Maidstone glanced down the hallway as the outer door slammed shut. "Ah, here's Mr. Aires now for a meeting. I wish you a good day, Mrs. Montgomery, and thank you for a most illuminating visit."

Savannah stumbled from the office and down the corridor in a dazed stupor. She barely had the sense of mind to open the door before walking into it. As she emerged onto the front stoop of the Home, she glanced around her. Night was falling with a brisk, cool wind blowing, scented by the recent rain. Shivering, she pulled her coat tighter around her as though to ward off the wind and the pain rendered by the matron's words. Rather than turning for the trolley stop and Sophronia's, she ventured farther into the maze of the North End.

***

"WHAT'S THE MATTER, SAVANNAH?" Richard asked as he studied her standing on his doorstep. "Why don't you come in? It's too late to be wandering the streets alone, and I know Florence would like to see you. It's been days since your last visit, and the baby's already grown." He clasped her arm, squinting to study her further as he noted the subtle trembling of her arm.

"I'll put the kettle on for tea. Our mum always said there was little a good cry and a cup of tea couldn't cure." He led Savannah into the back room where Jeremy was placing the finishing touches on dinner. Florence reclined on the dilapidated sofa, the baby asleep against her chest and a black cat purring its contentment next to her. Aidan sat at the scarred table, a mug of tea warming his hands.

"Savannah," Jeremy murmured. He set down the plates and walked toward her. He reached out to push a loose tendril of hair behind her ear, stroking her neck before dropping his hand. "You look terrible."

Savannah nodded. "I was just at the ... at the ..." She shook her head, her voice cracking as tears streamed down her face, and uncontrollable sobs escaped.

"Come here, darling," Jeremy said as he pulled her into his embrace, tucking her head under his chin. He shared a long look with Richard and Florence before he caressed her back and rocked gently to and fro.

Aidan rose, taking over Jeremy's duty and finished setting the table. He stirred the stew pot on the stove, sliced a loaf of bread and poured water into the glasses. Rather than retaking his seat, he remained standing in the kitchen, watching Jeremy and Savannah.

"Forgive me," Savannah said with a hiccup, easing away from Jeremy.

"Savannah, you must have learned by now that holding it all in does no good. And we're family," Florence said. She nodded toward a chair as she continued to rock side to side. "Sit. You'll have some supper that Jeremy made and tell us what this is all about."

Savannah crumpled into the chair, curling into herself as she sat sideways. Jeremy crouched in front of her. "We can hold dinner so you can tell us what happened. I think you need to speak of it, and waiting is only going to make it worse."

Savannah met his worried gaze, tears continuing to leak out. "Yes," she whispered on a stuttering exhalation. She glanced up, looking toward Florence, Richard and Aidan. "I need your help too."

Florence inched to the edge of the sofa and then heaved herself to a standing position. She waddled toward the chair Richard held out for her, smiling her thanks as he winked at her. She sat with a loud sigh, her hands cradling the baby's bum and head. Richard sat in the chair next to her, nibbling on his lower lip as he studied Jeremy and Savannah. Aidan moved and sat across from them, his hands folded on top of the table.

"I visited my uncle Sean's wife today. You've met Mrs. Sullivan." At their murmurs of assent, she continued. "She's bankrupt. She overspent her husband's earnings two to one in the redecorating of her home. That's why she was desperate for an influx of cash, to pay her creditors."

"Her desperation was our gain," Richard said with a sardonic smile. Aidan nodded.

Savannah rose, the chair making a scraping noise with her harsh movement. She paced in the area between the sparsely furnished living room and the dining room table. "She's no way to pay her bills. Has no friends who will come to her aid. Not even your aunt."

"That's not surprising. I imagine Aunt had her reasons for friendship with her, ones we'll never fully understand. She'll feel no compunction at abandoning her now that Mrs. Sullivan is of no use to her." Jeremy shared a rueful glance with Richard.

"And now she's decided she must forego any unnecessary expenses."

"Seems sensible," Florence said. She patted her son, nuzzling his downy head as she watched Savannah with mild curiosity.

"She's brought her daughter to the Home. Left her there as though she were an orphan. Unwanted and unloved." Savannah met Florence's stricken gaze, watching as all color leached from Florence's face.

"Good Lord, she couldn't have," Florence whispered. Richard reached for her hand, squeezing it in support.

"She did."

"Then you must go there, demand they give you Melinda. For she needs to know she's wanted. There's nothing worse than thinking you're not wanted," Florence said as her voice broke.

Savannah nodded, swallowing visibly before she took a deep breath. "I did. And was told that Melinda would never be given into my care. That a woman such as me would only warp her mind and spirit."

"That witch!" Florence shrieked, waking the baby. A lusty wail rose, and Florence calmed only to soothe her son. After a moment, when little Ian had quieted, she whispered, "Melinda knows who you are. Mrs. Maidstone knows you have the means to care for her. To love her. You're her family."

"Yes, but what would the patrons think if she consorted with one such as me?" Savannah asked, dull pain in her eyes.

"That she has some sense!" Florence hissed. She rocked little Ian as he fretted.

"Florence, love, hush," Richard soothed. He reached for Ian and settled him against his chest.

"Don't tell me to hush, Richard," she snapped as she rose. She moved toward the kitchen and stirred the stew pot, banging the wooden spoon with such force it cracked.

"There's more you aren't telling us, Savannah. Being denied your cousin would make you as mad as Flo. But something happened at the Home to bring you despair." Jeremy leaned forward and clasped her hand, lacing his fingers with her and tugging her toward him. He coaxed her into leaning against him.

"She knows where my baby is. My baby lived."

"Oh, my God," Richard said as Florence moaned and fell into her chair.

"That woman lied, all those months ago. Telling me no baby had come to the Home. Sending me on a wild chase to the other orphanages around

Boston. Having Sophronia solicit the aid of her friends. And the whole time, she knew where my baby was."

"Why would she do such a thing?" Florence whispered. "That's not the woman I remember." They all jerked as Aidan rose and turned to look out the window facing the empty lot. Nothing was visible on this dark January night, and the window acted as though a mirror, reflecting his troubled visage.

"Uncle?" Richard asked. Aidan shook his head and appeared lost in thought as he continued to stare out the window.

Savannah swiped at some of her tears, meeting Florence's worried stare and answering her question. "I don't know. If I had to guess, it's that Jonas paid her handsomely."

"And his money was worth more than your agony?" Jeremy rasped, now standing. "I've a mind to go there and ..."

"Jer," Richard said, a warning note in his voice. "No." He glared at Jeremy until he'd settled back into his chair.

Aidan turned, resting a hand on Jeremy's shoulder for a moment, his touch aiding in easing some of Jeremy's tension. Aidan pulled a chair away from the table, sitting with his legs crossed. "This Mrs. Maidstone, what is she like?" Aidan asked.

"She's a widow. She has been since I was a girl. I always thought she was kind and concerned about us," Florence said. "She began working there shortly before I left to work with Mrs. Kruger. I liked her. She was young and seemed to truly care about us."

"Middling height, salt-and-pepper hair, brown eyes, forgettable once you left her company," Jeremy said.

"And yet you didn't forget." Aidan rubbed at a spot on his gray wool pants, his mouth pulled down in a frown.

Jeremy shrugged. "It had to do with Savannah. I wouldn't forget."

Aidan nodded, rising and moving toward the stove. He picked up the cracked spoon and began to dish out the stew, setting filled bowls on the table. "Let's eat. Nothing is ever determined on an empty stomach."

"I never imagined the woman I knew then would act this way toward you now, Savannah," Florence said.

Jeremy sat with a distant look in his eyes. "She seemed to take an inordinate delight in talking about your family perishing. Didn't seem to have the sense to know to be quiet."

"Either didn't have the sense or, in fact, relished causing you pain," Richard growled. He stood, rocking baby Ian in his arms, allowing Florence a few moments to eat supper. He stroked Florence's nape, soothing any grief wrought by his words.

"Why would she dislike me?" Florence played with her spoon, stirring the stew in her bowl.

"For some women, living such a life for so long leaves them bitter. As I imagine it would many men as well. If I hadn't found you," Aidan said as he glanced around the table, "I could easily imagine myself as bitter and angry at the world for being alone in it."

"You are too understanding, Uncle," Jeremy said. He reached for Savannah's hand, as he tilted his head to one side, watching his uncle with deep curiosity.

"Would you mind if I approached her? I refuse to believe she would spurn such a profitable donation as one I could provide to the orphanage," Aidan said as he rose and paced anew. He rubbed the back of his neck, his shoulders bunched tightly under his well-fitted white cotton shirt and gray waistcoat.

"Uncle, you can't believe we expect you to always aid us in such a way. I—" Jeremy shook his head, unable to voice his concerns.

"Jeremy, I have more money than I will ever know how to spend. If I can help you in any way by using a small portion of it, then that pleases me. I know I would be as welcome here if I were poor and had nothing but my love to offer. That is the gift you have bestowed upon me."

"As long as you understand, Uncle," Richard said. He walked toward Aidan and handed Ian to him. "Why don't you hold your great-nephew and allow me to eat? He needs time with you if you are soon to be off adventuring again out West."

"When will you visit the orphanage, Aidan? I'm worried others will visit and see our little Melinda and want to adopt her," Savannah said.

"I'll go tomorrow, as soon as it is acceptable to call." He nuzzled little Ian's head, a contented sigh escaping him.

CHAPTER 48

AIDAN ENTERED THE ORPHANAGE, the heavy wooden door swinging shut behind him. He paused for a moment to allow his eyes to adjust to the dim hallway, glancing around to see if anyone would greet him before walking purposefully toward the office at the rear. He remembered Florence's and Savannah's descriptions of the orphanage. Pausing outside the partially opened door, he listened to a gentle humming. The contented sound harkened back to a long buried memory, and he paused, unable to recall it. He rapped on the door and pushed it open, coming to an abrupt halt as he saw the woman seated behind the desk.

"Delia?"

Mrs. Maidstone glanced up from her ledger, becoming as pale as Aidan's starched shirt. "May I help you, sir?"

"Don't act as though you don't know me, Mrs. Maidstone," Aidan said, recovering his composure as he stepped into her office, shutting the door firmly behind him. "I'd recognize you anywhere."

"How dare you ..." Mrs. Maidstone, Delia, half rose, her indignant blush fading as she beheld Aidan standing in front of her.

"I find I have business with you."

"Why are you here after all these years? I assumed you had died, like Ian."

"No, I kept my promise never to return. Until it became unavoidable due to business," Aidan said, now seated in the wooden chair in front of her desk. He brushed out a crease from his black trousers, continuing to watch her with intense curiosity. "I can't believe the woman I knew is acting in such a shameful way."

"How dare you speak to me in such a manner?" Although her voice was angry and she held herself with rigid control, she continued to stare at him greedily, as though noting changes and comparing the man she saw in front of her to the man she remembered.

"I can admire your tenacity. Your ability to continue to hate me after all these years is commendable. However, to turn your venom onto innocent children is going too far, Delia."

"How dare you!" she rasped, her cheeks regaining their color and blooming red with her anger. "You sit there in all your finery and attempt to convolute what happened that day into my fault? You left me. You abandoned me! When I needed you."

"Much of what we yelled at each other was in anger. You must know I didn't mean half of what I said."

"Why did you say it at all?" She bit her lip, attempting to stop its trembling.

He sighed, his deep blue eyes haunted. "I'd arrived home, with a bag full of gifts for my nephews after my travels, exotic teas for their mum, coffee for my brother, a surprise gift for you, and, instead of finding a ready welcome, I was told my family was lost to me. Dead from that wretched fire. When last we spoke, my torment barely seemed to register with you. All you were concerned with was what I would be able to provide you. I'd just lost what remained of my family, and you were asking me to give up the only life I knew. Wanting me to find a job, become a landlubber sitting behind a desk, in this wretched city that had just taken my whole family from me. I couldn't."

"You wouldn't. I didn't mean enough to you," she rasped, her hands gripped together on her lap.

"No, you meant ... meant more than I knew. But I hated feeling forced into anything. If Ian gave me anything, he allowed me to live the life I wanted and never showed any disappointment at my desire to sail the seas. He gifted me with his love, understanding my need for freedom. I couldn't lose that, along with my family, in a matter of days. I wasn't strong enough."

Tears flowed from her eyes. "Why did you say those words to me?"

Aidan winced and shook his head.

"Why did you say that you'd find another woman, just as good, just as meaningful, at every port of call? That you'd be more satisfied with your ...

doxy than you'd ever been with me?"

Aidan exhaled loudly and ran his fingers through his hair. He looked toward her, regret and shame shining in his blue eyes. "I was hurt and angry and frustrated. I wanted to hurt you too." He flushed. "Until that moment, when I saw your love turn to hate in an instant, I'd never fully understood the power of words. In my need to lash out at the world, I lost you too.

"I never wanted to return to Boston, and you wouldn't leave. It seemed hopeless to me. And yet, when I realized I had no reason to return, because even you hated me, I found myself wanting to come back."

"You knew I couldn't leave! My mother was sickly, and I had to care for her." She sniffled into her handkerchief. "And I did hate you. I've hated you every day since you walked away from me. All you had to do was come back and tell me ... tell me ..." She stifled a sob.

"That I was a fool and that I was sorry," Aidan whispered. "I'd hoped you'd marry. Have children. Live a full life." After a moment, he said, "I hope Mr. Maidstone was good to you. Better than I was."

"You have no right to ask me about him." She shook her head. "I've been here for years. I'll continue to be here until I'm no longer able to manage as I'd like." She pierced him with an intense stare, her brown eyes bruised and haunted. "Did you have such a life? A life like you had hoped for me?"

Aidan flushed and nodded. "I married, yes. And we had two short years together. She died in childbirth. The baby died a few weeks later."

"Oh, Aidan. I'm sorry," she whispered, new tears falling.

"There's the Delia I remember. The Delia who only showed me love and was always excited to have me home after my long journeys at sea. I've never understood why things were so damned different the last time I was in Boston. You were more concerned about yourself, about whether or not I'd provide the life you'd decided you wanted, than about the fact I'd lost my family."

"I needed you to want me. To choose me. And you didn't." She glared at him before heaving out a sigh. "I know rehashing the past isn't what brought you in today. We'll never come to an understanding. You're here about the Sullivan girl, aren't you?"

"Yes, and the Montgomery baby. I'd never thought you'd stoop so low as to separate a mother from her child." He blanched at the hatred in her eyes. "Delia ..."

"Don't you ever speak to me about what I would or wouldn't do for mothers or their children. I've done everything in my power to help these children who have been forsaken by their parents, and I won't be judged. Not by you, Aidan."

"Delia …"

"I was advised by Mr. Montgomery that his wife was … unstable, and that, if the child returned to her care, there was a risk of maltreatment and the potential of an early death for the child. When I met her, she seemed stable enough, but I had already given my word to him and accepted a large donation to help our flagging accounts. The winter was very cold." She gazed at her desk, staring at the ledger.

"Her baby is with a good family, one who will care for her well and raise her as their own." She closed her eyes. "Although I know that is unacceptable to you and to her, for it means she remains separated from her child."

"Why say such cruel things to Savannah?" Aidan asked.

"She is flaunting the rules the rest of us are forced to obey. It hardly is fair, although I know I was too harsh on her." She met his implacable gaze. Finally she whispered, "And I was jealous."

"Why?" Aidan cocked his head as he watched her.

"Do you know what it does to have you look at me like that? Like you used to?" She shook her head. "Because your nephew wants her enough he doesn't care about the scandal. Because she's brave enough to live the life she wants, one not dictated by society. And that made me jealous."

"Don't force her to suffer for my past transgressions, Delia," Aidan implored. "She's a good woman who has suffered greatly."

Delia held up a newspaper, her index finger tapping at one of the morning's headlines. "*Socialite Flees Abusive Husband in Back Bay, Seeks Solace in Carpenter's Arms.* So it seems. Her husband appears to be the villain in this tale."

"Never doubt it." Aidan shifted in his chair and watched Delia. "What are we going to do about the children?"

She steepled her fingers as she thought. "We will need to fill out some paperwork, but you may leave today with Melinda. I must speak with the parents who fostered Mrs. Montgomery's child. And I want a promise from you." She pierced him with a fierce stare.

Aidan tensed as he awaited her words.

"I want you never to return here. Never to seek me out. Never to speak to me again. If we pass on the street, do not acknowledge me. Our association is at an end."

"I can't promise you that, Delia. You've suffered enough, and I refuse to now gift you with my indifference. You've lived with my callous disregard long enough."

***

STOOPED OVER SO THAT their hands clasped, Aidan walked hand in hand with two-year-old Melinda. As their pace slowed to one where they barely made any forward progress, he glanced to see her stumbling on bricks. He bent down and picked her up, resting her weight on one of his hips. She held herself stiffly for a minute before resting her head on his shoulder and wrapping her small arms around his neck.

With one arm clasped around the back of her knees, the other at her upper back was able to caress her head. "Don't worry, Melinda. I'm taking you to your cousins. Do you remember them? Clarissa and Colin's cousins," Aidan said in what he hoped was a reassuring voice. The child relaxed at her siblings' names.

He entered the alley and knocked on his nephew's door. Colin opened it and gave a whoop of joy as he beheld Aidan holding Melinda.

"You got her!" He reached forward and stroked a hand down Melinda's back. "Melly, do you remember me? I'm your brother, Colin. I visited you with Clarissa a few months ago."

Melinda raised her head and looked at Colin with wary eyes. She nodded once.

"Come here, precious girl," Colin said, reaching out for her. Melinda was transferred from Aidan's arms to Colin's and hugged tightly. "Oh, how I've missed you, dear sister. We have so many games to play together. But first we need to fatten you up. You're far too skinny." He turned to carry her into the house.

"Look who's here!" Colin called out as he entered. He shushed at Florence's exasperated wave, baby Ian having just gone down for a nap. "Sorry. I'm just so excited. Little Melly, this is part of your family." He turned her so she could see the group waiting for her.

"These are your cousins, Florence, Jeremy and Savannah. Lucas and

Richard are at work." He stroked a hand down her back and leaned in to listen as she whispered something into his ear.

"No, Clarissa isn't here. She went home to be with her husband. She lives far away." Colin moved to the couch and sat. He stroked a hand down her back until she was asleep in his arms. He eased her out of his arms until she was lying on the couch with a pillow under her head. Colin rose and joined the group around the table.

Jeremy turned to study his uncle. "You seem out of sorts. What happened at the orphanage?" He clasped Savannah's hand to bolster her spirits.

"Ah, Savannah. It is as you suspected. Mrs. Maidstone knows where your daughter is and will attempt to restore her to you," Aidan said.

Savannah collapsed forward, burying her face in her skirts as she began to sob. Jeremy stroked her back, leaning over her, attempting to bring her comfort and kissing her nape. "When?" she croaked out. "When can I hold my baby?"

"I'm not certain but soon," Aidan soothed, reaching out to clasp her offered hand.

"Thank you," Savannah murmured.

"How did you convince her to tell you the truth?" Florence asked, swiping at her own eyes as she watched Savannah, overcome with emotion.

"It helped that the story about Savannah's abuse at Jonah's hands was the headline today. She was reading it and appeared distressed by it," Aidan said.

"As she should be," Jeremy said. At Aidan's pronounced pause, he asked, "Uncle?"

"She and I were acquainted many years ago. It came as quite a shock to see her again."

"Was this before she married Mr. Maidstone?" Florence asked.

"Yes. I imagine just before. I … acted in ways that shame me now, said unpardonable things to her and left in anger." He turned to spear Colin and Jeremy with intense glances. "Never leave after saying what you believe is the unutterable. Always grovel. I was too …" He shook his head, his eyes filled with remorse as he stared sightlessly at the tabletop.

"What happened?" Florence asked.

"It was when I had returned home to find my family dead. As you know, I thought all of you had died in that fire, not just my brother and sister-in-law. Devastation doesn't begin to describe what I felt. I was desolate and filled with an unbearable despair. And then Delia and I fought. And I was vicious, spewing all my anger and pain at the death of my family onto her. And, for my folly, losing her."

"If you had apologized, she would have understood," Florence said.

"Some things you can never take back, Florence. And I was foolish enough to hire on with a different crew, leaving Boston immediately. I never returned until I was compelled to for business a few years ago."

"Is this why she changed toward me, when she realized I was a McLeod?" Florence asked.

"She'd have known there was some connection when she saw who escorted you. Jeremy looks too much like me for her to think otherwise," Aidan said, pinching the bridge of his nose. "To answer your question, yes. She's nurtured her resentment against me and all my kin, as though needing it as sustenance to be able to survive."

"Poor woman," Colin said.

"I wouldn't pity her. She separated me from my child, then took great joy in gloating about it. I have no sympathy for her," Savannah snapped, smearing at the tears on her cheeks. She accepted the handkerchief from Aidan and scrubbed at her face.

"Delia," Jeremy murmured. "I remember that name from when I was a little boy. I'd sneak out of bed and listen to you and Da talk late into the night. You spoke about her."

"Yes. With greater frequency. She was the only woman I contemplated giving up seafaring for. After the fire, I couldn't imagine any more changes in my life, not even for her."

"But you did settle down, Uncle. You have a successful business in San Francisco," Jeremy said with a frown.

"Only because I met another woman, six years later, who inspired a similar sentiment." He half smiled with regret. "We had two good years together."

"How did she die?" Colin asked.

"In childbirth. The babe died a few weeks later. Thus, Savannah, until I met Gabriel's Clarissa at that fancy soiree in your house in the Back Bay two years ago, I'd thought I was truly alone in this world. I'd thought my nephews, and everyone I'd ever loved, were dead or lost to me."

"But now you've found Delia again," Florence said. "Along with your nephews."

Aidan nodded absentmindedly, rose and grabbed his coat. "I'm glad Melinda is restored to you. I'm off for a ramble." He donned his hat and moved toward the hallway.

Jeremy followed him. "I feel like our roles have reversed, Uncle, where I'm the one worried about you for a change."

Aidan blew out a breath in a mirthless laugh.

"Come back for dinner tonight. I know Rich will want to see you."

"Don't waste your time worrying about an old man's folly, Jeremy." He shook his head as though he could dispel the regret roaring through him. "I'll return in a few hours."

Jeremy watched his uncle walk down the alley, his long lope quickly taking him from view before Jeremy shut the door.

CHAPTER 49

"SAVANNAH, HAVE YOU HEARD anything from Jonas since the newspaper stories came out?" Richard asked a few weeks later.

Savannah sat at one of the chairs around the table as Richard and Jeremy did the dishes. Her attempt to help had been declined, and she'd been relegated to a chair next to Florence, to enjoy the company of little Ian. Aidan sat silently at the head of the table, sipping a cup of coffee, while Melinda slept on the couch "I received a message from his lawyer that he is considering suing me for libel if I don't cease the publication of my stories in the papers," she said.

Florence rubbed a hand down little Ian's back. "Do you think he will follow through with his threat and sue you?"

"I doubt it. If he hasn't taken action after the stories that have already been published, I doubt he will now," Savannah said.

"Does he know you've discovered the location of your daughter?" Richard asked. He poured himself a cup of coffee and sat across from Florence.

"I doubt it. I also doubt he'd truly care," Savannah said, unable to hide her bitterness. "I have yet to hear from Mrs. Maidstone about the possibility of meeting my daughter."

"Well, as to that, Savannah," Aidan said, "I heard from Delia today. She's spoken with the parents who took in your daughter."

Savannah held herself rigid, her hands clasped in her lap. Jeremy reached out and gripped her hands, giving them a soft squeeze of support. "What did they say?" Savannah asked.

"They'd like to meet you tomorrow at the Home." Aidan watched her with compassion glinting in his blue eyes.

"Will they bring my daughter?" Savannah whispered.

"Most likely."

Savannah let out the breath she'd been holding, her posture wilting. Jeremy scooted his chair closer to hers, and she leaned into him.

"I'll be with you, Savannah," Jeremy murmured in her ear as she burrowed into him, tucking her head under his chin. "Thank you, Uncle."

Savannah straightened and swiped at the tears on her cheeks. "I can't believe tomorrow I could hold my daughter in my arms. She's fifteen months old, and I've never held her in my arms."

Aidan strummed his fingers on the table. "There is concern that your daughter will have become attached to her foster parents and that her return to you will not be an easy one."

"I fear that too. However, she is my daughter. I have every right to be with her."

"I know, Savannah, but you must be aware that you will be taking her from the only home she's ever known. She could act out."

She met the worried glances of everyone around the table. "I understand the concern. But I need to see my daughter. Hold her in my arms. Ensure she understands she was always wanted."

Florence nodded her understanding, blinking away tears. "No matter how much they love her, she needs to know her mother loves her and wants her. Always wanted her."

Richard gripped Florence's hand as everyone became silent for a moment.

"Tomorrow it is then, Savannah," Aidan said.

Savannah nodded, trepidation and anticipation filling her.

***

SAVANNAH ENTERED THE ORPHANAGE the following day flanked by McLeods. Aidan preceded her into the orphanage while Jeremy followed her. Savannah paused in front of Mrs. Maidstone's office, running a damp hand over her periwinkle blue wool skirt.

"Hello, Delia," Aidan said. "Are they here yet?"

Delia rose and met Savannah and Jeremy in the hallway. "They are in the private front room." She met Savannah's tormented gaze and Jeremy's glare with an implacable one, her shoulders tensing before she turned to walk past them, leading them back down the hallway to a closed oak door. She rapped on it twice before opening the door.

"Hello, Mr. and Mrs. Woodhouse. I would like to introduce you to Mrs. Savannah Montgomery."

Savannah moved into the room, her eyes scanning for her daughter. A robust man in his late thirties, wearing his Sunday-best suit, rose to stand in front of her, blocking her view of the woman sitting on the couch. He clutched his slightly tattered brown hat in his hands before handing it to the woman behind him. He nodded to Savannah, his piercing gaze of sleet-gray eyes roving over her fine dress. "Ma'am."

"It's lovely to meet you, Mr. Woodhouse," Savannah said. "Thank you for traveling to meet me."

"Does she, John?" Mrs. Woodhouse asked, concern evident in her voice.

"Yes, Harriett." Jeremy and Aidan shared a curious glance, but then Mr. Woodhouse stepped aside. "I believe you'd like to meet your daughter."

Savannah gasped and held a hand to her mouth as though she were holding in a sob. "Oh, oh, my baby." The child looked up at her, in complete ease on Mrs. Woodhouse's lap, her blue eyes a match for Savannah's. Her wispy hair was beginning to darken but still held a hint of the strawberry blonde she must have been for the first year.

Mrs. Woodhouse patted down the child's worn rose-colored dress. "I never believed our daughter's mother would come back to claim her. We thought her mother dead, her father unable to care for her, and that there was no other family."

"No, not dead. I was told by my husband that my baby had died," Savannah whispered as she moved to a chair near the settee. She reached out a finger to the girl and smiled as it was grasped tightly. "So strong," she marveled.

"Much stronger than any of us could realize," Mrs. Woodhouse said. "Why don't you sit next to me so she can accustom herself to you?"

Savannah sat next to her on the settee, her hand caressing her daughter's curls, her shoulders, her arm. The little girl smiled at her and reached forward to trace the shiny brooch on Savannah's dress.

"Why don't you hold her?" Mrs. Woodhouse kissed the child on her forehead and handed her to Savannah. The girl abandoned the brooch and began to play with a button on Savannah's dress before moving on to clasp an earring.

"I see you'll keep me on my toes, little darling," Savannah said as she tilted her head back. "What's her name?"

"We called her Hope. I know that might not be a fancy-enough name for you, but that's what she was to us," Mr. Woodhouse said. He clasped his wife's hand as he watched Savannah holding their daughter.

"What do you do?" Jeremy asked. At their curious stare, he said, "I'm Jeremy McLeod, and this is my uncle, Aidan. We're close friends to Mrs. Montgomery." He watched Savannah flinch at him calling her by that name, regretting the necessity of using it.

"I am a mason." His voice was laced with pride.

"A wonderful profession," Aidan murmured. "I imagine you're quite busy."

"Busy enough in Lowell," he said. "Although there are quite a few of us from my family and other families, so the work is becoming harder to come by."

Aidan and Jeremy nodded as they watched Savannah cradle her child, whispering things in her ear and tickling her belly. She beamed at Jeremy when Hope squealed her delight.

Mrs. Woodhouse, a plumpish woman with wheat-colored hair and inquisitive brown eyes, frowned as she watched Savannah. She twined her fingers together on her lap, her work-roughened fingers resting on a worn chocolate-colored dress. "We are concerned that our Hope will be exposed to, please forgive me, but to a scandalous life should she return to you. Your story is all anyone talks about."

Savannah blushed. "I understand your reticence, and I thank you for taking such good care of my daughter. I can assure you that I have no desire to expose her to ridicule."

"Although you yourself are the source of gossip? You plan to live with a man outside of marriage, if the papers are to be believed. How could this be a proper place for our Hope to grow up?" Mr. Woodhouse asked, his face reddening. "Marriage is a sacred commitment. One that should be honored and cherished."

"As long as both parties honor and cherish, I agree," Savannah said in a low voice. "However, when one of the pair fails to show such regard for their chosen mate, it leads to great suffering."

"As I explained to you first in my letter and then again when you arrived,

Mrs. Montgomery was unaware that her husband had given away her child. She has suffered as she mourned the loss of her child," Delia said.

"Is that the reason you left your husband? Because he lied to you?" Mrs. Woodhouse asked.

"No," Savannah said as she paled. She kissed the top of Hope's head, attempting to find solace from her child. "I left him because he attempted to break my spirit in every way imaginable. I finally realized I could fight for a different life or consign myself to a life of misery and succumb to the early death he envisioned for me."

"I find it very difficult to believe any man could be that cruel," Mr. Woodhouse sputtered. He reached over and grasped his wife's hand.

"Believe it," Jeremy and Aidan said at the same time.

"I've met Mr. Montgomery," Delia said, speaking in a hesitant voice as she broke the tense silence. "He seemed a man determined to obtain whatever it was he desired, in whatever manner he deemed necessary. I imagine he would have been a difficult man to be married to."

Savannah nodded her agreement.

"That does not condone abandoning your home and exposing your daughter, our daughter, who we consider a part of our family, to scorn. To ostracism by anyone of decency in society. We cannot countenance our beloved Hope to suffer such a future." Mrs. Woodhouse took a deep breath and squared her shoulders. "If we are to be expected to return her to you, then you must also be willing to make sacrifices. For giving her up will be the greatest sacrifice we have ever made."

Savannah watched them with a guarded expression, holding Hope so tightly that she squirmed and arch her back in protest. Savannah relaxed her arms, and Hope settled. "What sort of sacrifice do you want?"

"If you truly want your daughter back, then you must be willing to create a loving home environment for her. You must return to your husband so that she can be raised within the respectability of marriage."

Mrs. Woodhouse nodded her agreement to Mr. Woodhouse's decree.

"Never," Savannah whispered. "I will never return to him. And a loving home environment is not dependent upon my having a husband." Savannah raised her gaze to theirs with one filled with righteous defiance.

"Then we cannot agree to have our daughter returned to you," Mrs. Woodhouse said.

"She's my daughter," Savannah snapped as she rose, hitching Hope onto her hip "You have no right to keep her from me."

"We fostered her in good faith," Mr. Woodhouse said. "We've shown her nothing but love. She is our daughter now." Mr. Woodhouse rose and approached the door with a pointed look to his wife.

"Please," Savannah whispered as tears poured down her cheeks. Hope had begun to squirm to the point Savannah set her on the floor. Hope rose, gaining her balance and walking while holding onto objects, nearly teetering and falling along the way, until she reached Mrs. Woodhouse again. She smiled broadly and snuggled into her as she was lifted and settled onto her adoptive mother's lap. Savannah collapsed onto her knees on the floor, as she watched her daughter choose Mrs. Woodhouse over her.

"Mrs. Maidstone, we will take our leave of you." Mrs. Woodhouse rose. She paused as she watched Savannah, kneeling on the floor, a look of absolute dejection and hopelessness on her face, her shoulders racked with silent sobs. She stood with Hope on her hip, but, rather than turn toward her husband and leave the room, she moved toward Savannah.

She placed Hope on the floor and watched as the little girl toddled over to Savannah. Hope patted at Savannah's face, looking at her hands and laughing to find them wet. Savannah smiled blearily, reaching out to trace a loose tendril of her daughter's darkening strawberry-blond hair.

"Harriett," Mr. Woodhouse said from the doorway.

"Not yet, John," she said. She knelt on the floor and continued to watch Savannah. Savannah started as Jeremy touched her on the shoulder, a momentary flash of fear replaced by acceptance.

"What did he do to you, Mrs. Montgomery?" Mrs. Woodhouse asked. At Savannah's silence, she persisted. "You remind me of my sister," she whispered.

Savannah raised curious eyes to her, waiting for her to continue.

"My family and I believed she'd married a good man. A man who'd provide well for her. But he was a beast. Treated her abominably. Derived his greatest pleasure in hurting her. Until one day, he went too far." Her voice broke off. "We'd be condemning you to the same fate, wouldn't we, Mrs. Montgomery?"

"Yes," Savannah rasped as tears continued to leak out of her eyes.

"My husband never knew her. He never met him. It all occurred before we married." She took a stuttering breath. "I was raised to live a good life. A proper life. One deemed worthy by religion and society. I'm not one to go against the norms, Mrs. Montgomery." She sighed. "But you have given me much to consider."

She rose, turning to her husband. He nodded his agreement to her silent communication. "We will return to Boston in a few days as we continue to determine what would be the best course of action. I remain unconvinced that living in a household of scandal would be the best place to raise our Hope. Might we call again in a few days, Mrs. Maidstone?"

"Of course," Delia said.

"Thank you," Savannah whispered as she squeezed her daughter's hand one last time before Mrs. Woodhouse scooped her up. "Thank you for taking such good care of her."

"We shall see you soon," Mr. Woodhouse said as he ushered his wife out the door.

Jeremy settled next to her on the floor, pulling her into his arms. He scooted over until he was leaning against the settee and held a sobbing Savannah. When her sobs turned to gentle shudders, she finally spoke.

"They'll never let me have her, Jeremy." She burrowed into his embrace. "It's such a sweet torture holding her in my arms but knowing I'll not be the one to raise her."

"Hush, love. It's too early to know what they will and won't do. You must give them time to come to terms with losing the child they love." He kissed her forehead and rubbed his hands up and down her back in an attempt to impart comfort.

Delia sat in the chair across from them. "I'm relieved they didn't reject you out of hand, Mrs. Montgomery. For a moment I thought you'd lose all chance of seeing your daughter again."

"I wish there were a way all of you could have a hand in raising her. It appears they are doing a good job, and a child can never be surrounded by enough love," Aidan said.

Delia sniffed and rose. "I find I agree with Mr. McLeod. Now, if you'll excuse me, I must see to a few business matters." She departed, closing the door with a silent click and granting them privacy.

"Tell me what you need," Jeremy coaxed.

"I need time to consider what occurred and what might be the best for my daughter. She is with good people, and I don't want to harm her by taking her away from them."

"You're a good person and have every right to want to raise her," Jeremy said.

"Thank you." She blinked away tears. "She doesn't know me. And I fear tearing her away from them would only cause her pain."

"Florence would say that the greatest pain the child would suffer as she grew would be to think that her mother hadn't wanted her. I'd think you'd want to alleviate that for her," Aidan murmured.

Savannah nodded. "I know. However, the thought of causing her any pain is almost more than I can bear."

***

SAVANNAH NODDED an absent hello to Poole as he answered the door, handing her heavy wool coat, hat and gloves to him before walking up the stairs with Jeremy. They entered the front sitting room, well lit by lamps and warm with a fire roaring in the grate, to find Sophronia reading.

Sophronia's smile faltered as she looked Savannah over from head to foot. "You look wretched, Savannah." She shared a concerned glance with Jeremy. "Was Mrs. Maidstone incorrect in believing that girl to be your daughter?"

"No, she's my baby. She has my eyes. My mouth." Savannah bit back a sob and shook her head.

Sophronia raised an eyebrow and looked toward Jeremy for an explanation.

"It seems they are upstanding members of society and do not wish to see the daughter they've raised as their own exposed to ridicule by a woman living outside her marriage vows."

"Succinctly stated," Sophronia said. "Are they fools to believe you should return to that abomination of manhood?"

"At first I believed them to be, but then, as Mrs. Woodhouse was just about to leave, she shared that her sister had suffered at the hands of her husband and had died from his abuse. I think she might understand, although she worries about Hope." Jeremy stroked a hand down Savannah's quaking shoulder.

"Hope?"

"That's what they named my daughter," Savannah whispered.

Sophronia nodded. "An appropriate name, wouldn't you agree, Savannah dearest?" At Savannah's nod, Sophie sighed. "It appears to me that we need to find a way that she is raised by you, but that her foster parents remain involved in her life. Where do they live?"

"Lowell," Jeremy said. "And that's what my uncle said."

"He's sensible then." Sophronia frowned as she thought. "Lowell isn't that far away, but it's not nearly as convenient as someplace in the city. Would they be interested in moving?"

"I've no idea. He's a mason. He admitted work is harder to come by." Savannah rubbed at her eyes.

"Excellent," Sophronia said. "Then there's always a way to entice a man with the promise of a good job. Especially if that means he and his wife will not be separated from the child they've come to love as their own. For I imagine that is what they claim?"

"Yes, although I believe it to be more than a claim," Savannah said. "They were attached to her and her to them."

"That's how it should be," Sophronia said.

"I know. But it's hard to reconcile all the time I've lost with my daughter." Savannah rubbed at her temples. "Those first months when I believed she was dead and then all that time due to Mrs. Maidstone lying to me. I know Mrs. Maidstone is helping me now, but I lost nearly nine months with Adelaide … with Hope …because of that woman's deceit."

"Did you ever suspect, even for a moment, that she might have been threatened by your husband? You did mention, months ago, that you'd seen him in the North End. I wonder if he'd been calling on her."

"What could he possibly have said to her that would cause her to persistently lie and mislead us?" Jeremy asked.

"Fear is a tremendous motivator, as I'm sure you both understand. And we all have secrets, although we like to think we don't. Determine what he was using as leverage, and then you might find it within you to have a little more compassion for the woman." Sophronia sighed. "As for the Woodhouses, we must formulate a strategy that will entice them to our way of thinking."

***

"I THANK YOU, DELIA, for attempting to help Savannah." Aidan collapsed onto the hard wooden chair in front of her desk. "I can only imagine how much it meant to her to be able to hold her daughter."

"What would you do if you were to hold your daughter in your arms again?"

"Weep while I rejoiced," Aidan murmured, a distant look in his eyes. He shook his head as he focused on Delia. "But that's not to be. I held my dead infant daughter in my arms. I know she's lost to me."

"What was your wife like?" Delia blushed as the question burst forth, unintended.

"Tall, buxom, opinionated." He paused with a faint, fond smile as he remembered. "She had a vitality, an insurmountable amount of energy. Always saw everything in a positive manner. She wouldn't allow me to rot away in my office or warehouse. Insisted I participate in all the events she organized. She was very social, was never happier than when she was with her friends."

"She doesn't seem the type of woman you'd like." Delia frowned at his description.

"She forced me to embrace life, rather than wallow in my grief, as was my desire." His smile was bittersweet. "In fact she reminded me of you."

"Of me? She doesn't sound a thing like me," Delia sputtered.

"Well, I agree, not physically. But you were passionate like her. Full of life."

"Please, Aidan," Delia said as she held up her hand. "Please stop. Forget I asked such a foolish question."

"I'm glad you did. There remains too much between us that's unsettled."

"It's not possible to set to rights all that's wrong between us." Delia shuffled a pile of papers on her desk from one side to the other.

"I'd like the opportunity."

At his soft, emphatic words, she met his gaze. After a few moments—where she stared into his eyes, seeing regret, loneliness and hope—she shook her head, breaking eye contact. "Too much has happened, Aidan."

"Do you have someone else? A deep, dark secret that shames you?" he teased. "We're old enough, Delia, for honesty."

"I'm married to the orphanage. All my energy must go to the children here. I've nothing else to offer anyone."

"I refuse to believe a woman as vibrant as you is satisfied by this half-life. You must want more. You deserve more. If only you had the courage to seek it. That's an important lesson my wife taught me. The only limitations on our happiness are the ones we fasten for ourselves."

Delia flushed with anger. "You have no idea what my life is like. What it's been like. Don't you dare judge me and intimate that all I need do to fashion my own happiness is to imagine it, and it will blissfully appear. As though all I needed to do was stroke the lamp and harken the genie. Life isn't that simple, Aidan. Anyone who believes differently is a fool."

"Do you believe I don't know how hard it is to struggle every day to find happiness? I held my wife in my arms and watched her life's blood seep from her, impotent to aid her in any way. I watched as my infant daughter struggled for every breath she took until finally the struggle was too great, and she died. I know what it is to claw myself out of apparently insurmountable grief by my fingernails. And I won't be called a fool for believing I have the ability to create my own happiness."

He breathed out through his nose in an attempt to calm himself, a brilliant flush limning his cheeks and fire lighting his deep blue eyes. "If you truly believe I was in any way trying to demean you, or the life you've led since I left Boston sixteen years ago, you never knew me." He took a deep breath as he watched her with sorrow. "And I never knew you."

Delia's eyes filled with tears. "Of course you knew me. If you didn't, then who else besides my mother has ever truly seen me?"

Aidan studied her during a tense silence. "Where is my courageous Delia? The one who stood up to me and showed me what a fool I was? What happened to her?"

"She learned how cruel and unforgiving life could be. That the world is not kind to women who don't follow societal norms. It's better to be unremarkable than to be noticed and suffer for the attention."

"What happened to you?"

"I loved the wrong man." She met his gaze with a defiant tilt to her head.

He sat back in his chair as though he'd been struck. "Me?" When she remained silent he asked again, "Me?"

Her sorrow-filled eyes were her only response, and Aidan held a hand to his head. "There's no hope, is there, Delia?"

"None, as I attempted to tell you the last time you were here. Any association between the two of us is best come to an end."

He studied her with inscrutable eyes. "So you've said." He rose, heaving out a sigh. "I wish you a good day."

"Do I have your word you'll not return to the orphanage?"

"No, I can't make any promises when I can't see up from down." He paused at the door, waiting a moment before he faced her and murmured, "I've never believed I loved the wrong woman." He opened the door to the sound of her quiet sob.

CHAPTER 50

A LOW FIRE WAS LIT in the fireplace in the front parlor in the orphanage. Savannah moved from picture to picture, looking at the photos hanging on the wall. She paused at one, studying a girl standing in the second row. "Jeremy, look at this."

He approached her, tracing a hand down her arm until he laced his fingers with hers. "Yes?"

"Is this Florence?" Savannah asked as she pointed to the grainy picture and the girl.

He leaned forward, squinting at the photograph. "I think so. I'd have to ask her to be certain, but I don't know as she'll ever want to return here."

Savannah spun to face the door as it opened. Mrs. Maidstone entered with the Woodhouses. Mrs. Woodhouse carried little Hope. Mrs. Maidstone nodded to Savannah and then backed out of the room, closing it behind her, granting them privacy.

Hope squirmed when Mrs. Woodhouse stopped walking and was set down. Savannah knelt, calling out to her. Hope walked to her, her short legs tottering a little until she found her balance. She then moved with amazing speed.

Savannah held out her arms, and Hope approached her, watching her with curiosity. Hope reached out, tugging on Savannah's sparkling bracelet before tracing the pink glass. She gurgled something to Savannah, smiling as she climbed onto her lap. Savannah laughed, tilting her head backward to keep Hope from pulling too hard on her matching earrings. She reached up, unfastening them and handing them to Jeremy, who slid them into his pocket.

Hope frowned, reaching forward to trace Savannah's ear, pulling on her now bare earlobe. Savannah giggled at her feather-light touch.

"That tickles, darling," Savannah said, reaching to tickle Hope's belly. Hope chortled with glee, arching her back and squirming. After a moment, Savannah stopped, leaning forward to hug her and kiss her on her forehead.

Hope pushed away and began to explore the room. Savannah glanced toward the Woodhouses and saw them studying her. She smiled and then turned to watch her daughter.

Mrs. Woodhouse moved to a settee with her husband standing behind her. "It is good to see you again, Mrs. Montgomery."

"Although the scandal only seems to grow with each new day," her husband said. "How many newspaper articles are there?"

"Quite a few I'm afraid," Savannah said as her daughter returned and crawled onto her lap. She curled up and fell asleep, allowing Savannah the opportunity to lean over and kiss her head.

"Why would you court such notoriety?" Mr. Woodhouse asked. "I've tried to understand. I can comprehend leaving a violent man. However, I'd think you'd want it done as quietly as possible. I wouldn't think you'd court infamy."

"It was either I told them my story or they reported falsehoods, and I'd never have the opportunity to speak my truth." Savannah took a deep breath, appearing to calm as she stroked her daughter's silky hair.

"Even if the notoriety means you will lose access to your daughter?" Mr. Woodhouse asked.

Savannah jerked, her ministrations to her daughter pausing for a moment before restarting again. "I'd like to think we could come to some sort of understanding."

"John," Mrs. Woodhouse said in a firm tone. "What my husband is attempting to say, in his blundering way, is that we remain concerned that your reputation will harm dear Hope."

"I understand your concern."

"That is why we cannot allow her to be returned to you to be raised by you," Mrs. Woodhouse said.

"Please," Savannah whispered.

"We can't allow it until the time arises that you are a married woman living with your husband. If that were to occur with Mr. McLeod, that would be acceptable. You'd still have the tarnish of divorce, with a tinge of notoriety associated to you, but you'd be within the respectable societal norms."

"I see," Savannah whispered. She bent over Hope, rocking to and fro. "Does this mean this is the last time I'll see her until things are settled?"

Mr. Woodhouse set a hand on his wife's shoulder, but she spoke. "No. I've spoken at length with John, and I believe you should play a role in Hope's life. If not as her mother raising her, then as her aunt visiting her. Lowell isn't that far away, what with the trains."

"I see," Savannah repeated. "I'd hoped you'd be willing to move to Boston."

"No, ma'am," Mr. Woodhouse said. "There's little that could entice me to live in this big city. I like Lowell just fine. We have family there, and my work will likely pick up again, like it always does as the spring nears."

"I'm happy for you, sir." Savannah cleared her throat as her voice had thickened. "When can I see her again?"

"We plan to return to Boston in a few weeks. Why don't we meet at your friend's house?" Mrs. Woodhouse said.

"The first part of March," Savannah said. "Yes, that would work nicely." She kissed Hope one last time as Mr. Woodhouse moved from behind the couch to lift her in his arms.

"She's been sleepier than usual lately," Mrs. Woodhouse said with a smile. "I think she must be growing."

"I look forward to seeing you in a few weeks," Savannah whispered as they moved toward the door. She remained on the floor watching, even after the door clicked shut.

Jeremy sat in the chair behind her. "Are you all right, Savannah?"

"I'm attempting to discover my courage to face Jonas in court."

"Your daughter means that much to you?" Jeremy stroked a hand down the side of her neck.

She saw his selfless concern and also his personal hurt in his eyes. "You do too, Jeremy. But no one's told me that I'm barred from you unless I divorce him." She leaned into his touch. "For if they did, I fear I might have done far more than publish articles in a newspaper. I can't imagine being separated from you." She whispered into his ear, "Do you think you could love her, Jeremy? I know she's not yours, but I hope you can."

Jeremy joined her on the floor, embracing her. "Put that fear to rest, my sweet Savannah. I'll have no trouble loving little Hope." His voice shone with wonder and happiness as he said, "A part of me already does. I'm sorry you've thought me indifferent to her, but I haven't wanted to interrupt the time you have with her by joining you."

"Thank you, Jeremy. I don't know how many times I can manage the separation from her."

"The Woodhouses seem like decent people. They want you to be a part of her life, and that's a start." He held her closer. "I think they fear losing her as much as you're eager to recover her."

Savannah sighed her agreement, kissed him on his chest and then pushed to rise. He helped her to a standing position and rose with easy grace. "Let's enjoy this day," Savannah said as she slipped her arm through his.

"Will you join me at the workshop for a while?" He opened the door, holding it for her as she walked through it first. "We'll have to search out food at some point, but I'd love to have you in my shop. We haven't had time to speak about our place recently."

"When will we be able to move in?" Savannah asked, looping her arm through his as they walked down busy streets.

"Hold that thought," Jeremy said as he ducked into a baker's shop. Savannah followed him in and stood behind him, watching him laugh and talk with the owner as he purchased both sweet and savory items. She closed her eyes, inhaling the scent of rising dough, of bread in the oven, all tinged with a mixture of licorice and chocolate. She sighed as she breathed deeply again.

"Ciao, Signora Castellini," Jeremy said as he grasped Savannah's hand, and they left. "It's as though all your cares fall away when you enter their shop. Don't you agree?" Jeremy asked.

"I've never smelled anything so delicious," Savannah whispered.

"When we left my aunt's house, Gabriel said that our visits to the bakery had to end. Somehow he always managed to scrounge together enough money to buy us one treat a week. Eventually he gave one of us the money so that every third week, we had the chance to choose the treat for all of us. That was my favorite day. Knowing I could go into that shop and be surrounded by that glorious food."

"And see Mrs. Castellini," Savannah murmured.

"Even then she was motherly. The best times were when one of us entered the shop and no one else was there. We'd often linger and act as though we didn't know what we wanted just to ensure we had the shop to ourselves."

"Why?"

"Because she'd slip a little something extra in the bag. When she realized the three of us were related, which didn't take her long as we all look alike and she's smart, she began to slip in three macaroons."

"She sounds like a lovely woman," Savannah said.

"She is. She one day apologized, saying they were the previous day's cookies, but Gabe, Rich and I didn't care. They were treats. And someone was showing us kindness." He sighed as he looked at the busy intersection near Haymarket for a way to easily cross the street. "It wasn't often anyone showed us three orphan boys a kindness."

He looked down at her and frowned, raising a hand to stroke her cheek. "Why the tears, darling?"

"I hate the thought of anyone treating you cruelly. You never deserved it."

"I know." His thumb continued to caress her cheek. "I realized, when I met Florence, no matter how rough I had it, that at least I had Gabe. He protected me from the worst aspects of life. She was left to fend for herself, at about the same age I lost my parents."

Savannah lowered her head, breaking eye contact.

"What is it, darling?"

"I'm continually ashamed at how I abused Florence to Clarissa before I married Jonas. I was awful."

"You were fortunate enough to change into the woman you were meant to be. Feel pride, Savannah. I know Florence bears you no ill will."

Savannah sniffed and turned to face the intersection, her brow furrowing. "How are we to cross?"

"I think we need to race to the middle trolley stand and then regroup before we race to the other side. Are you up for it?" he asked with a gleam of delight in his eyes. "Careful with your skirts."

"Yes," Savannah said, giving out a small whoop as Jeremy gripped her hand and they raced first toward the center of the intersection and then to the other side.

"Oh, that was exhilarating," Savannah gasped when they stood on the opposite side of the intersection.

They began the short walk to his workshop. "Returning to your earlier question, the first apartment I'd hoped to rent suffered water damage when there was a fire next door. We were supposed to move in the first part of March, but now that's impossible."

"And I can't imagine you'd want to live there," Savannah said. She gripped his arm gently. "Too many memories."

"Yes. It was close to where I'd lived with my parents and where we suffered the fire. It would have been difficult to live there." He squeezed her hand. "I'd hoped to have us in a place by early March so we could celebrate your birthday in our new home."

"Jeremy, that doesn't matter. I don't particularly like celebrating my birthday."

"What was your last birthday like before you had Hope?"

"Clarissa was still in Boston, but she was never invited to our house. Jonas loved having large parties while I dangled on his arm as though I were some sort of prize. I'd just stand there and nod, smile when something clever was said. Or when the person who said it thought they'd been clever."

"It sounds boring."

Savannah laughed. "Oh, it's freeing to admit it was. I hated every second of it. And I hated that birthday the most. For some reason, Jonas decided we should have a costume ball to celebrate my birthday. And since my birthday is March 15, that it should be Roman inspired."

"So that people could stab each other in togas and act like they were killing Caesar?"

"Exactly. By the end of the night, I'd hoped someone had actually brought a real sword and would stab Jonas." Savannah shuddered as she thought about that evening.

"Well then, no birthday celebration similar to that. I imagine we'd have a cake and quiet time with family."

"That sounds perfect," Savannah said as she squeezed his arm.

"As for our home, I've found another place, but it won't be available until May first."

"That's fine. I'm eager to start my life with you, but I can wait. Now that the stories are in the newspaper, we no longer have to worry about newspapermen. It's not as though there's much of a scoop to say that I'm an unhappy woman living outside the bounds of marriage."

"I'd sue them for using the word unhappy. For I've never seen you more radiant."

***

"DELIA," AIDAN SAID as he knocked on her door, poking his head in, noting another woman in the room with Delia. "I beg your pardon. I didn't mean to interrupt." He stilled his movement in the doorway, as though poleaxed, studying the young woman in front of him. She attempted to scoot around him and out of the room, but he blocked the only exit from the office. He reached forward and gripped her arm, causing her to look up at him in confusion.

He glanced at Delia, noting her pale expression and worried eyes. However, the young woman fascinated him, and he focused on her again. She was tall for a woman, nearly reaching his shoulders in height and had straight black hair tied back in a bun. Her bright blue eyes flashed with irritation, and her high cheekbones were flushed.

"If you'd let me pass, sir," she said in a soft voice.

Aidan shook his head, kicking the door shut with one foot and inviting the girl to sit. He looked toward Delia, catching a glimmer of fear before she steeled herself into expressionlessness.

"Delia?" he demanded. "Is there anything you'd wish to explain?"

"Let her leave, Aidan. She has her chores to do."

"Do you live here? Are you an orphan?" Aidan asked, clutching his hands to his side.

"Of course not," the young woman said. "I live with my mother, Mrs. Maidstone, in the small apartment at the rear of the orphanage."

Delia groaned softly and closed her eyes. "Zylphia, will you please leave us?"

"Zylphia," Aidan murmured, his eyes taking in her stature, impeccable posture and work-roughened hands. He watched as she shut the door behind her before spinning to face Delia. "How could you? How could you have our child and never tell me?"

"Keep your voice down," she hissed. "I'm a respectable widow, raising my only daughter alone under difficult circumstances."

He slammed his hands on the desk, causing the inkstand to bounce and topple over. She gasped, righting it and placing paper on top of the spilled ink to blot it. "Who is Mr. Maidstone? Did you trick him into marrying you, knowing you were carrying my child?"

She glared at him. "There was never any Mr. Maidstone. What was I supposed to do? You left!"

"Delia—for what, fifteen, sixteen years?—you've had the raising of her, and you never thought to tell me? To ask for my help? How could you think so little of me? Of what we shared?"

"You refused to stay. I begged you. I needed you here, but you wouldn't stay. Roaming the seas was more important to you than me. Than our child."

"Dammit, I didn't know we were to have a child. How could I have suspected? You promised me that you'd tell me if you needed my help."

"And you promised you'd stay, give up seafaring, if ever I asked. And you refused. That's the value of your promise, Aidan McLeod."

"I was out of my mind with grief. My family was dead. I couldn't believe all I'd lost, and you were indifferent to it. Then suddenly it seemed I was losing you too." He moved around her desk, and she swiveled to face him. He knelt in front of her, clasping one of her hands in his. "I would never have left had I known."

"Don't say that. Don't turn this into my fault," she said as she blinked furiously to prevent tears from falling. "I needed you to stay for me. If you only stayed for the child, what would you have done had something happened to the baby? Then you'd have resented me and been resigned to living a life with a woman you didn't want."

"I would have thought you'd known how much I wanted you in my life by the number of times we snuck out of your mother's house," Aidan said. He reached forward but dropped his hand as she flinched at his touch. "I can't believe you consigned our child to a life working in an orphanage, fatherless, because of your pride." He rose, pacing away, any concern turning into anger.

"How could you sit there and ask me how I'd feel if I were to hold my daughter in my arms again when you knew I had a living child? A child who stares at me as though I were a stranger. I'm her father. She should never doubt that I'd cherish her. Love her." He exhaled, sitting heavily into the chair again and staring at Delia as though seeing her for the first time.

"How could you be so cruel as to not tell me? I've been back for weeks, and you never thought I had the right to know?"

"How was I to know you wouldn't leave again? That you would concern yourself for her?"

He slammed his hand against the chair, then rose, kicking it viciously. "Because you should know me. You should have understood, watching me with my nephew Jeremy, hearing my stories. You should have listened, truly listened, and understood how much I value family. Instead, you've held your old hurts to your heart, refusing to grant me an opportunity to know my own child."

"Don't look at me like that," Delia pleaded.

He raised an eyebrow and waited for her to continue.

"Not as though you despise me."

"I do. At this moment, I do." He took a deep breath. "The last time I was in Boston, I left with horrible words between us, and I fear the same could occur again." He took a deep breath, closing his eyes and unclenching his fists. "Only you, Delia, have ever been able to move me to such anger."

"That's another reason we shouldn't be together."

"I disagree. I've never felt more alive than when I'm irritated or challenged by you." He paused, and Delia saw the pain in his eyes. "And I've never felt a greater agony than upon realizing you still don't trust me and that you might never trust me."

Delia closed her eyes, a resigned sigh escaping her. "Aidan, I wrote you. I sent letters on ships leaving Boston, asking them to be delivered to you. I spoke with your Captain McIntyre. I never heard a word. I thought you'd died."

"You tried to tell me? You wrote me?" he asked, unable to hide the eager desire from his voice to find some way to vindicate her actions.

Delia met his gaze, hers shattered while his was hopeful. "Yes. I wrote a few weeks after our argument. Even though I hated you for the things you'd said to me, my mother insisted I write you. She said, no matter what happened, it would bring me peace because I would know I'd done all I could for my child." Delia lowered her head for a moment before meeting Aidan's eyes again.

"When I never heard from you, I convinced myself it was because you had died. I couldn't bear to believe it was because you no longer wanted me. That you'd forsake your child. I invented Mr. Maidstone, dead at sea. I knew enough of what seafaring life was like from your stories to concoct credible tales about our marriage. And I found a way to survive."

"I swear, on my brother's grave, I never received your letters. And when

I left in such haste after our fight, I joined the crew of Captain Aloysius. I never saw Captain McIntyre again." Aidan clamped his jaw for a moment. "I want my daughter to know me."

"Aidan, what good will it do her to know you when her entire life she has believed her father dead? You refused to remain here, and this is our life."

"How can you want so little from your life?" He leaned forward with his hands on his knees, watching her with a keen intensity.

"When you stop wishing for more, you become content with what you have."

"Well then, maybe that's why I've never been content, because I always want more. I want my daughter to be a part of my life. I will not bend on this, Delia." He rubbed his forehead, unable to hide the incredulousness he felt. "I want to have dinner with the two of you. During that dinner, if I deem it appropriate, I will tell her who I am."

Delia flushed, glaring at him and slamming a book on her desk. "Will you listen to yourself? It's all about what you want and what you'll do. It's nothing to do with what I might want or need. Nothing about us. Can't you understand I've raised her for fifteen years and sharing her with you now will be …"

"Difficult," Aidan said with a gentle smile.

"Heart wrenching," Delia whispered. "She's the one thing in my life I did well. I refuse to allow you to take her away from me."

Aidan frowned. "I'll never try to separate you from our daughter, sweetheart. I just want to have the opportunity to know her. To be a part of her life."

Delia blinked away tears, rising to turn to stare at the bookshelf in the room.

"Why are you afraid?" Aidan rose, touching her shoulders in a whisper-soft caress. When she leaned backward slightly, Aidan traced patterns down her stiff back.

"That she'll want your world more than mine and leave me. Then forget about me," Delia admitted in a hoarse whisper.

Aidan gripped her shoulders and spun her to face him. He grasped her chin between his fingers. "If she's anything like you, it'll take more than a nice meal out and a few sweet words to charm her. She'll be loyal and stead fast." He pulled Delia into his embrace, holding her as she cried. "I'd never attempt to take her away from you, Delia. I know you have little faith in my promises, but I do promise you that."

CHAPTER 51

"LUCAS, WILL YOU PLAY something for us?" Savannah asked as she settled on a settee near the fire. She wrapped her ivory shawl more closely around her shoulders, covering the rose-colored wool of her fitted gown.

"Yes, Lucas, why don't you play the new song you performed last night? I thought it was quite good," their father said. He settled into his gentleman's chair, and reached out his hand for Matilda's but was ignored.

"I can't believe you wouldn't dress better for your own birthday celebration," Matilda hissed as she watched Savannah take in the changes in the room.

"I have to learn to live within my means now, Mother, and they aren't as extensive as they once were." Savannah stroked a hand down her skirts. "This is a comfortable, fashionable and practical dress."

"You should want more from life than that. I taught you better than that." Matilda's eyes flashed their displeasure.

"You attempted to teach me to look for gold in tarnished tin. I know better now, Mother," Savannah said. She closed her eyes as Lucas played, ignoring her mother's persistent glare.

"Savannah, how is our granddaughter?" Martin asked.

"I believe she is well. I haven't seen her for a few weeks because she has been ill and unable to travel. Her foster parents write me as often as they can, and I just received word that it appears she is recovering. I'm hopeful to see her in a few days."

"When can we meet her?" Martin asked, unable to hide his eagerness. Matilda made a small grunting noise of displeasure.

"I'd think the next time I see her, you'd be able to meet her, Father. And you also, Lucas," Savannah said with a smile. Lucas played a joyous tune and winked at Savannah.

"I'd hardly consider attending a meeting with those who should never have had a hand in raising her proper. She should be with you, in your home, with her father," Matilda said.

"I refuse to cause my daughter further torment by separating her from those who have raised and loved her as their own. Although I want her with me, I will find a way so that all of us are satisfied with the arrangement," Savannah said. She smiled as Lucas played a gentle child's lullaby as she spoke.

"The only satisfactory arrangement is for you to make your home with your husband," Matilda snapped.

"Never," Savannah rasped. "That was never my home and will never be again."

"How are your plans with Mr. McLeod?" Lucas asked, a tune mimicking the wedding march sounding from the piano.

"They are proceeding. I'll move in with him soon," Savannah said.

"Savannah, don't do this to the family," her mother implored.

"After what she has suffered, she should be free to determine her own fate," her father said with a severe frown at his wife.

"She will never be free of the scandal! How can you be so selfish?" Matilda asked as she leaned forward in her chair, her jaw clenched tightly as she bit back even harsher words.

"Matilda, you know we've discussed this. Savannah and our granddaughter will always be welcomed here, no matter their living arrangements. Their safety and happiness are of our utmost concern," Martin said with a hint of steel in his voice.

"So you decree. But I will never believe it. And I will never believe Jonas intentionally sent away your daughter," Matilda said as her lips turned down in a frown.

Savannah shook her head in wonder. "I should no longer be amazed at your callous disregard for me, and yet, every time, it's as though you pierce my heart with a thousand pinions."

Savannah held a hand to her forehead, taking a deep breath. "Lucas, will you play me something joyful? Something to help me celebrate my birthday?"

"Of course, Sav. And I can't wait to be a doting uncle," he said with a wink. Lucas began playing "Bill Bailey, Won't You Please Come Home?" He inflected humor into the lyrics, while playing the piano and repeating piano solo pieces.

Savannah and her father clapped and gave small cheers when Lucas finished with a flourish. "Well done, Lucas!" Savannah said as he sat back from the piano, and the fierce concentration left him, focusing again on the room rather than the piano. "I agree with Sophie. You are wasting your talents only performing for us. They should be shared with a wider audience."

Lucas smiled, flexing his fingers and massaging them as he relaxed.

"An interesting thought, Savannah," Martin said. "I—"

"Isn't this a heartwarming scene?" Jonas said as he strolled into the room.

Savannah started at the sound of his voice, tensing for a moment before trying to relax. "This is a family gathering. You are not welcome." She tilted her head up with defiance, refusing to show him any fear.

"Ah, then I'm sure I'm most welcome as I am still a part of this family. Aren't I, Mrs. Russell?" Jonas said as he approached Savannah.

Lucas sprang up from the piano seat, moving to sit beside Savannah.

"Matilda?" Martin asked. "Were you aware he was to visit tonight?"

"I am tired of the gossip surrounding our family, Martin. I've told you again and again that I will never agree with your decrees about Savannah and her life. It is time Savannah returned to her husband, as is her duty. Especially now that she has her daughter back." Matilda sat with a rigid posture, her mouth turned down in what was becoming her customary countenance.

Jonas pinned Savannah with a severe glare, looking around as though for his daughter.

"She's not here, Jonas," Lucas hissed.

"I see you continue to be the unreasonable woman I discovered you to be after our unfortunate marriage. I'd have thought you'd be thankful for my sparing you the presence of such a ... creature in your life." He glowered at Savannah.

"Hope is a beautiful girl, and I'm only thankful she's been spared being raised by someone like you." Savannah clamped her jaw shut to hide its trembling.

"Brave words, wife," Jonas said as he slapped his gloves against his palm, each cracking sound of leather against flesh eliciting a flinch in Savannah.

Martin stood, standing next to the settee where Savannah and Lucas sat.

"You are not welcome here. Savannah and her daughter will never return to you, no matter how you may have been led to believe otherwise by my wife. I ask you to leave."

Jonas's expression lightened to one of mocking amusement. "You mistakenly believe because you outmaneuvered me with regard to your business loans that you have some influence over my personal life. You are under the impression you have any say in the matter of whether Mrs. Montgomery, my wife, returns home with me or not. You have none. She is mine, to do with as I please. And it pleases me to have her at home with me. You granted me that distinction when you gave me her hand in matrimony."

"Consider it rescinded," Martin snapped. "I will not have a maniacal, brutal man near my daughter again. I will not have you anywhere near my granddaughter. Do you understand me?"

"Do you truly believe that one such as you can act against one such as me?" Jonas smirked as he watched Savannah who had begun to tremble on the settee. "Mrs. Montgomery, come here. Now."

His low, harsh words provoked a shudder and whimper in Savannah. She raised tormented eyes to him, but, rather than the defeated look he was accustomed to, she smiled with defiance. "Never. You may have been able to control me in the past with your threats and brute force, but never again. I would rather die than return to that house with you."

Jonas appeared amused. "Interesting you should say that, my dear." He extracted a small pistol, pointing it at her. "You are returning with me now." He pointed it at her and then to a spot next to him. "Come along. I've had all I can take with the newspaper stories and the loss of esteem among my business partners from your errant ways. You have much to repent for."

"Mr. Montgomery, you would never act in such a way," Matilda stammered. She paled as Jonas waved the gun around.

"I warned you that he was such a man, Matilda, but you wouldn't listen," Martin growled. He continued to focus all his attention on Jonas. "You believe you can march in here, on my daughter's birthday, and ruin our celebration? You are mistaken." He moved toward Jonas, placing himself between Jonas and Savannah, causing Jonas to back up a few steps. "Leave, now, before I call the police and file charges against you."

"Hey, Sav. Sorry I'm—" Colin stopped abruptly, his glance moving from Jonas to his uncle to Savannah, and then to Lucas on the settee, partially obscured by Martin. "Is that a gun?" He paled, putting up his hands as Jonas veered the gun toward him for a moment. "Whoa. Calm down, Jonas."

"Calm down. Calm down? After months of being played a fool by my worthless wife, you're telling me that I must continue to suffer due to her perfidy? You are to come home now, madam!" he yelled, swinging to face her again, pointing his gun in her direction. Her father moved to block her completely from Jonas's view.

"Do you have any idea what it's been like, living with such an infamous wife? Reading the sickening lies in the paper of my purported abuse? You knew how you were to behave, and any aberration warranted punishment." In his agitation he was nearly panting. He swung the gun in a constant arc from Matilda to Colin, keeping all of them within his sight. "You should have known your role rather than run away to an unnatural woman who doesn't know her place.

"And then, to read that you are replacing me with a man not even worthy to clean your boots? How could a woman I chose as my wife deign to allow such a man near her?" He shook with fury as he spoke of Jeremy. "I repeat, you are to cease your rebellion and return to me this instant!" In his agitation, he pulled the trigger, shooting Martin. Martin gasped, grabbing at his chest as he crumpled to the floor, a stream of blood seeping onto the carpet.

"Father!" Savannah screamed, unaware in her concern for her father that she was now fully exposed to Jonas. Lucas jumped up, pushing Savannah down onto the floor, covering her as Colin attempted to wrestle the gun from Jonas.

"Let go, you fool!" Colin growled. "You've already shot an innocent man. Don't make it worse than it is." He and Jonas were in a sort of primitive dance, continuously circling, bending, and bowing as one of them tried to obtain the upper hand.

"Father," Savannah whimpered, reaching a hand out to him. She grabbed his arm in an attempt to impart some sort of comfort.

"Stay down," Lucas grunted, grabbing her arm and forcing her to curl in on herself. He pushed her backward, in a futile attempt to push her under the settee.

Another shot rang out, and plaster fell on top of them from the ceiling. Colin shook his head to clear his eyes and attempted to keep Jonas's arm pointed upward as they continued to scrapple. However, Jonas kicked Colin in his thigh, and he momentarily lost the battle to keep Jonas's arm raised. The gun lowered, and another shot rang out.

Colin glanced up to see Lucas clutching his side. He continued to fight Jonas for control of the weapon but was unable to wrest it away from him.

"Lucas!" Savannah screamed, pushing him to his uninjured side.

"No, Sav," Lucas protested weakly, "stay down. Stay protected."

Colin's grip on Jonas firmed, and he fought with a lethal intensity. "God dammit, you're going to hell for what you're doing to my family."

Jonas sneered at him and then gasped, releasing his grip on the gun. He fell to his knees, a groan emerging. Colin wrested the gun from his lax fingers and blanched at the blood blooming under Jonas's right rib cage. Jonas gasped for air, small droplets of blood gurgling forth with each breath.

Colin spun to see Savannah standing, dazed and yet determined, a sharp letter opener in the shape of a dagger in her hand. She gripped it tightly, watching Jonas. "Never threaten me or my family again," she rasped before dropping it and turning to kneel in front of her father and brother.

"Don't worry about me, Sav," Lucas whispered. "It's just a nick." He reached a hand out to his father. "Father?" He grasped his hand.

Savannah leaned over her father, pressing her previously pristine ivory shawl onto his shoulder wound. She grimaced as he hissed with the pain. "I'm sorry, Father, but we have to stop the flow of blood." She remained focused on her father and Lucas, who held first his and then Colin's hand-kerchief to the wound in his side, ignoring the chaotic bustle of servants around them. She resisted firm, competent hands easing her aside until she realized it was the doctor.

"Mrs. Montgomery, perhaps you should tend your husband," he said with gentle reproach.

"Help my father and brother, please," Savannah said, releasing her hold on her shawl. She rose, grasping Colin's arm for support as her shock-weak-ened legs buckled. She continued to ignore Jonas's prostrate form on the ground. Colin led her to a side table with a pitcher of clean water and helped her wash her hands and wiped away a smudge of blood from her cheek.

"They will be conveyed to the hospital," the doctor intoned. "The am-bulance is here, and the hospital is only a short distance away."

"Thank God the servants had the presence of mind to call the police and send for the doctor," Colin murmured as he watched the doctor tend

Lucas and his uncle.

"What more can be done for them?" Matilda asked, coming out of her momentary shock.

"Pray infection doesn't set in," the doctor said, as he nodded to Colin to help him carry first Martin and then Lucas. When they were both in the ambulance and ready to go to the hospital, the doctor said, "There's no need to come to the hospital until tomorrow. All that can be done for them will be done."

When Colin arrived upstairs, he found the police officers circling the room. A sheet had been draped over Jonas.

"Would you care to explain, ma'am, how your husband died?" an officer asked. He held a small book in one hand and a sharpened pencil in the other, while watching her with unveiled fascination.

"He interrupted my birthday celebration with my family, charging in here with a gun. Demanding I return home with him. He shot my father. My cousin, Mr. Sullivan, attempted to free him of his gun, but he shot again, wounding my brother. I ..."

Savannah took a deep breath and met Colin's worried gaze. He nodded to her and smiled gently. "I speared him with the letter opener." She bit her lip at the pride-infused words. "I meant to hit him in his shoulder, but he stumbled, and it hit him lower."

"You murdered your husband," the policeman said. "You're admitting it."

"On the Ides of March," his colleague muttered.

"I was acting in self-defense," she whispered. "He had already attempted to kill my father and brother and was determined to come for me."

The policeman read the name she'd supplied and then studied her. "You're the one who left her husband due to mistreatment. The one the newspapers are full of."

"Yes."

The policeman sighed and turned to his partner. "I'm sorry, ma'am, but we must bring you in, for further questioning and to ensure you don't attempt to flee."

Savannah paled. "Please, not a jail. I've done nothing but protect myself."

"I'm sorry, ma'am," the policeman repeated as he reached forward and grasped her arm, pulling her firmly toward the hallway. "If you cooperate, I won't handcuff you."

Savannah nodded, attempting to forestall tears, and stumbled as she was propelled by the two policemen.

"As for you," the policeman nodded to Colin and Matilda, "I'd plan to remain in Boston for the foreseeable future. You were witnesses and will need to be questioned further."

Colin followed them down the stairs to the front door, grim faced as he watched Savannah led into a paddy wagon. "Where are you taking her?"

"The county jail. She'll have a private cell there."

Colin bristled at the image of Savannah in a cell. "Expect a vocal contingent of supporters tomorrow morning," Colin said and attempted to smile reassuringly to Savannah.

Savannah held up a hand, through the bars of the enclosed rear of the wagon. Colin gripped her fingertips, giving them a squeeze for courage. "I'll see you soon, Sav."

"Tell Jeremy," she said through tears. "Tell him ..."

"Never fear. You aren't alone, and we'll ensure you're released almost as soon as those doors are closed." He released her fingers as the wagon rolled away, watching its departure with a burning anger.

CHAPTER 52

AIDAN STOOD IN THE FOYER to the Parker House Hotel, awaiting the arrival of Delia and Zylphia. He practiced again and again what he wanted to say to Zylphia, but, the more he thought of his daughter, the more muddled the words became. Bright light shone from numerous chandeliers onto the rich wood in the foyer. Gold-framed mirrors along the hallway reflected the light, enhancing the warm glow.

"Mr. McLeod," Delia said from behind him.

He spun to face her, surprise and then delight shining from his eyes. "Mrs. Maidstone, Miss Maidstone," he murmured. "I am delighted you were able to join me for dinner." He watched as both Delia and Zylphia paused to stare at the fine furnishings in the lobby. "Shall we?" he asked, ushering them toward the dining room.

Delia and Zylphia removed their coats before following the waiter to the table set in a small nook to one side of the large dining room. Other patrons sat scattered throughout the room, but at discrete distances from each other, allowing privacy.

"Why are we having dinner with you?" Zylphia asked, after she accepted a menu from the waiter. She attempted not to gape at the splendor of the dining room with its marble pillars, coffered ceilings and mahogany paneling.

Aidan grinned at her sharp question. "One reason would be that I know you had a birthday last week, and it seemed a shame not to celebrate it."

Zylphia frowned as she studied the refined man in the impeccable clothes. "Why should you care about my birthday? No one bothers about someone living in an orphanage turning sixteen."

445

Aidan shared a long look with Delia, who nodded subtly, granting her consent. "I knew your mother many years ago. Unfortunately we parted in anger, and I did not know she was to be the mother of my child."

Zylphia frowned, looking from her mother, who was playing with her silverware, to Aidan, sitting with forced calm across from her. "You are mistaken. My father is dead, sir."

"I am not dead, Zylphia," Aidan said fervently. "I only learned of your existence yesterday. And, if you cared to look for it, the family resemblance is impossible to ignore."

"Where have you been for sixteen years?" Zylphia demanded, leaning forward as her blue eyes flashed their anger.

"First I was away at sea, and then I've been in San Francisco," Aidan said.

"You abandoned my mother, and now you've finally returned, thinking your sweet words and money will woo us to want to be with you?" She glared at him. "I've never been in need of a father, and I have no need of one now."

"Zylphia," Delia said, unable to fight the tremor in her voice, "this is not Aidan's fault. He never knew he was to be a father."

"I know you, Mother, and you must have had a good reason." She turned to Aidan with a fierce scowl. "Did you treat her badly? Have another woman on the side?"

Aidan blanched, while Delia sighed. She glanced at Aidan apologetically. "It's one of the disadvantages of having been raised in the backrooms of an orphanage. She's been exposed to the seedier aspects of life."

"At too early an age," Aidan growled. "Zylphia, you will never know what joy it has brought me to know I have a daughter. Or what sorrow to realize all the years I lost with you. All I ask is that I be given a chance to know the woman you are now. I …" He broke off what he was going to say when he saw Jeremy rushing toward him. A waiter trailed him, attempting to prevent him from approaching the table, but Jeremy shook off his hand and strode to the table. At a glance from Aidan, the waiter faded away.

"Uncle, if I might have a word?" Jeremy said, gasping a little. He clutched the rim of his hat in his hands, his suit sprinkled with dust from the workshop.

"Jeremy, sit down before you fall down." Aidan pointed to the empty chair at the table. "My nephew, Jeremy McLeod. I believe you've met Mrs. Maidstone. Her daughter, Miss Maidstone."

"Ma'am, miss." Jeremy nodded in their direction but looked at his uncle beseechingly. "I need your help. Savannah's in trouble, and I don't know what to do."

"What kind of trouble?" Aidan asked, his eyes sharpening.

"Colin's waiting in the lobby. He found me at the workshop. Told me that Sav's been arrested. For murder. Her father and Lucas are in the hospital."

Delia gasped. "Is she all right? Has her husband harmed her?"

"I don't know. I haven't seen her. I doubt they'd let me see her," Jeremy said, fear and impotent fury lacing his tone.

"Delia, Zylphia, will you please excuse me? This is an unfortunate turn of events, and I must render what aid I can to my nephew's friend." Aidan clasped Delia's hand for a moment before rising. "Please, enjoy dinner. I'll call at the orphanage as soon as I can." He rose, speaking with the waiter as he strode out.

"What in God's name happened?" Aidan asked as he and Jeremy met Colin on the sidewalk outside the hotel. They began the short walk toward Sophronia's.

"Savannah insisted on accepting her parents' invitation to celebrate her birthday with them. She's missed her father and wanted to show her mother she was well. They asked that it be a strictly family affair, thus I was excluded."

"And Jonas? Why was he there?"

"Aunt Matilda invited him," Colin said. "Said she was tired of the ridicule and gossip surrounding the family."

"Seems she's only garnered more after tonight," Aidan said. "How can they have charged Savannah with murder?"

"Because she killed Jonas," Colin said, meeting Aidan's incredulous stare. "He had a gun and had already shot Lucas and Uncle Martin, and I think he would have shot all of us if he could have. He gave no indication that he was going to leave without Savannah."

"How did he die?"

"She stabbed him with a letter opener," Colin said. "In an instant, he was brought to his knees, gasping for air."

Jeremy pounded on Sophronia's door, and the three of them were led immediately upstairs to a pacing Sophronia in the formal sitting room.

"About time you arrived," she said in her scratchy voice. She nodded her thanks to a maid who delivered coffee and tea, following her to the door and firmly shutting it behind her. She waved the men to various chairs as she sat in her lady's chair. "A letter opener, Colin?"

"It's what was at hand, ma'am. And it proved quite sharp."

Sophronia frowned and tapped her fingers on the wooden arm of her chair. "I've sent for my lawyer. I'm certain he'll be most displeased at being disturbed at such an hour, but it can't be helped. How are her father and brother?"

"I don't know. They were brought to the hospital, and we were instructed we could visit tomorrow. They were both shot by Jonas and bleeding heavily."

Sophie glanced toward the door at a gentle tap. Poole opened the door, admitting Sophronia's lawyer. "Ah, Mr. Jurdaine. Thank you for coming at such an hour."

He nodded, setting his briefcase next to his chair and sitting down. He crossed his legs, his chocolate-colored pants pleating with his movement. His deep brown eyes took in the three men sitting across from Sophronia. Aidan, impeccably dressed for dinner in a black suit, white starched shirt and polished shoes. Jeremy, covered in a thin sheen of wood dust and wearing worn pants and a long sleeved shirt. Colin, whose light-blue shirt was marred with splotches of blood. All three men wore the same resolute, determined look as they met his stare.

"If you could bring me up-to-date?" he nodded again, this time giving his thanks for a cup of black coffee.

Colin spoke, giving a brief overview of the evening's events.

"And you're certain she told the policemen that she killed the man?"

"I'm certain," Colin said. "It's why they took her away and put her in a paddy wagon." Jeremy grimaced next to him. "However, they granted her the courtesy of not handcuffing her."

"This is highly irregular. There are mandates set forth by various court cases such as *Runyon v. State of Indiana* or *Beard v. United States*. They stated that a person has the right to protect oneself from attack, particularly when one is in one's home. And I will argue, what had previously been one's home and should be as her home, as is the case for Mrs. Montgomery, thus negating the argument of *Allen v. United States*."

"You'll be able to free her then?" Sophronia asked.

"It shouldn't be too difficult. There is a strong court precedent for it, and there is a well-documented history of abuse."

"I thought you stated the staff would never speak out against Jonas," Jeremy said, his shoulders relaxing slightly at the lawyer's show of confidence.

"They wouldn't while he was alive, although I wonder if it will be different now that he is dead." He shook his head. "No, that's not what I meant. One of the doctors who had associated with Mr. Montgomery died last week in a trolley accident. I spoke with his colleague about the potential court case and the concern for a history of abuse at Mr. Montgomery's hands just yesterday. For some reason this colleague allowed me to see the notes taken. The abuse detailed is rather … extensive."

Jeremy tensed. "Imagine living through it," he hissed.

"I'd rather not. But, if this were to go to court, which I doubt it will, there will be a substantial amount of evidence as to the past abuse and the concern for future abuse at her husband's hands, had he succeeded in forcing her home with him. That threat alone would warrant her need for self-defense. I suspect I will merely need to speak in front of a judge."

"How soon can Savannah be released?" Colin asked.

"Hopefully tomorrow." He shared a sardonic smile with Sophronia. "I remember her saying she did not want to have the details of her abuse made public. I'm afraid she'll become the most talked-about woman in Boston for a time."

***

AIDAN KNOCKED on Delia's door at the orphanage the following afternoon, uncertain of his welcome. At her short, "Enter," he pushed open the door. "Hello, Delia."

She glanced up from reading the headlines proclaiming "Abused Socialite Takes Law into Hands, Skewers Savage Spouse." She asked Aidan, "Is this true?"

"Yes, I'm afraid it is." He closed the door behind him and, as was becoming customary, sat in the chair in front of her desk. "Savannah suffered greatly at his hands, and he attempted to force her back with him last night. He shot her brother and father in his attempt."

"Would he really have shot her too?" Delia continued to look from the lurid paper to Aidan.

"Colin believes so. He struggled with the man in an attempt to force him to release the gun, but Jonas was determined to hold onto it."

Delia held a dazed hand to her head, a relieved smile flitting over her lips before she subdued her emotions. She met Aidan's curious stare and shrugged.

Aidan tilted his head to one side, running one of his hands over the fine linen of his black pants as he studied her. "Why would you be pleased that Mr. Montgomery has met his maker?"

"Did you never wonder why else I might have acted as I did, Aidan? That there might have been something other than anger or resentment motivating my actions toward Savannah?"

He studied her a long moment, his features hardening while his gaze became implacable. "What did he threaten you with?"

"Exposing my secret about Zylphia. He had learned, somehow, that there'd never been a Mr. Maidstone and threatened me that, if I ever aided Savannah in any way, I'd ensure not only the loss of my post but that the orphanage would be destroyed. That all the children would be thrown out onto the streets."

"You had to have known he was bluffing, Delia," Aidan said.

"For the first few days I was so scared I didn't sleep at night. All I could envision was the scandal and the loss of everything I've worked for. Zylphia on the streets. These beautiful children forced to suffer even more." She closed her eyes and exhaled a deep breath. "Even though I realized that most of what he'd said was pure bluster, that he would never have the clout to shut the orphanage down, he still retained the ability to destroy my life. Thus, I acted to protect myself."

"And your daughter. Our daughter," he murmured.

"Yes." She firmed her lips. "And I'd do it again. There's little I wouldn't do to protect Zylphia."

"I have no plans to hurt her, Delia."

"I know, but, when you left precipitously last night, she was more confused than you can imagine. You didn't even acknowledge that Jeremy is her cousin."

"Delia, forgive me."

Delia held up her hand, forestalling any further rush of words on his part. "I understand it was a crisis. I'm sorry for reacting the way I am. I worry for Zylphia. She's seen the harsh realities of the world too quickly, and I can't bear for her to be disappointed now."

Aidan rose and moved toward her, tracing a hand along her desktop. He stilled as he saw a small pink shell on the corner. He picked it up and traced its fragile shape. "Delia?"

"That was the last thing you gave me. From the trip before everything changed. You brought me home a set of pearls and that shell. For some reason that shell was always more precious to me."

"What happened to the pearls?" Aidan caressed the shell once more before setting it down.

"I sold them. Years ago when Zylphia became ill, and I needed money to pay for a doctor."

"Good." Aidan reached out long fingers to stroke her cheek. "I wish I'd been there with you, to share the worry. The joy. The indescribable terror as she grew and demanded her independence."

"Aidan," Delia rasped.

He crouched in front of her, at the same height as she was, while sitting in her chair. He caressed a hand to the nape of her neck, moving his thumb along her cheek. He leaned forward, his lips brushing hers, waiting a moment for her to press him away. Instead, her hand curled into his shoulder, and he deepened the kiss.

He broke the kiss when they were breathless and nibbled his way up to her ear, whispering, "I've missed you, my Delia." He leaned away, brushing at her hair, smiling to find it still in place.

"Aidan," Delia murmured, pushing at him and rising when he leaned away. She walked to the bookshelf, gripping one of the shelves with one hand, the other on her hip.

"I'd like to have a gathering where you and Zylphia can meet my nephews and their families. I want them to know you even though I understand if it needs to be secret." He watched her stiffen with his words. "I'd prefer to proclaim my interest in you. Have the world know you are the woman I—"

"Don't, Aidan," Delia pleaded, still facing the bookshelf.

"Don't speak the truth to you? I thought we promised each other honesty. Why won't you allow me to speak of my feelings?"

"You don't know what you're saying."

"I'm almost fifty-five years old. I would think I'd know what I feel by now." Humor laced his voice.

"Don't laugh at me," she whispered.

"Oh, Delia, I'm not. Well, I'm laughing at the two of us. For not grasping at our chance at happiness. We shouldn't squander this opportunity, Delia. It won't come again."

"When are you leaving Boston?" She traced the spine of one of the texts, and Aidan couldn't make out the name of the book.

"I've no fixed schedule. I have competent people at my offices in San Francisco, and I will continue to rely on them as I remain here."

"I'd hate for your business to suffer on my account."

He gripped her shoulders and spun her to face him. "My business can go hang, Delia. I care about you. And Zylphia. About my nephews and their families. Everything else is secondary." He watched her with such intensity shining from his deep blue eyes that she shivered. "I hope someday you'll come to believe me."

Delia remained frozen in place, her face a mask of impassivity. She watched him with eyes dulled from years of unfulfilled hopes, failing to respond to the yearning in his eyes and gentle grip on her arms.

He backed away a step. "If you'll excuse me, I have a few appointments I need to keep." His shoulders stiffened when she remained silent as he walked away from her. He paused at the door. "Although I don't agree with you, Delia, I find I don't have the heart to continue to deny you what you want. I will no longer call at the orphanage to see you. If you'd like to see me, you know where I'm staying. I will write Zylphia to determine if she is amenable to seeing me again."

He paused, waiting for a response, but Delia remained resolutely silent. He exited her office and closed the door, leaning against it for a moment before continuing outside to visit his great-nephew.

***

JEREMY SAT AT THE DESK in Sophronia's back parlor, attempting to write Gabriel and Clarissa. He'd written no further than *Dear Gabe and Clarissa*, before his mind began to wander, imagining what could be occurring at the jail. He glanced out the rear window, tapping the tip of the pencil on the sheet of paper as he stared at the bare tree limbs. Images of Savannah behind bars caused his grip on the pencil to tighten to the point of snapping it in half. As he heard a commotion in the hallway, he bolted out of the chair, thrusting open the door to see Savannah headed to her third-story room.

He followed on her heels, taking the stairs two at a time, and tapped on her door a moment after it closed. He poked his head in to see Savannah leaning against one of the posters of her bed. She wore the rose wool dress she'd donned for her birthday celebration, splatters of dried blood marring the fine fabric.

"Darling," he whispered, entering the room and taking her in his arms.

She stiffened a moment before relaxing, burying her head in the crook of his neck. A moment later, a sob escaped as he pulled her close. He led her to the chaise longue, sitting and tugging her onto his lap. The door opened, and Jeremy shook his head at her maid, who discreetly backed away, closing the door behind her.

After many minutes, when her crying abated, Jeremy whispered, "Shh … love, it's all right. You're fine. You're safe." He leaned away, frowning as he again saw her soiled dress. "Let's get you out of this, darling." He helped her to stand.

He turned her, deftly unbuttoning her dress until it billowed around her waist. He shucked it down her legs along with her petticoats, lifted off her ruined corset cover and then began work on her corset ties, easing that away, all without comment from her. "Savannah?" he turned her to face him, seeing a distant, glazed look in her eyes. The skin on the upper part of her bosom was splotched with blood, while her previously pristine chemise was rust colored.

He moved away from her, flinching as he heard a whimper escape her lips, and searched for a nightgown and robe. He poured water into the nearby bowl, dipping the edge of a small towel into it and returned to her. "Here, love, let's get you cleaned up." He swiped away the blood on her skin and eased away her chemise. When she made no move to cover herself or to reach for the cloth, he gave her belly and arms a quick sponge bath.

"Raise your arms, my sweet Savannah," he murmured as he lifted the nightgown over her head and let it fall to her feet. He eased on her robe and returned her to the chaise longue.

"Talk to me, Savannah," he urged, hugging her close as he felt tears wet his shirt. He ran his big hands over her back and down her arms in an attempt to impart comfort.

"I can't believe you'd want to be near me. When you didn't come to the jail, I thought …"

He pushed her back, brushing tendrils of hair and tears off her cheeks. "You thought I no longer wanted you? Savannah, I couldn't be more proud of you for defending yourself and your family last night. And I couldn't be more devastated that you were forced to do what you did. The thought that such violence touched you, again, is almost more than I can bear." He kissed her once, softly.

"I was forbidden to go to the jail. By everyone. They feared I would taint the judge's good opinion of a woman defending herself, if they saw her lover waiting in the wings." He met her eyes with a reverent solemnity. "Never doubt my desire to be there for you. To stand proudly by your side."

She collapsed forward onto his chest, a sigh escaping her. "Do you have any idea the number of newspapermen who were there? The number waiting outside Sophie's?"

"Yes. It's why I didn't leave last night. I slept in the back parlor, away from any prying eyes."

"Did anyone see you come in?"

"I doubt it. When we arrived, news of Jonas's death hadn't spread, nor that of your arrest. By the time the lawyer had arrived and we'd formulated a plan, a mob of reporters huddled outside Sophronia's. Thankfully Colin had the sense to look outside from her upstairs window before we attempted to depart. Uncle, Colin and the lawyer left, but I remained here, hidden away."

"Why?"

"If I'd left, I didn't know when I would have been able to see you again. At least not without engendering speculation and gossip. I wanted to spare you that, if I could."

"They'll speculate why you're staying away, now that they haven't seen you," Savannah said. "They'll do anything they can to twist the story to their liking, to garner more readers."

"I'm afraid they won't have to do much to embellish the stories to induce an increase in readership." He kissed her head to take away the sting of truth from his words.

"Jeremy, do you have any news about Lucas or my father?" Savannah's fingers clasped his arms to the point of bruising.

He leaned forward and kissed her forehead. "By all appearances, your father's wound was the least severe. Went through the upper part of his shoulder and out the other side. He lost quite a bit of blood, but he's recovering. They're hopeful, if he doesn't become infected, to have him home in a matter of days."

"And Lucas?"

"He's fighting for his life, love," Jeremy whispered. "His wound is already infected, as it was in his belly. They're doing all they can."

"He can't die. He can't! Not because of me." Savannah stared unseeingly, with no tears falling.

"No matter what happens, it will never be because of you. Jonas caused this tragedy. From the very moment he mistreated you the first time, he's to blame. Not you." He tilted her head back and forced her to meet his implacable gaze, waiting until she nodded her agreement.

"Thank you, Jeremy." She sighed, snuggling into his arms. "I thought I wanted to be alone, when what I really needed was the comfort of my best friend."

His grip on her tightened, and he continued to stroke a hand down her back. He held her in companionable silence as the afternoon light faded.

"What are we going to do, Jeremy?" Savannah asked, nearly an hour later.

"What do you mean?" he asked, kissing her head.

"I know I agreed to move in with you into a place in the West End." She stroked his arm as he tensed underneath her. "I know we continue in our attempt to convince Hope's foster parents to move here so that we can all raise her together. But now that all this has happened, I don't know as I can live here with the notoriety of being the woman who killed her husband. Of having everyone whisper about me as I walk past."

Jeremy scooted so that they lay side by side on the chaise, facing each other. He traced a hand down her face. "Wherever you go, for as long as you live, there will be someone who whispers that behind you as you walk by. Even though you acted in self-defense and will not be charged, you won't escape the murmurs, my love. You must learn to accept what happened and take pride in the fact you didn't continue to be his victim."

"My mother didn't do a thing to help. Not while Jonas was acting out. Not when my father and Lucas lay bleeding on the floor. She just sat there." Her jaw firmed as she envisioned the scene. "And did nothing."

"Not everyone is strong enough to act when it is a crisis. Don't judge her too harshly."

"I couldn't judge her any more harshly than I already do for allowing that monster into our family. For encouraging me to marry him. For—"

"Hush, love. Such anger will only destroy whatever hope you have for a future happiness. And you do have that."

"I want to be brave like Clarissa," Savannah whispered.

"What makes you think you aren't?" He kissed her nose. "She stood up to Cameron, just like you confronted Jonas. She built a life with the man she loved, as I hope to build one with you. I can't see much difference between the two of you."

"Clarissa and I had a dream of raising our daughters together. So that they'd be close, like we were."

"What if she has a son?"

Savannah giggled. "We didn't plan on that." She sobered. "I've needed to live here with Sophronia. To find my strength again. And Aunt Betsy's support has been more than I could have hoped for. But I want to live near Clarissa. I realized that when she visited this fall."

"Why didn't you say anything to me about how you felt?"

"I'm not accustomed to asking for what I want and need." She took a deep breath and met his gaze. "I'm telling you now. I will miss Lucas and my father. I know I'll have days where I long for Sophronia's friendship and Aunt Betsy's support. But I want to travel to Montana, to see the life Clarissa is living. Determine if that is a life I'd like to lead."

He watched her for a moment, stupefied. "Savannah, are you sure you aren't simply trying to outrun your demons? Your memories of Jonas? For I can promise you, you can never run far enough or fast enough to escape them. They'll be with you, always."

She blinked tears and snuggled her head on his chest. "I see."

He squirmed around until she was forced to meet his concerned gaze. "I don't think you do. I will travel with you, darling, wherever it is you want to go. I will defend you against any and all gossip. I will never cease loving you."

"Trust me to know what I want, what I need," she whispered. "It may only be for a short time, but I need to leave all that is familiar to me. I have a yearning in me to … to …"

"To explore and not be confined by the limitations of your birth," Jeremy murmured.

"Exactly." She smiled tremulously, tracing the side of his face and raking her fingers through the soft pelt of his beard. "I've lived my life to fulfill the expectations of others. Now I want to fulfill my own."

"What about Hope?" he whispered.

She frowned. "Do you think the Woodhouses will want to travel with us?"

"It's a bit different deciding to move from Lowell to Boston than to move all the way to Montana. And if you determine you don't want to stay there, that could prove difficult for a man trying to provide for his family."

Savannah sighed, rubbing her head against Jeremy's chest. "I can't bear the thought of being separated from her again."

"Let's ask them and see what they think," Jeremy murmured as he nuzzled her forehead. "I can't believe I might see Gabe again." He reached toward the other end of the chaise longue and lifted a throw blanket over them, curling into her as she slept.

CHAPTER 53

FOUR DAYS AFTER THE ATTACK, Savannah walked up the front steps of Boston City Hospital with Colin. They entered one of the large red-bricked three-storied mansard-roofed buildings facing a courtyard with paths for strolling on warm days. The patients convalesced in this wing, whereas the operating rooms and doctor's offices were in the other wing. In the center of the courtyard sat an imposing rectangular building with pillars and cupola.

Savannah gripped Colin's arm as she entered the hospital, the strong antiseptic smell causing her to sneeze. "It's as though they believe, if they make it smell bad enough, the germs will disappear," Colin said with a wry twist of his lips.

Savannah squeezed his arm at his attempt at levity and followed him up a flight of stairs to her father's room. "I wish it had been that simple for Lucas." The large ward had sixteen beds in it, the majority full. Privacy screens separated a few of the beds, although most of them were open to their neighbor. She saw a few men sitting up and talking, although most appeared to be sleeping.

"I'm certain you do not need to expose yourself to such … to such unseemliness." A shrill voice behind Savannah gave them pause.

They turned to see a middle-aged man rushing toward them, his clothing covered by a graying overcoat that used to be white. "Excuse me?" Colin asked.

"The young lady. I'm certain she can wait outside or at home for any news about a gentleman here. She has no need to be in such a place. I'd hate for her to see things that are, well …" He shrugged his shoulders, not finishing his thought, and raised a hand, waving it around the room as though it were Exhibit A.

"There's little about a man that would shock me, kind sir, and seeing as my father is here, this is where I need to be. Good day." Savannah turned, and Colin smirked at the man as they continued their walk down the long ward, stopping near the end at Martin Russell's bed.

"Father," Savannah said. She sat in the chair next to his bed, reaching forward to push his hair off his forehead. "How are you? How do you feel?"

"Stop worrying about me. How's Lucas? How are you, my dear daughter?" He gripped her hand. He sighed as though a great weight had been lifted. "You don't know what it does for me to see you. To see that they released you." He turned grateful eyes to Colin. "Thank you, Colin."

"Don't thank me. Thank her friends, Aidan, Jeremy and Sophronia. They got a lawyer who was frightfully competent, and he knew how to free her in a matter of hours."

"I'll never be able to repay them," Martin said. "Are you all right, Savannah?"

She nodded, gripping his hand. "It seems as though it's been a bad dream, and then I see you here in the hospital, and I realize it truly happened."

"And your mother?"

"I don't know. I haven't seen or heard from her since that evening. I … I won't ever forgive her for inviting him. I won't ever forget that she just sat there while you bled and I stabbed Jonas."

Martin closed his eyes as though pained. "I will always be thankful you were strong enough to stand up to him."

"Thank you, Father." Savannah blinked away tears.

"Any news on little Hope?"

"She's in Lowell. They were supposed to come down to see me after my birthday, but, with all that happened and her not feeling well, they didn't come. I pray she can come this week or next. I miss her." She smiled ruefully. "It's amazing how much I've come to love her, and I've only seen her a few times."

"That's what children do for us. Fill our hearts so full of love and fear that you don't know what to do." Martin squeezed her hand.

"Why fear?" Colin asked.

"Having a child is to walk around with your heart residing in another's body. You love them with such an intense ferocity that any harm that befalls them also befalls you," Martin said.

Savannah sniffed as tears coursed down her cheeks and shared a long look with her father.

"Tell me, how is Lucas?"

"He's stable," Colin said after a long pause. "His fever is no better or worse, and it's hoped that he will fight off the infection. They are doing all they can."

"I wish I could visit him, but they insist I remain here, recuperating without overtaxing myself. Even though I argue that I should be up and moving about, they warn that too much too soon could lead to a relapse."

"Please follow their advice, Father. I need for you to improve. And Lucas needs you to be strong for when he does return home."

Martin nodded. "Always sensible, my Savannah." His eyes fluttered as he became weary. "Off with you now. You're both too young to spend your time in a hospital."

"I'll try to have Mother visit," Savannah whispered.

"Thank you," he whispered.

Savannah watched him a moment as he slept, before turning to slip her arm through Colin's and walk toward the front entrance. She breathed deeply when they exited the hospital, sharing a rueful smile with Colin.

"I know your mother dislikes the South End, but she should be thankful you live so close to the hospital. I think it's because of that that both of them have a chance of making a good recovery."

"Colin, will you do something else with me?" At his nod, she asked, "Will you come with me to visit my mother?"

"Of course. As long as I can come with you when you return to Sophronia's. I want to see Melly again." Savannah smiled, grasping his arm and walking toward her old home.

"Relax, Sav. He's not there to hurt you. He'll never hurt you again."

"Knowing that and believing it are two very different things, Col. And I'm beginning to realize Jeremy is right. No matter where I am, I'll always have my memories. I need to make peace with them or I'll never be free."

"I'd start focusing on the good memories," Colin said with an impish smile. "And the ones you hope to create. For, unless I'm greatly mistaken, you are now quite an heiress." He raised an eyebrow at her. "And you own one of the most desirable homes in Boston."

Savannah paled, gripping Colin's arm to remain upright. Her breath left

her in a *whoosh*, and she gasped, trying to catch her breath. Soon she was on
the verge of hyperventilating.

"Shh, … calm down, Sav. It's fine. I was only kidding."

"No, you weren't. Everything you said was true. I am to inherit everything. At least I think I am as his wife." She watched Colin with dawning
horror. "Are they saying I killed him for the money?"

"It doesn't matter what anybody says. Those who matter know the truth.
And I'm glad you'll receive his money. It's the least that could happen after
his mistreatment of you." He urged her forward, and they continued the slow
walk down Washington Street. He extracted a key and urged her inside the
shop.

"It's been closed?" Savannah asked as she noted the darkened interior.

"Yes, for four days now. Your mother hasn't wanted anyone in the house
or shop. Hasn't wanted the gossip."

"Father will be irate. He'd want her to go on as usual."

"Try explaining that to her," Colin muttered as they moved upstairs.

They entered the parlor to find Matilda sitting in the same chair she'd
occupied the night of Jonas's attack. The blood-stained rug and settee had
been removed, replaced by two new gentleman's chairs in slate blue and a
new forest-green rug.

"It's nice to see you've had time to visit the shops," Savannah said as she
strolled inside. Colin squeezed her shoulder, easing some of her tension at
entering the room again.

"Why are you here?" Matilda asked. Her dark steel-gray dress enhanced
the circles under her eyes, aging her.

Savannah stopped short, studying her mother, and quivered with anger.
"Don't tell me you are mourning?"

"Someone must mourn him. His own mother is dead."

Savannah met her mother's defiant eyes and stomped her foot in frustration. "How could you continue to care one whit about that man? About
propriety in the face of what he did? You should be giving thanks that his
mother is already dead and didn't have to live through the disgrace of discovering what her son was truly like."

"I will not have you speaking poorly of the dead," Matilda snapped.

"But you'll malign those living? Why are you acting like this? The grandparents are never going to forgive you for your transgressions when you were

a young girl." She nodded as her mother gasped. "Aunt Betsy told me all about what happened before I was born." Her mother glowered at her, but she barreled on.

"The baby you lost is never going to be returned to you. And Anita is lost forever. And now I am too." Savannah exhaled a deep breath. "The only difference between the baby you lost and Lucas's dead twin is that I'm still alive. Yet I'd rather be dead to you than to acknowledge you as my mother."

Savannah spun on her heels, failing to meet Colin's mournful eyes.

"Savannah, wait," her mother pleaded.

Savannah paused at the door, waiting for her mother to speak.

"You must understand I only wanted what was best for you."

"No, you didn't. You did what was best for you. If I'm charitable, I will try to believe you hoped it would also be what was best for me." She glared at her mother. "Good-bye, Mother. If you have any decency left in you, you'll deign to visit your husband. He protected you, even when you were too stupid to realize you needed protection."

She stormed out of the room, rushing through the hallway and down the stairs, coming to a halt in the shop. She leaned against the counter as she began to sob.

"Shh, ... Sav," Colin said.

She turned and flung herself in his arms. "I don't want to be filled with this anger, Colin. I want to be happy."

"You will be. You've lived through quite a lot in the past few days. You have to give yourself time to recover. And when you do, you might find that you're not quite so angry with your mother."

"I'll never be able to forgive her."

"Never's a long time, Sav." He patted her back. "Don't allow yourself to become hardened due to the actions of others. Or your perceptions of others. Live your life the way you want to live it." He handed her a handkerchief, swiping her face when she didn't take it from him.

"Let's go to Sophronia's. I know Melly is looking forward to seeing you." Savannah grabbed the handkerchief from him, wiping at her nose. "Thank you, Colin. I can understand why you were a comfort to Clarissa when she traveled to Gabriel."

Colin's cheery expression faded. "I hate that both you and Clarissa suffered at the hands of such men."

"I think I can speak for Clarissa when I say that we agree with you." She took a deep breath as she looked around the storefront. She looped her hand through Colin's arm and walked to the door. "I hope Sophie saved us some tea cakes."

Colin smiled and shut the door behind them.

**

SAVANNAH AND COLIN SAT on the floor in Sophronia's front parlor, playing with Melinda during an afternoon when Sophronia was out making calls. A robust fire roared in the fireplace, augmenting the forced heat from the heating vents. Bright sunlight entered through the windows, casting a golden glow on the room. A cough at the door by Poole heralded Jeremy's entrance to the parlor. He carried a small rocking horse constructed in sturdy maple.

Savannah's face lit with pleasure as she watched Melinda eye the toy with feigned nonchalance. "This is beautiful, Jeremy."

"I thought Melinda might like it," Jeremy said with a quick stroke along Melinda's head to her shoulder. He smiled as she leaned into his touch.

"It's for me?" Melinda whispered. Her wide blue eyes filled with a mixture of hope and the echo of disappointment. She bit her lip as she reached out to trace the horse's curved head and nose but dropped her hand before touching it.

"Of course. I don't think any of us would fit quite so well on it. Although I could always give it a try," Jeremy said with a wink to Savannah as he acted like he was going to swing a leg over the rocking horse.

Melinda giggled and pushed him. "No, Jeremy, it's mine!" She spoke in a normal voice, laced with joy. She patted the back of the horse; leaning over it, she whispered to it.

"What are you doing, Melly?" Col asked, sprawled on his side, leaning on his elbow.

"Naming him," she said with a proud tilt of her head.

Savannah laughed and caressed Melinda's blond curls. "If you don't look just like Clarissa right now. What are you naming him?"

"Reginald," Melinda said with a touch of defiance.

"A fine name," Colin said.

"Ahem," Poole said from the doorway to the sitting room. "A Mr. Wood-house is here to see you."

Savannah and Jeremy shared a quick glance. "Please, ask him to join us. Thank you, Poole," Savannah said.

"Melly, why don't you and I bring Sir Reginald upstairs to your bedroom? I think he should see where he'll spend most of his time." Colin stood, picked up the rocking horse under one arm and clasped Melinda's hand with his free hand, leading her from the room.

A few moments later, the sound of footsteps approached the sitting room, and Savannah took a deep breath as she faced Mr. Woodhouse. "Thank you, Mr. Woodhouse for agreeing to meet with us. I know it is a long journey from Lowell. Won't you have a seat and enjoy a cup of tea?" She waved toward the chairs and settees, but he shook his head. He remained in his heavy coat and rolled the brim of his hat through his fingers as he stood in the doorway to the front sitting room.

Savannah watched him with growing alarm as she thought through events. "How did you know we wanted to meet with you? I sent the letter in the late post yesterday. It's too early for it to have arrived already."

"May I take your coat?" Jeremy asked, reaching out a hand.

"No, I can't remain long and thought it best to come and share the news. Harriett was unable to travel with me, and I didn't believe a letter was appropriate. I didn't receive your letter, ma'am. I have news." He raised tortured eyes to Savannah. "I'm so sorry," he whispered.

Savannah collapsed into a chair, gripping the edge of it as she awaited his words. Jeremy moved to stand next to her, a hand on her shoulder. She reached up to clasp it, whitening his fingers with her firm grip.

"You must know we did everything we could. We paid for the best doctors. But there's nothing you can do for typhoid." He choked down a sob, and Savannah flinched as though struck at the mention of typhoid. "She was our little girl, and we loved her so much. I can't believe she's gone."

"I know she's been sickly recently," Savannah said, shaking her head in denial. "No one mentioned typhoid. I would have come immediately. I would have ensured …"

"At first we thought she simply had a cold or a touch of flu. I think Harriett wrote you." He sighed when Savannah nodded. "Then we realized it was more serious, and we became focused on her. On her recovery. We ensured she saw the best doctors. Nothing more could have been done." Mr. Woodhouse scrubbed at his eyes, unable to meet Savannah's or Jeremy's gaze.

Jeremy approached him, tugging him forward until he fell into a chair. "When did she die?"

"Last night. The doctor said she was getting better, but then the fever returned two days ago, and she had no ability to fight. She hadn't fully recovered from the high fevers, and she just slipped away." He swiped at his cheeks, reaching in his pocket for a handkerchief. "I meant to telegram, asking you to come, but, as she failed, I didn't leave her bedside. I couldn't leave Harriett. Forgive me."

"There's nothing to forgive," Savannah croaked out, reaching a hand toward him. "She was surrounded by those who loved her, and I could want nothing more for my Hope. My Adelaide." She stuttered out a sob. "How is Mrs. Woodhouse?"

"Inconsolable." He rubbed his nose again before folding the handkerchief and placing it in his pocket. "Hope was the daughter she'd always dreamed of having. Beautiful, bright, cheerful. She prayed we'd be able to find a way that all of us would have a part in the raising of her, because she couldn't bear the thought of giving her up."

"I will forever be thankful to you for caring for my daughter as your own. For she was yours, the daughter of your heart," Savannah whispered as she fought tears.

"If you will forgive me, I must return to Harriett." Mr. Woodhouse rose. "The services are planned for the day after tomorrow in Lowell. I'll leave the information with the butler."

"Thank you," Jeremy said as he rose and walked with Mr. Woodhouse to the front door. When he returned, Savannah was curled on the settee, a throw pillow clasped to her middle as sobs burst forth.

Jeremy knelt beside her, hugging her as best he could. He pulled her to him and rocked her in his arms, sitting on the floor with her in his lap. Running his hands over her head and shoulders, again and again, he attempted to impart wordless comfort.

Sophronia came in as Savannah sobbed and met Jeremy's tormented gaze, her aquamarine eyes glistening at the sounds of Savannah's distress. She sat in a chair, waiting for Savannah to calm.

"You'll go with me?" Savannah asked.

"You don't need to ask," Jeremy whispered into her ear. "Can I tell Sophie? She's sitting behind you." Savannah nodded her agreement, rubbing her face up and down on his chest. "Mr. Woodhouse visited today," Jeremy murmured.

"He refuses to travel with you and wants Hope to have no further contact with you?" Sophie asked, her anger and indignation rising.

"No. We didn't even ask him about Montana. They'd sent messages that Hope's been ill with a cold. I guess it must have been more serious than they told us because she had typhoid. She died last night."

"Well, I never," Sophronia said, as she held a hand to her chest. "Why didn't they tell you so you could visit?"

"She was recovering and then became suddenly more ill again. Unexpectedly. He meant to send a telegram but didn't want to leave her bedside." Jeremy kissed Savannah's cheek as another sob stuttered out.

"Admirable," Sophronia whispered as she watched Savannah. "Oh, my dearest. There are no words to ease this torment. What can I do?"

"Come to the funeral with me," Savannah whispered. "I can't go to it alone."

"Nor will you be," Jeremy vowed. "I'll speak to Colin, and I know he'll be there. Richard can man the forge. I doubt Florence will want to travel such a distance with the baby. I'll speak with Uncle Aidan, and I know he'll be there."

"What will you do afterward?" Sophronia asked.

"There's no reason we can't travel now," Savannah whispered. "I want to see Clarissa. Go west. Leave all this behind."

Jeremy shared a worried glance with Sophronia. "Her father and brother are improving and are expected out of the hospital in a day or so."

"When they are home, we should make plans to leave," Savannah said.

Jeremy kissed her head, holding her more tightly against his chest. "Soon, my love, soon."

***

March 22, 1903
Dearest Mrs. Maidstone,
I promised to honor your wish and remain away from the orphanage. I am

endeavoring to remain true to that vow. Rather than bring this news in person,
I write with the hope the news reaches you in a timely manner. Mrs. Montgomery's
daughter, Hope Woodhouse, died from typhoid yesterday, and her services will be
in Lowell at 10:00 a.m. the day after tomorrow. We are meeting at North Sta-
tion at 7:30 a.m. to travel together to the funeral. I believe it would be acceptable
for you to join us.
    Sincerely,
    Aidan McLeod

***

SAVANNAH STOOD TO ONE SIDE of the mourners with Jeremy, Colin, Sophronia and Aidan forming a wall around her. She need but reach out and one of them would seek to offer her comfort. However, she bowed her head as the pastor intoned a prayer, fueling impotent rage rather than imparting solace as intended. She gripped her hands to her sides, holding herself with a rigidity not experienced since living with Jonas, encouraging the deep numbness settling over her.

Sophronia sniffed, and Aidan placed a consoling hand on Savannah's shoulder moments before she moved forward to sprinkle dirt on the tiny casket. She bent, lifting the dirt and holding it over the yawning hole in the barely thawed earth, her arm shaking as her fingers refused to release the dirt. After a few moments, she held her gripped fist to her mouth, kissed it and then, with visible effort, released the dirt. As it fell, it created a tinkling sound on the casket.

"Good-bye, my beloved," Savannah whispered. She returned to stand near Jeremy, but moved so that no one would touch her. A few moments later came a ponderous "Amen" from the pastor, and the service concluded.

Savannah moved toward the Woodhouses, dressed in unrelieved black. "I'm terribly sorry for your loss," she whispered to first one and then the next, and moved on as the line of mourners grew behind her.

"Ma'am," Mr. Woodhouse said, gripping her hand to prevent her from slipping away. "Will you come by the house? You and your friends? There are things we'd like to show you."

Savannah nodded and moved away. Jeremy approached her, a quizzical expression marring his features as he studied her. "Savannah? What did he say?" He reached out to stroke her arm, moving his hand up and down, even though she tensed with the contact.

"He invited all of us to their house. There are things they wanted to show us."

"Of course," Jeremy said. "Aidan had planned a meal at a nearby tavern. We'll go there first and then to their home."

Savannah allowed herself to be led by Jeremy, climbing into the hired carriage to ride the short distance to the tavern. Upon their arrival, Aidan descended, marching into the tavern to speak to the owner as Jeremy and Colin helped Sophronia and Savannah out.

"As I had requested, there is a private room for us," Aidan said. "I've been told the food here is quite good." He nodded for them to enter and intercepted Savannah. "My dear niece, for I think of you as my niece, I hope you know you can ask me for any support you might need."

"The only thing I need, no money will ever be able to buy," Savannah snapped as she attempted to march around him. Aidan blocked her movement, remaining in front of her.

"You're correct of course. Nothing will ever bring your daughter back, and I'm sorrier than I can say. If there was anything Jeremy or I could do, you know we'd do it." He tilted her chin, forcing her to meet his gaze. "I know what it is to lose a child, Savannah. I know you'll never be whole again."

Savannah blinked away tears and firmed her jaw. "I'm fine."

"You're far from fine," Aidan argued. "Find comfort where you can, Savannah. Don't attempt to recover from such a loss on your own." He gave her a gentle shake. "I tried, and it only made everything harder. Let that man inside, who loves you past reason, comfort you."

"I'll consider what you have to say," Savannah murmured as she extricated herself from his grasp and moved into the tavern.

***

SAVANNAH LED THE SMALL GROUP to the front door of the Woodhouses' brick three-story home on the outskirts of Lowell. A barn and chicken coop stood nearby, with a large oak tree providing shade to the house.

Before Savannah could knock on the door, it swung open. "I thought you wouldn't come," Mrs. Woodhouse said. Grief had etched fine lines around her mouth, and she appeared much older than her thirty-five years.

Savannah instinctively grasped her hand in a comforting grip. "I'm so sorry."

"I should be saying that to you. We did all we could. I promise. There was nothing more to do."

Savannah nodded, blinking away fresh tears. She followed Mrs. Woodhouse into their home. They entered a small entryway and then immediately into a front sitting room with light-rose-colored wallpaper. A pair of chairs and settees formed a semicircle facing the fireplace. Formal portraits of dour ancestors hung on the walls while a closed door prevented Savannah from seeing into the rear of the house. Mrs. Woodhouse motioned for everyone to sit while Mr. Woodhouse entered carrying a tea tray.

"Would you mind coming with me, Mrs. Montgomery?" Mrs. Woodhouse asked when everyone was settled.

Savannah rose and followed her into the small foyer and up a flight of stairs. They paused outside a closed door.

"I've had the room cleaned, but I haven't touched any of her things. I wanted you to see them, to have anything of hers you wanted."

Savannah took a step back before firming her spine and motioning for Mrs. Woodhouse to open the door. Savannah entered the small corner room. Two windows allowed in bright light. A small bed with a pink blanket and lace ruffles sat against the far wall while a trunk sat under one of the windows. A stuffed doll and lamb lay on top of the bed.

Savannah crept into the room, listening intently, as though waiting for the echo of her daughter's laughter. "May I have a few moments?" she said with a quavering voice. Mrs. Woodhouse nodded, leaving Savannah alone.

Savannah moved to the bed, sitting for a moment as she hugged the stuffed lamb to her. She rose, leaving the lamb, sinking in front of the trunk. Inhaling deeply, she opened it. She closed her eyes as Hope's scent enveloped her. After a moment, she reached into the trunk, pulling out a christening dress, a tiny pair of baby shoes, a red velvet dress for Christmas. She traced her hand over the clothes, imagining her daughter, smiling and cheerful, wearing them.

She placed a hand to her mouth, swallowing a sob. She was unable to fight the tears, and they burst forth. She bent forward, keening as she cried, her hands wrapped around her middle.

"Savannah, darling," Jeremy whispered as he entered the room. He caressed her head, bending forward to whisper in her ear. "I lied and said I needed to use the bathroom. I really needed to find you. But I'll leave, if you want me to."

"No," Savannah implored, shaking. "Stay with me."

Jeremy wrapped her in his arms, rocking her from side to side. "Cry, my love. Cry. Don't keep this inside."

"These were her clothes, Jeremy. They still smell like her. How can my precious baby be dead? I had such little time with her." Savannah shuddered as her sobs quieted.

"I don't know, my love. Very little about this world makes sense."

After a few moments he kissed her head and leaned away. "Are you ready to return downstairs?"

"Yes. They said I could have anything of hers. But this all must be precious to them." Savannah glanced around the room.

"What do you want?" He swiped at the tears that continued to fall.

"I want her stuffed lamb," Savannah whispered.

"Then take it. I'm sure they'd want you to have it." He rose, reaching to help her to her feet. She was unsteady and leaned into him as she regained her balance.

"Forgive me, Jeremy." At his confused stare, she said, "Forgive me for my coldness earlier. I couldn't allow myself to feel. I couldn't break down at the funeral."

"Darling, do you think I didn't understand?" He leaned forward and kissed her forehead. "I understood your need to act as though nothing was affecting you. You like to believe you can live in a state where you don't feel pain or emotions. I know it's false and that it will only be a matter of time until something provokes a deep sentiment in you."

"How do you know that?"

"You've too much life, too much passion in you, to be restrained behind a wall of ice," he said as he kissed her on the forehead again.

Savannah looked around her daughter's room one last time before moving to the bed to grasp the small stuffed lamb. She clutched it to her breast, before kissing it. "I'll never stop loving you, my Hope," she whispered as she placed her hand in Jeremy's and followed him out of the room.

CHAPTER 54

AIDAN ENTERED THE PARKER HOUSE HOTEL, walking toward the front desk area for his key. He smiled to the man at the front desk who handed him an envelope along with his key. Aidan turned, walking toward the elevators and his room, scanning the message as he waited for the elevator.

"Damn," he muttered, turning away from the elevators and ascending the stairs one floor. He walked a short distance until he reached a formal sitting room, filled with overstuffed furniture covered in chintz fabric. He glanced around, finding Delia sitting near one of two fireplaces.

"Mrs. Maidstone," Aidan said as he approached, bowing before sitting across from her. "I hadn't expected to see you."

"Mr. McLeod," Delia said as she smiled at a young woman who delivered a fresh pot of tea with one cup. "I'm sorry. I just ordered for myself. Is there anything you'd like?"

"Coffee," Aidan said with an absent smile of thanks before the serving girl walked away. He tilted his head to one side as he studied Delia. "Why are you here?"

"I received your note, but I wasn't able to leave the orphanage. I'm sorry, Aidan, for Savannah's loss."

"Yes, well, she's finding it difficult to come to terms with her daughter's death. She'll need time to recover." His jaw tightened. "Although I know she'll never fully return to who she was before this loss."

Delia moved forward in her chair as though she were to grip his hand but then stilled her movement with the arrival of the serving girl. Delia waved her away with a smile and poured tea while Aidan poured himself a cup of strong black coffee.

"I don't mean to be rude, Delia, but it's been a hard day. Is there anything you need from me or can it wait until tomorrow?"

Delia paled as she studied him. "I'd hoped to impart some sort of comfort. I would never mean to distress you."

Aidan pinched the bridge of his nose, breathing deeply a few times. "I don't have it in me to fight, today of all days." He raised shattered eyes to her. "Please, save whatever it is you had to say to me for another day."

She reached forward and clasped his hand. "I wanted to be here for you, as your friend, as I envisioned you battling your own memories. I can only imagine it resurrected memories of your lost daughter."

Aidan's eyes shone with grief before he closed them, leaning his head against the back of his chair. He gripped her hand, giving it a gentle squeeze. "Thank you, Delia. More than anything else, I've missed your friendship."

"And I yours. I've been too much a coward to admit it. However, your absence these past days has forced me to examine my life. Every time there was a knock on my door, I hoped it was you. I hadn't realized how much your visits had soothed an old ache." She paused, taking a sip of tea and a fortifying breath. "I love what good I've been able to do at the orphanage. The lives I've helped."

"And yet," Aidan whispered, still holding her hand.

"And yet I realized, with your return, I want more. I've been too afraid of the changes it would bring to admit it."

"Delia, I'm not the same man I was sixteen years ago. I've lived through enough loss and disappointment to realize I need to grip my happiness to me, not thrust it away. Give me a chance to prove it to you. It's all I ask. Another chance."

Delia took a deep breath, her cheeks flushed as she hesitated. "Many would call me a fool. I'd have called any friend of mine thus. But I will give you another chance. Because by giving you an opportunity to prove yourself, I'm giving myself the hope for the future I thought lost to me."

"And Zylphia?" Aidan asked, unable to hide his eager hopefulness from Delia.

"She's sixteen, Aidan. A young woman. I must respect her enough to allow her to decide for herself if she wants to have you as part of her life or not."

"You won't prevent me from attempting to see her? From forming a relationship with her as her father?"

Delia's expression softened. "No. I've realized, as she's asked about you these past days, how much she's yearned for a father but thought it impossible. All I ask is that you decide now to either walk away or to fully commit to her. I couldn't handle seeing her hurt or disillusioned."

"Only time will show you the man I've become. Thank you." Aidan sighed with contentment, leaning his head against his chair once more, holding her hand for a moment before raising it and kissing it. "You'll come to a dinner held at my nephew's house?"

Delia nodded. "Yes. I'd like that very much."

***

AIDAN WALKED INTO a coffee shop near the orphanage. A thin sheen of steam covered the windows, engendering a sense of intimacy to the room. The rich smells of coffee and anise caused him to pause, his eyes closing momentarily, harkening back to memories of foreign travels when he was a sailor. His shoulders relaxed on the deep exhale, and he approached the table where Zylphia sat. He frowned, noting her stiff shoulders and the tight grip on her purse.

"Zylphia, thank you for agreeing to meet me." Aidan pulled out the chair across from her and sat down.

"I read about the infamous actions of your nephew's fiancée," Zylphia said.

"Forgive me for leaving you and your mother precipitously at dinner. Jeremy and Savannah needed my help."

Zylphia gripped her purse tighter. "I understand your desire to help those you are closest to."

"Zylphia." Aidan reached forward, placing his fingers over her fisted hand. "I may have just discovered I have a daughter, but I would come to your aid. If you needed my help, nothing could prevent me from rendering it."

Zylphia inhaled a stuttering breath and sniffed. "My mother and I have done well for years without you."

Aidan smiled as he watched his daughter, pride shining from his eyes. "You have every right to be wary of me. To worry I'll fail you or your mother again. Only time, and my constancy, will prove my sincerity."

Aidan smiled absently to the waitress, ordering tea and coffee with cakes. He met Zylphia's frank gaze as she watched him.

"I would think you'd relish your freedom," she said with a challenging lift of one eyebrow.

Aidan laughed, and his blue eyes sparkled with joy as he beheld his obstinate daughter. "You couldn't be more incorrect. I thought I was destined to be alone, until I learned my nephews had survived the fire that had killed my brother and sister-in-law. To find your mother again, and then you …" His blue eyes gleamed. "… it's wondrous."

"Mother informed me that you'd had another child," Zylphia said, her defiant countenance transforming into one of embarrassed concern as Aidan flinched. "Forgive me. I spoke out of turn."

"No, you are correct. And you have the right to know about me. I'd like for you to know me." Aidan sighed, meeting Zylphia's gaze with a tormented one. "I had a baby daughter. She was a part of my life for a few short weeks. Precious weeks," he murmured.

"You mourn her still." Zylphia watched him with evident confusion.

He tilted his head to one side as he studied her. "Yes, as I mourn all those I have loved and lost. As I had mourned your mother, until I walked through that door in the orphanage and found her."

"You don't mourn your daughter more than your wife? Than your brother?"

"It's a different pain, although, when the scars are written on your heart, they feel much the same. When I lost my brother, I had years of memories to mourn. When my daughter died, I had years of dreams to mourn. I mourn them still." He half smiled as he looked at Zylphia. "Meeting you has made me imagine what she would have been like. Feisty. Independent. Loyal."

Zylphia blushed but continued to meet his gaze.

"I understand you were raised in an orphanage, but I know your mother, and I know she would have showered you with love." Aidan watched her with confusion. "Why do you doubt the ability of others to love you?"

Zylphia flushed and looked into her teacup. "She did. And I knew she would never give me away, unlike the fate of many of the children in the orphanage. But I understood what my fate would be if something were to happen to her. And it terrified me."

She closed her eyes for a moment, her fingers gripping the teacup. "I didn't want to be consigned to the life of an orphan. To an adoptive home. I hated my father for dying. For leaving her destitute." She raised angry eyes to Aidan. "And when I learned of you, I hated you. For abandoning my mother."

"For abandoning you," Aidan said after a long pause. "I hope someday you'll believe me, although I know it sounds a weak reason to a woman who's spent years yearning for a father, that I didn't know I was to be so blessed." He smiled as Zylphia's eyes flashed with emotion, and she blinked tears. "Yes, my daughter, blessed. For, if you believe nothing, I need you to understand you were created out of an abundance of love."

"Why did you leave? Why did you consign my mother to endless nights crying into her pillow?" She swiped at an errant tear and lifted her chin away to prevent Aidan from tapping at her wet cheeks with a handkerchief.

"Your mother and I fought, said cruel things to each other, and I lost her. In my grief over the loss of my brother and his family, I lost your mother. I never knew I was losing you too."

"If you had known, would you have stayed?"

Aidan's expression softened, and he clasped her hand fiddling with the teaspoon. "Nothing could have caused me to leave." His expression darkened. "But I can't rewrite the past, Zylphia."

She sniffed, her gaze focused on the steamy windows for a moment. "I believe you." She smiled ruefully as Aidan exhaled deeply. "I want to know you, but I think I'll find it difficult to have another parent giving me instructions."

"We all must adjust," Aidan murmured as he reached forward and brushed a hand over her dark hair before clasping her hand again. "I'll only ever want what's best for you, Zylphia, and will find joy even in our squabbles."

Zylphia blinked away tears. "It is almost too much to understand. I have a father," Zylphia whispered.

"Yes, and cousins. I'd like for you to meet them at a gathering to be held at their home here in the North End. Will you attend with your mother and me?"

"Will you tell them who I am?"

"Of course. I'm eager for my nephews to meet their cousin, my daughter." He smiled tenderly at her. "I know it's difficult, Zylphia, but I hope someday you find as much joy in discovering you have a father as I do in my discovery of you."

Zylphia bit her lip before whispering, "I have, Father. The joy I've felt at the prospect of truly having a father has terrified me."

Aidan's eyes flashed, and he reached forward to grip her hand. "You won't lose me, Zylphia. I can promise you that."

Zylphia nodded, turning her hand over to squeeze his.

CHAPTER 55

SAVANNAH STOOD ON THE FRONT STEPS to the McLeod house in the North End and took a deep, fortifying breath. Jeremy opened the door, pulling her in for a quick embrace before leading her down the hall.

"Savannah," Florence said as she rushed toward her, holding little Ian. "It's wonderful to see you. Thank you for coming."

Savannah nodded, tracing Ian's head before attempting a smile. "Hello, Florence, Richard."

Florence tugged her to the settee, shooing away the cat. "How are you?"

Savannah cast a quick glance to Richard and Jeremy who appeared deep in conversation in the kitchen area. "Not very good," Savannah whispered. "I wake at night, hearing Hope calling for me. It's almost more than I can handle when I realize she's gone."

Florence gripped Savannah's hand. "I'm sadder than I can say, Savannah. I regret not being able to travel for the funeral."

"I wouldn't have expected you to. Besides, I wasn't aware of much that happened that day," she admitted in a whisper. "It's as though it all happened to someone else."

Savannah looked up as Colin, Lucas and her father walked in, with Colin carrying Melinda. "Lucas!" Savannah exclaimed. "I hadn't expected you to come." She rose and threw herself in his arms.

"Sav," Lucas said, holding her tight. "I've missed you these past few days and had to see for myself that you were doing all right." He brushed a hand over her head, marring her simple chignon.

She leaned in again for another embrace. "All I care about is that you are recovered."

"It's going to take a few weeks before I feel like my old self," he admitted. "I still don't have much strength, and the doctors don't want me to do much heavy lifting. Other than that, I'm fine."

Lucas reached out a hand to clasp Jeremy's, keeping one arm around Savannah. "Thank you for keeping her safe," Jeremy said with an emotion-laden voice.

"Always," Lucas said. "It's something else we have in common."

Savannah stepped out of her brother's arms and turned toward her father. She was unable to battle her tears, and they poured forth as he pulled her into his strong arms.

"Ah, my Savannah," he whispered, blinking away tears. "I'm sorry you've suffered as you have." He patted her back as Savannah attempted to control her tears.

Lucas collapsed into a chair and accepted a glass of water from Florence.

"Lucas, you shouldn't be exerting yourself by coming here," Savannah admonished, swiping at her tears.

"I'm fine, Sav. We took a carriage here, and now I'll spend the entire evening sitting down."

"As long as you continue to follow the doctor's orders," Savannah said, sitting next to him. He slung an arm over her shoulder, and she leaned into him a moment. Colin sat next to them, balancing Melinda on his knees. She reached out her arms to Savannah and squirmed on Colin's lap.

"Here, Sav, I think she'll only settle once she's with you."

Savannah stifled a sob as she held her small blonde cousin, fighting memories of her daughter. She nodded and sniffled her acknowledgment to Colin and Lucas that she was fine, cuddling Melinda on her lap as she settled. She smiled as Colin extracted a small doll from his pocket, and Melinda played with it silently.

"You've become very attuned to the needs of a child," Lucas teased Colin.

Colin played with Melinda's wispy curls. "She needs to know only love from now on," Colin murmured. Lucas and Savannah mumbled their agreement, their focus on Melinda shifting at the sound of new arrivals.

Aidan entered with Zylphia and Delia, and the small room felt as though it would burst with everyone in it. Although a cool day in mid-April, Jeremy leaned over to open the kitchen window.

"Mrs. Maidstone, Delia, I believe you know most everyone present," Aidan said as he quickly introduced those she didn't know. "This is Zylphia, her daughter."

"Nice to meet you," Martin said as he offered one of them his chair. The table now had six chairs around it but were still three short, even with Melinda and baby Ian sitting on two of the adults' laps.

Jeremy and Richard stood, studying Zylphia. They shared a long look, nodding to her and then furrowing their brows in confusion as they communicated silently. "Uncle," Richard said. "There's something we wanted to show you in the alley."

"Not now, Richard," Aidan said. "You can show me at a later time."

Delia sat next to Savannah after Colin rose and joined Richard and Jeremy. Delia fidgeted with her dark blue dress, adorned only by a silver belt with its large buckle. "Florence, Savannah, I owe you both apologies."

Florence raised an eyebrow, remaining silent, and Savannah followed her lead.

"I'm afraid I treated you both poorly once I realized you were in any way affiliated with a McLeod. As Aidan pointed out, I'd held my bitterness to me like a shield, and I attempted to maim you with my disappointment. It wasn't fair of me, and I'm sorry."

Florence watched her with keen interest, running her hand over Ian's back as though she found the motion soothing. "Is what you said true about my parents? My family?"

"Everything I said was true, but I should have been much more tactful. I should never have imparted such information in a callous manner. I'm sorry."

"Do you know of any way to locate them? My siblings sent on the orphan train?" Florence bit her lip as she fought hope.

"I believe it will be very difficult. The Children's Aid Society keeps records. However, once your siblings were on the train, the recordkeeping wasn't as good as it should have been. I will do what I can to help."

"Thank you, Delia. If I could find them ... You don't know what it would mean," Florence whispered as she bent to kiss Ian's head. Delia nodded and tried to smile.

Savannah looked at Delia with grief-stricken eyes. "I believe I've already made my peace with you. You helped me find Hope, and I was able to hold her in my arms a few times. For that, I will always be thankful."

Delia nodded, blinking away tears. "I'm terribly sorry, Savannah."

Savannah nodded, cuddling Melinda. Lucas stroked Sav's shoulder and gripped it gently in support. She looked for Jeremy, seeing him standing next to Richard with his arms crossed, a formidable frown on his face as he stared at his uncle. For the first time since Aidan had returned, Jeremy didn't seem pleased at his uncle's presence.

"Uncle, was there some reason you wanted us all together?" Jeremy asked.

"There were a few reasons. You and Savannah will travel soon, and I don't know when I'll see you again. I wanted to have this opportunity to have the family together."

"You have a home in Missoula, Uncle. I'd think you'd visit it soon or why else own it?" Richard asked.

"It would please me greatly if you and Savannah would consider living in it in my stead during my prolonged absence. I have great faith in my house-keeper, Mrs. Egan, but I would feel better if one of us were also living in it. Gabriel refuses, due to an excess of McLeod pride, but I'd appreciate it if you would consider my request."

"Savannah and I will discuss it," Jeremy said. He continued to watch his uncle with a quizzical expression.

"I also wanted us all together because I have an announcement to make. I believe most here are aware that, at the time of the fire in November of 1886, I was romantically involved with Mrs. Maidstone. We separated due to grief-stricken, idiotic comments I made after the loss of what I understood at that time was my whole family. I believed my grief insurmountable."

His solemn gaze moved to Savannah. "I've since learned that most grief subsides and takes up residence in a small portion of one's heart, making it-self known at inopportune moments, but not preventing one from living a fulfilled life."

Savannah nodded as she wiped away tears.

"What I had not realized, back in '86, when I had sailed away under a different crew, planning to never return to Boston, was that I was to be a fa-ther." At this Jeremy and Richard nodded, nudging each other in the sides with their elbows. "I've only just discovered that Zylphia Maidstone is, in fact, my daughter."

"Oh, how wonderful," Florence enthused, rising from her chair to give one-armed hugs to Aidan and then Delia and Zylphia. "After all this time of believing you were alone, to now find you have your own family."

Savannah handed Melinda to Lucas and rose, embracing Aidan. "I'm so happy for you, Aidan."

"I'm sorry if this brings you pain, my darling niece," Aidan said.

"I just hate that I'm envious," she whispered, releasing him.

"I'm not. It means you'll continue to fight the darkness." He turned to accept slaps on the back from Jeremy and Richard, who then studied their cousin.

Richard watched Zylphia. "You're a fair sight prettier than our other cousins."

"And I hope nicer," Jeremy said. At Zylphia's confused stare, he said, "We were orphaned at a young age and raised by an aunt. She wasn't very kind, and her sons took joy in tormenting us."

Lucas smiled warmly. "I imagine it's overwhelming to meet so much family so quickly."

Zylphia nodded, moving closer to Delia.

"And there's more in Montana!" Aidan said. "My eldest nephew, Gabriel, lives there with his wife."

"Our cousin," Savannah said, pointing to Lucas and herself.

Zylphia bit her lip as she tried to determine how everyone was related.

"Don't worry. We can draw you a diagram later. For now let's enjoy supper and get to know one another," Richard said as he moved toward the large stew pot. "It's stew tonight because of our number."

He handed out bowls and mugs, with just enough to go around to everyone.

Jeremy approached Savannah's father as they waited for their bowls of stew. "Sir, if I could speak with you for a moment?"

Martin nodded, stepping aside toward the rear door. He smiled encouragingly toward a seated Savannah who watched them with a frown. "What is it, Jeremy?"

"As you know, Savannah and I are planning our journey to Montana. I would like to ask your permission to marry her when we arrive there."

"Why wait? Why not marry before you travel?"

"I'm aware that we may cause gossip traveling together when we are unmarried, but I know Savannah will want Clarissa with her at her wedding."

Martin's gaze became distant for a moment before focusing on Jeremy again. "You're correct." He studied Jeremy before sighing. "I know Savannah loves you. You've shown her tremendous loyalty and compassion throughout everything that has occurred."

"I love her, sir."

"I believe you do. I failed her once, and I dread failing her again."

Jeremy's shoulders stiffened at Martin's words.

"However, she chose you this time. Not the family. I must trust her, as well as my instincts, that you will never harm her."

Jeremy bristled. "Never, sir."

Martin smiled sadly. "Then I give you my consent. Although I'll never be more distraught than the day I receive the letter describing your nuptials, knowing I wasn't there." He clasped Jeremy's shoulder before walking with him toward the kitchen area.

Jeremy smiled and winked at Savannah, and she relaxed in her chair.

In a conversational lull and after most everyone had eaten, Richard asked, "What does this mean for the orphanage?"

"For now, I'm continuing on," Delia said.

"But I thought this meant …" Florence bit her lip before saying anything to offend Aidan.

"In time, Florence," Aidan murmured.

"When does the train leave?" Lucas asked.

"In a little over a week," Jeremy said.

"All is settled with Jonas's estate?" Martin asked.

"I've spoken with the lawyer. There is no movement to press charges or to move forward with any legal action against me, thus everything will be out of probate soon."

"Will you keep the workshop, Jeremy?" Martin asked.

"Yes. As it is uncertain we will remain permanently in Montana, I think it best to keep the space. I'd also hate to lose all those tools."

"What about you and Jeremy?" Lucas asked Savannah.

Jeremy wandered to stand behind Savannah, resting a hand on her shoulder. She raised her hand, intertwining her fingers with his. "We'll be married in Montana, with Clarissa and Gabe present. I don't want another Boston society wedding," Savannah said, sharing a long look with her father, who sighed in agreement.

"I can promise you, our wedding will be nothing like the first," Jeremy said, kissing Savannah's hand.

CHAPTER 56

Montana, April 1903

"THAT WAS A DELICIOUS MEAL, Amelia," Ronan said as he stretched in his wheelchair. "Thank you."

Gabriel played with his fork, crumbling the piecrust remains on his plate. "It was good to have reason to celebrate. It seemed as though the trial would never end."

"Thankfully Cameron received the justice he deserved," Ronan said.

"There is no such thing as justice for a man like Cameron," I said. "But we are all better off now that he's in prison for the rest of his life."

"The Bouchards seemed unaccustomed to eating crow," Ronan said with a satisfied smile. "I've enjoyed watching them and some of the townsfolks' effusive praise of Sebastian's integrity and work ethic. It's been a joy to watch them attempt to backpedal after all the vicious things they said."

"I agree," Sebastian said. "Especially after their rush to judgment."

"Although I doubt they've truly learned any lessons. People like Mrs. Bouchard do not change overnight," I said with a rueful shake of my head.

"I'm sad to see you depart tomorrow, Seb," Gabriel said.

"As am I. However, I'm looking forward to the challenge of starting a mill almost from the ground up. Picking the men I want to work with. Ensuring I have the men in charge that I want, not ones who were inherited. And Darby isn't that far away."

"Isn't it a small town?" I asked.

"Yes, much smaller than Missoula. Although it is supposed to be quite beautiful." Sebastian took a sip of tepid coffee. "Your Mr. Pickens can never say enough good things about it, although I'm not sure he's ever been that far south."

"I know. You'll have to write and tell us if you agree," I said. "It always seemed a bit too wild."

"It's less than a hundred miles from here, Rissa," Amelia said as she rose and entered the kitchen.

"Sorry," I whispered, sharing a chagrined glance with Sebastian.

He raised an eyebrow and shook his head in resignation as we heard her go into one of the back rooms to check on the children.

"It's not easy on her," Sebastian said.

"Of course it isn't. She's survived the loss of one good man. She can't relish the loss of another," Ronan said as he frowned at Sebastian.

"Sebastian, Gabriel informed me that you no longer have your house here in Missoula," I said as I bit my lip in concern.

"I was forced to sell rather than lose it to the bank. I'm hopeful to be able to find a similar home in Darby."

"I'm sorry, Sebastian," I said as I reached forward to clasp his hand for a moment. When I released his hand, I rubbed my open palm over my belly, silently marveling at the movement of the baby within.

"I was too, Clarissa. But I've found another dream, and it comforts me." He smiled reassuringly and glanced toward the doorway to the kitchen.

Amelia reentered the dining room and cleared away one armload of plates. I moved to help her, but she waved me away. "No, Rissa. Rest. You'll have little enough opportunity when the baby comes." She continued her circuit back and forth between kitchen and dining room, her movements becoming more agitated with each trip.

I raised an eyebrow and tilted my head in the direction of the kitchen while looking at Sebastian. He nodded and rose when she came into the dining room for the last set of plates. He grabbed a few glasses and a bowl, ignoring Amelia's frown.

I shared a smile with Gabriel as he winked at me. "Let's go to the office," I whispered, and Ronan and Gabriel nodded their agreement. Gabriel grabbed his coffee mug and I my water glass as we moved to grant Sebastian and Amelia some privacy.

***

"AMELIA, TALK TO ME," Sebastian said as he followed her into the kitchen. He glanced through the doorway and saw Clarissa leading Gabriel and Ronan to the office, leaving him with Amelia, virtually alone on this side of the house.

"There's so much to be done to ensure you are ready for your travels tomorrow, Sebastian," Amelia said as she picked up a hearty loaf of oatmeal bread and began to slice thick slabs. She slathered on butter with jerky motions, her head lowered as she focused on her task.

Sebastian reached for her hand, stilling her movements. "Amelia, look at me." The soft entreaty provoked a sniffle and a shake of her head. "I know you're angry with me. There's no need to deny it. But I'd rather talk with you about it now than have it between us when I'm away."

Amelia wrenched her hand from under his and spun around. She dropped the knife in the sink and then gripped the edge of it, her shoulders shaking with silent sobs. "Forgive me." Her reedy voice emerged above a whisper. "I'm thinking only of myself."

Sebastian turned her to face him, placing his index finger under her chin and tilting her head up to meet his eyes. "If you weren't upset, I'd be devastated."

Amelia bit her lip as she fought a smile and then leaned into his large palm as he cradled her cheek. "I know you promised we'll be together again. And I tell myself you speak the truth. And yet I have this tremendous fear. That I'll never see you again. That I'm destined to always be alone. And it overwhelms me."

"We won't be separated for long, sweetheart. I have money from the sale of my house. I want to have the mill up and running before you come to Darby."

"The thought of any separation is beyond my ability to bear." She leaned into his touch, accepting the soft caress of his thumbs over her cheeks. "Promise me that you'll let your men do the dangerous work. That you won't run into a fire, putting yourself at risk again."

"I can't promise you that," Sebastian said, his light-brown eyes shining with intensity. "I can't promise I'll be less of a leader to my men. That I'd let any of them come to harm because of a promise I made to abate your fears."

"Sebastian—"

"Life is full of risk, Amelia. Full of danger, uncertainty and cruelty. I can't promise you that life will be as we wished. But I can promise you that I'll do everything in my power to remain healthy and whole. To be able to love you and the children until we're old, when the wildest thing I can imagine is holding your hand while sitting in my rocking chair."

Amelia sputtered out a laugh, unable to prevent her tears from spilling. "I'd rather be sitting on your lap in the rocking chair."

Sebastian smiled appreciatively. "There's my girl," he said huskily, leaning forward to kiss her with a yearning tenderness. After a few moments he leaned away, his forehead against hers. "Never doubt my desire to forge a life with you. To raise Nicky and Annie as though they were mine. I want this life with you."

A soft smile bloomed, and a rosy blush enhanced Amelia's beauty at Sebastian's declaration. She began to speak but then bolted back a step, bumping into the countertop and wincing in pain, as the sound of a throat clearing was heard in the living area. Sebastian chuckled, although it was tinged with frustration.

"Seb?" Gabriel's deep voice called out. "We're heading out soon."

Sebastian traced a hand down the side of Amelia's face and neck, and then turned to the living room, his boots thumping on the hardwood.

Amelia stood in the kitchen, her hands behind her, braced on the edge of the countertop as she attempted to memorize the feel of Sebastian's hands caressing her face. She heard the front door opening, quiet murmurings and the sound of a carriage rolling away.

"Glad Gabriel finally learned to drive a carriage. He can help Ronan travel here now," Sebastian said as he reentered the kitchen.

"Yes," Amelia murmured.

Sebastian grinned, reaching forward to clasp her face again. "Where were we, sweetheart?"

All teasing left Amelia's countenance as she stared into his eyes. "I want this life with you too, Sebastian. I hope you realize I'd never run off—"

"Hush, love." His eyes glowed with a fierce emotion. "I've watched you raise your children. Mourn your husband. Support your friends. I know the woman you are. I know you're not that type of woman."

He took a deep breath as he closed his eyes for a moment before meeting her gaze again. "All I ask is, when I disappoint you—because I know I will— that you tell me. Tell me plainly when I hurt you or fail to do something you wanted."

"I will," Amelia said.

"I promise the same." He leaned forward, kissing her forehead. "To love you." A kiss to one cheek. "To cherish you." A kiss to the other cheek. "To never take for granted your love." A kiss to her mouth.

He moved to back away and say something else, but she clasped him around his neck and held him tightly to her, deepening the kiss.

"Establish the mill soon, my dearest," Amelia whispered. "Send for me and the children."

CHAPTER 57

A WEEK AFTER SEBASTIAN LEFT, I waited in our apartment for Gabriel to come upstairs after work. When I heard his boots on the stairs, I moved toward the stove and put the kettle on for tea.

"How was your day, Gabriel?" I asked.

"Fine. More of the usual. Amelia came by with the children while you were at the depository. She's impatient for word from Sebastian, and I can tell she's having a hard time waiting for Sebastian to get the mill running and to find acceptable housing for her and the children."

"They'll be reunited again soon," I said as I poured steaming water into the teapot.

"What's this?" Gabriel asked as he picked up a yellow envelope propped against a glass on the dining room table. He raised an eyebrow as he looked at me. "It's a telegram addressed to you, Rissa." He flipped it over. "And you've yet to open it."

"I know," I whispered.

He set it down again on the table and moved to his chair. After he'd settled, he nodded to the envelope.

I picked it up, holding the telegram in my hand, afraid to open it. The last telegram I'd received had contained the news of my father's death. I bit my lip as I continued to stare at it as though it were the harbinger of unwanted news.

"Open it, Rissa," Gabriel urged. He clasped his hands together with feigned patience, watching as I stared at my name on the front of the yellowed paper.

I met his amused gaze and overcame my fear as I ripped open the envelope. "I don't understand," I whispered as I held the telegram to Gabriel.

"*On our way. Be there Tuesday. Much to discuss.*" Gabriel gripped the paper so tightly he almost crushed it. "*Savannah.*"

"Yes, and Jeremy." I moved toward his chair, sitting on his lap and provoking a groan as I settled my pregnancy weight on his legs. I reached for his hand and eased it open, clasping my fingers through his. "How can they be coming here? I thought their plan was to rent an apartment in the West End." I raised a hand to my forehead, my mind spinning.

"I suspect there's much we haven't been told. The last letters have been from Florence. Filled with information about little Ian"—Gabriel cleared his throat as his voice thickened at his father's name—"but little other real news."

"I wonder that Savannah has had the strength to leave Boston and Jonas behind," I said.

"It seems you're not the only independent cousin," Gabriel said. "If they're scheduled to arrive on Tuesday, that's tomorrow."

"Why wouldn't they have written sooner?"

Gabriel sighed and settled me in a more comfortable position on his lap. I didn't fit as easily as I used to with my protruding belly. He kissed me before leaning over and placing a soft kiss to my belly. "We'll know soon enough."

***

I STOOD NEXT TO GABRIEL, attempting not to fidget as we awaited the train's arrival. I peered around his shoulder, down the train tracks, hoping to see the puff of steam from the engine heralding its arrival. The sun had yet to burn through the low clouds blanketing the town, and I could not see the tops of the mountains. A sprinkling of snow covered the tips of the hills and half of the mountains, and I worried more snow was on its way. I tapped my toes to keep them warm in the cold, early May weather.

"If you're chilled, why don't you wait inside?" Gabriel asked as I shivered. He placed his arm across my shoulders, and I snuggled into his embrace, thankful for his warmth.

"I want to see them as they descend the steps," I said into his lapel. I breathed in his masculine, musky smell with a hint of cedar. "How can it be this cold in May?"

"It's Montana, love."

"I didn't believe Mr. Pickens when he said it could snow in June. This year I fear he could be right."

Gabriel chuckled and kissed the top of my head. "Here they are," Gabriel murmured, unable to hide the joy from his voice.

I leaned away from his embrace but wrapped my hands around his arm, gripping it in my excitement. The shiny black steam engine groaned to a halt, and, within a few moments, passengers disembarked. I bounced from foot to foot as I searched for Jeremy and Savannah.

"Colin?" I asked incredulously as I looked toward the steps. "Colin!" I screeched as I raced toward him in an uneven gait due to my pregnancy. He stood at the base of the steps, appearing handsome in a disheveled way with a two-day-old beard and wrinkled clothes.

"Rissa," Colin said pulling me into a long hug. He leaned away, his blue eyes sparkling with merriment. "Oh, it's good to be home."

"I can't believe you didn't tell me that you were coming," I said as I leaned in to hug him again. I looked behind him and saw Savannah and Jeremy descending the stairs. I released Colin with a smile and walked toward her. "Sav," I breathed and launched myself at her, gripping her tightly. "Sav," I repeated as I rocked to and fro with her in my arms, tears falling unheeded as I beheld her, healthy and safe.

"Clarissa," Savannah whispered. "I thought we would never arrive." She squeezed me tightly. "I can't believe I'm seeing you again and in Montana."

I finally released her and swiped at my cheeks. "Let's find Gabriel and Jeremy," I whispered as I turned toward the station.

"Wait," Savannah said, stilling my movement, waiting at the foot of the steps by the train.

I watched as an unknown woman descended the steep train stairs, clinging to a wriggling bundle with one arm and the bar with her other hand to balance herself on the steps. Savannah turned to the woman, murmuring soft, cooing words to her bundle. A blond head emerged from the swaddled mass of blankets and coats, and reached out her arms to Savannah. As she turned sapphire blue eyes toward me, I gasped.

"That can't be," I said, barely above a whisper.

"Melinda, this is your sister, Clarissa. I've been telling you all about her. You might remember her from when she visited you around your last birthday." Savannah brushed down yellow curls as I watched Melinda lean her head closer to Savannah. If I hadn't known better, I would have thought Savannah was Melinda's mother.

"Sav? You brought her?" I reached out to grip Melly's small hand, and she let go of Savannah, reaching out her arms for me. Savannah passed my sister to me, and I hugged Melinda tight, reminding myself not to crush her in my enthusiasm. "Thank you," I whispered.

Savannah smiled as she again brushed at Melinda's curls. I kissed Melinda's forehead, overcome with emotion to see both Savannah and my baby sister again.

"Look," Savannah murmured as she nodded toward the brothers standing a short distance away.

Gabriel stood tensely, gripping his hands together at his sides as he studied Jeremy intently. It had been nearly five years since they'd seen one another, and I saw them silently cataloging the changes in each other. I kissed Melinda's head, glanced toward Savannah and moved toward them as suddenly Gabriel pulled Jeremy into his arms in a bear hug. They slapped each other on the back a few times and rocked to and fro. After a few moments they broke apart. Gabriel reached up to clasp Jeremy's face and then pulled him in for another hug. Not long afterward they released each other once more. Gabriel kept one arm slung around Jeremy's shoulders as he turned toward me, his blue eyes bright with unshed tears.

"Rissa," he said, holding his hand out for me to join them. I moved toward him and Jeremy, shifting Melinda to carry her on my hip and to free one of my hands.

"Jeremy," I said, touching him gently on his arm.

"Miss S ... Mrs. McLeod," he said with a shy smile. I leaned forward and hugged him, careful not to squish Melinda.

I whispered into his ear, "It is so good to have you here." I gave him a gentle squeeze and then backed away. "And I think by now you should call me Clarissa."

Jeremy smiled and reached out a hand for Savannah. Colin stood talking to a nearby porter, making him laugh with one of his tales, before he rejoined us. He grabbed Melly from me, lifting her high overhead and causing her to squeal with delight. "I'll carry her, Rissa," Colin said as we began to walk down the boardwalk toward downtown.

"We're to stay at Uncle Aidan's place," Jeremy said.

"Does Amelia know?" I asked as I peered up at him.

"Uncle said he wrote her," Jeremy said. "I asked him not to tell you that we were thinking of coming here. We wanted to surprise you."

"I couldn't be more surprised. Or delighted," Gabriel said as he looked at his youngest brother again as though fearing he were an apparition. "How long are you staying?"

"We are uncertain," Jeremy said after sharing a quick glance with Savannah. "If we like Montana, we could be here for a good long while. Otherwise, I didn't let the workshop, so I could always return to Boston."

"I never knew you wanted to travel," I said to Savannah.

"There's been little else I dreamed of lately," Savannah said, refusing to meet my gaze.

I frowned, and Gabriel squeezed my arm. I bit back the multitude of questions wanting to burst forth and instead focused on the joy of having Savannah, Jeremy, Colin and Melinda here.

Gabriel appeared to mirror my sentiments as he said, "All that matters is you're here now. Amelia mentioned something about preparing the house for visitors, but I didn't press her for details. Col, you should stay there too, until you're settled."

Colin nodded his agreement as Melinda patted at his face, running her fingers over his rough cheeks. He acted as though he were going to eat her fingers, causing her to laugh even more.

"I'm sorry. I'm Clarissa," I said to the woman who trudged along behind us.

"I'm Araminta," she said. She wore ill-fitting clothes that were too tight across her bosom and waist, giving the impression the worn pale blue cloth was about to burst open at any moment. She walked with a slight hitch to her steps but had no trouble keeping up with the brisk pace set by the long strides of the McLeod men.

I looked to Savannah for more of an introduction, but she appeared too absorbed in taking in her new surroundings. At one point she stopped and stared at the large hills surrounding the city, her head tilting backward as she looked up. "Snow?" she asked with confusion while staring at the very tops of the mountains that had cleared with their arrival. When I nodded yes, she shook her head with wonder.

We walked along the boardwalk, avoiding the muddy street as much as possible. "Horse-drawn trolleys?" Savannah asked as one trundled past.

"Yes, things aren't as advanced here, Sav. You'll get used to it. In fact I rarely take a trolley. I tend to walk everywhere."

"If you're feeling adventurous, after the baby's born, you should both learn to bicycle," Gabriel said with a teasing smile. "Then you'll be able to explore a bit more together."

"I can only imagine the havoc Rissa could cause on a bicycle," Savannah teased.

I laughed my agreement, and we were silent for the rest of our walk. By this point, I'd pulled on Gabriel's arm to slow him down, and we walked at a more leisurely rate.

"Here we are," I said as we turned into the walkway of Uncle Aidan's house. The whitewashed two-storied house gleamed in a momentary break in the bleak day as a shaft of bright afternoon sun beamed down on us. A bench and two chairs sat on the long covered porch to the left of the door. Black shutters to the side of each window were open and were more decorative than practical. A row of pansies, their petals fluttering in the light wind, lined the walkway.

Savannah smiled, her shoulders relaxing. "I hadn't thought it to be this nice." She looped her arm through Jeremy's.

Gabriel led the way up the front stairs, knocking on the door. Nicholas answered, jumping up and down when he saw us. He yelled, "They're here, Mama! They're here!" and abandoned his post at the front door, running into the house.

"That's Nicholas," I said, following Savannah, Jeremy and Araminta inside with Gabriel on my heels.

Colin and Melinda were the last ones inside, and he closed the door, handing Melinda to Araminta. Nicholas raced back toward us, and Colin scooped him up in his arms, holding him upside down while Nicholas squealed with glee. "There's my boy," Colin said.

Amelia emerged from the kitchen, removing a stained apron. She swiped at her flour-dusted cheeks and extended her hand.

"You must be Amelia," Savannah said. "I feel as though I know you already after all Clarissa's written. It's nice to finally meet you."

"And you. You're very welcome," Amelia said. "I imagine you'd like to freshen up, have a little time before supper. I've a roasted ham, mashed potatoes and one of my last jars of pole beans planned for supper tonight."

"And cake?" Colin asked hopefully. "You always have cake."

"There is something for dessert," Amelia said with a smile.

I hadn't seen her this happy since Sebastian had departed.

"Whoopee!" Colin said twirling in place with Nicholas in his arms. When he stopped spinning, he nodded to Araminta, and they both set down their charges.

I watched as Melinda became acquainted with Nicholas, his natural tendency to friendliness overcoming any impulse to keep Colin for himself. When Nicholas showed Melinda his favorite marbles, I sighed with relief.

"There's enough for all of us, isn't there?" Gabriel asked as I poked him in the side.

"Yes," Amelia said while Colin laughed.

"I haven't felt like cooking as much now that the birth nears," I protested.

"It's still more than a month away," Gabriel said. "Thankfully the nearby café is decent."

"You should plan on having supper here most nights," Amelia said. "It'll be like old times with our big family gatherings."

Colin and Araminta remained in the living room with the two children, and I saw Gabriel give Jeremy a silent tilt of his head, indicating he should follow him.

Savannah smiled as she followed Amelia upstairs to the bedrooms while I lumbered up after them. "You have the choice of room, Miss Savannah," Amelia said.

Savannah flushed as she poked her head into the three bedrooms. "I like this one," Savannah said, indicating the one at the end of the hall.

I'd never been in it and giggled as I peered inside. "Of course you like it. It's the grandest bedroom in the house." I looked at Amelia. "This was Aidan's."

Sturdy oak furniture filled the room, including the bed frame, two nightstands and a pair of bureaus. An ewer and basin sat atop large lace doilies, most likely tatted by Amelia, on the taller bureau, while above the lower bureau was a mirror reflecting the room. A lamp sat on each of the bureaus and the side tables. A sturdy rocking chair placed in front of one of the two windows allowed for moments of quiet contemplation.

"I always wondered where he put the rocking chair Gabriel made for him," I said as I moved to it and traced the fine lines. I gave into my fatigue and sat into the comfortable chair, although it was too large for me.

"He says he does his best thinking staring out the window, looking toward the mountains with the birds in the trees singing to him," Amelia said. "To answer your question, yes, this was Aidan's room, although he hasn't been here in over a year. In the letter he wrote me, he indicated that he wanted them to use any bedroom they desired. With the three of you, and the maid, I don't know how we'll all fit."

Savannah blushed. "Ah, well, as to that. Jeremy and I are engaged. We'd like to marry here, with all you present. Thus, the room situation shouldn't be much of a problem for long."

"Oh, that's wonderful!" Amelia said. "We'll have a feast here at the house. Although you should have a private place for your wedding night. Not a house full of children and relatives." She frowned.

"They should rent a room in the Florence Hotel," I said. "I remember staying there when I first arrived, and it should prevent you from being chivareed."

"Chivareed?" Savannah asked with a small catch in her voice.

I laughed as I remembered my wedding night. "It's when the men from the town come to your window and make a racket, and won't cease until your husband leaves to buy them drinks at the saloon."

"I think it's because the single men in town are jealous of the husband's good fortune," Amelia said.

I sobered after a moment, frowning. "Sav, what about Jonas?" I whispered. "You can't be married to two people at once."

Savannah paled. "Didn't Aunt Betsy write you? Inform you of everything that's happened the past few months?"

"No. I haven't received any real news from either Sophie or Aunt Betsy in a while. At least, not as pertains to you." I frowned. "Aunt Betsy's rheumatism must be bothering her, as she said she'd never dictate to a maid any overly personal matters in a letter."

Savannah grimaced. "With all that happened, I'd forgotten about Aunt Betsy's rheumatism. As for Sophie, she did no end of muttering that some news one had to share oneself."

"I should leave you to catch up," Amelia said as she moved toward the door.

"By all means stay," Savannah said, waving toward the other side of the bed. "I'm sure it will become common knowledge soon enough, and I'd rather have you hear the truth from me rather than as mangled-up gossip."

"There wouldn't be much they could say about you that would shock me," Amelia said.

"What if they told you that I skewered my husband with a letter opener and felt no remorse?" Savannah asked.

I gaped at her while Amelia gasped.

"He'd already shot my father and Lucas, who are both recovered, and it appeared he'd stop at nothing to have me return to him."

"Good God," I muttered. "Are you all right? Are you sure Uncle Martin and Lucas are well?"

"I assure you, they're fine, Rissa. Lucas was quite ill for a while, and I worried he'd die from an infection." She blinked away tears before she firmed her jaw, and I saw steely indignation take the place of any sadness or grief. "I'm filled with regret I didn't do it sooner," Savannah whispered. "I know that makes me a wretched person, but I can't help it. He took undue pleasure in tormenting me."

"Thank God you are free of him," I said.

"Even though he's gone, I'll never be fully free of him." Savannah shared a long glance with me, and I saw the echo of pain and loss in her eyes.

"I know," I murmured, and Savannah nodded her understanding.

Amelia shook her head as though coming out of shock. "You killed your husband? You defended yourself against the man who stole your child and beat you? Who would have tried to kill you had you returned to him?"

Savannah nodded.

"I don't know what I feel," Amelia said, "but it's not disgust. I'm embarrassed to admit it might be admiration."

"If you're uncomfortable and would prefer me to stay elsewhere, I'm sure Jeremy would be willing to find rooms at that Florence Hotel you mentioned." Savannah traced patterns on the quilt on the bed, not meeting our eyes.

Amelia raised an eyebrow, frank amusement shining from her eyes. "You imagine I worry for myself sleeping in my bed at night in the same house as a woman who … killed her violent husband? No, I have no concerns, although I'm sure the sisters Bouchard and Vaughan will relish the retelling of this story."

I shuddered at their names. "Don't worry about them, Sav. They are townswomen who live to gossip. Now you'll be their most interesting target as our stories have worn thin," I said pointing to Amelia and myself.

Savannah took a deep breath and met my eyes. "The other news, Rissa, is that I met my daughter, Hope."

"Where is she? Why isn't she with you?" I demanded.

"She died," Savannah whispered.

I pushed myself out of the rocking chair, arching my back to gain the leverage I needed to free myself from the chair. "How?" I sat next to her, pulling her into my arms as Amelia closed the door gently behind her, granting us privacy.

"She caught typhoid and died. No one knew how severe it was. Even the doctor thought she was recovering. She didn't and she died." Savannah sobbed, leaning into my embrace.

She tried to pull away, but I kept a firm hold of her shoulders, restraining her from rising and placing any distance between us.

"I'm so sick of crying. I worry Jeremy will become tired of me and yearn for a different woman." Savannah sniffled.

"Sav, how could he want you to be anything other than who you are? It's normal to mourn your daughter. How could you not?" I stroked her head, shoulder and arm in an attempt to impart comfort where no comfort was possible.

I glanced at my belly, patting it. "I'm sorry." When she shook her head in denial, I said, "It's normal to resent me or to wish you too could be expecting a baby with Jeremy."

"I haven't given up all hope, Rissa. Even with what the doctors said, and with everything that happened with Hope, I'd cherish any child I was blessed enough to have."

"Even though it would mean another birth?" I asked biting my lip.

"Even then," Savannah said, squeezing my hand. "I know the thought of birth might scare you, but you won't be alone. Amelia and I will ensure you receive the best care."

"I know. It's the unknown that terrifies me," I admitted.

"Just as there's no cure for my sorrow, there's nothing that will prevent you from feeling trepidation as your time nears. It's normal, Rissa."

"Thank you for bringing little Melly here. Gabriel teased me for worrying as much as I did, even though I knew she'd been rescued. Thank you for caring for her all this time."

Savannah bit her lip and firmed her shoulders. "You're to be a mother, Rissa. Something I've always dreamed of. Deep inside, I know I'll never have a child. Could you consider allowing Jeremy and me to raise Melinda? We already love her, and ..." She broke off.

I paused for a long moment before answering. "I can't answer right away, Sav. I'd always thought I'd raise her, as she's my sister. And yet I see the bond that's already formed between you." I smiled as I saw a tremulous hope in Savannah's eyes. "Can I think about it for a day or two?"

Savannah nodded, blinking away tears.

I hugged her and rose. "Why don't you wash and then try to relax a little? One of us will come for you when it's time to eat."

"Would you mind terribly if I slept through supper?" Savannah asked, biting back a large yawn.

"Of course not. I remember my fatigue when I first arrived in Butte." I opened the door and glanced back, watching Savannah burrow under the covers, fully clothed. "We'll check to see if you're awake later." I smiled as she mumbled her agreement, already half asleep.

***

GABRIEL LED JEREMY into their uncle's study while Colin sprawled on the living room floor, playing toy soldiers with Nicholas while Melinda played with Nicholas's marbles.

"A word to the wise," Gabriel said as he shut the door. "I wouldn't let Nicholas know you were in the army unless you want to be barraged with questions. Almost daily he has one of us act out Teddy Roosevelt's charge up San Juan Hill, with Nicholas, of course, always the victor."

"That happened years ago. Why's he focusing on that now?"

"One of Rissa's semisenile friends got to talking about the army and told Nicholas about it one day when they visited them at the depository."

"Don't they have a library here?" Jeremy asked.

"Not yet, although they're starting to build one. Missoula's best architect, Mr. A. J. Gibson, is to design it. Another word to the wise, never confuse the architect, A.J., with Clarissa's friend, A. J. Pickens. They couldn't be any more different."

Jeremy nodded as he filed away the information.

"It's hopeful the new library will be finished sometime early next year." Gabriel sat in one of the two leather chairs in front of his uncle's desk, and Jeremy took the other.

"I'm sure you understand how glorious it feels to sit on something that isn't moving." Jeremy closed his eyes as he rested his head against the top of the chair for a moment.

Gabriel smiled, his eyes continuing to rove over the brother he hadn't seen in years. "You look different, and yet I'd recognize you anywhere."

Jeremy rubbed a hand over his closely trimmed beard.

"It's not just the beard," Gabriel said with a shake of his head. "It's how you hold yourself. With an air of command, of responsibility." His smile held a touch of regret. "You've grown up, and I wasn't there to see it."

"I missed you and Richard every day I was away," Jeremy said. "I needed to go on my adventure, become the man I was meant to become, but I always knew I wanted to return to Boston. Naively I thought we'd all live near each other. Raise families together."

"I couldn't remain in Boston any longer, Jer. Besides putting you on that train, or watching our home burn, leaving was one of the hardest things I've ever done."

"Although you seem happy," Jeremy said as he watched his older brother, a look of wonder passing over his face to be in the same room as him.

"I am now. Clarissa was brave enough to travel to me. We are to have our first child soon. You are here." Gabriel's brow furrowed. "With Savannah."

Jeremy huffed out a laugh. "You don't have to act like the older brother anymore, Gabe. I can take care of myself."

"You'll always be my baby brother. I had the raising of you for too long not to worry."

"I know." Jeremy sighed as he settled his long legs in front of him. "The moment I saw Savannah again, I knew I wanted her. At first I tried to tell myself it was because she had been abused, and I wanted to help her as a friend. I think I knew all along I was deluding myself." He smiled a half-mocking grin to himself as he stared at a point in the distance.

Gabriel took a deep breath. "I always imagined that's why you were attracted to Savannah. The damsel in distress."

Jeremy bristled at Gabriel's raised eyebrow. "There's much more to it than that."

"I should hope so if you're going to last for longer than a few months." He held up a hand to forestall an argument. "Before you become righteous in your anger—which Clarissa says we McLeods thrive at—I've always suspected there was more to her than she was willing to admit while she was under the control of her grandparents. I want you to know that I'm very happy you're content with her."

"Content? Do you remember what Mr. Smithers said when you used that word as your goal for your future life?" He raised an eyebrow.

"'A namby-pamby word,'" Gabriel said with fond affection, as he recalled his old mentor and friend.

"I feel a hell of a lot more than content with Savannah. The extraordinary thing was that, the more time I spent with her, the more I genuinely liked her. I never saw her as damaged. She's always been the strongest woman I know."

"I may have to argue with you, as Clarissa's the strongest one I know." He shared an amused grin with Jeremy. "Why don't we agree they're tied and forgo an argument?" Jeremy laughed and Gabriel relaxed further, seeing the echo of his youngest brother he'd fought so hard to safeguard from harm.

"Tell me about Florence and Richard," Gabriel said as they settled in for a long conversation.

***

I KNOCKED TWICE on the study door before poking my head in. I heard loud laughter and saw Gabriel wiping his eyes and Jeremy doubled over, holding his stomach. Even though I had no idea what was funny, I giggled due to their infectious laughter.

"Ah, my darling, is it time for supper?" Gabriel asked as he swiped at his eyes.

"No, not quite yet. I thought I'd come to see how you were after I left Savannah. She's fallen asleep, and I think she'll remain abed through supper." I moved toward Gabriel but didn't sit on his lap. I wasn't sure if his uncle's furniture was as sturdy as ours and didn't want to test it with our combined weight. Gabriel rose, pulling out the chair behind the desk, and I sat in it at Gabriel's side.

"She didn't sleep well on the train. Never dosed for more than an hour," Jeremy said as he recovered from his laughing fit.

"What had you laughing so hard?" I asked, unable to stifle a sigh as I settled, rubbing my belly. Gabriel reached over to lay a hand there too, smiling as the baby kicked where his hand lay. After a few forceful kicks, the baby calmed, and I relaxed into the chair.

"Oh, just stories from when we were younger," Gabriel said, dropping his hand to clasp mine.

"I thought you lived with your aunt and were miserable," I said.

"Not every moment of our lives was devoid of happiness, Rissa." Gabriel lifted my hand and kissed it. "Aunt would have wished it so, but she wasn't able to destroy our sense of humor or our ability to find joy."

"I worried she had for you, Gabe," Jeremy said. "Always so serious, taking care of Rich and me. I can see you've stopped dwelling on the past, as Uncle Aidan recommended." Jeremy nodded to the two of us.

"His favorite advice, I think," Gabriel said with a wry smile.

"Jeremy, who's Araminta?" I asked. "Savannah and I spoke of other things, and then she was exhausted and fell asleep."

"She's a young woman who was going to age-out the orphanage with nowhere to live or work. Mrs. Maidstone was very worried about Araminta because she had injured her leg when she was younger. I think she broke it, and it didn't mend properly. At any rate, she can walk short distances, but she can't run or stand for long periods of time. She'll have that limp for the rest of her life."

"How is she going to care for Melly? For I assume she's come here to help with Melly," I said.

"In a way. She's here to help Savannah, help with Melly, act as a maid to Sav, cook or clean as she can."

"She seems a nice young woman," I said.

"She is, although she's afraid she'll be turned out once Melinda is older. I think finding Mrs. Egan was a shock for her," Jeremy said.

"I will need help soon." I paused as I thought of the distance between Uncle Aidan's house and our home. It had always seemed a pleasant walk to me when it wasn't the middle of a blizzard, but, for Araminta, it might prove too long. "Does she ride a bicycle? They're the rage here, and she would have much more freedom of movement."

"If she doesn't, we can teach her," Gabriel said.

Jeremy smiled. "You're as generous as I remember, Clarissa. Thank you." Gabriel grunted his agreement, and I flushed.

"Jeremy, there is a small problem that needs to be addressed," I said. "I don't know if Amelia will speak with you or not." I bit my lip, and Gabriel raised his eyebrows at me.

"What is it?" Jeremy asked, leaning forward in his chair.

"There aren't enough bedrooms for all of you here, not with Araminta and Melly," I said on a rush.

Gabriel sputtered out a laugh before attempting to calm it at my glare. "Jer?"

"I ... that is, Savannah and I are going to marry," Jeremy said.

"Yes, but, until you do, you shouldn't be causing more gossip than will already surround Savannah," I said. "I imagine Savannah dreamed of escaping Boston and the scandal surrounding her actions, but people gossip no matter where you go."

"I know, Clarissa, and you are correct," Jeremy said with a deep sigh. "How soon do you think we could marry?"

"Not soon enough, by the looks of you," Gabriel teased. "And, as you aren't married, you shouldn't be staying here. We could fix a cot up in our apartment."

"I agree," I added. "It's what will be best. And you can work with Gabriel again, in his workshop here."

"Gabe, would you mind?" Jeremy asked.

"No, I could use the help. It will give us a chance to catch up after all these years."

"How long does it take to arrange a wedding here?" Jeremy asked.

"Not long," I said with a broad smile as I squeezed Gabriel's hand. "We'll have to see if we can convince Amelia to cook a feast to welcome you and to celebrate your wedding. It shouldn't be too difficult, for she loves to cook, and there's no better reason to celebrate."

We laughed, rising for supper in the dining room.

CHAPTER 58

I SAT AT AMELIA'S KITCHEN a few weeks after their arrival, listening to Savannah's stories as she prepared the dinner and Amelia tended her children. I arched my back, trying to find a comfortable position, but nothing worked.

"How are you and Jeremy adapting to married life?" I asked as I rubbed my lower back.

"Life has only improved with marriage to Jeremy," Savannah said with a bright smile. "I no longer have to hide our relationship from inquisitive eyes, and we are free to spend as much time together as we like."

"I'm sorry the sisters made a fuss when they found out about Jonas." I grimaced as I remembered their pronouncements about being misled by too many from the East Coast.

"I've survived worse. Besides, I think the townsfolk are intrigued, and they like you and Gabriel. For the most part, we've been well received." Savannah finished kneading the dough and set it in a bowl to rise.

"You didn't mind the simple ceremony and feast here?" I arched an eyebrow as I watched her ease in the kitchen. "It was a far cry from your first wedding."

"And far more enjoyable," Savannah said with a laugh as her eyes became distant. "You can't imagine the joy I felt walking down the aisle to meet Jeremy, his eyes glowing with love rather than disdain. Or the delight in hearing the organist play one of Lucas's songs as we marched down the aisle as husband and wife. Or later when we were back in the house, listening to the children squabble, or Mr. Pickens wheezing out his sage advice, or Ronan's and Colin's whispered plans for the chivaree. It was magical, and all I'd hoped for in a wedding day." She looked at me with wondrous eyes, blinking tears. "Thank you, Rissa, for standing beside me again."

"With no unfortunate fall off the altar," I said with a smile, causing Savannah to laugh. "Melinda seems very happy to be here with you. When I heard her call you *Mama*, I knew this was where she belonged."

Savannah blinked away tears and nodded. "Jeremy loves her too. Thank you, Rissa."

"It was a family decision, and all I want is for her to never doubt she's loved." I paused for a moment as I heard Amelia's soft voice speaking with Nicholas. "I imagine she'll find it difficult when Amelia and the children leave."

"She will. She already thinks of Nicholas as an older brother and Anne, her sister. They're more her age. She considers you and Colin her aunt and uncle."

I smiled, thinking of the age difference between Melinda, Colin and me. Savannah sat across from me, a bowl of potatoes in front of her to peel. "You've become proficient in the kitchen, Sav," I commented.

"I prepared many of the meals at Richard and Florence's after the baby was born and before that terrible evening with Jonas. I wanted the practice, and I enjoy the entire process of cooking." Savannah smiled as I grimaced.

I squirmed in my chair again, unable to find a position that brought relief to the building tension and pressure I felt.

Savannah watched me with thinly veiled concern, but I smiled, hoping to allay her fears. "The baby's getting too big. It's hard to imagine I have a few weeks to go." I gave a gentle pat to my stomach.

"I doubt you really have that long, Rissa," Amelia said, entering the kitchen. "It seems about time for that baby to meet all of us."

"Well, the doctor says it should be mid- to late June." I heaved myself to my feet and began a slow walk around the kitchen and then the dining room. I stopped with a pain to my side and placed my hand on the wall until it passed. "Oh!" I gasped.

"How long have you been having pains?" Savannah asked, setting down her paring knife.

"A few hours," I whispered.

"And how often are they coming?" Savannah asked.

"About every ten minutes or so," I said. "But it's too soon."

"That's for the baby to decide, not us," Amelia said as she led me toward a bedroom. I saw Amelia and Savannah share a long look.

"Seems you waited a long time to share your concern," Savannah said.

"It's too soon," I gasped as I became out of breath easily with the exertion of climbing stairs. I paused at the top, when, with a *whoosh*, I felt a gush of water come down my leg.

"Well, too soon or not, you'll be holding a baby in your arms in a matter of hours," Amelia said. "Let's get you settled, and then we'll send for Gabriel and the midwife."

I laid on the bed where Sebastian had stayed during his recovery and which was now Colin's room. It was the larger of the two guest bedrooms, and Amelia and Savannah scurried around either side of the bed as they prepared it for a delivery. Now that I was resting, the pains were milder, and I felt like sleeping.

"Sav, I think you could wait before going for the midwife," I said as I was on the verge of dozing.

Savannah shared an amused grin with Amelia, patted my shoulder and ran out of the room. I heard her steps as she descended the stairs. I dozed for a few minutes, gentle pains roiling through my belly every once in a while, but nothing to cause undue distress. Through it all, Amelia puttered around the room, preparing for the birth.

I sighed when I heard Gabriel's deep voice calling my name as he entered the house.

"Do you want him in here, Rissa? Most men wait for news until after the baby's born."

"He should wait in the study," I whispered as the next contraction was stronger. "No, Gabriel, wait downstairs," I gasped as I saw him in the doorway as though through a haze.

He entered and pulled a chair over to the side of the bed, leaning forward to kiss my forehead. "Don't ask me to leave. Let me stay with you." He clasped my hand, interlacing our fingers.

"This is unseemly, sir," the doctor sputtered as he entered, a gasping Savannah on his heels.

"No more unseemly than you attending to my wife," Gabriel said with a glower.

"Where's the midwife?" I asked.

"Attending another birth," Savannah said.

"Never fear. I've attended many births," the doctor said as he turned toward the ewer of water on the washstand and scrubbed his hands before approaching me. He felt my belly, and the gentle pressure of his hands against my belly was an agony. I saw him frown, and I flinched as his touch became firmer.

"Tell me," I demanded when I saw him frown again.

"The baby's not turned right," he said. "I should feel the head here." He placed his hand to the lower part of my belly. "Instead, I feel it here." He placed it on the side of my belly.

"Can you do anything?" Gabriel asked, his voice shaking with his attempt to remain calm.

The doctor raised intense eyes to me. "Do you have any desire to push yet?"

"No, not really. The contractions are still quite mild." I gasped, proving the lie of my statement as the next contraction roiled through me.

"Don't push," he commanded as he placed his hands over my belly again. "We're running out of time, and, if I'm to do this, I must do this now." He looked to Gabriel for permission, and I became irate.

I snarled, "I'm the one in this bed having the baby. Ask me for permission." I met his startled eyes with ones filled with fiery determination.

He half smiled, and I saw respect replace the surprise. "Well then, ma'am?" he asked. I nodded, gripping Gabriel's hand. He placed his hands on my belly, tracing again the baby's placement within.

He raised apologetic, yet determined eyes to meet mine. "This will be painful." He waited until I nodded and then moved his hands on my belly. I arched in agony, unable to hold back a wail in protest. Gabriel gripped my shoulders, holding me down so the doctor could work with greater ease.

"Stop, please stop," I screamed, but the agony went on and on. It was as though I were enveloped in an unending vise of pain tinged with fire. As though my insides were rearranging themselves, and I was never to be put to rights again.

I don't know if I fainted or simply ran out of air to scream, but, after a while, I whimpered as the doctor touched my belly again. "Please, not again," I begged.

"The baby is partially turned now," he said with calm, almost cold, practicality. "We must try once more. For your sake as well as the baby's."

"Please, Rissa," Gabriel whispered, his voice breaking with worry, the only sound in my pain-induced fog that would induce me to undergo this torture again.

I nodded, reaching deep inside myself in an attempt to battle the pain. I couldn't prevent myself from arching as the intense pressure was applied to my belly once more, although I refrained from screaming. Either I had resigned myself to the pain or it didn't last nearly as long, because it seemed that Gabriel's hands went from restraining to reassuring much more quickly.

I flinched as the doctor felt again, and I sobbed as he murmured, "Yes, that worked quite well."

I met his focused gaze as another pain, stronger, roiled through me.

"Now, when you have the desire to push, by all means, push!" the doctor commanded. He rose and stepped away from the bed.

I nodded and dozed for a while, gripping Gabriel's hand and attempting to murmur my thanks as my brow was wiped free of sweat. Finally the pains became intense and closer together, and I had an overwhelming urge to push.

"I have to push," I gasped.

"Good," the doctor said, rising from his chair and washing his hands again.

I clasped Gabriel's hand, ignoring his grunt of pain as I focused on each contraction.

"Keep pushing. You're doing well," the doctor encouraged. "On the next one, take a deep breath and use all your might to push!"

I glared at him as I lay in the throes of agony until the next pain began. I took a deep breath and pushed as hard as I could.

"One more good push and we'll know if you have a boy or a girl," the doctor urged.

I pushed with the last remnant of my energy remaining, and Gabriel raised my hand to kiss it. I collapsed onto the bed, gasping for air as I listened to the commotion at the foot of the bed. A momentary lassitude struck, and I turned my head to Gabriel with a frown.

He smiled through his tears as he leaned to kiss me on my forehead. "A girl," he said with awe. "We have a baby girl." He gripped my hand, holding it to his lips as he released a silent sob.

I reached up to stroke his hair, soothing him. "I'm fine, my darling."

At my whispered words, he bent forward, burying his face in my neck. "I hate that you were in such pain," he rasped. "And yet I'm so proud of you. And so in love with our daughter."

I smiled a moment before focusing on the doctor and my child. "Why isn't she crying?" I asked worriedly but then relaxed as she gave a lusty wail.

I heard the splashing of water, and afterward Amelia brought my baby to me, swaddled in a towel. "Your daughter," she whispered with tears in her eyes. "Congratulations. I'm going to tell the others."

She slipped out the door as I held my daughter, tracing her head, her cheeks, her fingers. "I can't believe she has fingernails," I marveled.

Another pain gripped me, and I groaned. "Doctor, what's happening?" I gasped. I looked at Gabriel with panic-stricken eyes, and he reached for my hand. I shook my head, instead handing him our daughter. He cooed and stroked her cheek as he held her for the first time, momentarily distracted.

"It's the afterbirth. You'll be fine," the doctor soothed.

I groaned, causing Gabriel to hold our daughter in one arm and grip my hand with his other. The pains weren't as severe, but I barely had the energy to react. I glanced toward the doctor, taking comfort in his calm countenance. Soon the doctor was proven right, and I collapsed against the bed.

"Hold our daughter, Clarissa," Gabriel murmured, kissing her again on her forehead. He rubbed a hand over her downy soft head. "I think she's hungry." He smiled as she made small smacking sounds with her lips. He settled her in my arms, and I traced her ear, her cheek, her perfect fingers as she suckled her first meal.

I turned my weary head to Gabriel, reaching out the hand that wasn't supporting our daughter to rub the tears from his cheeks. "I'm fine, darling. She's fine."

"Thank you, my brave Clarissa." His eyes were filled with an equal measure of wonder, fear, joy and the torment recently lived. "I never want you to suffer like this again."

"Let's not argue about it now," I murmured sleepily, tracing his eyebrow. "I love you, Gabriel."

Gabriel's eyes flashed with intense love as he watched me with our daughter. "And I you, my darling. What should we name her?" He rubbed a hand over her head, his touch soothing. When our baby stopped breast-feeding, and I handed our daughter to him, my heart filled with an unbearable amount of love at the sight of him holding her.

I lay back, tired but not ready for sleep yet. "I thought Geraldine Agnes McLeod."

He raised startled, thunderstruck eyes to meet mine. "You wouldn't mind? Naming her Geraldine for my mother?"

"No, my love. My only regret is that our parents aren't here to meet her," I whispered as I fought tears.

"Today is a time for joy, my Rissa, not sadness." He leaned forward and kissed me, leaning back at the soft tap on the door.

Amelia and Savannah poked their heads in, smiling when they saw Gabriel holding baby Geraldine. "Gabriel, it is time for you to go downstairs and receive the congratulations from the men. We're going to tidy this room. Then you can return."

Amelia took the baby while Savannah shooed Gabriel out. We shared one last look before the door was closed on him.

***

AN HOUR LATER I was cleaned up; the bed was changed, and all evidence of a recent birth had disappeared. I lay on clean sheets with Geraldine in my arms. Savannah curled on the bed next to me, stroking a hand down Geraldine's back.

"Are you all right, Sav?" I whispered.

"Of course I am. I will always wish little Hope were here so that they could grow up together and become good friends like you and me." She raised luminous blue eyes with a deep sorrow hidden in their depths. "I will always mourn her, but I will never begrudge you your joy."

"Thank you," I whispered as I leaned into her shoulder, "for I desperately want her to know her aunt Savannah."

Savannah's smile bloomed at being called an aunt. "Jeremy once said the best part about being an uncle is that you can love them and spoil them without all the resulting responsibility. I think I'll enjoy that."

I laughed, looking to the door as Gabriel, Jeremy, Colin, Amelia and Mr. Pickens trooped in. I pulled the sheets up to my neck even though I was wearing a matronly gown.

"We all wanted to meet baby Gerry and see you," Gabriel said. He sat in the chair next to me, reaching forward to clasp my hand again. I moved to give him the baby, and he released my hand, holding the baby in the cradle of his large arms.

"There's a good girl. There's my beautiful baby," he whispered as he kissed her forehead. He rose, walking toward the foot of the bed so that everyone could meet her. They cooed and tickled her feet, laughing as she kicked them.

"Well done, Rissa," Colin said.

"If she's anythin' like my Missy, she'll keep her plenty busy," Mr. A.J. said as he tottered over to the other chair and collapsed into it.

"We'll be here to help," Amelia said with a broad smile.

"Here, Gabe," Jeremy said as he reached to hold her. "I'm your uncle Jeremy. Your aunt Savannah and I are going to spoil you rotten," he murmured as he kissed her head.

Colin traced her hand and leaned forward. "He's your uncle Jeremy, and I'm your uncle Colin. We'll take you fishing and teach you to ride horses."

"And then return you to your parents," Gabriel murmured to me as he sat next to me again. "How are you, my darling?"

"Very tired." I stilled his instinctive movement to clear the room. "Please, let them stay. I enjoy having everyone together, even if it is in my bedroom."

"Thank you for this life," Gabriel said, staring deeply into my eyes.

"I should be thanking you," I whispered as I was momentarily overcome with emotion. "Such a full life, filled with family and friends, was only a dream until I met you. Now we have a wondrous future to anticipate."

Gabriel smiled with intense joy as we held hands, watching as baby Geraldine snuggled into the crook of Jeremy's arms. I looked from Jeremy and Colin, teasing each other over who was the best uncle; to Amelia and Savannah, whispering in the corner, sharing confidences and forging a friendship; to Mr. Pickens, watching the scene with quiet contentment. I sighed, gripping Gabriel's hand and was at peace.

AUTHOR'S NOTES

Thank you for reading *Undaunted Love*. Never fear, dear reader, I'm already busy at work on the fourth book in the series. I hope you will continue to join me on their journey.

Would you like to know when my next book is available? You can sign up for my new release e-mail list, where you'll be the first to know of updates and special giveaways at http://www.ramonaflightner.com/newsletter/

Follow me on twitter: @ramonaflightner

Like my Facebook page for frequent updates:
http://facebook.com/authorramonaflightner

Reviews help other readers find books. I appreciate all reviews. Please consider reviewing on Amazon, Goodreads or both.

Most people learn about books by recommendations from their friends. Please, share *Undaunted Love* with a friend!

ACKNOWLEDGMENTS

It's an honor to write books and have fans eagerly awaiting the next installment. Thank you to all of my readers!

Thank you, Margo and Brian, for your unwavering enthusiasm and interest.

I couldn't ask for more ardent fans than the Ladies of Somerset. Thank you!

To my dedicated, wonderful editors, Caroline, Gary and Denise at BubbleCow, thank you for helping me see plot holes and ways to enrich my story.

Thank you to everyone who has helped spread the work about the Banished Saga. A big Montana thank you to all of the wonderful internet book bloggers, especially Charlie, Punya, and Kayla. Thank you!

Finally, thank you to my family. Your endless patience as I discuss random historical facts, lose the thread of a conversation because my mind has wandered to a new plot point, or I disappear to write is priceless. Mil Gracias!

www.ingramcontent.com/pod-product-compliance
Lightning Source LLC
Chambersburg PA
CBHW020626020726
47494CB00001B/63